Molly's Boudoir

The 4th Jasmine Frame novel

Molly's Boudoir

The 4th Jasmine Frame novel

P R Ellis

Molly's Boudoir
First published in Great Britain by Ellifont, 2018

Ellifont, 20 Llangattock Court, Dixton Road, Monmouth NP25 3PX
www.ellifont.wordpress.com

ellifont

British Library Cataloguing in Publication Data.
A catalogue record for this book is available from the British Library.

ISBN 978-0-9933647-8-5 Print edition
ISBN 978-0-9933647-9-2 eBook edition

Printed and bound by CPI Group (UK) Ltd, Croydon, CR0 4YY

This book is a work of fiction. All names, characters, places and events are either a product of the author's fertile imagination or are used fictitiously. Any resemblance to actual events, places or people (living or dead) is purely coincidental.

To Lou – again, as ever.

1

Smoke, or was it steam, gleamed silver in the fire appliance's spotlights as it drifted from the shattered frontage of the shop and rose into the night sky. DI Tom Shepherd peered through his windscreen as he parked behind one of the vehicles. He got out and stood, looking up at the row of brick built terraced houses and shops. Water was no longer being sprayed on the building but hoses wormed across the pavement with puddles of water dammed between them.

Tom pulled his jacket tight around him to shield him from the cold wind which blew up Broad Street, and took a few steps along the pavement. He nodded to a uniformed police officer who recognised him and held up the police tape high enough for him to duck under. Coming towards him was DC Sasha Patel. She tilted her head to look up at him.

'I recognised your car, Sir.'

'You've been here a while, Sasha?'

They turned and walked side by side beside the fire engine.

'Not as long as the fire service and response team. I was just leaving home when the call came through on my phone so didn't have to go far.'

'Oh, yes, I forgot that you live in Thirsbury. Your patch then.'

'I don't know it that well, Sir. We only moved in six months ago.'

They stopped as a couple of fire officers, still wearing breathing apparatus, returned to their vehicle.

'What have we got then?' Tom asked, 'I gather it's not a routine fire, if there is such a thing.'

'No sir. There's a body inside, and the incident commander doesn't think the death was due to the fire.'

'Ah. Can we have a look?'

'They haven't let me in yet, Sir, but I think they've put the fire out now. The commander thought the building might be unsafe. The flames were pretty fierce at the front of the building.'

'An accelerant?'

'Possibly or maybe the building was just a tinderbox.'

Tom stroked his chin. 'Hmm. What was it used for?'

'I'm not sure, Sir. The ground floor is a shop called Molly's. Clothes I think. I've never really noticed it.'

Tom turned and looked down the gently sloping main street of the small town. There was no traffic, not surprising as the fire and police vehicles blocked the road, but there was now a small group of people, lit by the streetlights, waiting at the tape barrier that had been erected.

'It's some way from the main shops, so not a major retailer,' Tom said.

'No.'

Tom faced the shop and took a step forward.

'If the fire guys think the victim wasn't killed in the fire presumably the body is not where the fire was fiercest?'

'That's right, Sir. It's in a room at the rear.'

Tom looked up and down the street. 'Can we get to it by the rear entrance?'

'There isn't one, Sir. The Fire brigade had to fight the fire from the front. That's why they've got hoses going into the building.'

'We're going to have to go through the front door then, safe or not. Let's get overalled up. SOCO should be here by now.'

'They got here just before you, sir, and are waiting for permission to enter.'

As he tugged the one-size-fits-all disposable overall over his shoulders, Tom noted the similarity with the baby-grows his infant son was put in. There seemed to be room for two of Sasha Patel in hers. He signalled to the pair of scene of crime officers to follow and then advanced towards the blackened entrance to the shop with a hefty torch in his hand. A fire officer blocked the doorway; Tom guessed he was the incident commander.

'The fire's out but we're still damping down as a precaution. We're carrying out a preliminary structural survey. I wouldn't like to give odds against the ceiling of the ground floor coming down.'

'We need to get in to secure the scene of crime,' Tom said.

'I understand that. We'll escort you through. The rear of the building wasn't as affected by the fire and seems pretty sturdy.'

'Thanks. Lead on.'

The fire officer turned and entered the building with Tom behind and followed by Sasha and the SOCO officers carrying their bags of forensic kit. They stepped directly into a corner of a rectangular room about four metres by three. The only light was from the lights erected on the street outside shining through the shattered windows. There were heaps of sodden, charred material scattered over the blistered and buckled laminated floor running with water. There was also what Tom took to be the shards of a wooden desk. Tom switched his torch on and dispelled the shadows to reveal the fire-blackened remains of what was presumably the stock of a clothing retailer. He could tell the SOCOs were fretting about their and the fire officers' feet trampling over the floor which was a possible crime scene. They'd secure the scene as soon as they could have it to themselves.

They entered a narrow corridor directly opposite the entrance which had a stairway up to the left and then they passed into an even darker windowless room. The dancing light of torches revealed it to be a little larger than the front room, and square, though with one corner taken out by a now scorched wooden cubicle. The torch light bounced back at them from tall, cracked and shattered mirrors in the centre of each wall. Again, there were heaps of cloth reduced almost to ashes but amongst the debris were pale lumps of material that mystified Tom.

'What's that stuff? It looks like dinosaur eggs.' he said.

'Not sure what they were,' the Fire Officer replied, pausing as he crossed the room. 'It hasn't burned like the other materials. Probably a silicone rubber. It's non-flammable.'

'What are they doing here?' Tom asked.

The fireman shrugged. 'The body's through here.' He moved on to the exit from the room. Tom followed close behind. The floor changed from wood to stone. This was a smaller room, narrower than the others but with a door and window onto the dark garden. The body lay in the doorway. Before examining the deceased, Tom edged around the body and scanned the room. It appeared to be a kitchen, no, more like a scullery. There was a sink unit and cupboards but no cooker.

The Fire Officer directed his torch at a door on the side of the room. 'There's just a loo in there,' he commented.

'The fire didn't reach here then,' Tom said looking around.

'There's some smoke damage and superficial scorching,' the fireman said directing his torch at the beamed ceiling. 'There was a bit of flameover but we were lucky. Got here soon after the fire took hold and as it was apparently centred on the front of the building, managed to get water on it at a decent rate. Obviously, it wasn't lucky for her.' He nodded at the body. 'I guess she was dead already since she didn't get out of the back.'

Tom crouched to get a closer look at the victim. It looked female although Tom was a little surprised by the mode of dress. The victim seemed to be wearing an unusual flared black dress, that barely reached her knees, over a ruffled petticoat. The legs were clad in sheer nylon and the shoes on her feet had narrow heels at least three inches in length.

Sasha bent down at his side and directed her torch beam onto the victim's head.

'I think she's wearing a wig, Sir.'

The hairpiece had slipped revealing a bald skull which was covered in dark stuff.

'Mmm, yes, and I think that's blood not soot on her head. I'd say she was hit with a blunt instrument.'

'Drawing your own conclusions Detective Inspector?'

Tom swung round on his heels to see another overalled figure standing over them.

'Dr Winslade?'

'Yes, Tom. Do you think I could get to see the deceased?'

'Oh, yes of course.' Tom straightened up, wary that his head was just about at beam height. He stepped aside to allow the pathologist to crouch down beside the body. DC Patel also moved aside as the two SOCO officers manoeuvred into the confined space.

'We need light in here,' Winslade said as she peered at the corpse.

'Yes, I know, but we haven't even done a preliminary scan for evidence yet.' Tom replied.

'Well, let the experts get on with the job. You go and do what you're good at.'

The pathologist's bossying didn't rankle with Tom. She'd been doing this job for longer than he'd been a senior detective and she was right.

'Let's get out, DC Patel, and start asking questions.' They retraced their steps towards the front of the building, meeting the senior fire officer in the front room.

'What's upstairs?' Tom asked.

'Living quarters. One bedroom.'

'Can we go up there?'

'I'd prefer if you didn't, Inspector. We're still not sure whether the beams were weakened significantly. There was some transmission of the fire to the upper floor but we stopped it taking hold. I think it will be daylight before I can say whether it is safe for you.'

Tom wondered whether he could delay that long to start the search for evidence about the dead woman but decided that pressing the fireman was not sensible just yet.

'OK, please let me know as soon as you can.' He passed on out of the premises with Sasha at his heels. In the glare of the floodlights he turned to face her. 'Right Sasha, we need to know who the victim was, who lived here and ran the shop. Perhaps they are the same person. I presume the neighbours have been evacuated. There's plenty of people gawping. See what they know, but don't mention how or when the victim was killed yet.'

DC Patel nodded and marched off. Tom took his phone from his pocket and after glancing up at the peeled and dripping nameboard above the shop window began tapping the words "Molly's" and "Thirsbury" into the search box.

Tom was reading the screen with a growing sense of bemusement when a SOCO approached him from the burnt-out building.

'Sir. Dr Winslade says she'd like you to come in.'

Tom followed the officer back inside the burnt-out building. In the few minutes he had been concentrating on his screen, there had been considerable changes made. Two battery powered light-stands had been set up in the rear room providing a much more even illumination. Tom noted the white-painted walls stained with soot and trails of mucky water, and the white plastic floor-pads contrasting with the dark stone, but his focus was the body still lying on the floor apparently unmoved. Dr Winslade was kneeling, peering at the back of the head of the victim. She beckoned for Tom to join her. He too knelt.

'Your guess was correct, Tom.'

Tom smiled. 'My guess?'

'Yes, the victim was hit on the back of the skull with a heavy but blunt instrument. I can't be certain but I'd say death was instantaneous. The killer took a pretty good swing at it.'

'The weapon?'

'Can't say exactly, just yet. It doesn't seem to be here.'

'We need daylight to have a good look around. Is that all?'

'No. There was something else I wanted to tell you. I have

12

given the body a look over, well Tom, more a feel over actually.'

'Yes?' Tom was surprised that Dr Winslade wasn't getting to the point more quickly.

'Did you notice the clothes the victim is wearing?

'Sort of. An unusual fashion. Those shoes for a start look pretty uncomfortable.'

'It is a particular kind of outfit. But the main point is that the victim is not female, well, not a cis-female.'

Tom frowned. 'I've heard that term. Jasmine uses it.'

Winslade nodded. 'Yes, I think Frame is going to be needed on this case. The victim wasn't born female. He or she has a penis.'

Thanks to the pathologist's lead up, Tom wasn't surprised. 'A transsexual?'

Tom saw Winslade frown. 'I'm not sure that's the appropriate term in this case, Tom. She, he, has a contraption around her genitals.'

'A contraption?'

'I think it's a chastity device.'

Tom found his mind filled with questions he wasn't sure he wanted the answer to, but he remembered what he had been reading on his phone. 'I wonder? I'd just looked up the website for this place. If I understand it correctly I think they offer dressing up sessions for transvestites and gear for making them look female.'

Winslade nodded. 'I'm sure Jasmine can explain it to you, better than I can.'

Tom sucked his lip. 'There's only one problem. I'm not sure if Jasmine is up to it. It's only a month since her op. The big one.'

'She's had her Gender Reassignment Surgery?'

'That's it. She said before she went in for it that it would be a while before she was back at work.'

'It's a serious operation, Tom, so I'm not surprised, but perhaps she'd welcome a visit from you if she's been convalescing for a month.'

2

Jasmine pulled the dress over her head and dropped it on the bed. She reached behind her back to release her bra and lifted out her enhancers as the cups loosened. She felt her customary sadness at still requiring the fillers as she glimpsed a reflection of her breasts in a wall mirror alongside the cabinet by the side of the bed. *Now why*, she thought, *would they bother to put mirrors on the wall in a surgical ward*. Surely, none of the patients would relish looking at themselves after surgery. Perhaps it was there so they could check that their appearance was satisfactory when it came time to leave.

She was standing in just her knickers but, with the curtain pulled around the bed, she didn't feel self-conscious; no more than usual when she spied her naked body. For years, she had avoided looking at what was between her legs but now she felt an urge to do so. She slipped her knickers down and manoeuvred so that she could see below her waist in the small mirror. The shrivelled thing hung there between her thighs As she had shaved her pubes in preparation for her surgery and each hair on her scrotum had been eliminated by her electrolygist the appearance was unfamiliar to her. It didn't seem to be part of her, probably because it was already not fully her flesh, being bulked out by the two plastic balls that had replaced her testes last year. If she hadn't followed instructions and stretched the useless appendage every day it would probably look even more insignificant.

No regrets. That pleased her. The urge to move on and

become the woman she had long felt herself to be was as strong as ever. Tomorrow, or whenever she next felt up to examining herself she would look different.

'Are you ready, Miss Frame?'

Jasmine leapt at the sound of the nurse's voice beyond the curtains and hurriedly grabbed the hospital regulation gown from the bed. She pulled it over her head and removed her knickers.

'Yes,' she replied belatedly.

The nurse poked her head in, took in her clothed appearance, and drew back the curtains. Jasmine in a nightdress was revealed to the other five occupants of the ward. She had already made their acquaintance, although the lady who had been operated on today was still somewhat groggy in a morphine-induced haze. The others, in various more advanced stages of the recovery process, gave her a warning of what was to come for her – discomfort, plenty of it, plus a growing sense of achievement.

'Hop into bed then please. Your dinner is here.'

Jasmine responded to the nurse's instruction beginning to feel the truth of her institutionalisation. "Give yourself up to it", she had been encouraged, and that she resolved to do. She would be the model patient.

She was glad to be awoken early in the morning since her recurring nightmare had troubled her throughout the night. As it consisted of knives slashing at her flesh, it wasn't too surprising the night before major surgery but she greeted the morning tired and disturbed. Jasmine had to tell herself it wasn't the actual operation, with the very real cutting that was required, that bothered her, but the old fear of knife attack that she had to overcome. She was grateful for the start of preparations for her surgery. No breakfast of course, but the embarrassing and not very comfortable flushing out of her bowels. Then there was the final consent form signing session with her surgeon and her reassurances that she did indeed wish to go through with it. The day she had looked towards for years had finally arrived.

She walked to the theatre, but didn't walk back. She awoke, her mouth parched, tongue like old leather, her head heavy and mind foggy, her body not belonging to her. The nurse told her she was in the recovery room, almost five hours had passed, and everything had gone well. Jasmine thought, *I have a vagina, I'm a woman*, but really all she wanted to do was sleep. The nurse kept talking at her, asking questions until she was sure Jasmine was fully awake.

They wheeled her back to her ward. She noticed that one bed was now empty but the remaining four women greeted her with varying degrees of jollity but all with congratulations for making it to the ranks of post-op transsexual. She lay, slightly nauseous, but feeling a sense of achievement although to be honest all she had done was lie on the operating table. It was the surgeon who had transformed her, giving her the body she wanted. Gradually she regained the sense that her limbs belonged to her, the numbness of the anaesthetic replaced by a growing ache and soreness that was kept at a distance by the morphine being pumped into her arm.

She asked for her phone to be put in her hand and her mind was taken off the awareness that the next days would be full of pain. There were best wishes messages of course, from Viv and Angela, sister Holly and even her mother. The last surprised her as her mother had never given her blessing for Jasmine's planned surgery and only barely accepted that she no longer had a son. She flicked through social media, news and a light novel that she'd had the sense to load before leaving home, happy to have something to pass the time.

'How're yow doing, Jas love?'

Jasmine looked up from her screen on hearing the familiar Birmingham lilt. She felt a cute furry animal do a little somersault in her stomach when she saw the beaming smile of Viv. She hauled herself up the bed to a more conversational position.

'Fine, a bit numb at the moment, thanks to the morphine. That I'm grateful for.'

Viv pulled up a chair and sat beside her bed. He took her hand in his.

'It's all done? You're happy with it?'

'They say it went to plan. There's so much packing and padding down there I haven't seen a thing yet,' Jasmine nodded towards her lower half. 'Not sure I want to yet. I've heard it's a bit of a horrid sight for the first day or so.'

'Ah, yes, I s'pose so.' He lifted a brown paper bag onto the covers, 'I wasn't sure whether to bring you flowers or grapes or what, so I decided on chocolates.'

Jasmine drew the shiny box from the bag and smiled at him. 'Thanks. I don't think I want one now. Do you?'

Viv shook his head. 'No, they're for you, and the nurses and,' he glanced around the ward, 'the other, er, ladies.'

Jasmine smiled, 'I'm sure they'll be appreciated.'

'Have you had dinner?'

'A while ago. I didn't feel like much,' in fact the thought of eating had made her feel sick, 'I managed a few mouthfuls of soup.'

'Oh, are you not feeling well?' There was a look of concern on Viv's face.

'As well as expected. Look, we went through this Viv. I know it's going to be pretty uncomfortable for a while.' In fact, all the reading she had done had warned her that the next few days, once the morphine was withdrawn, would be about as painful as it could be.

'Yes, I know, but, I was sort of hoping...'

'That I was superhuman or something, able to cope with major surgery without batting my eyelashes. Sorry.'

Viv looked infant-like. 'No, I know, it's silly, but I don't want you in pain.'

'It comes with the consent forms, Viv. It won't be for long.' She didn't feel quite as relaxed as she sounded. The impending pain was not something she welcomed as a challenge. They chatted on for the duration of the short visiting time. When a bell rang, Viv leaned over the bed and placed a kiss on her cheek.

He stood up straight. 'Um, I have a meeting in Bristol tomorrow…'

'Don't worry, Viv, I never expected you to come from Kintbridge every evening to see me. I'll be home in a few days, and anyway, the next day or two I may not want visitors.'

He gave her a thin smile. 'Well, imagine I'm here and you're holding on to me tight when the pain gets bad. See you soon, love.' He waved farewell and she blew him a kiss with the hand unimpeded by the infusion. Jasmine settled back on the pillow hoping that sleep would come soon.

The next two days were as bad as she feared with paracetamol and Ibuprofen hardly taking the edge off the pain. Weirdly, much of the discomfort seemed to be in the appendage that she no longer had, an example of the "phantom limb" syndrome. The padding was removed and she looked at her bruised and bloody groin with distaste, but it was the packing stretching her newly-constructed vagina that caused the greatest discomfort. Somehow, she got through the days and she was grateful for having the foresight, gleaned from previous patients, to have sleeping pills prescribed for the nights. At least they provided a few hours of semi-blissful unconsciousness.

The following evening, she was trying to read through the pain, and largely failing when another familiar voice makes her look up. The sight of Angela gave her a lift she found surprising.

'Hey, you're looking great, Jas.'

'I don't believe you.' Jasmine managed a chuckle. 'Thanks for coming.'

'I couldn't not come and see you when you've finally got what you wanted all these years. And anyway, I've been up in the City all day, so I was in need of a bit of relaxation. Pity we can't crack a bottle of wine.'

'I don't think that's on my prescription just yet.' Jasmine

looked around and saw that most of the other patients were dozing. 'Let's go to the day room for a chat.'

'Can you move?'

'With difficulty.' Jasmine slowly swung her legs off the bed. A passing nurse disconnected her catheter from the urine bag and leaning on Angela's arm they walked the few yards from the ward to the small television lounge.

'I feel like an old woman.' Jasmine said as she lowered herself into an upright armchair.

'At least you are a woman.' Angela said. In moments, they were chatting as if they still lived together. Jasmine had never lost her love for her ex-wife although she accepted they had moved on.

'How's the new love in your life?' she asked, knowing that Angela had a new boyfriend.

'My toyboy?'

'Is he?'

'Well, he's three years younger than us; tall, dark and handsome.'

'A change from me then.'

'Yes,.' Angela's face turned serious as a memory or two seemed to flash through her mind but then she brightened, 'but we're getting on well.'

'In all ways?'

Angela blushed, 'Yes.' She took a breath, 'And you and Viv?'

'We're getting on fine, and looking forward to me being fit.'

'So, you can do it properly?'

Now it was Jasmine's turn to flush. She nodded.

Angela hurried on, 'And you're settled in the new house?'

'Yes. You must come round with, er, …'

'Simon.'

'Yes, that's it, both of you.'

For a while Jasmine was almost able to forget her discomfort and when it came time for Angela to leave she was surprised how well she had coped. It gave her hope that the worst of post-operative pain was passed.

She reassessed that optimistic feeling the following morning when the time arrived to remove the packing from inside her. The extraction of the bloody mess of gauze and dressing almost made her faint but with the catheter also removed she was then able to have her first real pee as a woman, and a shower. Then though, it was on to the task which would fill her with anticipatory fears for the next months – dilation. Jasmine started with a heavily lubricated one-inch diameter test-tube-like dilator, which she eased into her vagina, gently twisting it and holding it in place for five minutes. She slid it out gently almost expecting to see a flood of blood, but apart from a few dark flecks of dried blood it was clean. Then it was the turn of the wider dilator to be kept in place for ten to fifteen minutes. She felt as if she was going to tear in half, but in fact the fears were unfounded. The specialist nurse who had trained any number of trans-women in this task nodded with approval.

'That's it. Three times a day from now on.'

'Forever?'

'For the time being. You will be able to reduce it as you heal and the channel becomes established. Forget it and you'll quickly close up.'

Jasmine certainly didn't want that to happen. She wanted an adequate and useable vagina so she listened to all the advice the nurse had to give.

There was one more night of pill-induced sleep, and then a day of waiting, hoping that she would be given the all-clear to be discharged. She was more than impatient by the early evening when Viv arrived. She was dressed, coat on and sitting somewhat stiffly on the bed, when he appeared.

Jasmine waved goodbye to her fellow patients, all of whom had changed since she had arrived. She eased herself into the wheelchair that the nurse provided, grateful that she did not have to walk the couple of hundred yards to Viv's parked car. She was going home to convalesce and become familiar with her new anatomy.

3

SATURDAY 21ST SEPTEMBER
MORNING

Lee looked up at the sign above the display window. "Molly's", he read. This was it; he'd driven a hundred miles to get here, saved up for months – money and courage. He was a little surprised how small the shop appeared. For no real reason at all, he had expected a large emporium with neon signs and bold branding. But here was a small, discreet shop at the end of a country-town high street, keeping to itself what its purpose was beyond selling female clothes. The window was occupied by a couple of mannequins in tasteful dresses along with a few pairs of shoes and sandals, scarves and gloves. Now that he thought about it he was glad that the premises didn't shout out what it offered. He would have been even more nervous about approaching the door if it had.

He pushed the door open and an old-fashioned bell jangled. He stepped into a bright, if small, premises with a pair of racks of female clothes standing on the light, wooden floor. Two walls had floor to ceiling shelves and drawers. In front of him a woman was rising from her chair behind a low desk on which there was laptop.

'Good morning. May I help you,' the woman said in a sing-song voice that did not conceal its low register. She was a good couple of inches shorter than Lee but had a considerably wider girth. She was wearing a high-necked, dark purple, maxi-dress that was almost Victorian in its style.

'I'm Lee Clement. I made an appointment,' he said, trying not to let his voice waver.

The woman beamed and moved from behind the desk to welcome him with her arms reaching out to him.

'Of course. I was expecting you. I'm Evelyn. I'll be escorting you on your journey.' She moved behind Lee to drop the latch on the door and flip the "Open" sign to "Closed".

'Come on through,' Evelyn said, guiding Lee around the desk and through a short corridor into another, slightly larger room.

Evelyn stood in the centre of the space and stretched out her arms.

'Welcome to my boudoir,' she said, 'where all your dreams come true.'

Lee looked around. It was a windowless room lit by a dozen or more small ceiling lights which banished all shadows. There was another, closed, door in front of him and in the opposite corner, a curtained cubicle. In the last corner stood another mannequin which looked somewhat strange. It seemed unusually fleshy, and the skin looked soft instead of the usual shiny hardness. It was dressed in just a bra and pants. Wide, floor to ceiling mirrors occupied the middle of each of the four walls with banks of narrow chests of drawers on both sides with open shelves above them. The top shelf around the room was filled with dozens of wigs on stands. A couple of easy chairs and what resembled a hairdresser's chair were the only furniture.

'Let me take your coat and then you can have a seat,' Evelyn said.

Lee shrugged off his anorak and sat, as directed in the salon-style seat. Evelyn carefully hung the coat on a rack beside the cubicle. She turned, smiling and approached Lee.

'Now tell me what you would like today, Lee.'

'I'd like you to make me into a woman.' There he'd said it. The first time he'd spoken his desires out loud let alone telling them to another person. But he had to qualify it. 'I know you can't really turn me into a woman just like that, but, your website said you could make me look like an attractive woman.'

If anything, Evelyn's smile grew broader. 'That is exactly what we do here at Molly's,' she said, then, stepping closer, her voice dropped to a more conspiratorial level. 'Have you done anything like this before such as dressing, er, in female clothes.'

Lee felt his cheeks turning red. It was silly to be ashamed of what he did at home when he'd driven all this way to feed his urge to wear women's clothes. 'Yes,' he whispered, 'I have a few skirts and dresses that I wear at home and a pretty horrible wig.'

'You only dress at home?'

Lee shrugged. 'Mostly. I have gone out a few times, at night, but I just don't feel that I look feminine enough. My figure…'

Evelyn looked him up and down. 'Hmm. Yes. Stand up a moment, please Lee.' Lee did as he was told. Evelyn continued to consider his body. She pulled out a tape measure from a pocket in her voluminous dress and quickly circled it around his chest, waist and hips.

'Yes, your figure is, um, boyish, and you are quite tall, not too tall mind. Your face…,' she looked steadily up into his eyes. 'Yes, you are young; your features could easily be female. With cosmetics and a good wig, you will be an attractive young woman.'

A little bubble of joy grew inside Lee. Those words were what he wanted to hear. 'Thank you,' he said.

Evelyn was thoughtful. 'To make any woman look attractive, no matter how expensive her dress, she needs good foundation garments. And for a man to look like an attractive woman he needs a good foundation under the foundation garments.'

Lee was a little mystified. 'What do you mean?'

'We need to give you a woman's figure, and hide those bits that men have that women do not.'

'Ah, yes. I see.' Lee had examined Molly's website and had some idea what Evelyn was referring to.

'Go and undress in the changing room.' Evelyn pointed to the small cubicle in the corner of the room. 'Take everything off. You'll find a robe hanging up in there for you to put on. Come out when you are ready.' She stepped across the room and pulled the curtain aside. Lee went in and the curtain closed behind him.

The changing room was hardly that. Standing in front of a small bentwood chair there was just enough room for Lee to spread his elbows. He pulled off his clothes and hung them on the wall hooks. As he tugged down his pants he wondered what to with them. They could hardly be hung over a hook. He screwed them up and stuffed them in a pocket of his trousers. As he reached for the satin wrap he heard a noise from the ceiling above his head. Someone was pacing across the floor above. There is someone else here, he thought. He hoped that they wouldn't come down to interrupt the intimate business he was engaged in with Evelyn. He shrugged off his worries and pulled on the rich apricot, embroidered robe. He stepped out of the cubicle feeling that he had left his male self hanging on the hooks. Evelyn had opened several of the chests of drawers and was taking garments out. She turned around and smiled at him.

'Ah, that's better. Rid of that drab male stuff. Now the first thing is to hide away what you've got between your legs. You can either use one of these.' She held up a scarlet item that resembled a jockstrap. 'It'll hold everything thing and make you smooth at the front.'

Lee reached out for the garment and held it between his hands testing the elastic. It was strong and he imagined it gripping his genitals tightly.

'Or perhaps you would like to have the appearance of being female, even under your clothes,' Evelyn went on. She delicately picked up an item from a drawer and turning held it out to Lee. It appeared more like a piece of modern erotic art than something to wear. It was flesh-coloured and while shaped like a pair of knickers, the pouch was moulded into the shape of a woman's private parts, complete with a small tuft of pubic hair.

'This is the basic vagina knickers,' Evelyn explained, 'They'll hold you in but give you the appearance of having a vagina or a vulva to be accurate. There are others which let you to pee with them on and allow penetration.'

'I see,' Lee said, feeling a thrill at the thought of having his own fanny. 'I think I will try those.'

'But we need to check your flesh tone first, and your hair colour, unless you want the shaved version.' Lee shrugged. 'Do you mind opening the robe so I can match the colour.'

With trembling fingers, Lee loosened the cord holding the gown around her waist. He let the loose ends drop and slowly, very slowly parted the robe. For the first time a person other than his mother was looking at Lee's naked body. He felt a stir in his penis, followed by embarrassment and the feeling subsided.

Evelyn advanced towards him with a sheaf of cards in her hand in various shades from almost pure white to chocolate black. She selected a few and held them against Lee's midriff, apparently oblivious to Lee's stirring cock.

'Yes, I thank that's the one.' She stepped back, 'You can cover up now, thank you Lee.' Evelyn returned to the bank of drawers and having rifled through a couple of drawers pulled out two clear polythene encased items.

'Hair or not?' she called.

'Er, none,' Lee replied. All the girls in pictures he had seen had shaved pubes. Evelyn turned and handed over one packet.

'This is a close match I think and it's your size. Would you like to try it on? You can go back into the cubicle if you like. Make sure you tuck yourself in carefully. It should be comfortable.

Lee nodded and hurried into the changing cubicle. He tore open the packet and pulled out the garment. It had a rubbery feel to it but didn't smell of latex. He opened the dressing gown again and pulled the knickers up his legs being careful to do as Evelyn had instructed. The knickers clung tightly to his abdomen and when he looked down he got a thrill. There was just a smooth mound with the hint of pink crinkled lips between his legs.

Lee returned to face Evelyn.

'Let's have a look love?'

Lee opened the gown, boldly this time, after all he wasn't really nude anymore. Evelyn nodded.

'Yes, that looks lovely, much nicer, but a girl shouldn't be flashing her fanny should she. Here are some knickers for you.'

Of course, she was a woman now, with woman's bits. She took the black silk knickers from Evelyn's hand. They were almost weightless, almost not there at all. She bent and slipped them up her legs. There was just a small triangle of cloth that covered her fake vulva and a thin strap around her waist and between her buttocks.

'What should I call you now that you are a woman?' Evelyn asked.

This was something Lee had thought long about. 'It's still Leigh, but spelt differently, L, E, I, G, H.'

Evelyn nodded. 'That's convenient. My name serves for both male and female too and it saves getting muddled.' Evelyn went on, 'Now here's a matching bra, but you need some tits. I've picked out a C cup breast-form for you in your shade. These have nipples. Would you like me to help you?'

Leigh gulped when she saw the size of the breast sitting in Evelyn's hand. She nodded.

'Drop the robe then, love.'

Leigh slipped the dressing gown from her shoulders and let it fall around her ankles. Evelyn put the breast down and fastened the bra around Leigh's chest. Then she helped Leigh slip the silicone breasts into the cups. Leigh was astounded at the weight. Until now she had stuffed her bra with socks but had always been disappointed with the effect. These breasts felt as if they were part of her. She looked in the nearest wall mirror and saw a woman with a figure reflected over and over again. It was her. Happiness bubbled over inside her.

'Now you have the undergarments we can decide what to put on top to show the world,' Evelyn said. She went to one of the racks of dresses and pulled out a small black dress. 'Every lady needs a little black dress,' she added as she handed Leigh the hanger.

There was a noise from the front of the shop. Someone was hammering on the door and Leigh was sure she could hear a voice shouting, demanding entry. She looked at Evelyn and was surprised to see her face had turned white.

'You put that on. I'll sort out this interruption,' Evelyn said with her hands waving in anxiety. She started to move towards the source of the noise, but turned, picked a packet off one of the shelves and passed it to Leigh, 'Oh, put these on too.' It was a pair of sheer black stockings. Evelyn hurried from the room, her dress ballooning out.

Leigh picked up the robe and returned to the cubicle. She hung the robe and the dress on a hook and sat down on the chair. She carefully unwrapped the stockings and pulled them up her slender legs. They were hold-ups and when she stood she was delighted that they clung to the tops of her thighs. Now she was feeling really sexy. She took the dress from the hanger and worked her way into it. It was a bit of a struggle because it was made from a clingy fabric that fitted tightly to her body. She had to fight to get it over her large breasts, but then was able to tug it down over her stomach and bottom. She found the hem came just below her stocking tops. She stepped out of the cubicle in time to hear the argument going on in the shop.

'I want my money back,' a loud male voice said.

'I'm sorry Mr McLeesh I can't do that,' Evelyn's words were adamant but her voice had a high-pitched squeal to it that betrayed her.

'The quality is poor, I tell you. It tore the first time I tried to wear it.' McLeesh replied.

'You can't have followed the instructions I gave you,' Evelyn insisted, 'I did warn you that it is difficult to put on and you must dust yourself first.'

'I did all that. Look, it cost me a fortune. I want a refund.'

'I can't do that, Mr McLeesh. Now will you leave please. I am busy.'

'I'm not going till you pay me.'

'It's not my responsibility,' Evelyn said, changing tack, 'You'll have to try the manufacturer if you think it was substandard.'

'Damn right, I will. And you will be hearing from my solicitor.'

'Really. Will that be Stuart's or Stella's solicitor?'

Leigh heard a spluttering and then the door being closed with a slam. The bell was still tinkling when Evelyn reappeared, looking flushed and sweaty.

'I'm sorry about that interruption,' she said and then looked at Leigh admiringly, 'But don't you look a picture.'

Leigh basked in Evelyn's attention while also peering at herself in the mirrors. She liked what she saw.

'Now we're not finished yet,' Evelyn said, 'With your complexion you need a blonde wig, don't you think?'

Leigh nodded. Evelyn pushed a small stool against the wall, mounted it unsteadily, and reached up to the top shelf for a long blonde wig. She lifted it down and took it off its stand.

'Sit in the chair, please, love and I'll put it on you.'

Leigh sat down and held her head straight as the wig was lowered over her skull. There were a few minor adjustments then Evelyn stepped back and looked at her handiwork.

'That looks fine. Now sit still while I find some shoes. What size are you. Let me guess. Eights?'

Leigh nodded and Evelyn hurried to a cupboard, pulling out a shoe box. She took out a pair of black patent pumps with a three-inch heel.

'How are you with heels, dear?'

'I've practised at home,' Leigh said.

'Good. Let's try these then.' Evelyn knelt and fitted the shoes onto Leigh's stockinged feet. She stood up and stepped back. 'Now let's have a look at you.'

Leigh pushed herself on to her toes and somewhat shakily straightened up. Despite what she had said, wearing high heels was not an everyday experience.

'Take a few steps, and give us a twirl,' Evelyn ordered.

Leigh took two wobbly steps towards a mirror and looked at her image. She saw a tall, slim, woman with a head of shoulder-length hair.

'Gorgeous,' Evelyn said, 'Now there's just your face to do and add a few pieces of jewellery. Your ears aren't pierced, are they?'

Leigh shook her head, feeling the long hair brush her cheeks and neck.

'Right, well sit down and I'll get started.'

Leigh sat in the chair once again and relaxed while Evelyn applied foundation, eye shadow, mascara, blusher, powder, lipstick and finally fitted a pair of outrageously long gold-coloured earrings by clips to her lobes.

Evelyn stepped back to examine her efforts. 'Yes, I think you will like that.'

A voice from upstairs made Leigh jump.

'Evelyn! Evelyn! Come here at once. We need you.'

Leigh was surprised at Evelyn's reaction. She appeared to curl up like a hedgehog as if trying to make herself smaller. She immediately hurried to the stairs between the front and back rooms.

'Coming, darling,' she called in a plaintive, little girl voice. She paused at the bottom of the stairs as if just remembering her client.

'Have a look around. Make yourself at home. I won't be too long,' she said as she disappeared up the stairs.

Leigh sat dazed for a few moments wondering who the "we" were and why Evelyn should react with such alacrity that the call had to be answered without delay. A minute or two passed and she decided that Evelyn was not going to return immediately. She stood up and walked across the room and through into the front shop. She enjoyed the feel of the dress clinging to her body and of her nylon covered legs rubbing against each other. The high heels caused a little unsteadiness on her feet and the weighty breasts made her top-heavy, but she imagined this was a feminine feeling. She casually fingered through the multi-coloured frocks hanging on the rack. A noise came from the room above, the squeaking and rumble of a heavy piece of furniture moving on a floorboard in a rhythmic manner. There were other sounds too; faint gasps and cries.

Leigh could only think that she was hearing the sound of sexual intercourse but found it difficult to believe that Evelyn was the one servicing the female who had called for her, or his, attention. She felt uncomfortable listening to the intimate behaviour so returned to the "boudoir". She was drawn to the mannequin in the bra and pants that she had noticed at the start. It definitely had a different quality to the models used to display clothes. She reached out a finger to touch the model's stomach. It was soft on the surface, springy, not as smooth as plastic. She moved her hand up to the mannequin's breasts. Though firm, the flesh was depressed by her finger. It felt just like the breasts she was wearing and she realised the skin resembled the knickers she had put on. Then she recalled the body suits she had seen on the website. This was one of those, fitted onto the body of a regular mannequin. It was seamless and where it ended on the upper arms and thighs and around the neck, the line was almost indistinguishable.

With no sign yet of Evelyn returning, Leigh slipped her hand under the models' knickers. Her fingertips encountered labia. Although there was resistance from the dry rubber, they slipped into a channel that could swallow more than one extended finger. Leigh withdrew her hand amazed at the realistic appearance of the suit.

She stepped back to look at herself in a mirror. Her image had lost its initial semblance of perfection. She noted that although the dress clung to her body there was little sign of a waist and her bottom and hips were significantly narrower than her shoulders. Despite the big tits, she still had a boy's figure. The breasts too pulled down on her bra cups which in turn tugged on the straps over her shoulders. Her breasts were not really part of her and just hung from her chest. She glanced at the model. That was what she wanted – a full, female body suit.

She heard footsteps on the stairs and Evelyn reappeared. Her hair, or wig, was slightly mussed and her lipstick smudged.

'I'm sorry to leave you like that,' Evelyn said somewhat breathlessly.

Leigh pointed to the model. 'I want one of those.'

Evelyn's face showed bewilderment, then understanding and

finally joy. 'You'd like to buy a full female body suit?'

'Yes, I want to have a really feminine figure.'

Evelyn looked doubtful, 'You do realise the price. It's just under two thousand pounds for the full piece.'

'I know that. I've been saving for this. This is what I want.'

The smile spread across Evelyn's face, 'Well, I am delighted to oblige you madam.' She gave a little curtsey. 'Of course, I don't have one in stock for you; they are manufactured individually to your measurements and colouring from the best silicone rubber. Wearing one of those you can really be the woman you want to be.'

Leigh was already daydreaming of partying and clubbing, with her male and female friends and even perhaps meeting a man who would …

'I will need payment in advance,' Evelyn added.

Leigh blinked. 'Of course.'

Evelyn had changed into her evening outfit, the maid's uniform with the short black dress and petticoats, ready to begin her nightly chores. The corset made it a little difficult to breathe but she welcomed the constriction along with the other impediments that Harriet made her wear. She sat upright at her desk and tapped at her laptop. There were a few more emails to deal with, a few orders; not many though, not enough. She paused. That order from Leigh, however, paid in advance would tide her over for a while. If the cheque didn't bounce. She didn't think it would. Leigh seemed a genuine newbie tranny, and apparently had a well-remunerated job which enabled her to afford the expense of being who she wanted to be.

A knock on the door made her look up. She expected to see Harriet with her toy boy, Tyler, returning having gone out after Leigh left. It was however, two men she could see through the glass of the door. Evelyn recognised them but was not pleased to see them. One of them bashed their hand on the door again, hard, rattling it in its frame.

'Let us in or we'll smash yer door in,' he shouted.

Reluctantly, Evelyn rose from her seat and, trembling, went to the door. Would avoiding damage to the door result in damage to herself? She wasn't sure but unlocked the latch anyway and opened the door slowly. It was thrust aside as the two men crowded in, pushing her back against the desk.

'You don't keep us waiting outside, perv.' The bald-headed spokesman said, leaning over Evelyn with a clenched fist raised. His companion, a dark-haired, bearded man with an east-European appearance stood behind him, at ease.

Having made his threat, the tough guy, straightened up cupping his fist with his left hand. Evelyn slid around her desk putting it between herself and her unwanted visitors.

'Mr Griffiths, wants the instalment on yer loan,' baldy went on.

'Yes, yes, I know. I have it, well, I, er, don't have the um, cash,' Evelyn stuttered. 'I need to go to the bank.'

'Mr Griffiths is getting impatient. He doesn't like clients who delay paying what they owe.'

'No, of course not,' Evelyn nodded her head rapidly in agreement. 'I can get it on Monday when the bank is open.'

'Make sure you do. We'll be back Monday evening. And don't forget the extra, for the insurance.' He nodded to his companion. The silent fellow crossed the shop floor to the rack of dresses, took a grip of the rail and tipped it. The steel frame crashed over, spilling frocks across the wooden floor. 'Whoops. Accidents happen. You wouldn't want a bigger accident to happen if you delay paying, would you?' He turned, beckoned to his assistant and marched out of the shop.

Evelyn followed them, her whole body shaking. She pushed the door closed and dropped the latch once more. She lifted the clothes rail back on to its legs and methodically rehung all the dresses on their hangers. She hoped Leigh's cheque could be cashed on Monday.

She turned at the sound of a key turning in the lock. The door opened again to let in a slim elegantly dressed woman a few inches taller than Evelyn, but of similar age, followed by a younger, dark-haired man with broad shoulders and the stance of a bodybuilder.

'Oh, hello, Harriet,' Evelyn said standing with her head bowed and hands crossed in front of her

'Why aren't you upstairs preparing dinner, Evelyn? Tyler and I are starving.'

'I had a visit from Neville Griffiths' goons.'

'Those thugs! What did they want?'

'Money.'

'Of course they do. I told you not to borrow from that criminal.'

Evelyn sighed. 'I had no choice. You insisted that I pay off Gary Nicholls.'

'Don't go blaming me for your financial incompetence. If you'd made a success of this business, you could have bought out Gary with no problems and we'd be rid of him.'

'It was you that gave him a third share when you and he were…'

'How dare you make it seem that your troubles are my fault,' Harriet screamed, 'You're in for more punishment later, I promise you.'

'Yes, dear,' Evelyn replied, her voice weak and trembling.

'Now get upstairs where you should be. Tyler and I need a drink.'

As Evelyn climbed the stairs she heard Harriet speak in a much softer voice.

'Come along, my darling. Let's get you out of these horribly restricting clothes and think about the lovely things we can do to each other.'

4

Jasmine gazed out of the conservatory windows. The temperature outside may be autumnal, but the bright sunshine made the garden and the country beyond look warm and inviting. This morning she felt that she might have the energy to do more than a gentle stroll around the garden. She knew she shouldn't spend so much time just sitting more than a fortnight after her operation.

The first week had been difficult; she couldn't believe how tired she felt. Viv kept on telling her it was to be expected after major surgery, but she felt guilty doing nothing at home while he went out to work, even though she couldn't have stirred herself anyway. But now the fatigue was fading and the soreness between her legs was wearing off despite the infection that she had developed on leaving the hospital. It was getting a little easier doing the thrice daily dilations although her vulva was still swollen. There was little feeling in her clitoris, which wasn't surprising considering the manner in which it had been fashioned from the glans of her excised penis. Now she was beginning to get impatient, with herself as much as anyone, for not having the energy, the inclination, the simple "get up and go" to stir herself.

Part of the problem was perhaps the feeling of contentment. She knew how lucky she was. First, she was now the woman she had long felt herself to be and soon she would be fit enough to try out the new organ she had been given, although that in itself was another quandary – how would Viv feel? No one could now question her assertion that she was female, not unless they did a DNA test on her, but could Viv forget what she had been? He said he had always thought of her as a woman but did she believe him? She also realised how lucky she was to be living in this smart and spacious home, so much more comfortable than her old, dingy flat. That was Viv again of course. Okay, they had looked around potential properties together and both agreed that this was the one, but it was Viv's salary that secured the mortgage not her pitiful earnings as a private investigator, and her past as a rising police detective no longer counted.

The last nine months had passed in a whirl of activity – choosing the house, moving in, settling into a shared life with Viv, and the news that her gender confirmation was imminent. Now things had slowed, or had in fact stopped, while she recovered. She glanced at her watch; time for the first dilation of the day.

Jasmine climbed the stairs, still feeling a twinge of pain in her abdomen as she lifted each foot. She went into her bedroom; yes, it was hers not theirs. Viv had graciously given her the room with the ensuite while she prepared and went through with her confirmation surgery. The move to a shared room and bed was planned for the near future. That thought gave Jasmine both a thrill and and worry. Would she be woman enough for Viv? What would intercourse with a man feel like?

For now, the room was hers alone. Her clothes, a growing wardrobe, again thanks to Viv's generosity, occupied the small dressing room. Her laptop lived on the dressing table amongst her cosmetics, and the double bed was hers to spread out in.

She shrugged off the loose jogging pants and slipped out of her knickers – no longer the big, tight pants she used to wear. The feel of thin, light, pretty knickers was one of her daily pleasures. She lay on the bed, reached for the hand-mirror, spread her legs and examined herself. As the swelling reduced and her flesh took on a less vivid colouration she grew more and more amazed at the wonders the surgeon had wrought. For years, she couldn't bear to look between her legs; now it was an object of fascination. She put the mirror down and reached into the bedside drawer for the dilators. This wasn't a pleasure, more of a chore, but one she was resigned to now that it needed to be done. She felt that she was preparing herself for Viv.

………………

'Look at it from my point of view, Mr Bunting.'

Evelyn frowned while holding the phone to her ear. She didn't like being referred to by the male honorific but she wasn't in a position to correct her supplier.

'It's a firm order, Mr Rana.'

'I know it is, but will I get paid? You already have a big debt to repay, Mr Bunting, for previous orders.'

He's taunting me, Evelyn thought, he knows I've lived as a woman for years.

'Those bills will be paid, Mr Rana. This order is special.'

'Of course it's special. These all-singing, all-dancing body suits are bloody expensive and they are made to order. If I take the order and you don't pay for it, I'm stuck with it. That's why I need cash in advance.'

Evelyn sweated into her dress. She couldn't pay for the body-suit in advance because she had withdrawn the cash from the account to pay Griffiths. If she didn't hand over the cash to Griffiths' thugs this evening she wouldn't have a business and perhaps not a life. There was only one thing to do – lie.

'I'll put a cheque in the post Mr Rana. First thing tomorrow morning. I promise.'

'No Mr Bunting, I cannot accept your promises. Your cheques have a habit of bouncing. I need to see your cash or, of course you could transfer the funds from your bank account to mine like most businessmen do these days.'

'I'll do that, Mr Rana, I promise.'

'We'll see, Mr Bunting. Until then, no order.' The phone line clicked. Evelyn sighed and put the phone down. What was she to do. Leigh was already pestering her for a delivery date for her suit and knew that her cheque had been cashed, but Akash Rana wouldn't accept the order without payment in advance and Evelyn needed the money to pay off some of the loan from Griffiths which was used to buy out Gary Nicholls, her former partner. Meanwhile Harriet expected to live the life of a business tycoon with all the expense that that entailed.

She shook her head. The business was doomed anyway. Few people came all the way to Thirsbury to visit the shop and the website took few orders because browsers went straight to the big suppliers like Rana's company. Perhaps though there was a way. She pulled open the filing drawer beside her desk and rummaged through the papers. Eventually she let out a cry of success. She read the document word for word, and in particular the date at the end. Yes, it was all paid up and valid. She reached for the phone again and dialled Neville Griffiths' number.

....

Viv arrived home soon after five. Jasmine felt a little guilty that he was still striving to leave work as early as possible despite the responsibilities of his job.

'How have you been today, love?' he said having leant forward to kiss her lips.

'Improving.' It had been her daily mantra for at least the last week.

Viv tipped his head sideways. 'Really?'

'Yes, really. I've only taken one painkiller today, and I don't feel so tired.'

Viv's face crinkled into a broad smile. 'That's great. You're ready to entertain Angela and, what's his name, her new bloke?'

'Simon. Yes, I'm looking forward to seeing both of them. I've even been in the kitchen getting stuff ready.'

'You? In the kitchen?'

'Yes, I've opened two packets of nibbles.'

Viv laughed. 'Well, I'm glad you won't starve while I cook my one pot chicken.'

'Is that one of your father's specialities?'

'Of course, brought from Jamaica and entrusted to me, eventually.' He put his arms around her waist and pulled her towards him. She winced. Viv dropped his hands and stepped back. 'Sorry. Was I too rough?'

Jasmine was annoyed with herself. 'No, it wasn't your fault. Let's try again; a little more gently.'

Jasmine had been sitting by the front window as dusk darkened into night. While Viv busied in the kitchen, she was looking out for Angela and Simon's arrival, feeling apprehensive. There was no problem between Viv and Angela; she knew they both loved her. Angela accepted that she and Jasmine were no longer a couple and Viv had shown no sign of being jealous of the continued close friendship between Angela and Jasmine. Jasmine thought, and hoped, that he viewed them as long-time girlfriends rather than the former husband and wife that they had actually been. The problem was Simon, well, not necessarily Simon himself. Jasmine still felt a little raw at her encounter with Angela's first post-divorce lover, Luke. He had turned out to be a transphobe and Angela had hastily dumped him. It had taken her a long time to try again and Simon was the lucky fellow.

Jasmine didn't want to be judgemental, but she couldn't help wanting to be sure that Angela had found someone who would love and respect her as much as she herself had done when she had been James most of the time. She knew she no longer had the right to give her opinion to Angela but on the other hand Angela still seemed to want her approval, hence this evening's meeting.

After visiting her in hospital, Angela had rung and texted frequently and suggested this evening get together as soon as she felt that Jasmine was recovered enough. Viv of course was happy to oblige.

A car drew up outside and put out its lights. The shadowy shape of a man got out of the passenger seat and stood still until he was joined by the driver. Jasmine's first observation was that he was a good few inches taller than Angela which made him a good few inches taller than her. As they approached the illuminated porch Jasmine could see he was also slim and dark. She slipped off the couch and hurried to open the front door.

5

'Yes, Mr Griffiths, I understand. Everything will be ready. Thank you.' Evelyn heard the click of the line closing and she put the phone down on her desk with a smile spreading across her face. Everything was falling into place as she had hoped. She got up from her seat and went to lock the shop door. It was dark outside and the street quiet.

A call came from upstairs. Well, less a call, more of a screeched demand. Evelyn turned and hurried up the stairs, the hem of her long dress gathered in her arms. At the top of the stairs she turned left, into the bedroom. Harriet was lying on the bed, naked, with Tyler beside her also unclothed, kissing her left nipple.

'What were you doing downstairs, Sissy?' Evelyn's wife asked in an impatient tone.

'A phone call.' Evelyn answered, nerves making her voice quake

Harriet glared, ignoring the tongue caressing her breast. 'A phone call, what!'

'Mistress,' Evelyn bowed her head.

'That's better. Now, no more phone calls. You know what you should be doing.' Her voice softened into a sigh as Tyler's ministrations had an effect.

'Yes, Mistress,' Evelyn acknowledged.

'Well, get that ghastly dress off. Tyler needs you to prepare him.' Harriet smoothed the young man's short curly black hair. Evelyn admired how his gleaming dark skin contrasted with her wife's pale body. She reached down to pull her dress off over her head revealing the white satin corset she had been wearing all day. It cinched in her waist, tightly but not painfully and cupped her artificial D-cup breasts. Her legs were encased in white silk stockings held up by suspenders connected to her corset. She dropped the dress on the landing and stood upright waiting for her orders.

It was a few minutes before Harriet noticed her again. Tyler was working on her other nipple now and sliding a hand up and down between her legs. Harriet's eyes focussed and then she frowned.

'You're still wearing knickers. Remove them at once.' Her voice was stern. Evelyn obeyed immediately, tugging the almost insignificant garment down her thighs.

'You know I want to see it, pathetic little thing that it is,' Harriet went on. 'If you won't do as you're told, you won't get to have it released.'

Evelyn sighed. Harriet was always finding excuses for refusing to unlock the device that enclosed her penis. The anticipation was getting excruciating.

'Come and see to Tyler,' Harriet went on, 'I'm just about ready for him.'

Evelyn climbed onto the bed and shuffled closer to the dark man.

. . . .

Jasmine kicked off her shoes and sank onto the sofa. She sighed with gratitude as the fatigue oozed out of her. Why was she so exhausted? Well, it was the latest she'd been up since her op and the first time she had been out for an evening. But they hadn't had to walk far to the car and they'd only been sitting in a cinema after a light meal in a restaurant. When would she regain her old energy? She longed to get back to her daily run but that seemed out of the question at the moment.

Viv came into the lounge and looked at her sprawled over the chair.

'Tired, love?'

'Yes. I'm sorry Viv. I don't know why I'm still like this.'

'I do, you silly. It's still less than a month since you had your surgery. I think you're doing marvellous. This evening was lovely and you looked, you do look, stunning.' He sat down beside her, leant over her and kissed her on the cheek.

'Really?'

'Really.'

Viv's compliment reassured her because although the exhaustion had hit on the way home she had felt a new confidence while they were out. She was a woman with her boyfriend and that was all there was to say. On her first visit to a Ladies' loo since her op she had also felt the right that her new anatomy gave her. It was silly really, since how could any of the other women there have known what she did or didn't have between her legs?

'Ready for bed?' Viv asked.

'Mmm.'

'Do you want to join me? I can help you get to sleep.'

A fear stabbed at her. 'I'm not ready yet, Viv. The swelling…'

Viv shook his head. 'I wasn't suggesting that. Just a cuddle and kiss or two. Don't worry, love, we'll only do it when you're good and ready. I know now is much too soon.'

Jasmine felt reassured. 'Well, alright then. A cuddle sounds nice.'

. . . .

Evelyn sat at her desk with her dressing gown wrapped around her corseted body. Harriet and Tyler were dozing in each other's arms but she had a few emails to write to set the scene. There were only a few minutes available and she must return to the bedside before her absence was noted. Harriet needed little excuse to add to her punishments. She tapped in Gary's email address. It had been a while since she had contacted their old partner. This seemed a good opportunity to get a bit of a comeback on his wife's previous lover. Evelyn grinned as she typed out the message.

6

Tom Shepherd leaned against the bonnet of his Ford Mondeo and let out a long sigh. He noticed that the sky was lightening and he glanced at his watch; it was just after seven a.m. The night had passed quickly while they were getting the investigation started. Dr Winslade had completed her preliminary examination of the body and it had been taken away to the mortuary; SOCO were all over the building since the Fire Service's Incident Commander had decided that the upper floor was safe; and uniformed officers had got initial statements from neighbours who had been woken to warn them of the fire. The onlookers had dispersed hours ago once the flames had died down and the news of the discovery of the body had spread. Now there was just one fire engine left and the road was open to traffic.

DC Patel approached carrying two disposable cups. 'I got you a coffee, Sir. Milk and sugar.'

Tom's eyebrows rose in surprise. 'Thanks Sasha. Where did you get it?'

She nodded down the hill. 'A coffee shop down Broad Street opens early for commuters using the station. I use it some days before I drive into Kintbridge.'

'Ah, yes,' Tom nodded, 'Were there any other people there.'

'There were two or three in front of me and others came in after, the owner does a good trade. The, uh, incident was the main topic of conversation.'

'I bet it was. Did you ask any questions?' Tom realised it was a silly question. Sasha was a good detective; of course, she would ask questions.

'I didn't need to ask much once they knew I was a police officer. Most of them had something to say. Obviously, a fire in the main street and a death was of interest but few of them knew anything specific about Molly's or Evelyn Bunting. The proprietor knew her though. He said she came in for a coffee now and again and he knew she wasn't a real woman.'

'Did he know what type of business Evelyn ran?'

'He just thought it was some kind of clothes shop for trannies, but he insisted that it was all very discreet and that the shop wasn't a problem especially as it was right at the top of town.'

'So, if this coffee-shop owner is representative of the businesses in town they weren't too concerned about what Evelyn was getting up to behind her tasteful shop window.'

Sasha shook her head. 'Molly's USP isn't obvious from the window displays. I never took any notice of it and none of the customers in the coffeeshop seemed to either, or at least didn't want to admit to knowing.'

Tom sipped his coffee which was still hot despite Sasha having carried it up the street.

'So, what do we know then?' he asked.

'We have the owner of the premises, dead,' Patel began.

'Killed by a blow to the head with a heavy, blunt implement,' Tom added. 'and she is transgender but what that means in Evelyn Bunting's case I don't know. Her dress and that thing around her genitals – what does that mean?'

'I don't know, Sir, but she was married or had a partner.'

'Ah, yes. Where is Mrs Bunting? Harriet, isn't it?'

'Yes, Sir. She wasn't in the house when the fire service arrived and she hasn't returned yet. None of the neighbours knew where she might be.'

'But we're fairly certain that the fire was deliberate.'

'Yes, Sir. The Chief Fire Officer thought it was probably started in the front and that an accelerant was used. I think he means petrol.'

'So, we have an arson, a dead owner and a missing wife.' Tom noticed a large Volvo draw to a halt behind his own car. 'And we have DCI Sloane to answer to,' he added.

The DCI hauled his grey bulk out of the newly arrived car and with a few large strides, joined them.

'Good morning DI Shepherd, DC Patel. I understand you are running a murder investigation.'

'Yes, Sir.'

'Suspects?'

'None yet, Sir, although the deceased's wife is absent.'

Sloane glared at Tom. 'Absent? You mean you don't know her location?'

'That's correct, Sir. She apparently left before anyone responded to the fire alarm and has not returned. We haven't discovered where she went.'

'I see. Do you have a description?'

'Yes, Sir. No photos of her yet but some of the neighbours…'

'Good. If nothing else she needs to be informed that her husband is dead.'

Tom bit his lip. 'Um, yes, sir. Actually, I'm not sure that husband is the right word.'

Sloane frowned. 'Partner then. Is the dead person a woman?'

'We're not sure of her gender identity, Sir,' Tom replied noting the muscles in the DCI's neck tense. 'Physically the body is male but she apparently dressed as a woman most if not all the time.'

'A transvestite.' Sloane snorted the word. 'Looks like you had better have some words with Frame.'

'Yes, Sir,' Tom nodded.

'And I suggest that one of you gets some rest. I believe you've been up all night.'

'Yes, Sir, that's correct Sir.'

'Well, carry on, Detective Inspector. I want this case cleared up as soon as possible. Sounds as if the wife should be able to provide the answers when you have located her.' Sloane turned and strode back to his car. He got in, started the engine, reversed a few feet then did a swift three-point turn and drove off down the street.

Tom watched the receding car with DC Patel.

'Well, Sir. It looks as though the DCI is letting you run the investigation.'

Tom took in a deep breath. 'It does, doesn't it, and the first thing to do is for you to go home and get some rest. We'll meet back at the police station at...' he glanced at his watch, 'One p.m. when I've found out who else Sloane is assigning to assist us.'

'Thank you, Sir.'

Tom walked around his car and opened the driver's door.'

Patel called out, 'What are going to do now, Sir? Don't you need a bit of sleep too?'

'I'm going to do what both Sloane and Dr Winslade suggested – have a chat with Jasmine Frame.' He got into his seat.

The brief ring on the doorbell made Jasmine jump from her bed. She grabbed her dressing gown and wrapped it around herself, covering her nightdress, then hurried down the stairs, just wincing slightly as she strained her groin muscles. The silhouette seen through the crinkly glass of the front door immediately revealed who her early morning visitor was.

She opened the door with a cheerful greeting, 'Hi, Tom.'

Tom appeared a little confused as his eyes flicked up and down her clothes. 'Hi, Jas. Look, I'm sorry if I got you up.'

'You didn't. I was still in bed but I've been awake since before Viv went off. He likes to get to work early.'

'That's good. I'd pressed the button before I thought that you might still be um, convalescing.'

'I am, but it doesn't mean I'm stuck in bed all day. Come in, it feels pretty chilly out there.'

Tom stepped inside the door and once Jasmine had pushed it closed he followed her into the lounge. She watched him looking around, taking in the comfortable and smartly furnished room.

'Have a seat,' she said, 'Coffee?'

'Uh, yes please.' Tom settled onto the sofa stretching out his long legs in front of him. Jasmine took in his heavy eyelids and the way that he slumped.

'You look knackered. Have you been up all night?'

'Yes.'

'I don't suppose you've had anything to eat, have you?'

'Er, no.' The mention of food seemed to come as a surprise to Tom.

'Toast do you?'

'Mmm, yes, thanks.'

Jasmine went through to the kitchen-diner put the kettle on and dropped a couple of slices of bread in the toaster. She put coffee into a couple of mugs.

'Nice place you've got here.'

Jasmine turned around to see Tom leaning against the doorway.

'Yes, it is, but of course, it's Viv's place really. I'm just the lodger.' She poured the boiling water into the mugs and added milk and sugar to one which she handed to Tom. The toast popped.

'Lodger? I thought it was a bit more than that; you and Viv.'

Jasmine felt herself blushing. Although she knew that she and Viv were a couple, that they were even sharing a bed, she still felt uncertain about what other people thought, even people she knew as well as Tom.

'Well, yes, we are, but it's still Viv's house, at least for now.'

Tom's eyes wandered around the well-equipped kitchen while Jasmine prepared the toast.

'Well, you've done well, the two of you.'

'I like it. Viv does too although he grumbles that we could have got a bigger place up where he comes from.'

'Birmingham?'

'That area. Here.' She handed the two slices of toast on a plate to Tom.

Tom took the plate in the hand not holding the mug. 'What about you?'

'I'll have the next slice. Go and sit down and eat.' She shooed him back into the lounge where he resumed his seat on the sofa. When the next batch of toast was ready she joined Tom. She picked up one slice and dropped it onto Tom's plate.

'There, I'm sure you can manage three.' She settled herself down in the chair and picked up her own plate.

'Mmm, thanks.' Tom said through a full mouth. He examined her.

'There's something different about you Jas. Your hair?'

Jasmine reached for her locks of hair that almost touched her shoulders. 'I've let it grow since before I went into hospital. I've never had hair this long before; not my own anyway.'

Tom swallowed, 'I'm sorry Jas. I should have asked sooner. Hospital, operation. How are you?'

Jasmine smiled. 'I'm fine. Getting there. I hope I don't look too bad. Of course, I haven't put any make-up on yet this morning…'

'No, no, you look great. But your op. You had it, er, all done?'

'Yes, Tom. I'm now the woman I wanted to be with all the correct bits.'

It was Tom's turn to flush.

'Mind you,' Jasmine went on, 'I felt like wanting to die afterwards.'

'Oh, was it bad then?'

'Indescribable. I would have got myself hooked on morphine if the nurses had let me. You know, Tom, despite all the preparations and reading about other tee-esses, the pain and discomfort after the op was still incredible.'

'You're better now?'

'As I said, getting there. Moving about and walking is getting easier but I still get tired pretty quickly, and,' she gave him her conspiratorial smile, 'the exercises I have to do down there, you, know, to stretch it, take it out of me a bit.'

Tom's blush turned a deeper shade of red. 'You mean you have to stuff things up inside you.'

'Yes, Tom, if I want to be a functioning woman.'

Tom shook his head and the hand holding the slice of toast. 'Enough! Don't tell me anymore.'

Jasmine giggled. 'OK, Tom. What about your news; you've made Detective Inspector.'

Tom smiled and looked proud. 'Yes, it came quicker than I was expecting, but with the changes and Sloane being given more admin, I suppose they needed a DI in the unit.'

'So, you're running the Violent and Serious Crime Unit now?'

'Well, Sloane is still nominally in charge, but he's not in the office much.'

Jasmine had a thought. 'I guess I'm honoured to have you drop in at last.'

Tom frowned, 'I'm sorry, Jas. I should have come to see you when you sent out your new address, but Sloane's kept us pretty busy and then Soph had Abi…'

'Oh, gosh, Tom. I forgot. You're a Daddy.' Jasmine clapped her hand over her mouth. She felt dreadful that she had been teasing Tom for not visiting her while she had been so full of her move with Viv and having her GRS. She had forgotten about his expanding family. 'How are they? Sophie and Abi, did you say?'

'Yes, Abigail. She's lovely, not sleeping much though. Giving Sophie a pretty hard time of it since I'm rarely around to do my share.'

'No, I understand.' She didn't really. She and Angela hadn't had children, of course, and she couldn't imagine really giving birth and bringing up a child. She was a woman, she was sure of it, but she would never have that female experience. 'I'm sorry Tom. I should have given her something.'

'It's okay Jas. We've both been pretty busy one way or another.'

'Well, you're here now and it's great to see you, but I don't suppose this is a social visit.'

'No.'

'What is it?'

'A case, Jas.'

'I guessed.'

Tom described the fire at Molly's, the discovery of the body, the missing wife and their investigations through the night.

'Why have you come to see me so quickly this morning? Surely there's a lot of information gathering going on.'

'Of course, there is, Jas, but Sloane and Winslade think you may be able to help.'

'Sloane and Dr Winslade? You mean there's a trans angle.' Why else would DCI Sloane suggest her involvement. It seemed that she popped into his mind when anything transgender was mentioned. But the pathologist too; that was interesting.

'You got it. The victim is physically male but was dressed in female clothes. Apparently, she did all the time.'

Jasmine nodded, her suspicions confirmed. 'A pre-op TS then.'

'Perhaps, Winslade discovered that her, or his, I don't know which; his I suppose, anyway, his genitals were encased in some sort of metal frame. She said it may be a chastity device. Do you know what I mean?'

'Yes, Tom. A chastity cage, locked around the penis and testicles, it stops the wearer from getting an erection. I presume there was a lock.'

Tom shook his head and shrugged. 'I don't know.'

'Winslade's doing the post-mortem?'

'Yes, she had the body delivered to the mortuary a couple of hours ago.'

'Well, you'll soon be able to see what a chastity cage is. But I think it means that your victim wasn't TS in the same sense as I am, or was. I didn't want to remember I had that dangling between my legs let alone emphasise it by locking it up.'

Tom seemed to squirm on the sofa. 'He, er she, must have been aware of it all the time.'

'Exactly. Who is she and what is the shop that burned down?

54

Did you say it was called Molly's?'

'Her name was Evelyn Bunting, there doesn't seem to be a Molly.'

'Evelyn. Interesting, one of those male-female names.'

'That's right. She owned Molly's. There's a website too.' Tom dug in the pocket of his jacket and pulled out his phone, 'She sold clothes and other gear for transvestites and offered them dressing sessions. Look.' Tom thumbed the screen and when he'd got to the webpage he passed it across to Jasmine. She flicked through the site.

'I see. And all this was happening in staid old Thirsbury?'

'The shop was very discreet, apparently, and although Bunting's retail activities were known, there doesn't seem to have been any problem with the neighbours.'

'I don't suppose many transvestites made the journey to Thirsbury. Probably most of the business was online. But she was taking a bit of a chance.'

'Why?'

'Well, Tom, have you never heard of mollyhouses?'

Tom's face was blank. 'No, should I?'

Jasmine shrugged. 'Probably not. Homosexuality was legalised long before we were born.' She took a breath. 'In the eighteenth and nineteenth centuries mollyhouses were where gay men met. Some of them dressed as women. They may have been transsexuals or cross-dressers – they didn't have those names for them then. Or they were drag-queens who did it to service the other gay guys or even straight men fancying something a bit different.'

Tom's mouth hung open. It was a few moments before he closed it. 'I see. So, Bunting was signalling what her business was.'

'Sort of. Perhaps trannies would understand, if they know their queer history. I'm not saying that she was running a gay brothel or anything. It may be just what the website says it is; somewhere for trans guys to visit to be transformed into women.'

'You've just given me an idea, Jas. We hadn't come up with a motive earlier unless it was a domestic between Bunting and his missing wife; but, what if someone found out that Bunting was running a mollyhouse like you described and didn't like it and decided to shut it down.'

Jasmine shrugged. 'It's possible but you said that you haven't heard any rumours of discontent about the shop or anger directed at Bunting.'

'No, nothing like that.'

'Well, it's an idea, but I think you need to look more closely at Bunting and his wife. The clothes you described sound a bit kinky – a sexy maid's uniform, very high heels, and the chastity cage. Evelyn Bunting sounds a bit like a sissy to me.'

'A sissy?' Tom was wide-eyed again.

'A man forced into women's clothes. Well, I say forced; they love it really. A male submissive with a dominant woman.'

'Harriet Bunting?'

'Pretty likely.'

Tom put the final morsel of toast into his mouth and hauled himself to his feet.

'Well, I'd better make sure she turns up to answer some questions.'

'A good idea. If she's alive.'

Tom froze. 'I hadn't considered she might not be. God, another complication. Thanks Jas.'

Tom headed towards the front door with Jasmine behind him. He paused and turned. 'Look Jas, see what else you can find out about Molly's and Evelyn Bunting, and this sissy thing. Perhaps you can come over to Thirsbury and have a look around. There's stuff in that shop that I don't get.'

'Er, yes, Tom, but I'm not really running around or driving just yet.'

'I'll pick you up. This afternoon. I'll give you a call. It will be like old times – you and me.'

'Not quite, Tom, you're a DI now, but, okay, I'll be ready.'

'Good. See you later.' He turned again and almost seemed to

hurry out through the door and back to his car. Jasmine watched him depart.

Jasmine carried the mugs and plates into the kitchen and headed back upstairs to her bedroom. She was going back to work. Well, it felt like that although she realised that Tom probably wouldn't need much assistance from her. During her weeks of recovery, she hadn't thought much about her career as a private detective but now she felt an excitement as if her brain had clicked on and was already analysing the case.

She showered and performed her exercises, not perfunctorily, as she knew how important they were to her future as a woman. Then she dressed, not in the sloppy bottoms and loose tops that had been her normal wear since the operation, but opaque tights, a skirt and blouse – her work uniform. All the time she was thinking over what Tom had told her.

Once she had applied some foundation and lipstick she made space on her dressing table to open up her laptop. She quickly found the Molly's website and went through every page. What she saw revealed a lot about Evelyn Bunting's business. Then she explored the topic of "sissies". Not totally ignoring the porn, she soon confirmed that the description of Evelyn matched some characteristics of this subset of effeminate males and raised some questions she would like to ask of Harriet.

She was totally absorbed in her research when her phone buzzed. She grabbed it; Tom.

'Hi Tom. Have you got more news?' She glanced at the time and was surprised to find that three hours had passed since Tom had left and that it was now gone eleven o'clock.

His audibly tired voice replied, 'Yes. Harriet Bunting has turned up. She returned to what is left of her home a short while ago. A couple of the officers that were on duty at the scene are bringing her in for a chat and then we'll go to see Dr Winslade and formally identify the body.'

'That's good news. There are plenty of questions she needs to answer.'

'Yes, I've got a few. Perhaps you've got some more.'

'Just a few dozen.'

'Oh! I guess you've been thinking about it.'

'And doing some background research.'

'That's great. I knew you'd be a help.'

'Yes, well, it's an interesting case.' Jasmine wondered where the conversation was going. She couldn't exactly interview the woman herself as she wasn't a police officer.

'Look, Jas. I wonder if you'd mind coming in and giving us some advice on what questions to ask.'

'Yes, okay, but...'

'I'll get someone to come and pick you up. It'll probably be Terry Hopkins. Sloane has assigned him to the case.'

'Oh, he's still with you, is he?' They had once been colleagues, she and DC Hopkins, but never buddies. Her opinion of the older detective constable was somewhat soured by his attitude to her transition.

'Yes, he's still here, the same old Terry. He's a plodder but he does the business.'

'I suppose so. Okay, I'll be waiting for him. I hope he's civil.'

'I'm sure you can handle him if he's not.' Jasmine heard a chuckle in Tom's voice as the call ended.

Jasmine dropped some essential items into her bag, the first time that she'd had to prepare to go out for anything other than a gentle stroll or a brief evening out with Viv. She put her woollen coat on and stood in the lounge looking out at the road wondering how long it would be before Hopkins arrived.

She was surprised when after only a few minutes an unmarked Ford Focus drew up outside the house; Tom must have had the car on its way as he rang. The familiar round-shouldered figure of DC Hopkins got out. Jasmine didn't wait for him to reach the front door. Throwing her bag over her shoulder, she went out of the door and pulled it closed behind her.

'Oh, you're ready, Frame,' Hopkins said, glowering at her.

'Nice to see you Terry,' she said, 'I didn't want to keep you waiting.'

'No? Just as well. There's a lot of work to be getting on with.'

Jasmine wondered if he resented being used as a chauffeur. 'Of course. Shall we go?'

Hopkins nodded and returned to his seat in the car leaving Jasmine to get in to the passenger seat.

They were already heading towards town when Hopkins spoke.

'Shepherd says you're not driving.'

'Well, not at the moment. It's still a bit, um, uncomfortable.' She wondered whether that was more information than Hopkins wanted. His grip tightened on the wheel and he stared ahead through the windscreen.

'Not sure why he's dragging you in. Open and shut as I see it. The wife bumped off the weirdo and set the place alight to cover it up.'

Jasmine shrugged. 'If that's what the evidence suggests it's a reasonable guess.' That's all it was, a guess and Hopkins knew it. He was letting his prejudices sway his opinions. 'Is there evidence?' she added. Hopkins sniffed and said nothing.

Jasmine went on in a cheery tone. 'I gather that DCI Sloane suggested that DI Shepherd give me a call.'

'The guvnor's on his way to retirement.' Hopkins commented as if that was an excuse for his unorthodox action.

'Is he?' Jasmine couldn't imagine the Violent & Serious Crime Unit without Sloane at its head, but everyone retired one day. Hopkins drove without further conversation.

They pulled into the police station carpark and both got out. Hopkins lead Jasmine into the building but failed to hold the door open for her. They passed through the outer office without the desk officer raising his head and entered the secure part of the building. Tom Shepherd was standing in the corridor.

'Hi Jas. Thanks Terry. Get on to Winslade. See if she's ready for Mrs Bunting to come and identify the body yet.'

The DC grunted and moved on.

'Thanks for coming,' Tom went on. 'We've got Harriet

Bunting in the family suite for now. We're not questioning her directly as yet. She seems pretty upset.'

Jasmine was interested. 'What has she said so far? Where was she last night?'

'She says she was away for the night staying at a hotel in the Cotswolds. Left home yesterday afternoon. We're checking out her story.' Tom frowned and concentrated his gaze on Jasmine. 'You said you'd been doing some research. Anything useful.'

'How much time have you got? I've got some thoughts on the business and about Evelyn Bunting.'

'You mean this sissy thing?'

'Yes. If I'm right and Evelyn was a sissy – your description of her fits pretty well – and it was Harriet who was her dom, then the relationship between them was intense. Perhaps not what you and I would consider a normal loving partnership but there was a strong bond between them.'

'I'm not sure I get it. You're saying, she, that is Harriet, made Evelyn wear that chastity thing and the weird clothes but that that was what Evelyn wanted.'

'That's it. The Master, or rather Mistress/Slave relationship. They depend on each other.'

'But Evelyn ran the business?'

Jasmine felt a pang of uncertainty. She didn't really understand the behaviour she was attributing to the Buntings, just going on what she had googled. Nevertheless, she thought she could see how both Evelyn and Harriet could lead visible and hidden lives.

She tried to explain. 'The, er, intimate activities of the relationship probably went on in the bedroom. They both lead outwardly normal lives but it seems that Harriet, if it was her, made Evelyn wear and do things to remind her of her power over her.'

'Like the thing around his penis and the maid's outfit.' Tom shook his head.

'That's it.'

'Well, it must be Harriet who was her, er, dom. It couldn't be anyone else, could it, with them living together?'

Jasmine shrugged. 'Unlikely unless there was a third person who dominated both of them.'

'Oh heck, this is getting ridiculous,' Tom spluttered. 'Look, I have a woman in there in tears apparently caused by grief at her husband's, or wife's or whatever you call it, murder. Could she have done it?'

Jasmine shook her head. 'I don't know. It's possible. If for some reason Evelyn wanted to end their arrangement, Harriet may have killed her to stop her escaping from her and now is feeling remorse. These relationships are complicated.'

Tom sighed and sagged. 'You said it. But if Harriet isn't the killer, who was it. There aren't any leads.'

'Not yet, but something will crop up. Harriet may offer some suggestions when she's calmed down a bit.'

'Mmm, yes.' Tom straightened up and looked more cheerful. 'You're right. Oh, there was one piece of good news.'

'Oh?'

'Yes. We found a lap top in the front shop. It looked pretty well knackered by the fire. The screen was broken and the keyboard melted, but the tech guys think they may get some files out of the hard drive.'

'That's good,' Jasmine said. 'Now what do you want me to do?'

Tom thought for a moment. 'Look, I'm not questioning Mrs Bunting formally yet. Why don't you come into the family suite with me? Have a chat with her and see what we get.'

'Okay if you don't think it'll jeopardise your investigation.'

'We'll keep it unofficial for now. You're just there to help her cope with the bereavement.'

'Let's get started then.'

7

Jasmine followed Tom into the family room. It was brightly lit and decorated in cheerful colours of yellow and green. There were a pair of comfortable sofas and another pair of easy chairs arranged around a low table. Behind one sofa was a sideboard on which there was a hot drinks machine and supplies of cups, and beverages. Mrs Bunting sat on the edge of one sofa, with her knees squeezed together and a hanky pressed to her nose. She was wearing a smart tweed skirt suit with her legs covered in sheer, flesh-coloured nylon. Jasmine judged her to be in her mid-fifties like her partner but taller and slimmer. She looked up as they entered and dropped her hand from her face revealing tear trails down her made-up cheeks and strands of her shoulder-length hair sticking with the moisture.

'Hello again, Mrs Bunting,' Tom said in a soothing voice, 'This is Jasmine Frame. She will help you at this difficult time. Do you feel able to talk about what has happened?' He sat down on the sofa opposite her. Jasmine lowered herself into the chair alongside her.

Harriet nodded, but then sobbed. 'Who did this?'

Tom set his face in a sympathetic expression. 'I'm sorry we don't know at the moment, Mrs Bunting. Perhaps you have some information that could help our investigation.'

Harriet shook her head, 'I don't know who could have killed Evelyn.'

'Someone Evelyn knew? An enemy?' Tom offered.

'He didn't know many people,' Harriet sniffed. 'He usually

stayed at home, looking after the business.'

'Perhaps there was someone to do with the business, a customer, or a supplier …' Tom ran out of ideas. Harriet shook her head and said nothing.

Jasmine leaned forward. 'Did you help with the shop, Harriet?'

Mrs Bunting looked at her, faintly surprised. 'Oh no, that was Evelyn's job. I was a partner but that was just for the paperwork.'

Jasmine went on, 'So, you knew how the business was doing, the accounts and so on.'

Harriet tossed her head, 'Not really.'

'You had other things to do while Evelyn was doing her *chores*, then?' Jasmine wondered if Harriet Bunting would notice her choice of word. It seemed that she had because the woman glared at Jasmine, examining her.

'Of course I had other things to do.'

Tom spoke, 'Such as going to a hotel for the night, without your partner.' Jasmine thought his tone was a bit judgemental. Was it deliberate?

Harriet turned her head towards Tom. She had lost the tearful, grief-stricken appearance. Now she held her head up. Jasmine saw a proud, dominant woman not used to having her actions questioned.

'Evelyn had work to do while I was away.'

'Was she expecting a visitor, a friend perhaps?' Tom asked.

Harriet scowled. 'There may have been a business caller, but Evelyn didn't have friends visiting. Are you going to keep asking questions or will you let me see my husband's body?'

'Yes, we're arranging that now Mrs Bunting, but if we are to find who killed your *husband*,' Tom emphasised the masculine word, 'and set fire to your home and business, we will need your help, as much as you are able to give us. That's why we're asking questions.'

Harriet still looked irritated. 'I understand Inspector, but I have no information to give you.'

Tom looked as though he was going to respond but then stood up. 'I'll see if it is possible to view Mr Bunting's body. Jasmine will keep you company.' He stepped out of the door. Jasmine noted that Harriet was unmoved by references to Evelyn's maleness, but surely if Evelyn customarily wore female dress she must have expected his gender to be questioned. Jasmine decided to question her on the topic.

'Did Evelyn consider himself a man?' she asked.

Harriet frowned. 'That is a very personal question.'

'I know,' Jasmine said with care, 'but you have referred to him as your husband while he was discovered wearing feminine clothes and we are told he always wore female dress.' She wondered whether Harriet considered Evelyn to be male or female; both or neither.

'You are referring to matters that are private.'

Jasmine pressed her, 'But Evelyn appeared in public as a woman. Was she transgender?'

Harriet Bunting examined her again for a few moments before speaking. 'Do you mean did he want to be a woman? No, he didn't. But he accepted that he wasn't the sort of man who gives out orders, takes what he wants, grabs any woman that he fancies.'

'Your relationship reflected that,' Jasmine said.

'Our marriage satisfied us both. I cherished him... and he obeyed me.' She glared at Jasmine, daring her to question her statement.

Jasmine pressed on regardless. 'Cherish? What does that mean exactly?'

'I ensured that his needs were met.' She blinked, 'Look, I don't know what this has got to do with finding my husband's murderer. I thought you were some sort of bereavement counsellor. Why are you asking these questions?'

How should she answer? 'I'm not a trained counsellor, Mrs Bunting, but DI Shepherd thought I might be able to help by having some understanding of Evelyn's situation. I'm not sure if I do.'

Harriet was examining her again, looking her up and down. 'Are you a transvestite then?'

The "t-word" cut at Jasmine and she felt a momentary anger. 'No, I am a woman. I was transsexual.'

'Oh, you mean you've had the chop. Evelyn would never have that. He liked the feelings he got from his cock.'

'Is that why you kept it locked in a chastity cage?'

Mrs Bunting's mouth opened but no words came out. Her face reddened. Finally, she spoke.

'How do you know that?'

'The pathologist who examined Evelyn's body discovered it, of course. DI Shepherd informed me because he didn't know what it was for. But it was a sign of your dominance wasn't it. You had control over Evelyn's sex-life.'

Harriet took a deep breath. 'He preferred to be subservient. I decided when he could have an erection. You wouldn't understand, especially as you've had yours cut off.'

'Oh, I understand desire, Mrs Bunting, and the urge to achieve what one wants. I have wanted to be a woman for years and now I am one.'

The woman sneered, 'Just because you've got a cunt instead of a cock, doesn't make you a woman. You can never feel what a real woman feels during her life: puberty, periods, pregnancy. You may think you're a woman because a man can stick his cock inside you, but you're no more a woman than if you were wearing one of the suits Evelyn sells.'

Jasmine felt hot and tense. This was supposed to be a gentle and soothing talk not a bitter argument. She tried to organise her thoughts so that she could respond calmly. She didn't have to. The door opened and Tom came in. He looked to one woman then the other. Jasmine thought he could tell that tempers had been raised.

'We can go to view the body now, Mrs Bunting. The mortuary is at the hospital, so I can take you in my car.'

'Good. At last.' Harriet said rising to her feet. Jasmine thought she looked a formidable woman with an excellent figure.

'Would you like, Miss Frame to accompany us?

The widow turned and looked down her nose at Jasmine. 'If she must.'

Tom frowned and looked at Jasmine who gave him a shrug and a smile.

'Right. We can leave now,' Tom said, holding the door open for the two ladies to leave the room.

Tom lead them out of the station to his car and they drove out of the town to the hospital. Harriet and Jasmine, sitting side by side on the back seat each looked out of their windows not speaking to each other.

They parked outside the pathology department of the hospital and one of Dr Winslade's assistants let them into the mortuary. Jasmine was pleased that they weren't guided to the laboratory where the pathologist carried out her autopsies but instead to a more tastefully decorated small room where the only furnishing was the cloth draped trolley on which lay the body. Only the face was visible with the body covered in a white sheet with a white cloth laid loosely over the head.

The three of them stood just inside the doorway, not one wanting to take another step closer.

'Ah, you've got here,' Dr Winslade said, striding in from the corridor. 'Hello Tom, oh, and Jasmine, nice to see you again.'

'This is Mrs Bunting,' Tom said.

The doctor held out her hand to shake Harriet's. 'I'm sorry to meet you on this sad occasion,' she said, 'we just need you to have a quick look and confirm the body is that of who we think it is.'

Harriet Bunting nodded and with Dr Winslade at her side approached the trolley. The doctor lifted the cloth. The widow took a glance then turned her head and stepped back.

'That is Evelyn,' she said with just a hint of sob.

'Thank you,' Tom said. 'There's no hurry. You can stay with Mr Bunting if you wish.'

Harriet shook her head and lifted a hand to her neck. She tugged on a chain and pulled a small key from between her breasts. She undid the clasp on the chain and dropped the key into her hand. She held it out to Dr Winslade.

'I think you may need this. There is no point keeping Evelyn locked up anymore.'

The pathologist took the key without a comment and Mrs Bunting headed towards the door.

'I don't want to stay any longer. Take me home please.'

'Yes, of course,' Tom replied, 'But your home is still a crime scene and the fire has left it uninhabitable.'

'I realise that, Inspector, but perhaps I may be permitted to pick up some items before I go to stay with friends.'

'We can do that if the items have been documented and are not required as evidence.'

'Evidence of what?'

'Murder, arson, whatever the motive was for the attack on your husband or home.'

Harriet sniffed and marched off to the exit and the car.

'Thank you, Doctor,' Tom said to Winslade, 'I hope we can speak again soon.'

'Yes, I've got a few observations for you, and now we've got this,' she waved the key, 'we can get that contraption off his penis. I was thinking I was going to have to use the bone saw. Nice to see you again Jasmine.'

They left the doctor and her assistant wheeling the trolley back into the path lab.

Tom drove speedily to Thirsbury and pulled up several metres short of the burnt-out frontage of Molly's. Harriet stepped out of the car and stood staring at the shattered windows, charred window and door frames and blackened brick. Jasmine stood beside her and examined her face for the emotions that surfaced. The widow's lips appeared to tremble slightly but she pursed them to prevent a sob escaping.

'Can I go in?' she asked in a shaky voice.

Tom strode to the tape that cordoned off the crime scene. 'I'll check to see where SOCO have got to.' He spoke to the police officer that was standing there while Harriet continued to peer into the glassless windows. Jasmine was equally interested in the state of the building. The appearance of the front of the building suggested a very hot and fierce fire. She looked forward to seeing the rest of the property.

Tom returned and beckoned to them. 'SOCO are glad you're here. They've finished the forensic sweep upstairs. They'd like you to come in and check to see if any of your and, er, your husband's property is missing.'

'Missing?' Harriet asked.

'Yes,' Tom nodded, 'We are not sure whether the murder of Evelyn and the arson are directly connected and whether there was any theft. Perhaps the fire was set to cover up a burglary and your husband got in the way.'

Harriet didn't reply but pushed past Tom and headed into her home. Tom hurried after her.

'You must put the overalls on first Mrs Bunting.'

The woman stopped and looked at Tom with disdain. 'Overalls?'

Tom bent down and pulled a packet from the box by the entrance to the house. He opened it out and revealed the garment to Mrs Bunting.

'I have to wear that?' she said showing some disbelief.

'I'm afraid so. It's the only way to go inside while the forensics are being done.'

Harriet sniffed and took the proffered overalls. Jasmine stepped forward and offered to help her put them on, but she brushed her away.

'I think I can dress myself, thank you.' She stepped into the legs and pulled the top over her shoulders.

'You too Jas?' Tom said offering her another packet.

Soon, all three of them were encased in the protective covering. Tom led them to the open and shattered door.

'Please don't touch anything and only walk on the footpads,' He said pointing to the floor. 'There is wet wreckage everywhere.'

Jasmine followed them into the shop but did not climb the stairs. From the sounds overhead, the first floor seemed quite full of people. Having taken in the heaps of wet and charred clothing she moved in to the middle room. There was very little light, just some autumn daylight filtering in from the window in the room at the rear. There was a similar mess as the front room, but the fire damage appeared a little less severe. The mounds of white material on the floor, that Tom had mentioned, stood out, almost glowing amongst the blackened textiles. She bent to look at them and gently poked one with a latex-covered finger. It was soft but elastic and confirmed her guess. It was silicone rubber used in the prostheses that Bunting sold – breasts, buttocks and thigh padding, and one larger lump must be the remains of a full-body suit. Jasmine recalled the pictures from the website. Men bought these items to give themselves a more feminine body shape, but she struggled to imagine what it must be like to wear them.

Jasmine moved on to the back room, where the body had been discovered. Now there was just an empty space. She looked around hoping that clues might leap at her, but they didn't. She heard steps coming down the stairs and returned to meet Tom and Mrs Bunting.

'Anything missing?' Jasmine asked. Tom shook his head.

Harriet looked indignant. 'Apparently I can't remove any of my own belongings. What am I supposed to do for clean clothes? And where am I to stay tonight.'

'We can help you to arrange accommodation, Mrs Bunting,' Tom said, 'And reimburse you for any expenses caused by our investigation.'

'It's not money I want, but my knickers and bras and all the rest. I'm not in the mood to go clothes shopping; and there's my toiletries…'

'We understand,' Jasmine said and soothingly as she could, 'You've been away. Don't you have a suitcase.'

'I don't know where that went,' Harriet said. She glared at Tom. He tried to calm her.

'It's at the police station. You had it with you when we took you there.'

Harriet, sniffed, 'Well, take me back there. I obviously can't stay here.'

'Yes, of course,' Tom said, 'And we can take you anywhere you want to go to stay tonight.'

'I'll take a taxi thank you. I don't want to be taken in a police car again if I can help it.' She marched towards the front of the shop and the exit. Tom shrugged.

'Are you coming, Jas?'

'I haven't got any transport either, Tom. I'm with you.'

The silence for the return journey to Kintbridge hung even heavier in the car than on the way to Thirsbury. When they reached the outskirts of the town, Tom asked a question.

'Now you've seen inside your home, Mrs Bunting do you have any more thoughts on who might have set the fire and killed Mr Bunting?'

'No, I don't. I think it's your job to find out who did those things.'

'What time did you leave yesterday?'

'It was four o'clock.'

'And how did you travel to your Cotswold hotel.'

'By car.'

'Oh,' Tom showed interest, 'Where is your car now?'

'It wasn't my car. I don't drive. I was driven there.'

'A taxi?'

There was a pause before Mrs Bunting answered. 'Not a taxi, no.'

'A friend?' Jasmine interrupted.

'Yes, that's right, a friend.'

'So, you weren't alone at this hotel,' Tom said.

'Um, No.' Harriet's voice had lost its boldness.

'Who was your friend?' Jasmine asked.

'Tyler. Tyler Smith,' she replied.

'Tyler?' Jasmine asked. 'Is that a male name?'

'Yes, of course it is. He's a friend; of us both.'

'But he accompanied you to this hotel while your husband remained at home,' Tom went on.

'Evelyn had work to do. I wanted some relaxation. Tyler offered to come too. There's no law against that is there.'

'No...' Tom said, 'But we'll have to meet Mr Smith to confirm your movements last night.'

Harriet leaned forward to speak to Tom. 'Am I a suspect in my husband's murder, Inspector?'

'Just routine questions, Mrs Bunting. We have to establish where everyone was when your husband was killed. Here we are, back at the station.'

Tom and Jasmine escorted Mrs Bunting into the building where she recovered her small suitcase. Having provided her mobile phone number, she marched out.

Tom and Jasmine watched her leave from the foyer.

'Do you think she did it?' Tom asked.

'I think she is determined enough to get whatever she wants and that could include murder and arson,' Jasmine began, 'but she almost showed emotion when she saw the state of her house and whenever her husband was mentioned. I don't think it was her, but I think we need to find out how she and her husband and this Tyler Smith are linked.'

'Hmm. I think I agree, Jas. I don't get this sissy thing though, and what's with that cage around his penis?'

Jasmine frowned. She was quite sure she didn't understand it either. 'It's a complex relationship. She's dominant, he's submissive, but he's also got a gender identity issue stirred into the mix.'

'Does she only dominate him do you think, or has she got others? This Smith bloke for example?' Tom asked.

'Is she a professional dominatrix, do you mean? Perhaps, but it could be just in her relationship with Evelyn.'

Tom shook his head, yawned and raised a hand to his mouth.

'You're shattered,' Jasmine observed. 'Have you had any rest today?'

Tom shook his head. 'No. I sent Sasha home this morning and was going myself after I called on you but then Harriet Bunting turned up, so I didn't make it.'

'I think you'd better get some sleep now before you fall off your perch.'

Tom sighed and his shoulders slumped. 'Yeah, you're right. I'll just go up to the office and see what's happening.' He turned towards the secure door.

'What about me, Tom?' Jasmine called after him. 'I haven't got my car, remember. We've missed lunch and I need to get home to do my exercises.'

Tom paused and turned. 'Exercises?'

'I thought I mentioned it this morning.' She pointed at her crotch.

Tom's pale face turned red. 'Oh, yes, you did. Look, I'll take you home. Wait here, I won't be long.' He stabbed the key pad by the door and pushed the door open. Jasmine turned to scan the public area. The familiar figure of Sgt Gorman leaned against the desk examining her.

'Hello GG,' she said.

'Back again, *Mizz* Frame. It's been a while since we saw you in here.'

Jasmine noted that he still had to emphasise the Ms, but she tried to answer civilly. 'I've been a bit busy since I was last here.' She tried to remember when she previously entered the police station. It was over a year ago.

'Have you indeed. You look a bit different.'

I should hope so, Jasmine thought. Years on the hormones, completion of her GRS; a year ago she had been nowhere near the woman she wanted to be. Now she was there, or nearly.

'Probably grown my hair a bit longer,' she offered.

GG nodded, 'I suppose that's it. Assisting DI Shepherd again, are you?'

'Apparently,' Jasmine said and added, 'DCI Sloane suggested it.'

Sgt Gorman sniffed as if that was enough to dismiss the idea of Sloane requiring the help of someone like Jasmine. 'Don't think the guv'nor will be around much longer.' He turned away and went to the far side of the office, his back to Jasmine.

He's the second person to suggest that Sloane is about to retire, Jasmine thought. Perhaps it's true. She turned her attention to the various posters on the wall of the waiting area. Some advertised services for victims, others warned about knife crime and hate-crimes. She was beginning to feel like sitting rather than standing when Tom re-emerged through the door.

'Let's go, Jas,' he said wearily.

'All under control?'

'Yes, Sasha is back on duty. She'll collate the reports of SOCO and the house to house. Perhaps we'll have more from Dr Winslade by tomorrow. There's not a lot to do until we get some names of people to question.'

'You can get some sleep then.'

'Yes, Sasha will ring me if something comes up. Let's get you home so you can do these exercises of yours.' He seemed to have got over the embarrassment of contemplating her stuffing a dilator into her vagina, or perhaps his cheery reference to it was to mask his discomfort with the thought.

Jasmine accompanied him out of the station. 'Actually, it's something to eat I need first. What about you? I don't suppose you've had anything since I gave you that toast.'

Tom shook his head. 'No, but Sophie's still home, with Abi. She'll have something ready. You're right though. I'm starving.'

They got into the car and Tom pulled out into the afternoon traffic.

Jasmine waved to the departing Mondeo and turned towards her front door. Viv's Audi was parked on the drive and she felt a small leap of joy tempered by apprehension. Viv would be concerned about her being out. As she reached out with the key the front door opened. Viv stood there, a frown on his face.

'I saw you get out of the car, Jas. Was that Tom Shepherd?'

Jasmine nodded and stepped inside. Viv helped her take her

coat off and hung it on the hook.

'Does that mean you're working?' Viv went on.

'Yes. A murder in Thirsbury.' Now she was in her own home Jasmine felt tired. No, exhausted. A day out, okay some of it sat in a car, but going from place to place, picking up the facts of the case from Tom and watching and listening to Harriet Bunting, had drained her of energy. Missing lunch hadn't helped either.

'You look like you need to sit down, Jas. Do you feel alright?'

That confirmed it. If she looked tired then she must be.

'I'm fine, just not used to it.'

'Used to what?'

'Being on my feet, working, living.' She went into the lounge and slumped onto the sofa. She glanced at her watch. It wasn't five yet. 'You're early.'

Viv frowned again. 'Yeah. I finished what had to be done today and I thought I'd get home to see my girlfriend, only to find you weren't in.'

'Sorry.'

'It doesn't matter,' he said in a tone that suggested it did. 'Tell me all about your day.'

Jasmine forced herself back onto her feet. 'I will but I need to get my dilations done first.'

'Of course. I'll get supper on – '

'Great, I'm starving.'

'I'll pour a glass of wine and then you can tell me all about your new assignment.'

Jasmine put her fork down in her dish and smiled at Viv.

'That was wonderful, thanks.' She always enjoyed his spicy chicken risotto, especially when she had fasted almost all day.

'My pleasure as always. How do you feel now after a day's work?' Viv's expression showed that he meant what he said and wasn't kidding her after her weeks of inactivity.

'It was tiring, but I needed Tom to push me into taking the leap.'

'You think this case will occupy you for a while?'

'Unless, Harriet Bunting suddenly confesses I think it's going to take some work. There are no other obvious suspects and I don't think it was her.'

'But this relationship she and her husband had…' Viv shook his head, 'I know there are people who are into BDSM but I don't get it.'

Jasmine shrugged. 'I don't either but I think I'm going to have to understand it to get a grasp of the case. There's the matter of him being a sissy too.'

'That's another thing. If he wants to dress as a woman why is it a punishment?'

Jasmine laughed. 'I'm as confused as you, but I think it's a question of gender identity and sexuality not being the same thing and both being complicated.

'Well, good luck to you I say.' Viv stood up and started clearing the table.

Jasmine leapt up and made a grab for the dishes. 'Let me clear up. You did the cooking.'

Viv tugged the bowls back. 'No, If you're going to be a working girl again, you need to rest. Go and put your feet up. I'll be with you in a few minutes.'

8

THURSDAY 17TH OCTOBER
MORNING

A noise penetrated her sleep. An alarm? No, she hadn't set one; hadn't needed to for weeks. What then?

'Jas! It's your phone.' Viv's voice jogged her fully awake. She opened her eyes, reached an arm across the bedside table and lifted her mobile. She was aware of Viv standing by the bed. In the dim light, she saw he was half-dressed.

'What time is it?' she mumbled as she pressed the answer button.

'Seven,' Viv growled.

'Hello, Jas. Are you awake?' It was Tom's voice sounding particularly cheery.

'I am now,' she replied.

'Good. We need you here, in the office.'

'Why?'

'We've made some progress overnight. Evelyn Bunting's phone and mobile logs have come through and forensics have managed to get some files off his/her, damn I'm still not sure which it is, laptop.'

'You've got a suspect.'

'No. There may be a clue amongst what we've got but there's work to do, and DCI Sloane has insisted you're on the case. He thinks all this sissy and BDSM stuff needs your input.'

'I'm not sure it's quite my thing…'

'You know Sloane, Jas. I need you. Now when can you be here?'

Jasmine sighed. She used to be able to leap out of bed, grab some clothes, any clothes, and be at her desk in minutes. 'I can't rush things yet, Tom.'

'Yes, I know that, Jas.'

'And I'm not driving yet.'

Viv bent down beside her, 'I'll bring her in, Tom.'

'Oh, hi, Viv. That'd be great. When can I expect you then Jas?'

How long did she need to get her dilations done, get showered, dressed, have breakfast, and not tire herself by rushing?

'I'll be with you by half eight.'

'Great. We'll have a plan organised by then. Bye, Jas.' The line clicked off.

Jasmine rested back on the pillow and groaned. Viv leant over her and placed a kiss on her lips.

'Are you sure you want to do this, Jas? You don't have to.'

She sat up. 'Yes, I do. It's my job.'

Viv shrugged. 'Okay then. The bathroom's yours. I'll get breakfast for both of us. No need to rush yourself – Tom, and Sloane, will wait for you.'

'Thanks.'

Jasmine stepped into the V&SC unit's office. It was just as she remembered, despite it being over a year since she had lasted visited. The feelings she had now, she wanted to explore. Once she had felt pride at being part of the team, investigating murders and serious crimes. Then it had been frustration and anger at being side-lined in cases when she had started her transition. When she had been called back as an "advisor" rather than as an official police officer she had been uncomfortable as if she was returning to somewhere she shouldn't. Now there was little of that discomfort; she felt more confident. No one could question her femininity since she had had the surgery. Physically, if not genetically, she was a woman.

Tom Shepherd was standing at the whiteboard with half a dozen men and women facing him, some of whom Jasmine recognised but a couple that were unfamiliar. Tom saw her enter and smiled.

'Ah, Jas, come and join us. We're just going over what we know.' The other faces turned to look at her, some welcoming her with a smile, one or two looking bemused as if wondering who this interloper was. Jasmine joined them. Sasha Patel shuffled to the side to make space in the circle. She greeted Jasmine with a grin. They had met a year before on another case when she had been the "advisor" but Sasha had joined the team since Jasmine had left the police service.

Tom addressed the group. 'Jasmine has joined us because the nature of the case suggests that she will have particular knowledge and opinions that may be useful to us. DCI Sloane has approved her presence as an advisor. In fact, he suggested it. Now I think you all know the bare facts of the case, but I invited Dr Winslade to join us to give us the details about the victim, Evelyn Bunting.'

The young pathologist who had been standing at the end of the line stepped forward.

'Thank you, Tom. Great to see you again, Jasmine. Now as you know, Evelyn Bunting's body was found in the rear ground floor room of the property she shared with her partner Harriet Bunting. The body had a covering of soot and other products of the fire but was not burned. The fire was not the cause of death. Mr, er Miss, Mizz, . . which is it Jasmine?'

Jasmine was disturbed from her listening mode. 'Um, I'm not certain how Evelyn identified herself. She apparently usually wore female clothes but I'm not sure that necessarily means she considered herself female. I think we need to leave her gender open until we find out more.'

'Thanks, yes, well, the victim was killed by a blow to the head with a blunt instrument.'

'A hammer?' Terry Hopkins offered.

'No,' Dr Winslade replied, 'This is the murder implement, we think.' She lifted up a large, clear plastic evidence bag from the desk behind her. There was a long, narrow black object inside.

'It was found amongst the debris in the front room of the shop.'

'It's a baseball bat,' Hopkins said, leaning forward to peer into the bag.

'Yes, DC Hopkins. It's not just covered in soot. It was partly burned in the fire so it's fairly fragile. Because of that we're not going to get any DNA from the assailant off it or any fingerprints, but its size and shape fits the wound to Evelyn's head.'

'You can't prove it was the weapon used?' Sasha said.

Tom interrupted, 'No, but it looks likely and gives us some questions and perhaps answers. Go on Doctor.'

Dr Winslade put the package back on the desk. 'The cause of death is therefore fairly certain but the timing is not. All I can say is that it was before the fire started. There is no smoke in the victim's lungs.'

'So Bunting didn't start the fire?' Hopkins asked.

'No,' Winslade said slowly as if uncertain. 'However, we did find a trace of an accelerant on her hands, face and feet.'

A young dark-skinned man standing between Sasha Patel and Terry Hopkins who Jasmine didn't recognise, spoke. 'Accelerant?'

'Petrol?' Terry offered.

'That's right,' Winslade replied.

Terry Hopkins had a triumphant look on his face, 'The killer spilled petrol on her when he was setting the fire.'

Tom looked doubtful. 'Not necessarily. The petrol is only on specific parts of Bunting's body. It doesn't look as if she was doused with it.'

'Oh,' Hopkins was crestfallen.

The young detective spoke again, 'Does it show that it was Bunting that was spreading the petrol?'

'Good point, Hamid. It looks a possibility,' Tom said, giving the junior detective a smile.

Sasha Patel summed up what Jasmine was thinking. 'Bunting is implicated in the arson but did not actually start the fire.'

Tom nodded. 'That's what it looks like. We'll come back to that in minute, but we'll let Dr Winslade finish so that she can get off.'

'Thanks Tom,' the pathologist smiled at the group. 'There were other injuries on the body. There were marks on his buttocks and backs of the thighs and on his wrists and ankles. The marks vary in size and age – some have almost faded away and others are recent. We believe that these, er, injuries are unrelated to the death of Evelyn Bunting but were representative of his, um, lifestyle. Jasmine, I think you can explain.'

Explain was not a word that Jasmine would have chosen. Describe, narrate, or report, perhaps, but definitely not explain. She paused before responding to the doctor's appeal.

'Yes, well, I can't say I understand it but we have established that Evelyn Bunting and his, er wife, Harriet had a submissive-dominant relationship. Evelyn was the submissive and Harriet the dominant. Evelyn was forced – perhaps forced is the wrong word because he did it willingly – he had to wear certain female clothes and wear a chastity cage on his penis. It also appears from Dr Winslade's description that he was spanked or beaten frequently and perhaps regularly.' Jasmine stopped but realised that she wanted to add something. 'I don't have any personal experience of this kind of BDSM relationship but since yesterday I have been looking into it. Harriet Bunting has confirmed it but has not gone into the details of their relationship.' She looked at her colleagues and saw Terry Hopkins looking at her leerily, while Hamid, the new detective, had a lip curled in disgust.

Tom gave her a grateful smile. 'Thanks Jas. I should add, that when SOCO searched the living accommodation above the shop they found a drawer containing a variety of wrist and ankle restraints and collars.'

'A pair of nutters,' Terry Hopkins muttered.

'We're not here to judge their relationship,' Tom said.

Dr Winslade went on, 'And there is no direct link between Evelyn Bunting's death and their lifestyle. The blow to the back of his head was unlikely to be part of some BDSM scenario.'

Tom continued. 'But we're not saying that there is no connection between the relationship Evelyn and Harriet Bunting had and the arson and murder. We have to keep an open mind.'

'Is Harriet Bunting a suspect?' Sasha asked.

'Yes,' Tom replied, 'although she appears to have an alibi and seemed distressed on hearing that Evelyn was dead. We will be looking at all possibilities. Which brings us to DS Lockyear.'

All turned to look at the female at the end of the row.

'Charlotte is a member of the SOCO team. Over to you Charlotte.'

The woman stepped forward and faced the group. 'Thanks DI Shepherd. We are still investigating the scene but have drawn a number of conclusions that I can share with you. First of all, the fire started at the front of the building. We believe the ignition was caused by something thrown through one of the windows; some glass was found inside while most of the windows were blown out by the fire. There is evidence that the accelerant, petrol, was spread around the front and middle rooms prior to the fire starting.'

'Er, let me get this right,' Terry Hopkins said. 'DI Shepherd said that Bunting poured the petrol in the place but was dead before the fire was lit.'

'That's right,' Tom said.

'So the killer started it,' Terry added.

Tom shrugged. 'It's a possibility. We don't know. The killer had to get out. Whether he did that before or after the fire started is uncertain.'

Sasha Patel raised a hand and spoke, 'There could be three people involved – Evelyn who spread the petrol and then was hit on the head by her killer and someone else who started the fire by throwing something through the window.'

Tom nodded, 'That's right, or the killer and the arsonist may be the same person.'

'We're looking for DNA all around the building,' Charlotte

Lockyear said. 'There's not much chance of getting any from the front and middle rooms where the fire was fiercest, as DI Shepherd has commented on in connection with the baseball bat, but we have found a number of possible samples upstairs as well as those instruments that were mentioned. They could reveal if the Buntings entertained, er, guests.'

'We'll have to wait for DNA results,' Tom added, 'But DS Lockyear does have some more immediate information for us.'

'Yes,' Charlotte said, 'We have Bunting's laptop. It was pretty badly damaged in the fire but we have managed to retrieve some files from the hard drive. These seem to relate to the business and include the accounts. I've made the files available to you.

'Could the fire have been an insurance scam?' Sasha blurted out.

Tom chuckled, 'Very good, Sasha. We need to check his insurance, if he had any. But of course, it doesn't explain his death. We do though have some of his emails and phone records.'

The group leaned forward expectantly. This was what they were hoping for – names of family, friends and acquaintances that may become suspects when questioned.

'There are quite a lot of names,' Charlotte said, 'but only a few appear a number of times.'

'They're the ones we will start with,' Tom added. He turned to write on the white board, 'There's Akash Rana, Gary Nicholls, Lee Clement, S Mcleesh, and Neville Griffith.'

'Neville Griffith?' Terry said. 'That name's come up before. Isn't he involved in some shady stuff?'

Tom nodded, 'I recognised it too, Terry. Could be the same guy. Those are the ones we want to know more about. Who are they? What was their connection to Bunting?'

Jasmine felt urged to speak, 'What about Harriet and that friend she spent the evening with, Tyler Smith.'

'Good point, Jas,' Tom said, 'Thanks for the rundown, Charlotte. We need to find out more about these people and their connection to Evelyn Bunting.' He looked at DC Hopkins,

'You take Griffiths, Terry. Find out if it is the guy we know and how he and Bunting came to be in contact. Hamid, you look into Rana and Nicholls. Sasha – take Clement and McLeesh. I'm going to have another chat with Mrs Bunting and I'd like you with, me Jasmine.'

He was about to send them all off with a wave of his hand, when Hamid spoke, 'Um, can you explain what Bunting's business was. I don't understand.'

'Yes, of course,' Tom said, 'Jasmine, can you give us an outline.'

This was something Jasmine felt happier with. 'Bunting supplied clothes and other stuff to transgendered people. He advertised online so did postal deliveries but also sold across the counter in the shop.'

'What do you mean, other stuff?' Hamid asked.

Jasmine took a deep breath, 'Basically, aids to help men look more like women or at least let them feel more like women.'

Hamid still looked confused. Jasmine went into more detail. 'Wigs, false breasts, special knickers to hide their bits, and give them a bigger bum. He even had a line in body suits that can give a man a female figure, big tits, wide hips, a vagina.'

Hamid's eyes had widened as if he could barely believe it.

'Are you a customer?' Hopkins chuckled.

Jasmine tasted acid in her mouth. 'No, I never have been and I certainly am not one now.'

'Moved on have you?' Terry said.

'Now, Terry.' Tom cautioned. Tom had seniority of rank but not of age. Hopkins glowered at him.

Jasmine felt sad. Despite going through her GRS she was still going to get these snide remarks from people like Hopkins. People who didn't seem to think it rude to tease someone about their gender identity to their face. She realised that what she had said wasn't completely true; she was still stuffing enhancers into her bra to give herself the illusion of fuller breasts. Nevertheless, she was disappointed that she was still going to have to fight for her identity with the Hopkinses of the world.

The team was dispersing to their desks and Dr Winslade and Charlotte Lockyear were hurrying out. Jasmine stood still, not sure where she was to go. Tom saw her and stepped towards her.

'Are you okay, Jas? Sorry about Terry. His attitudes still haven't got into the twenty-first century.'

Jasmine shrugged. 'I suppose I am still going to meet people like him. Who's the new boy?'

'Hamid? DC Sassani. Just joined us having transferred from the Met. He told me his parents came from Iran in the 1980s. Seems a keen lad but inexperienced. It'll be good if you get to know him.'

'Perhaps, but I'm not planning on spending much time here, Tom. I've got a business to run, or I hope I have once I get back to it.'

Tom looked a little sad at that. 'Yes, of course, Jas, but you can give us a bit of help, can't you?'

Jasmine smiled. To be truthful, she was loving being back among the team investigating a murder. Not the gore or filth of the body or contemplating the pain the victim may have suffered of course, but the buzz from the search for clues, of finding connections, and teasing information from witnesses and suspects; of bringing criminals to justice an inch at a time. 'Of course. What do you want me to do? You said you wanted me with you for another interview with Harriet Bunting.'

'Yes. We'll do that, but I've got some admin to do first. Why don't you look through the data we've collected so far? You used to be good at that. Oh, and find out about this Tyler Smith character.'

'OK, but how do I do all that. I'm not on the system anymore.'

Tom didn't hesitate. 'You can use my desk and log-in.'

Jasmine shrugged. 'Which is your desk?' Tom pointed to the back of the room. 'Oh, you haven't moved.'

'No, but I'm in and out of Sloane's office these days.' In confirmation, he headed towards the self-contained office of the DCI.

Jasmine walked to the desk Tom had indicated and sat down noting that he had already logged himself into the police computer system. Soon she had called up the corrupted files that the forensic team had dug out of Bunting's fire-damaged laptop. She immersed herself in the emails, accounts and business files, such as there were. Some were intriguing snippets, others just names and addresses. An hour had passed when she paused. She chuckled to herself. She had hated this work when it was the only task she had been given once she started to transition. It was one reason for her resignation. Now, almost two years later, it gave her purpose again and a sense of being part of the team. Nevertheless, she needed to ease the stiffness in her groin. She stood up and went to the corner of the office where the drinks machine still was. As she waited for the machine to fill a paper cup with black coffee she was joined by the middle-eastern detective. Jasmine looked at him wondering when police officers, detectives even, had started to look young. It wasn't long since she turned thirty and she didn't feel old herself but the Iranian's smooth, olive skin made him look barely out of college.

'Miss Frame,' he said as introduction.

'Call me Jasmine. You're Hamid?'

He nodded, 'Yes. Hamid Sassani.'

'Settling in?'

'Yes. It's different to the Met, but I am enjoying being a detective.'

'I did too.'

'Ah, yes. Terry said you worked in the unit when you were a man.'

Jasmine felt her face take on a grimace. It was typical of Terry to out her. Actually, she could take him to court for revealing her gender history. Her Gender Recognition Certificate had arrived a few months before her operation. It was supposed to protect her from having her history revealed. But, she reflected, her chances of just being known as a woman in this environment were limited; so many people had known her as James Frame or were aware of her transition.

Instead of launching into a self-defensive tirade she nodded. 'That's right. I started my transition right here.'

Hamid bowed his head. 'I am sorry. It is an intrusion, but I don't know much about transsexuals.' He pronounced the word as if it was an unfamiliar part of his vocabulary.

'Not many people do.'

'But I have a cousin who is one.'

Jasmine's expression surprise. 'Really?'

'He, I mean she, has had the, er, treatment. Now she is a good Moslem woman. She wears the niqab and she hopes to have a husband.'

'I don't know much about Moslem transwomen, or men,' Jasmine confessed. She was thinking what concealing her body, as many Moslem women did, would mean to her. Would it also mean making herself subservient to a husband as it seemed Islamic women often were? She wanted her relationship with Viv to develop, but had not thought of marriage or becoming a wife.

Hamid nodded. 'It is difficult. Her parents are traditional and have disowned her saying their son has dishonoured the family. Even my parents have criticised her and they haven't been practising Moslems since they got out of Iran during the revolution.

'What do you think?' Jasmine asked, testing Hamid's attitude. He looked sad.

'I'm not sure. I think everyone should have the freedom to follow their beliefs, whether it is their religion or their personal feelings, but I don't really understand her. I have only met her a couple of times. She seems content now that she is a woman despite all the difficulties and rejection that has brought her. She has been attacked by Moslem men and some have threatened to kill her.'

Jasmine reflected. 'It is a very deep urge to be the person you feel yourself to be. I am sure that is as strong in everyone regardless of their race or religion. I admire your cousin for going ahead with her transition and I hope she stays safe.'

'You have had no such difficulty?' Hamid asked.

Difficulties? Well there had been a few but Jasmine couldn't imagine that she had faced the pitfalls that Hamid's cousin had met.

'It hasn't been easy,' she admitted, 'particularly the wait for my surgery, but I've had support from my boyfriend and my ex-wife, and my family.' Well sister Holly more than Mother, but they got along.

'The reassignment surgery ...'

'We call it Gender Confirmation now. My surgery confirmed me as the person I know myself to be. I've always felt feminine and now my body is too.' Almost, she acknowledged. Nothing could change her broad shoulders, almost non-existent waist and narrow hips. 'Actually, the hormones have more effect on outward appearance than the surgery. They soften the features and re-distribute some fat to give a more female figure.'

'You are an attractive woman,' Hamid said then hesitated, '''I'm sorry, perhaps I should not comment on your appearance. You may consider it harassment.'

Jasmine laughed. 'No, I'll take any compliments I can get. But I know I have some way to go. A speech therapist is helping me adjust my voice. Some transwomen have surgery on their larynx to raise their tone of voice. I still give myself away to some people. Mrs Bunting recognised what I was almost immediately, yesterday.'

'It must be annoying for you being labelled as transsexual.'

'Yes, especially as I don't consider myself that anymore.'

'No?' Hamid appeared confused.

'I was transsexual before and during my transition. Now I am fully female; I'm just a woman and my certificate says so.'

'Oh!'

Jasmine decided to move the conversation away from herself. 'What about you Hamid?'

The young man looked suspicious, 'Me? I am not trans.'

Jasmine chuckled. 'Of course not. I meant as a member of a

minority. Have you met any prejudice?'

Hamid shrugged. 'A little. I don't let it bother me.'

'What about Sasha?'

The officer was confused. 'DC Patel?'

'Yes. Do you get on – you being Muslim and her Hindu?'

'She has been very helpful to me since I joined the unit. We don't let our religions interfere with our work.'

Jasmine realised that she was in danger of speaking out of turn but she couldn't stop herself. 'How about Terry? He wasn't too "helpful" to me when I was transitioning.'

Hamid drew in a breath. 'DC Hopkins is a proud Englishman.'

Jasmine was impressed by Hamid's reticence then became aware of a looming presence. She turned her head to see Tom standing beside her.

'I'm glad you two have got to know each other,' he said.

'Hi, Tom. We were having an interesting conversation. Are you ready to call on Harriet Bunting?'

'Yes, but we're paying a visit to the scene of the crime first. Charlotte has called to say they've found something.'

'What?'

'A cellar.'

Jasmine was surprised. 'A cellar. Didn't they know it was there?'

'No. The access door is in that middle room. It was hidden behind debris from the fire and they've only just started doing a thorough sweep in there.'

Jasmine recalled standing in the poorly lit room with the corners in shadows. She could see the heaps of burnt and sodden stock and the mysterious remains of the silicone body parts. It was easy to imagine a door to a lower floor being mistaken for a cupboard.

'Charlotte says there are things we might like to see down there which may or may not have a bearing on the investigation.'

Jasmine was excited. 'Sounds intriguing. Let's go.'

'You come too, Hamid,' Tom said, 'We have to question the neighbours again.'

Tom navigated them through the Kintbridge traffic and out on to the A road to Thirsbury. Jasmine saw his eyes in the mirror looking at her.

'Did you get anywhere with those files, Jas?' he asked.

Jasmine was pleased to respond. 'Hmm, sort of. I was able to piece together some of Evelyn's business accounts.'

'And?'

'The business was in a poor way. Cash flow problems.'

'Bad enough to burn the place down for the insurance?' Tom asked

'Possibly. She did have at least one policy. I found the name of the brokers and have asked them for details.'

'Good.'

'Oh, and it looks as though she recently paid out a large sum to the Gary Nicholls who appeared on the list of contacts. It is balanced by an almost equally large sum paid into the account, but I can't tell where that came from.'

'Sales?' Tom suggested.

'It seems too large for that, certainly compared with the level of business she was getting normally.'

'Hmm,' Tom mused. 'You were looking into Nicholls, Hamid. Get anything?'

'Some,' the young officer said gladly, 'he lives just outside Kintbridge and seems to own a few small businesses. In fact, he was listed as a director of Molly's.'

'Really,' Tom said, 'so what was his relationship with Evelyn and Harriet Bunting?'

'A partner?' Jasmine said, 'Perhaps Evelyn bought him out.'

'I wonder why,' Tom said as they pulled up outside the burnt-out shop.

9

Jasmine got out of the car and looked around. There were still a few police cars and vans parked in the high street close to the Bunting's property. With Tom and Hamid, Jasmine ducked under the tape marking off the restricted zone, nodded to the bored police officer and headed towards the entrance. They paused to pull on the disposable overalls. Jasmine was getting familiar again with the task of doing up the zip of the garment over her skirt. Once all three were encased they stepped inside and moved straight into the middle room. There were more lights in there now and a door under the stairs was open. Jasmine recalled that the remains of a mannequin and the melted remains of a body suit had stood there previously. Tom stepped towards the entrance to the cellar and called out.

'Charlotte! Are you down there?'

A reply came from below. 'Hi, Tom. Come on down.'

'There's Jasmine and Hamid too.'

'That's okay. There's room.'

Tom ducked his head as he passed through the doorway and started down the steps. Jasmine followed. The open stone steps descended into a space that wasn't quite as large as the two rooms the shop occupied on the ground floor and had a low ceiling. Jasmine stepped onto a stone floor.

There were electric lights on stands on both sides of the stairs illuminating the two halves of the cellar. Before she took in what she could see it was the feel of the place that Jasmine experienced. The lights had not banished the shadows and it felt cold, colder than the floor above. There was a smell too that mystified her; not damp or mould, but a more human mixture of sweat and urine.

To her left, Tom was standing with his neck bent, wary of the ceiling just above his head. The lights picked out a wardrobe, a chest of drawers, a dressing table, all in dark wood, and a high backed easy chair. It seemed to Jasmine to be a bedroom without the bed. She turned and looked to the right and saw a different scene. In the far corner was a cage, about a metre in height, slightly more in length but less in width. Inside the cage was a steel dog bowl and old-fashioned china chamber-pot. In the middle of the floor of the room was an object resembling a low vaulting horse covered in shiny brown leather. There were small rings at the base of each of the four legs. Against a wall was a wooden rack containing a collection of implements. Jasmine did not need to examine each to decide that they were whips, paddles and crops.

'Excuse me, Jasmine,' a voice said behind her.

'Oh, sorry, Hamid.' Jasmine moved to Tom's side in the homely surroundings of the dressing room. Charlotte Lockyear was facing them.

'What have you got?' Tom asked.

'I think this is where Evelyn Bunting kept her clothes and where she dressed and made up,' the crime scene examiner said. 'We were wondering why we didn't find her belongings upstairs in the bedroom. Only Mrs Bunting had stuff in the cupboards and drawers up there.'

'Okay,' Tom said turning around, 'and the other side?'

'I think you can guess,' Charlotte said. 'The Buntings didn't keep a dog so I think we know who spent time in the cage.'

'It's a dungeon,' Jasmine said, 'where Harriet kept Evelyn and punished her.'

'What do you mean by "punished"?' Hamid said. His eyes were wide as they surveyed the cellar.

'Those marks that Dr Winslade found on Evelyn's buttocks and thighs,' Jasmine explained, 'were the result of whippings and spankings using the implements in the rack over there. I imagine that Evelyn was fastened by her wrists and ankles over the leather stool there in the middle.'

'Why was she punished?' Hamid asked.

'For her and Harriet's satisfaction,' Jasmine said. 'It's all part of their sub-dom relationship.'

Hamid shook his head. 'How could a man allow a woman to do that to him?'

'It turns some men on,' Jasmine offered as an explanation.

Tom interrupted. 'Is there anything relevant to the murder and fire?'

'It doesn't look like it,' Charlotte answered. 'It's unaffected by the fire – the walls and floor are stone and the ceiling is very well insulated, for heat and sound. The fire wasn't able to penetrate from the floor above.'

'What are you looking for?' Jasmine asked.

'Any other DNA material,' the CSE replied, 'Is there evidence that people other than Harriet and Evelyn Bunting used this space.'

Jasmine nodded. 'That would give us a fuller picture of how their relationship worked. When will you know?'

'A couple of days to find out how many different samples we have. Rather longer to identify them, if that is possible in all the cases. We have Evelyn's and Harriet's DNA. It's the other persons who might turn up that may be the problem.'

The three detectives nodded in unison. Tom glanced at his watch.

'Okay, we'll leave you to it Charlotte. We're late for our appointment with Mrs Bunting. Hamid. I'd like you to visit the neighbours again, including the houses behind. We know now that at least one person was at the property after Evelyn died. Let's see if anyone saw anything. Also see if anyone can corroborate the time that Harriet Bunting says she left. Oh, and see what people know about Gary Nicholls.'

Hamid was scribbling in his notebook. 'Got it, Sir.' He turned and hurried up the stairs. Jasmine followed, a little more slowly. Tom came along behind, cursing when he banged his head on the ceiling.

They exited the shop and dragged the overalls off, dumping them in a plastic box provided for them. Hamid went off alone.

'Mrs Bunting is staying in The Anglers. Seems she likes the best,' Tom said.

'Thirsbury's not short of good hotels,' Jasmine replied.

'Do you know it?'

'Angela and I had dinner there once, I think.'

'It's just down in the centre of town, isn't it? Shall we walk? Are you okay?'

'I'm not an invalid, Tom. I need to exercise.'

'Yes, of course. Well, come on then.'

They set off down the gentle hill, soon finding themselves amongst the townspeople going about their business. They reached the old coaching inn and Jasmine followed Tom inside. He approached the reception desk and showed his ID.

'Mrs Harriet Bunting is expecting us,' he said.

The male receptionist nodded and pointed into the lounge. Jasmine looked and saw Mrs Bunting relaxing on a leather sofa.

She looked up as Tom and Jasmine walked towards her.

'Ah, Inspector. You're late.'

Tom and Jasmine stood in front of her. 'Yes, Mrs Bunting, we've just been visiting the cellar in your property.' The gentle hubbub of the other guests died away a little as some guests stopped their conversations and listened in.

Jasmine noted that there wasn't a hint of a flush on the woman's cheeks. Having the scene of her sexual adventures with her husband revealed did not seem to embarrass her. However, she did rise to her feet.

'I suppose you want to ask more questions,' she said, 'it may be better if we went somewhere more private. We don't want to shock the guests do we.'

'That might be the case,' Tom agreed.

'Come to my room.' She led them from the lounge, back into the foyer and up the grand central staircase. On the first floor, they walked a short way down a corridor lined with pictures of fish until Mrs Bunting stopped and opened a door. They stepped inside a large bedroom with a king size bed and the fresh smell of potpourri. A couple of easy chairs stood by a window looking over the High Street. Mrs Bunting went to sit down. Tom picked up an upright chair that was beside the dressing table.

'You take the other chair, Jas,' he said. He placed his chair between the two easy chairs and when it was clear that Jasmine and Mrs Bunting were comfortable he sat down.

'Now why do you want to see me,' Harriet said in a voice that made it clear that she wasn't prepared for small talk.

'We wondered if you had thought of anything else we should know since we last met,' Tom said.

'My husband has been killed, my home destroyed, my clothes ruined, and my private life revealed for your grubby little minds to whisper about. What else can I say?' The woman's nostrils flared.

Jasmine was impressed by Tom's calm response. 'We are doing all we can to find who killed Evelyn and set fire to your property, Mrs Bunting, but we do hope that you can assist us in any way that you can.'

Harriet was hardly mollified but she answered. 'Well, ask your questions. I haven't got much time. I'm moving out shortly.'

'Oh, where have you found to stay?' Jasmine asked in her sweetest voice.

'A friend has invited me to their home.'

'We do need to know how to contact you,' Tom said.

'Of course, Inspector. I shall give you the address.'

'Who is the friend you are staying with?' Jasmine asked wondering if it would be a name that had occurred previously.

'Oh, I am not staying with them,' Harriet said, 'They are loaning me their house for the time being.'

'Oh,' Jasmine said, lost for words. Harriet obviously had generous and well-off friends.

'It's not your friend, Tyler Smith's home, is it?' Tom asked.

'No, it isn't.'

'We haven't tracked him down yet to ask him some questions,' Tom went on.

'What questions?'

'Well, mainly to check the times that you gave us for when you left home on the day of the fire.'

'You can ask him that in a minute. He's coming to pick me up any time now.'

'He's acting as your chauffeur again, is he?' Jasmine said.

Harriet glared at her. 'He is a friend who is willing to assist me at this troubling time.' She focussed on Tom. 'Now do you have any more of your questions, Inspector.'

'Well yes, there are a few,' Tom said, 'Can you tell us anything about Gary Nicholls.'

'I know him,' Mrs Bunting replied.

Tom persisted. 'How well do you know him?'

'What do you mean?'

'Is he a friend, or a business acquaintance?'

'He was a friend and he took a share in Molly's when we started out, several years ago now.'

Jasmine asked. 'Is he a shareholder now?'

Harriet looked at her for a moment before answering. 'No. Evelyn bought his share.'

'That must have stretched your finances,' Jasmine commented, 'Was the business able to sustain the expense?'

'Of course it did.' Harriet replied, 'What are you suggesting? That Molly's was going bankrupt.'

'How was the business doing?' Tom asked.

'I've told you before that Evelyn looked after Molly's,' Mrs Bunting did at last appear to Jasmine to be a little flustered, but Tom pressed on.

'Was your fire insurance up to date?'

'What has that got to do with Evelyn's murder?' the wife countered.

Tom spoke quietly, 'There is a suggestion that the fire was started deliberately in order to claim the insurance money.'

'Ridiculous!' Harriet replied.

There was a polite tap on the door and after a very short pause it opened. Jasmine turned to see a tall young man with dark skin – very dark – enter. He was wearing a designer suit in a medium blue.

'Ah, Harriet,' he said in a smooth, southern English accent. 'Reception told me you were in.'

Harriet rose speedily to her feet and crossed the room to present her cheek to the visitor. He stooped to give her a chaste peck.

'Tyler. How good of you to come,' she said.

Tom also got up from his chair and advanced towards the couple.

'Tyler Smith I believe.'

'That's correct. You are…?'

'Detective Inspector Shepherd, and this is Jasmine Frame,' Tom gestured towards Jasmine, 'We're asking some questions relating to the death of Mr Bunting and the fire at Molly's. I gather you were with Mrs Bunting the night that happened.'

The speed of Tom's greeting and question appeared to confuse the young man.

'Yes, that's right. It's, er, terrible what's happened.'

'You picked up Mrs Bunting from the premises in your car?'

'That's right.'

'At what time?'

Tyler looked to Harriet, who shrugged.

'Um, about four, I think, I'm not sure.'

'You drove into the Cotswolds, I understand,' Tom went on.

'Yes,' Tyler replied.

'Where did you stay overnight?'

'The Royal Hotel, Faringdon.'

'There,' Harriet said, 'Now you know where we were while my poor husband was being beaten to death and our home and livelihood destroyed. Does that answer your questions, Inspector?' She stared at him as if daring him to disagree.

'Yes, I think so,' Tom replied.

'Just let us know where you are staying from now on,' Jasmine said.

'Of course,' Mrs Bunting replied and moved to the dressing table where she picked up a pen. She scribbled on the pad of hotel paper that lay there. When she finished, she tore off the top sheet and handed it to Tom.

'Now, if you please I would like to be allowed to get on with our move.'

'Yes, of course, Mrs Bunting,' Tom replied, 'We will speak again.'

'I hope it is when you have discovered my husband's killer.'

Tyler went to the door and pulled it open. He stood, holding it while Tom and Jasmine left the room.

Jasmine found herself with Tom in the corridor with the door closed behind them.

'Well, she was glad to get rid of us,' she said.

'Yes. She's quite a powerful woman isn't she. With Tyler at her beck and call and friends handing over houses to her.'

'And she likes the high life, here and Faringdon,' Jasmine said, 'which I can't believe was supported by Molly's. Not on the evidence in the accounts I've seen.'

'Hmm. There's more to discover I think. Let's go and find Hamid.' Tom headed off towards the stairs.

They walked back up the High Street towards Molly's. Tom had his phone pressed to his ear. As they approached the burnt-out shop Hamid stepped out of a neighbour's house.

'Find anything?' Tom asked as they met.

Hamid shook his head. 'No-one I've spoken to saw anything that night. The neighbour who alerted the emergency services says he heard a window smashing followed by a sort of slow explosion. When he took a look, he saw the fire but that's all.'

'Hmm, not helpful,' Tom commented. 'How far did you get?'

Hamid pointed to the antique shop they were standing outside. 'I haven't been in there yet.'

'Well, let's give them a go,' Tom said, pulling the door open and stepping inside. Jasmine followed, glancing at her watch. It was past lunchtime and she was getting concerned, but not about needing to eat.

The smell of old dust greeted them as they were approached by a grey-haired man in a tweed jacket and brown trousers.

'May I help you,' he said.

Tom waved his warrant card. 'We're police officers. Are you the proprietor?' He pocketed his card and took out his notebook.

'Yes. Ed Simm. That's with two m's. How can I help?'

'We'd like to know if you saw anything on Tuesday evening.'

'When the fire happened and Evelyn was killed?' the antique dealer asked.

'That's right,' Tom said.

'I'm afraid I'd closed up and gone home,' he answered. 'I don't live on the premises.'

'Does anyone?' Tom asked.

Simm shook his head. 'No, we use all the rooms for storage.'

Jasmine spoke, 'You knew Evelyn Bunting, though.'

The shopkeeper frowned. 'I knew, him, er her; not well though.'

'Enough to know Evelyn was transgender,' Jasmine commented.

The man flushed slightly. 'Well yes, didn't everyone. Evelyn always wore dresses but when he spoke you knew immediately he was a man. We met in the street occasionally and always had a few words for each other.'

'You didn't meet socially or for business?' Tom asked.

Simm shook his head. 'Evelyn didn't attend Chamber of Trade meetings and I never saw him or his wife at social events in Thirsbury.'

'But you knew Mrs Bunting too,' Tom added.

The shopkeeper shrugged, 'Like Evelyn, we exchanged greetings in the street, but she was less friendly. A bit haughty.'

'Do you know a Gary Nicholls?' Jasmine asked.

'Gary? Yes.'

'In passing, like Mr and Mrs Bunting?' Jasmine pressed.

'A bit more. Gary was a customer.'

Jasmine looked around at the mixture of furniture, stuffed animals, pictures and other assorted antiques, or junk. 'What was he interested in?'

The dealer gave a small shrug of his shoulders. 'He said he was interested in anything relating to horse riding and carriage driving but all he bought from me were a couple of riding crops and a driver's whip.'

Jasmine felt her heartbeat increase. 'Did he say what he was going to do with them?'

'Display them with the other items he had, I expect.'

'He was a close friend of the Buntings?' Jasmine said.

'I don't know. He was a partner in the business, I think.'

'Do you know what the business was?'

Mr Simm raised his eyebrows, 'It was a small boutique wasn't it. Clothes. For a particular clientele.'

'And what clientele was that?' Tom asked.

The flush had returned to Simm's cheeks. 'Well, people like Evelyn I presume, transvestites.'

'That was common knowledge, was it?' Jasmine said.

The dealer waved his hands, 'I should think so.'

Jasmine went on. 'Did anyone show any concern about Molly's clients?'

The dealer looked confused now. 'Concern?'

'Anger, disgust, that sort of thing.'

Simm caught on to Jasmine's reasoning. 'Do you mean, do I think someone, a neighbour, would set fire to the place?'

'It's a possibility, don't you think?' Jasmine said.

Now the man was affronted. 'In Thirsbury? Never. I haven't heard anyone comment adversely about the Buntings and their business. It wasn't as if there were queues of trannies outside the place, clogging up the pavement. Certainly not recently.'

'Oh, business was quiet, was it?' Jasmine changed her line of questions.

'Well, one tends to notice people coming and going this end of the High Street and I can't say I've seen many people visiting

Molly's recently.'

'Do you recall any of the callers?'

Simm shrugged. 'They were all men, I think, but there wasn't anything distinctive about them; nothing that's stuck in my mind anyway.'

Jasmine glanced at her wrist watch. 'Thank you Mr Simm. You've been very helpful,' She started to move towards the exit. Tom and Hamid were caught off guard, gave brief farewells and hurried after Jasmine.

Jasmine paused and turned to face Simm. 'Was Evelyn ever a customer of yours?'

The dealer shook his head. 'Only once.'

'Oh, what did she buy?'

'About a month ago he bought a baseball bat I'd had in the window, nothing special.'

Jasmine was interested. 'Did she say why she wanted it.'

Simm chuckled, 'He said it was an expeditious precaution.'

'She was expecting trouble? A baseball bat is a useful weapon,' Jasmine asked.

Simm shrugged, 'I don't know, he never mentioned it again.'

'Thank you,' Jasmine said turning once again and striding to the exit.

On the pavement Tom caught Jasmine's arm.

'What was the rush?'

'We'd got all we were going to get, didn't we?' Jasmine replied.

'Well, yes, I suppose so. I don't know,' Tom muttered.

'We know where the murder weapon came from,' Jasmine said.

Tom nodded, 'Presumably the bat Evelyn bought was the one used to batter her to death.'

'Um,' Hamid muttered.

'Yes, Hamid?' Tom urged the young officer to speak.

'That means the killer didn't bring the weapon with him.'

Jasmine smiled, 'That's right, Hamid. So what does that suggest?'

Hamid shook his head. 'I'm not sure.'

'Perhaps the murder wasn't premeditated,' Jasmine said. She glanced at her watch again. 'anyway, I need to get home.'

Tom looked at his watch too. 'Oh, you need lunch.'

'No, Tom, I can do without lunch. Done that enough times. But there are other things I need to do – regularly, my exercises…'

There was a blank look on Tom's face for a few moments, then realisation spread like the dawn. 'Oh, yes, I see. Yes, Jas, your, er, exercises.'

Hamid continued to look confused by the conversation.

Tom went on, 'Come on Hamid. Let's get Jasmine home and then we can get back to the office and sort out where we're going.' He marched off to the police car.

'Have you got any idea where the investigation is leading, Jas?' Tom asked as they settled into their seats.

Jasmine buckled herself into the back seat. 'I think it's clear that despite what Harriet told us the business was in trouble and I think the insurance scam needs investigating further. I think Evelyn was expecting trouble from angry customers or others which is why she bought the baseball bat. Then, if Evelyn spread the petrol, who ignited it? Someone chucked something through the window that started the blaze.'

Tom nodded as he started the engine.

Jasmine continued, 'Then there's Gary Nicholls, a third person in the partnership who buys whips and riding crops. Were they a present for Harriet, or for Evelyn?'

'You mean he was involved in this S and M thing?' Tom asked spinning the wheel so that the car turned around in the road.

'Was. He's been paid off, remember. I wonder why?'

'Hmm, a good question.'

'Harriet Bunting interests me too,' Jasmine added. 'She seems to have little concern for Evelyn's business yet apparently enjoys a life of dinners in posh hotels, chauffeured by a handsome young man.'

'He was fit,' Hamid added.

'You noticed,' Tom said with a chuckle. Jasmine couldn't see the DC's face, but the back of his neck seemed to turn a redder shade of olive. Tom eyes flicked to the mirror. 'So, you think we need to dig into Harriet Bunting's life a little more, Jas?'

'I'm sure it will be educational, Tom. But let's see what the rest of your team have come up with on those other names we had.'

Jasmine waved to the departing Mondeo then scampered into the house. Since the operation she had rigidly followed her timetable of exercises and being late made her anxious. Of course, her new vagina wouldn't close up if she was late for one dilation, but the fear was there. She had to tend to her new anatomy; she wanted it to be fully functioning as soon as possible so that she could perform as a woman and give Viv what they both desired. She must carry out all the instructions of her doctors to the letter.

She shucked off her coat and hurried upstairs to her bedroom. The skirt was dropped to the floor and tights and knickers removed. She gave herself a wash then lay on the bed with the lube and the dilators beside her. The task was no longer painful although her flesh was still tender. She eased the largest tube into herself, gently twisting it. She took care not to push it too hard or too far. As she relaxed, the feeling of the dilator inside her became more than tolerable. A tingle in her clitoris surprised her and very carefully she touched it with a finger.

The sensation drew a gasp from her. It was an unfamiliar feeling, an almost forgotten pleasure. It had been years since she and Angela had had intercourse and just as long since she had relieved the tension of her own erect penis. Now the same tissue remodelled into a woman's erogenous zone was making her heart beat faster, her face flushed and erotic thoughts streamed through her head.

They passed. The remaining discomfort from her surgery

and the anxiety that it was still too soon took the edge off her excitement. She removed the dilator from inside her, rested back on her pillow. Sleep came unexpectedly.

She awoke. Jasmine sat up with a start. What was she doing sleeping? This was her first day back at something like work. Surely that can't have tired her out. She was shocked, disappointed and worried. How much longer would it take to get her old self back.

What did she mean, "old self"? She was a new person now, a woman. She must not look back but ahead at the new possibilities she had. She knew what Viv would say, anyone for that matter – just over a month since major surgery was nothing. She was still in recovery. "Stop being so hard on yourself".

Jasmine sat up. The nap had actually been refreshing. She felt full of energy now, her mind working. She got up and washed the dilators thoroughly before putting them and the lube away. This walking around with nothing on, on her lower half at least, was a new experience. Previously she had always, and that meant always, hidden her penis and testicles. Now she caught a glimpse of herself in the long mirror – no appendage but a short fuzz of re-grown pubic hair on her mound (would she have to think about trimming it to look neater?). There was just a hint of redness between her thighs; not bruising from the operation but the barely visible edges of the lips of her new vulva.

Why did Harriet Bunting spend a night in Faringdon? The facts of the case came into her mind along with the remembered conversations with Harriet, Tyler Smith, and Ed Simm, the antique dealer. Questions flooded after. Why go away without her husband? Was it anything to do with their relationship – sex, S&M, Evelyn being a sissy? Was Tyler just a chauffeur? Even Jasmine, (even?) could see that he was attractive and desirable. Where did Gary Nicholls fit in? Why Faringdon?

The last question stuck. Harriet had originally said they had gone to the Cotswolds and she had imagined somewhere like

Stow-on-the-Wold, or Chipping Camden, places that were over an hour's drive from Thirsbury. But Faringdon? It was barely in the Cotswolds at all. No distance.

Jasmine sat at her dressing table and opened up her laptop. It took a while to boot up – it was pretty old after all – but she was soon able to load a route finder website. She inputted Thirsbury to Faringdon. The result didn't surprise her at all. Forty-one minutes with clear roads. Why spend a night away so close to home? Well, you might if you had someone special with you.

She was eager to find out what Harriet had done during her night away and an idea formed in her head. She found the phone number of the Royal Hotel, rang the hotel and then sent a text message to Viv saying, "I'm taking you out to dinner this evening – if you'll drive.'

A glance at her watch showed that she could expect Viv home in under an hour and then they would have to set off soon for Faringdon. It was time for her to get ready and blow the cobwebs off her credit card.

10

Tom Shepherd marched into the V&SCU office with Hamid at his heels. He was pleased to see Terry Hopkins and Sasha Patel at their desks.

'Gather round, guys. Let's see what we've got.' Tom stood by the whiteboard.

'Where's Jasmine?' Sasha asked moving forward.

'She needed a timeout. It's still early days. You know…' Sasha nodded while Terry made a grunt.

'Right, well we've had an interesting time.' Tom summarised their visit to the Bunting's cellar, their conversation with Harriet Bunting, Tyler Smith and Ed Simm.

'She's shagging her toyboy,' Terry said when Tom finished.

Tom nodded. 'That is the obvious conclusion. The point is does it have any relevance to the case.'

'She did away with her husband so she could shack up with the young bull?' Terry offered again.

'In which case why offer the alibi of the night in Faringdon. We can easily check that.'

'Have we?' Sasha Patel asked.

'Not yet. That can be your next task Sasha.'

'What about this fella, Nicholls?' Terry asked, 'Is it a ménage?'

Tom shrugged. 'Could be. We need to speak to him. Hamid found his address. You can make contact with him Hamid.'

The young DC, nodded and looked in his notebook. Tom looked at the whiteboard checking what he had put up earlier in the day.

'Hamid. You were also looking in to Akash Rana. Did you find him or is it her?'

'Him. He's the supplier of the, um, gear, that Bunting sold on to the transvestites,' Hamid said.

'What do you mean?' Sasha asked.

'The wigs, false breasts,' Hamid was beginning to blush, 'things to cover their genitals, even suits to make men look like women even when they are naked.'

Terry chortled, 'Enjoy looking into that did you, Hamid boy.'

The Iranian detective glowered at Terry. 'I understand that they help some transgender people feel happier with themselves.'

'Aw, you've been talking to Frame haven't you,' Terry said.

Tom stepped in. 'Now Terry, stop teasing. Go on Hamid. What did you find out?'

'Rana's business is based in Manchester. I wasn't able to speak to him but his secretary confirmed that Molly's was a customer.'

Tom nodded. 'Right, well we need more on that. It looks as if the Bunting's business was struggling. Now, Terry, Sasha, how far have you got?'

Terry opened his hand to DC Patel, urging her to speak first.

'My two are both customers of Molly's. I've spoken to both of them. Mr McLeesh had been complaining about the quality the goods he had purchased and had been trying to get his money back. As well as emailing and phoning Mr Bunting he admitted to calling at the shop a few times. He lives in Bournemouth. He's a Scot and sounded as though he could be pretty belligerent if he wanted to be.'

'Enough to murder, Evelyn?' Tom asked.

Sasha shrugged. 'I don't know. A bit extreme, isn't it?'

'Still, a trip to Bournemouth may be useful,' Tom said, 'He may be able to give us a better picture of the business. What about the other one, er, Clement.'

'Oh, he was completely different. Very nervous when I spoke to him. Said he'd visited the shop a few weeks ago and paid

Evelyn a lot of money for the goods in advance but hadn't received them yet.'

'What goods?' Tom asked.

'One of those whole-body suits.'

'Bloody hell,' Terry said, 'Blokes actually buy them.'

'Yes,' Sasha said, 'They do, and Lee says he paid nearly two thousand pounds.'

Terry whistled.

'But not received anything yet?' Tom asked.

Sasha nodded, 'That's right. He'd been on to Evelyn a few times, but Evelyn had fobbed him off with saying that the suit had to be specially made for him.'

'But meanwhile Bunting was sitting on the two thousand quid,' Terry said.

'No. We know the money left his account quickly,' Tom said.

'Paid to Mr Rana?' Hamid asked

'There's no record of it,' Tom said. 'Where does Clement live, Sasha?'

'Essex. He was very shy but he told me he'd driven specially to Thirsbury to have a dressing session with Evelyn. A transformation, he called it.'

'With a wank thrown in?' Terry added. 'Who does who, do you think?'

'That's not necessary, Terry,' Tom said, 'There's no evidence that the Buntings were offering sexual services.'

'And no evidence that they weren't,' Terry added.

'What did you get from Griffiths, Terry?' Tom asked in order to change the topic of conversation.

'Well, it is the same Neville Griffiths that we know from past run-ins, but he's gone legit.'

Tom raised his eyebrows. 'Really?'

'He says so. He's running a loans business. Got a licence too. Reasonable rates of interest, so he says.'

'So, Evelyn has taken out a loan?'

'Yeah. A big one, hundred thou or so. Don't know why though.'

'I do,' Tom said with a satisfied grin, 'Jasmine found from the files on Evelyn's computer that he'd paid out that size sum to Nicholls to buy him out of the business. Harriet admitted that.'

'It's a lot of money to pay back,' Sasha said.

'And I wouldn't want to be in debt to Neville Griffiths even to save my life,' Terry added.

'Where's Griffiths based, Terry?' Tom asked.

'Reading. He's got a few businesses there.'

'I think we need a chat with him, you and me, Terry.'

'You think he's involved in Bunting's death?'

'I'm sure a bit of insurance related arson would be just his kind of way of getting his money back quicker than by instalments.' Tom said.

Sasha spoke, 'It's a bit obvious, isn't it? I mean, if Evelyn spread the petrol to make the fire catch, the insurance won't pay out will they.'

Tom frowned. 'You're right, Sash, but if Griffiths is involved and he is to the tune of a hundred thousand pounds, then we need to question him. Come on Terry, let's go.'

'What about me and Hamid?' Sasha asked.

'Hamid needs to speak to Rana and make contact with Nicholls. I'd like you to find out all you can about Tyler Smith and see what else you can get on McLeesh and Clement or any other disappointed or disgruntled customers.'

They were in a back street off a side street, a short distance from the town centre. There were closed up shops amongst blank-faced buildings, but one frontage was bright and welcoming. It read "Cash In Your Hand" in colourful bubble shaped letters with a cartoon hand piled with cash.

'This is Griffiths' place?' Tom said.

'Looks like it,' Terry replied, 'Jolly isn't it.'

'To entice in the people desperate to get some money in their pockets,' Tom said. He pushed the door open. The interior was as warm and inviting as the window, with primary-coloured easy chairs against the side walls and cheerful posters advertising short term loans – £100 for a month with just £120 to repay. A chest high counter divided the room, with a glass window up to the ceiling. It looked somewhat defensive, Tom thought. Behind it sat a young woman in a smart red uniform, perfectly styled blonde hair and immaculate make-up. Tom advanced to the counter and held up his warrant card for her to see.

'We'd like to see Mr Griffiths,' he said.

'Mr Griffiths isn't here,' she replied without a pause. 'Can I help?'

'We're interested in a loan that Mr Griffiths made.'

'You had better see our loan advisor, then. Mr Adams.' She had hardly spoken the name when the door behind her opened and a man appeared. Tom thought immediately that he looked like a smooth operator, smart tailored suit, slicked back black hair, smooth complexion, a look unlikely to be matched by his customers.

'What is it Mel?' he said looking at the woman and then at Tom and Terry.

'These policemen wanted to see Mr Griffiths about a loan, Mr Adams.'

'Ah, you'd better come through guys.' He moved to the side and leaned down. There were a number of clicks and thumps before part of the counter and window moved to allow Tom and Terry to enter. They followed Adams into a back room, which was decorated much more sparsely with a desk and a couple of office chairs.

'How can I help,' Adams said pointing to the chairs. Tom ignored the gesture and remained standing.

'You provide payday loans?' he asked.

Adams nodded. 'Short term loans to tide people over periods when they're short of cash. We don't call them payday loans.'

'But they pay back a lot more than they borrowed out of their pay or benefits,' Tom tried to keep his voice level but couldn't avoid sounding judgemental.

'Our rates are competitive.'

'Twenty pounds interest on a hundred-pound loan for one month,' Tom recited recalling what he had read. 'That's competitive? It's a rate of a couple of hundred per cent.'

'There's an arrangement fee in there,' Adams said, 'But, it is comparable, lower even, than our competitors. We provide a service to people who need cash for basic things like food and heating, and rent.'

'While making them even worse off.'

Adams glowered. 'Is this why you're here – to make accusations about a legitimate business. We're not doing anything illegal here.'

Tom realised he had been getting diverted by his feelings. That wasn't good for a detective.

'No, we're not here about what I suppose you'd call your small loans. We're interested in a loan Mr Griffiths made to Evelyn Bunting. A pretty large loan in fact.'

'We do offer bigger loans over a longer period, but I can't give you any details.'

'Oh, I think you can. You see Mr Bunting is dead and we think the loan he received from Mr Griffiths may have been a contributory factor.'

Adams' pale face became paler. 'You mean he committed suicide?'

'No, he was murdered. Now I want to know the terms of the loan and whether it was being repaid. I can demand your assistance you know.'

The young man sat at his desk and hurriedly tapped keys on his laptop. 'What was the name? Bunting?'

Tom moved to stand behind him and looked down at the screen. 'That's right, Evelyn Bunting. He ran a shop called Molly's in Thirsbury.'

Adams fingers ran over the keyboard and very quickly a page appeared that Tom saw bore Evelyn's name. There was a statement.

Adams described what was on the screen. 'Yes, he had a loan of £110,000 over three years. He'd made one monthly repayment of just over seven thousand pounds.'

Tom leaned closer to read the small characters. 'That was back in July. What about since then?'

The loan salesman, also peered at the screen. 'He doesn't appear to have made any other repayments. He's in arrears.'

Tom straightened up. 'I'm not surprised. Seven thou a month. I bet that's more than Bunting's takings in the shop.'

'If he was defaulting on the loan, we would have been taking steps to recover our money,' Adams said.

'And what steps would those be?' Tom asked.

Adams looked scared as if he had realised what he was implicating himself in.

'I couldn't say. Mr Griffiths makes decisions about non-payers.'

'I bet he does,' Tom said, 'But he's not here – is that right or just a story that your receptionist is programmed to hand out?'

Adams shook his head. 'No, he's not here. He doesn't come in very often, but he expects me to send a daily report by email.'

'We need to speak to him,' Tom said. 'Which of his properties is he using at the moment.'

'I don't know where he lives. I just contact him by email or mobile.'

'Well, give me his email address and number and we'll get in touch with him.'

Adams scribbled on a piece of notepaper and handed it to Tom.

'And you can put in your daily report that we will see Mr Griffiths very soon. Come on Terry.'

Tom and Terry left the young man visibly shaking in his chair. They nodded to the female receptionist in passing and left the loan shop. Terry paused on the pavement and brushed the arms of his jacket.

'I feel grubby after meeting that slimy little snake,' he said.

Tom was surprised. Terry didn't usually show much emotion.

'I feel the same, Terry.'

'Making a tidy living from other people's misery,' the DC went on, 'I've been in this job long enough to know people who have had to take out loans from people like him and then struggle to repay the interest. I'd like to see all these payday outfits closed down.'

'Yes, I know, but we have a particular loan to follow up this time. Let's give Griffiths a call.'

They returned to their car. Tom got out his phone and the scrap of paper Adams had given him. He tapped in the number. It rang for a few seconds before it was answered by a gruff voice.

'Who is that?'

'Mr Griffiths? Detective Inspector Shepherd speaking.'

'Police?'

'Yes, Mr Griffiths.'

The voice become smoother, 'How can I help you Detective Inspector.'

'We'd like to speak to you about a loan you made.'

'I'm not interested in the loans my company makes. That's what I pay my employees to do.'

'Yes, we've spoken to Mr Adams. This is quite a big loan and we believe that some repayments have not been made.'

'Are you offering to act as my debt collectors now, Inspector?'

'No Mr Griffiths, but we would like to talk to you about the loan you gave Evelyn Bunting.'

There was silence for a few moments.

'Ah. Mister or is it Mizz Bunting? I see. Well, you'd better come over.'

'Where Mr Griffiths?'

'My house.' He rattled off an address outside Reading.

'Thank you, Mr Griffiths. We're on our way.'

Tom ended the call and started the engine. 'Let's get there before he has much time to build his story.'

They drove through the electrically operated gates and pulled up in front of a modern mansion with a mock-Palladian frontage.

'Done alright for himself, hasn't he,' Terry Hopkins commented.

Tom scowled, 'A pity we've never been able to make anything on him stick. Perhaps this case will change that.'

'Griffiths is slippery.'

They got out of the car and approached the gleaming black front door. It opened before they reached it. They were confronted by a bald-headed man in a black suit and tie. From his bent nose and moth-eaten ears, his had not been a sedentary life.

'Police?' He growled. Tom and Terry flashed their cards. 'Mr Griffiths is expecting you.'

'I hope so,' Tom said in a cheery voice. The servant or bodyguard, Tom thought the latter was probably a more accurate title, stood aside to let them in, closed the door behind them and then lead them into a large lounge. Griffiths was standing by a fireplace. Tom recognised him from previous meetings and photos that had appeared in crime files as well as newspaper reports. Griffiths was either a master-criminal or a generous benefactor depending on which you read.

'Gentlemen,' Griffiths opened his arms in welcome, revealing his sizeable paunch. 'Can I offer you tea or coffee?'

'No thank you,' Tom replied, 'We just want to ask you a few questions about Evelyn Bunting's loan.'

'Yes, so you said, and as I told you, I employ staff to look after my businesses.'

'But you indicated that you know Evelyn and her gender confusion. You referred to her as "Mister or Mizz".'

'Yes, I do know about Evelyn Bunting and her business.' Griffiths made the concession without appearing dismayed by it.

'Perhaps because the loan is bigger than those normally agreed by your staff in the Reading shop.'

'That is true, Detective Sergeant.'

'Inspector.'

'Ah, you've had a promotion since we last met.'

Tom recalled that interview when they had attempted, and

failed, to pin a human-trafficking case on Neville Griffiths. He hadn't been so full of bonhomie on that occasion.

'So, you agreed to the loan to Bunting?' Tom persisted.

'I allowed it.' Griffiths nodded.

'And when Bunting failed to keep up with the enormous repayments...'

'Repayments are handled by my staff.'

'But you knew that Evelyn was unable to keep up? How he ever expected to I don't know.'

'We have procedures for assisting clients who get into difficulty.'

'And what measures do those procedures include?'

Griffiths smiled. 'We look for ways of helping the client repay the loan, perhaps by rescheduling payments.'

'And if that proves impossible such as if the client doesn't have any money or income?'

'Are you suggesting that Evelyn Bunting's business was in that state, Inspector?'

'I believe that he had no way of meeting the huge monthly instalments you demanded of him.'

Griffiths shrugged. 'He signed the agreement.'

Tom pressed on. 'But what do you do to clients that can't pay you back.'

'We don't do anything *to* them. We employ bailiffs to claim goods to the value of what is owed.'

'I doubt that the contents of Molly's came anywhere close to a hundred thousand pounds,' Tom said.

Griffiths shrugged. 'Bunting may have had other possessions that would have served.'

'Such as an insurance policy on the building.'

'What are you suggesting, Inspector – that we would benefit from the misfortune of a fire at Evelyn Bunting's premises?'

'You heard about the fire, then, and of Evelyn Bunting's death.'

'It was on the local news,' Griffiths said, 'A sad business. I should point out that the death of a client makes it more difficult for us to recover the loan, so the fire and death of Evelyn Bunting is hardly of benefit to my business.'

Tom was wary of accusing Griffiths of arson or murder as he would easily deny any involvement. 'But prior to his death, you can't tell me what steps you were taking to recover your money from Evelyn Bunting.'

Griffiths spread his arms and shook his head, 'No Inspector, I cannot. My staff were following the procedures I mentioned and had no need to involve me. Now, if you please, I do have other things to attend to.' He gestured to the door.

Tom realised that he had nothing more to ask, not without any evidence to back up his questioning.

'Well, thank you Mr Griffiths for answering our questions.'

Griffiths gave them a warm smile. 'I am delighted to help the police with their enquiries in this sad case. Preston will show you out.' The bent-nosed henchman had obviously been listening outside the door because he chose that precise moment to push it open and appear in the doorway.

Tom put his foot down and accelerated through the gateway.

'I'm glad to get out of there,' he said, 'I felt like James Bond in the villain's lair.'

Terry laughed. 'Yeah, it was a bit like that. I bet there were a few more like Preston in other rooms, waiting for the signal to spring into action.'

'And all we did was alert Griffiths that we're on to his involvement in Evelyn's death.'

'Oh, I think you did more than that, boss.'

'Really?'

'I was watching him carefully. Although he appeared to be very relaxed there was a lot of control there. Fat oaf that he is, his muscles were tense and when you mentioned fire insurance, his eyelids blinked twice.'

'You think that means he was involved, Terry?'

'In an insurance scam – yes.'

'But as he said. Having Evelyn killed separately to the fire doesn't help him at all.'

'No, and that was why he was desperate to disassociate himself from Bunting's death.'

'Hmm. So, the fire and the murder are two separate incidents.'

'Still looks like it, boss.'

'Stop calling me boss, Terry. Sloane's the boss. I'm still Tom Shepherd, even if I am technically your senior officer now.'

'DCI Sloane is hardly ever out on the ground these days. You're the guv'nor on this case, Tom.'

11

Jasmine stepped out of the Audi and onto her high heels. She felt a bit unsteady; it had been a while since she'd worn them. It had been a while too since she had dressed up to go out. This evening was exciting, and it wasn't only because she was out with Viv for the first time since she became a real woman. The investigation added to it.

Viv came around the car to her and offered his hand. She took it gratefully, not just to steady her on her feet, but because it was offered. It was a sign that they were a couple, herself and her partner. When she had split from Angela she had thought she would never have someone else to call "partner" and had never dared to hope that such a person would be a man that fancied her sexually.

Viv had been eager to take up her suggestion of an evening out with dinner, even when she admitted that it had a connection to the current investigation. He had said he was pleased that she was getting back to full fitness and was proud of her as his companion. He didn't grumble too much about being her stooge while she indulged in a little detecting.

They were welcomed into the Royal Hotel dining room by a small, thin waiter who spoke with a French accent. Jasmine couldn't decide whether it was genuine or not. The room was not busy, so there was plenty of room between the diners. The heavy curtains at the windows and the thick carpet ensured that they wouldn't be overheard in their conversation. The waiter brought the menus. Jasmine decided to make a start straight away – on the investigating.

'You were recommended by one of your guests,' she began.

The waiter showed interest, feigned or otherwise. 'I am pleased that you received a good report on us, Madame.'

'Yes, Harriet Bunting said she had a good evening here on Tuesday.'

The waiter's eyebrows rose. Jasmine guessed that he recognised the name.

'You know Mrs Bunting?'

'Yes, Madame, she is a not infrequent guest.'

'I believe she was here with her friend, Tyler Smith.'

'Ah, yes, it was Mr Smith on this occasion. There were two other guests of Madame Bunting on Tuesday.'

Jasmine hadn't expected that. She had imagined Harriet and Tyler having a cosy supper before retiring to their bed for their evening's entertainment. 'Oh, really, I wonder which of Harriet's friends they were?'

'I do not know them,' the waiter said and dropping his voice to a conspiratorial volume added, 'A man and a woman, although the woman appeared to be a man dressed as a woman.'

Jasmine giggled. 'Really? That sounds exciting. Did other people notice?'

'The restaurant was almost empty on Tuesday evening and anyway, Madame Bunting and her guests left early. It was the woman who was a man who paid for the meal.'

'All of it!'

'Only Madame Bunting and Mr Smith had had a full dinner. The other two ate very little.'

'How strange. I shall have to ask Harriet what was going on.'

The face of the waiter clouded and he sucked in his breath. 'Oh, please do not say that I told you all of this. I should not have indulged in gossip.'

'Nonsense. We're all friends.' Jasmine did her best to reassure the waiter and made sure that Viv ordered a good bottle of wine to accompany their meal.

'What was all that?' Viv asked after the waiter had left them.

'It's mysterious,' Jasmine replied, 'I thought that Harriet and Tyler had come here for a naughty night away but instead there are these other two, one apparently a tranny who paid for the meal which didn't go on very long. What were they doing?'

'I don't think you'll get any more out of the waiter. I think he's embarrassed that you drew so much out of him so quickly. They are supposed to show discretion.'

'Well, it seems that Harriet's antics got the better of him. He mentioned that she is quite a regular here. I wonder if she always meets other people?'

Viv shrugged and nodded at the waiter returning with their bottle of wine.

Jasmine got no more information out of the waiter, but it didn't matter because she enjoyed her meal with the two or three glasses of wine and the company of Viv. After a month when they had been unavoidably a little distant from each other while she was recovering from her surgery and coming to terms with her new anatomy, it was a relief that they enjoyed each other's company.

After tipping the waiter generously, they drove home. On entering the house, Jasmine took Viv in her arms, kissed him on the lips and whispered in his ear, 'I think we'll share a bed tonight.'

Viv's eyes opened wide with excitement. 'You're not ready to, you know, well... It's only been a month or so.'

'Five weeks actually. No, I'm not ready just yet, but there are other means to an end, and I think I'm ready to show you.'

Even through Viv's dark skin she could see the flush of excitement.

'Well, let's see what you're offering.' He took her hand and drew her up the stairs and into the master bedroom. It had been intended as their room when they moved in but since the operation it had been Jasmine's exclusively while Viv had been pushed into a guest bedroom. He hadn't complained.

Jasmine made a rush for the en-suite, removing her knickers, going to the loo and giving herself a quick wash before returning to the bedroom. Viv was already in the king-size bed, the visible part of his body naked.

'I'll close my eyes while you undress,' he said. Previously when they had shared a bed, Jasmine had always ensured she was in a nightie with tight knickers encasing her male genitals, before Viv joined her. Sexual fumblings had taken place under the covers with the light off. Now she had to get ready for bed with Viv watching, unless she took up his offer. But she didn't have to hide anymore. She had a female body. She was proud of it, well almost.

'It's OK. You can watch, but I'm not doing a striptease.' She let her dress drop to the floor, stepped out of it and reached behind to unclip her bra. Her enhancers dropped out. Damn, she'd forgotten them in her excitement. Her breasts were still a disappointment, a work in progress. Despite the female hormones they had not developed a great deal, and were still A cup bumps. She put that out of her mind. She was pretty pleased with her figure. Despite the inactivity caused by her recuperation, her stomach was flat but there was a little extra flesh on her hips and bottom – she had a figure.

'Face me,' Viv said in a tone that was a request not an order. She did as he asked and stood with her arms by her side and legs together.

'Beautiful,' he announced.

She covered her nipples with her crossed hands. 'My tits…'

'Are lovely. Come here. May I see you?'

'See me?'

'Between your legs?'

She swallowed. This was what she had been looking forward to and dreading. Revealing the core of her femininity for the first time. She nodded slowly.

Viv flung the duvet back and beckoned to her. She saw he was completely nude and aroused. She moved around the bed, sat down and swung her legs onto the mattress. She lay flat and slowly raised her knees and opened her legs. Viv pushed himself up, scrambled round between her feet and gazed at her. He stared as if mesmerised.

'Absolutely wonderful,' he pronounced. He leaned closer, examining her. She allowed it. More than that, she enjoyed his gaze.

'May I?' he said.

'What?'

'Touch you.'

'Um. Yes. It's still a bit tender, you know.'

'Yes, I understand. I'll be gentle.'

He reached out with his right hand. Fingers touched her vulva. She tensed as if expecting pain. There was none. Then a fingertip squeezed gently between the folds, found her clitoris. She gasped. An electric shock had shot up her back to the top of her head.

Viv withdrew his hand. 'Sorry. Did that hurt?'

Jasmine shook her head unable to draw breath to speak for a moment. Then, 'No, it didn't hurt. It was, I don't know, unexpected. I haven't had anything like that before.'

'The first time it's been touched?'

'No, I've touched it when I've been doing my, uh, exercises. But it's the first time someone else has touched it. It must be like trying to tickle yourself.'

Viv grinned. 'Again?'

'Yes, but perhaps some lube... I don't ...'

Viv nodded and reached to the bedside table where Jasmine's dilators and lubricant lived.

12

FRIDAY 18TH OCTOBER
MORNING

Jasmine drifted to the surface of consciousness but remained, eyes closed, curled up under the duvet reliving the pleasures of the night. A delicious sleep had followed the delightful discovery that she could orgasm, and she recalled the pleasure she had given Viv. *Is this what a woman feels after lovemaking*, she asked herself. Not quite perhaps, not until she could allow him to penetrate her, sometime not far away now. Then, yes, she would feel complete. Soon, she thought.

Other thoughts surfaced: the investigation; the hotel in Faringdon; Harriet Bunting's guests. She needed to find out more about what had gone on that Tuesday evening when Evelyn had been bludgeoned and the shop burned. This time it would not be by subterfuge. She would use her unofficial position in the police to ask questions.

Viv had already left, leaving her to doze on. She performed her exercises, showered, dressed and had breakfast. Ready to go to work, she went into the garage where her Fiesta had sat since before her operation. The tyres looked as though they needed a little air and the driver's door opened with a reluctant creak. She got into the cold seat, put the key in the ignition, turned it. Nothing. She tried again. More nothing. She thumped the steering wheel. She should have thought ahead and got the car checked over while she was convalescing, or at least put the battery on charge. The poor old thing had nearly had it anyway. It probably wouldn't pass the next MOT. When was that due anyway?

She got out and slammed the door. Returning to the kitchen she pondered how she would get to Faringdon. There was only one thing to do – contact Tom. She pulled her mobile from her bag.

'Hi, Jas, how things?' Tom said, answering immediately.

'My car won't start.'

'Your car? You mean that old Fiesta?'

'Yes. It's given up on me.'

'What did you need it for? Are you thinking of coming in to help us?'

'No, I want to go to Faringdon.'

'Faringdon? Why?'

'The Royal Hotel. Harriet Bunting's naughty night away with Tyler.'

'Yes, that's their alibi for Evelyn's murder. It checks out. Why do you want to go there?'

'To ask some questions about the other guests.'

'What other guests?'

Jasmine explained what she had learned from questioning their waiter the previous evening.

'Interesting, but I don't see what it has to do with the case. If they were there they weren't anything to do with the murder or the fire.'

'Perhaps,' Jasmine conceded, 'but I think there might be wider implications. Harriet Bunting seems to live the highlife which has little to do with the business that Evelyn was running.'

'Hmm, I suppose so. I'll send Hamid over. He can go with you. Won't be long.' Tom hung up.

Jasmine was looking out of the window when the Ford Focus drew up. She was out of the front door before Hamid had a chance to get out. She slid into the passenger seat.

'Hi again, Hamid. Thanks for giving me a lift.'

'We're going to Faringdon?' Hamid put the car in gear and they set off. 'I don't know where it is.'

'I'll give you directions.'

'OK. Why are we going there?'

Jasmine repeated what she had told Tom. Hamid shrugged and yawned.

'You didn't get much sleep last night?' she said.

He shook his head. 'Didn't get home till late. Sasha and I were looking into Evelyn Bunting's contacts.'

'What about Tom and Terry?'

'They were investigating this loan shark, Neville Griffiths.'

'Did they find anything?'

'No, but Terry said they're sure there was an insurance scam going on. But Terry went home, DI Shepherd was doing admin.'

'So what did you find out?'

Hamid shrugged. 'Not a lot. I did learn a lot more about the things Bunting stocked in the shop supplied by Akash Rana.'

'Oh yes.'

'Do men really get pleasure from making themselves look like women?'

Jasmine took a deep breath. 'For some men it's a pleasure thing, but for others it goes a bit deeper than that. It's a need. They'd do anything to get the physical appearance that they see in their head but not in the mirror. For some, the clothes and the silicone falsies go some way. For others that isn't enough, or, no, it's not a question of it being enough, it's not real enough.'

'You mean those men need drugs and surgery.'

'It's not just men wanting to be women. There are just as many F to M transsexuals.'

Hamid concentrated on the road ahead.

'You never used these "falsies"?'

'Well, yes, I did.' *I do,* Jasmine meant but didn't say. 'You have to if you want to have a feminine figure while you're transitioning. But I only used breast enhancers.'

'Not one of these body suits.'

'God no!'

'I think you don't approve of the men who buy these things.'

'They don't need my approval, Hamid. If they want to

purchase all that stuff it's none of my business, but it's not me. I've got no argument with people like Evelyn selling it.'

'That was the problem.'

'What?'

'He hadn't been selling much stuff.'

'Ah. You got that from Rana.'

'Yes. I spoke to him last night. Seems he and Bunting have been doing business for years which is why Rana says he hadn't been pushing Bunting for payment until recently. Bunting owes a pretty big sum for stock. Rana says he refused to supply one of those expensive body suits when Bunting ordered one recently unless he paid up front.'

'Another debtor.'

'Yes.'

'Do you think Rana could be involved in the fire or murder?'

'I didn't get that feeling. Should a policeman have feelings?'

'Oh yes, Hamid, hunches are important. They show your subconscious weighing up the evidence. So…'

'No. He seemed genuinely upset about Evelyn Bunting even though he's owed a lot of money. They seem to have been friends. And anyway, Rana, was up in Manchester at the time of the fire. We've checked his alibi.'

Jasmine was finding Hamid a useful informant. 'What about the other people you and Sasha were checking.'

'We didn't get anything useful. McLeesh and Clement are two customers of Molly's both of whom paid out large sums for stuff. McLeesh wasn't satisfied with the product and Clement didn't get a delivery.'

'Either a suspect?'

'Not really. McLeesh is quite belligerent but he crumbled when Sasha suggested he might have done something to Evelyn. His alibi checks out. And Lee Clement was just embarrassed that anyone could find out he is a transvestite or that he has spent nearly two thousand pounds regardless of whether he actually received the suit.'

'What about Nicholls? It would be interesting to find out his relationship with Evelyn and Harriet.'

'We've got his address just outside Kintbridge but he's not been seen there recently and isn't responding to calls.'

'Done a runner or on holiday?' Jasmine mused. Hamid shrugged. 'No-one else?'

'Not on Bunting's contacts. Sasha did find out a bit more about Tyler Smith.'

Jasmine sat up, her interest suddenly increased. 'And?'

'He's got a private income. Rich parents, or rather mother, they're divorced. Sasha wondered if Harriet had replaced his mother as the female in his life. Anyway. he's got plenty of money for the flash cars and nights in hotels.'

'No job?'

'No, spends all his time in the gym when he's not with Harriet.'

They continued to chat about life in the police force and other inconsequentials. Jasmine felt that Hamid wanted to ask her more about her transition, but was too embarrassed to do so. Soon they entered Faringdon.

'This is the place?' Hamid asked.

'Yes. The hotel is in the centre of the town. Why?'

'It hasn't taken long to get here,' he glanced at the clock on the dashboard. 'forty-five minutes. I thought we were headed on a longer journey into – what are they called – the Cotswolds.'

'I thought they'd gone further too until Harriet told us it was just Faringdon they'd come to. It isn't far from Kintbridge. That's why I brought Viv here for dinner last night. It didn't take long to get back home.'

Hamid parked in the carpark and they walked into the hotel together. The waiter from the previous evening, crossed the corridor in front of them. He glanced at Jasmine, his eyes showed recognition. He seemed about to greet her then his eyes moved on to Hamid. He ducked his head and hurried on.

Jasmine turned to Hamid. 'Did you see his reaction? I don't think it was because you're not the boyfriend I was with last night and I'm not in my nice dress.'

'Perhaps he's embarrassed by what he told you last night.'

Jasmine shrugged, 'Maybe you're right.'

They approached the reception desk. The female receptionist looked at each of them and narrowed her eyebrows at Hamid. He showed her his warrant card.

'We have some questions about some of your guests,' he announced.

'Yes, Sir,' she seemed relieved to have discovered that he was a policeman. 'Are they resident now?'

'No,' Hamid replied, 'They stayed on Tuesday night, Mrs Harriet Bunting.'

'Oh yes, Mrs Bunting. I know her.'

Jasmine intervened. 'She's a regular guest?'

The receptionist frowned as she composed her answer. 'Not really regular, or frequent. I suppose she spends a night here on average two or three times a year.' Jasmine nodded in agreement – not regular or frequent but quite often. The receptionist's fingers were dancing over her computer keyboard.

'That's right. She was booked in last Tuesday.'

'She shared a room with someone?' Hamid went on.

The receptionist nodded. 'Yes. Her gentleman friend, Mr Smith.'

They were pretty brazen about their relationship, Jasmine thought, to not register as Mr and Mrs Smith, but of course Harriet would have been the boss.

'I believe that they were joined by two other people for dinner,' Jasmine said.

The receptionist nodded. 'Yes, that is true, I was on duty and remember them.'

'A man and a woman?' Jasmine added.

The receptionist's mouth moved as she tried to compose an answer, but no sound came out. Eventually she just nodded. 'But they didn't stay the night,' she blurted out.

'They just came to dinner with Mrs Bunting and Mr Smith,' Hamid said.

The receptionist nodded.

'I have information that one of these guests paid for the dinner,' Jasmine said.

The woman nodded again, 'Yes, I do recall that. It was the, er, woman.'

'Do you recall every guest that pays for a meal?' Hamid asked.

The woman shrugged, 'No, I don't suppose so, but this one was different.'

'Why was that?' Jasmine asked.

'Er, *she*, paid by credit card but it was in the name of a man. It had "Mr" on it.'

'But you still accepted it?' Jasmine pressed.

'Well, yes, I could see it was really a man dressed in – what is it – drag. And as they were friends of Mrs Bunting I thought it would be alright.'

'I'll need details of the transaction,' Hamid said.

The receptionist turned pink. 'Oh, was I wrong to accept it. Will it be refused?'

'I shouldn't think so,' Hamid said.

'Dressing as a woman doesn't make a man's card invalid,' Jasmine said, a little more stridently than she intended. The woman flustered as she searched for the credit card details.

'Did these two guests leave after dinner?' Jasmine asked.

'No, I don't think so,' the women said shakily and then her voice became surer. 'No, I know they didn't. I think they went up to Mrs Bunting's room. They left later, some hours later.'

'How do you know?' Jasmine asked.

'Because they came to the desk, well, the man did, the one dressed as a man, and he paid for the room.'

Jasmine's voice showed her surprise. 'He paid Mrs Bunting's and Mr Smith's bed and breakfast?'

'That's right. The whole bill.'

'I think we'll need details of that transaction too,' Hamid said.

'Yes, of course.' The woman got busy.

'Which room did they stay in?' Jasmine asked.

The woman's eyes scanned the screen. 'One-oh-one. On the first floor. It's our largest bedroom apart from the suites on the second floor.'

'Can we have a look at it?' Jasmine asked.

The receptionist appeared overloaded with requests for a moment and then recovered. 'Yes, last night's guests have checked out. You can go up. Let me get you a key.' She tapped the keyboard some more and collected a plastic keycard as it emerged from a machine. She passed it to Hamid.

'You'll have those transaction details for us when we come down?' he said. The woman nodded eagerly.

Hamid and Jasmine climbed the grand central stairs together.

'What's going on?' Hamid asked, 'Why are these people paying Mrs Bunting's bills – the food and the room?'

'She seems to have a knack of getting things for free, like the house she's moved into.'

They reached the first-floor landing and walked across the thick carpet to the door to room 101. It was open. Inside Jasmine could see a maid working, surrounded by a pile of discarded bedding. Hamid and Jasmine stepped inside. She let out a silent whistle. It was a big room. The centre was occupied by a bigger than king-size, four poster bed, but it did not overwhelm the high-ceilinged room. There was space around it for a cluster of easy chairs, with a wardrobe, desk, bedside tables, and cabinet with drinks glasses alongside a sizeable fridge and still there was plenty of empty floorspace, lavishly carpeted.

'I wouldn't mind staying in a room like this,' Jasmine said.

'Me too,' Hamid said, 'but I couldn't afford it on my police salary.'

'Nor me. It was quite a bill that Harriet's guest picked up.'

Hamid approached the olive-skinned maid who had frozen and looked bemused. Again, he waved his card. She still looked confused.

'We're police,' Hamid said slowly. The girl nodded.

'Do you do this room every day?' Jasmine asked. The girl stared, shook her head, shrugged, flapped her hands.

'She doesn't speak much English,' Hamid said. He spoke in a foreign language. The girl's eyes widened then she spoke in reply. After a short exchange during which the girl briefly became bashful, Hamid turned to Jasmine.

'She's from Libya. Speaks Arabic. It's not my first language but I can get by.'

'What did she say?' Jasmine asked.

'Yes, she does do this room most if not all days. I presume the hotel gives her a day off each week.'

Jasmine was quick to add. 'I hope so otherwise we'll be asking some questions about their treatment of migrant workers.'

'Yes, anyway she recalls the older woman and young man who occupied this room on Tuesday night. She is a bit embarrassed but apparently the bedding was well-stained.'

'Um, bodily fluids.'

'I think that's the story.'

'So, Harriet and Tyler went at it.'

Now it was Hamid's turn to be embarrassed.

'Anything else?' Jasmine asked.

Hamid shook his head. 'I don't think so. Quite a lot of booze from the fridge had been used.'

'There were four of them here after dinner.'

Hamid nodded, 'But there's nothing else she can recall at all out of the ordinary.'

Jasmine took a turn around the room, looked out of the wide windows at the town and peered into the large ensuite bathroom.

'I don't suppose we're going to find anything here after three days,' she said, 'I guess she does a good job of cleaning after each set of guests.'

Hamid spoke again to the maid and she replied.

'That's right,' he said, 'Each room is given a thorough clean when it is vacated.'

'Well, let's go,' Jasmine said heading towards the door, 'Let's see if that woman downstairs has the names of the other two guests for us.'

Hamid followed her after bowing to the maid and speaking again in Arabic.

Hamid pulled up outside Jasmine's house.

Jasmine opened the door and paused. 'You'll find out all you can on those two guests and let me know as soon as you can?'

'Yes, I will,' Hamid replied.

'Good. Thanks for the lift.' Jasmine got out and pushed the door closed. The car pulled away and she turned to hurry into the house. It was lunchtime and there were things to be done.

13

Tom watched Hamid leave to pick up Jasmine, then wandered to Terry's desk.

'I've been thinking,' he began.

'That's dangerous, boss,' Terry said with a chuckle.

'I told you, none of this "boss" thing. I was thinking about what we learned from Griffiths yesterday.'

Terry nodded, 'What did we learn?'

'I'm sure there's something in this insurance scam between Bunting and Griffiths. If Griffiths was pushing for some or all the loan to be repaid and with Molly's in poor shape, then Bunting may have seen burning the place down and claiming the fire insurance as the only way out.'

'I'll go along with that,' Terry said.

'We need some evidence of collusion – emails, phone messages between Bunting and Griffiths or his employees.'

'Nothing's come to light yet.'

'Not from Bunting's end. Perhaps he didn't use his own phone or computer to make the contact.'

Terry nodded, 'That would be sensible of him.'

'Of course, Neville Griffiths himself wouldn't have made the contact. He wouldn't want any records of conspiracy to defraud in his name.'

'Definitely not.'

'So, we have to get at Griffiths' people.'

'The heavies he used to recover bad debts?' Terry looked doubtful, 'But as Griffiths pointed out, having Bunting die at the scene complicates matters. He would have wanted a nice clean fire, with no casualties, so Bunting could claim on his insurance and hand over the cash.'

Tom stuck with his idea. 'Perhaps that was the plan, and something went wrong. Maybe Bunting had second thoughts at the last moment and Griffiths' men got angry.'

Terry considered while various expressions passed across his face. 'It could have happened like that.'

'I think we need to speak to young Wayne again and find out who Griffiths entrusts the debt collecting to.'

'If he knows.'

'I can't believe that Neville Griffiths wants to be associated with the business of threatening debtors to hand over their possessions. Wayne will have a contact I'm sure. Let's go and have another chat to him.'

This time there was a customer in the loan shop. A small woman in a cheap, worn coat peered over the high counter. Mel was speaking to her but looked up as Tom and Terry entered. She frowned.

'We'd like to speak to Wayne again, please,' Tom said. He had barely got the words out when the door behind the counter opened and Wayne appeared. With his hair slightly less smooth than previously and his eyes darting from side to side he had apparently expected an emergency of some description.

'Why did you press the panic button, Mel? Oh, hello, officers.'

Tom gave him a broad smile. 'Good morning, Mr Adams. Could we have another chat, do you think.'

'Oh, yeah, okay.'

Again, he went through the process of unlocking the door in the counter to let them through and usher Tom and Terry to his office. Wayne sat at his desk and glanced at his computer screen. He reached out to turn it off.

'No, don't do that,' Tom said, 'You may need it in a minute.' He stood by Wayne's side so that he could see the screen. There was a list of names on it. Tom didn't look at them closely.

Wayne looked up at Terry and Tom.

'What else can I tell you? I thought I answered all your questions yesterday.'

'You did,' Terry said, 'but we've thought of some more.'

'Yes,' Tom added, 'We had a talk with your boss, Mr Griffiths, and it seems he has more faith in you than you suggested to us yesterday. You said that Mr Griffiths follows up non-payers, but he said you have a procedure to follow in those cases.

Wayne's pale skin became paler. 'Uh, there is a procedure.'

Tom leaned down to the young man. 'What is it?'

'I give the details of defaulters to the head of the collection team.'

'When?'

'He calls in most days at about eleven'

'He comes here?'

Wayne nodded. Tom looked at his watch. It was just after ten-thirty.

'Did you follow this procedure when Evelyn Bunting failed to make his second monthly payment?'

Wayne shook his head. 'No, I told you before. I don't have responsibility for the big loans. That's what I meant yesterday. Mr Griffiths would have instructed the collection team in Mr Bunting's case. It was nothing to do with me.'

Terry responded, 'Ah, that's lucky for you isn't it, young fella.'

'Do you have a phone number or email for this debt collector.'

Wayne shook his head. 'Mr Griffiths doesn't like there to be any record of our contact.'

'Probably a good precaution,' Tom said. 'Looks like we'll have to wait for the guy.'

Terry asked, 'Does he come through the shop or is there another entrance?'

Wayne nodded to the back of the building. 'There's a lane

and parking at the back. That's the way he comes in.'

'We don't want to both be in here when he arrives,' Tom said. 'You go out the back, Terry and keep out of sight until he comes. Once he's inside the building you come in.'

'Right,' Terry hurried out of the office. Tom sat on one of the chairs opposite the young manager and eyed up the coffee making facilities in the corner of the room. Wayne took the hint and offered Tom a drink. He spooned out the coffee. poured the kettle and returned with two steaming mugs.

Tom blew on the surface of his coffee and took a sip.

'Do you enjoy your job, Wayne?'

The young man shrugged, 'Yeah, the pay's alright.'

'You and Mel get on?'

'Yeah, she's a nice girl.'

'Neither of you mind taking money off people who can't afford it?'

Wayne's face reddened. 'They come to us. They don't have to take out loans.'

'Don't they?' Tom queried. 'At the end of the month when money has run out and perhaps the landlord is demanding the rent, or there's no food to feed the kids, they're looking for some cash to tie them over.'

Wayne nodded.

'So, you lend them the cash, and they're grateful to you, but they've not figured on the swingeing interest you're charging them which means that next month they're even worse off.'

'It's all legal,' Wayne complained.

'For now,' Tom said. 'but is it ethical?'

'They have a choice. They don't have to take our loans.'

'No, they can go to any one of the other loan sharks out there. Do you know what happens to the people if they don't make the repayments?'

Wayne shook his head. 'I've told you that's not my job. The collection team look after those people.'

'That's nice for you isn't it. You never have to see the results of being heavily in debt.'

Wayne turned away so that Tom couldn't see his face. Tom hoped he was reconsidering the morals of his job. They sat silently as the hands on his watch approached eleven o'clock.

A door slammed and footsteps came along the corridor from the back door. The office door swung open and a figure appeared. He stopped and stared.

Tom recognised him. He was the short, bald man who had let them into Griffiths' house.

Tom stood up. 'Ah, Neville Griffiths' doorman. I might have expected he'd have you on this job.'

'What yer doing here?'

'Waiting for you, in fact. I'm interested to see that your procedure for dealing with non-payers of loans gets off to an efficient start.'

'What d'yer mean?'

'Your daily call to pick up business.'

Baldy glared at Wayne. 'You told him I was coming?'

Wayne nodded and avoided Baldy's eyes.

'Now I'd like your name please,' Tom said, taking out his notebook and pen.

He looked as though he was contemplating refusing the request but thought better of it.

'Elvis Preston.' Tom's eyebrows rose. 'Don't say anything. My mother was a fan.'

Tom suppressed a giggle. 'You're employed by Neville Griffiths. What is your position?'

Preston shrugged, 'General duties, debt collector, bailiff, bodyguard, whatever he needs. Why're you interested?'

Tom composed a reply. 'I'm sure you are aware from our visit to Mr Griffiths yesterday that we are investigating the death of Evelyn Bunting and the fire at his premises, Molly's.'

'Yeah. So what?'

'Given your position in Mr Griffiths' business you must know that Evelyn Bunting took out a large loan and that he failed to keep up the payments.'

Preston glowered at Tom without giving a hint of an

affirmative or negative.

Tom had to ask the question. 'In your capacity as debt collector did you pay a visit to Mr Bunting.'

'Yeah. I did.'

'When was that?'

'Can't remember. A few weeks ago.'

'You don't keep a record of your meetings with clients.'

Preston shrugged. 'Not necessary. They pay up.'

'Did Evelyn Bunting pay up after your call?

Preston didn't answer.

'Did he?' Tom repeated.

'I 'aven't looked at the accounts.' Preston said.

Tom expressed disbelief. 'A loan of over a hundred thousand pounds not being repaid and you don't know what was happening? Come on, Elvis, you can do better than that.'

Preston's face grew red and his fists clenched. 'Mr Griffiths did not give me any instructions to extract a payment from Bunting.'

'And why do you think that was?'

Preston shrugged. 'Mr Griffiths did not tell me; 'ad his reasons no doubt.'

'Could it be because Evelyn Bunting agreed to hand over the proceeds from his insurance should his premises catch fire?'

'I wouldn't know,' Preston said.

'You didn't pay another visit to Molly's?'

'No.'

Tom examined Preston's face but could see no sign of doubt or weakening.

'Well, we know how to get in touch with you, Elvis, so we may have more questions for you.'

Tom slipped past Preston and headed towards the rear entrance of the shop. He exited into a small yard where a Mercedes was parked. Terry was leaning against the driver's door. He straightened up as Tom approached.

'Sorry I didn't follow the other fella in. Thought I'd ask this guy a few questions.'

Tom looked through the windscreen at the driver. He was dark, with a beard and glared back at Tom.

'Who is he?'

Terry answered. 'He hasn't got much English. Gave the name Karol Bednarz. From Poland. Took a while to get that much. Claimed he couldn't understand me.'

'I presume he understands Preston enough to put pressure on debtors. Did you ask him about Bunting?'

'Yes. He denied knowing the name, so I described him – bloke in dress. He remembered then. Says they paid a visit to Molly's a few weeks ago.'

'That's what Preston says but can't say exactly when.'

Terry looked doubtful. 'They can't have left it at one visit since Bunting didn't cough up.'

'Unless there was another plan...' Tom left the implication hanging. He urged Terry to follow him out of the yard. 'These guys know we've got our eye on them now. Let's leave them to stew. I'd like you to follow them for a while. So you take the car.'

'What are you going to do?'

'I'll head to the station here and get a lift back to Kintbridge. It's about time we tracked down Gary Nicholls.'

They reached the car. Terry got in, started up and drove around the block to watch the lane. Tom headed towards the town centre and the police station. He had some thinking and planning to do.

14

After a bit of lunch and a spot of relaxation – how long would it take to get her youthful energy back – Jasmine was ready to continue. But what could she do without transport? She called Viv. Unusually he answered.

'Hi, there, gorgeous. What's this call for? Suggestions for another evening? … heck, you're okay, aren't you?'

Jasmine struggled to fit a word in. 'Yes, I'm fine, but I needed someone to grumble at and you're it.'

'What's there to grumble about?'

'My car won't start.'

'That rusty old Ford. Why do you need it?'

'Because I'm working. I have an investigation. Hamid took me back to Faringdon this morning, but I don't want to be calling on Tom all the time to provide transport.'

'No, I see. Where do you want to go? Far?'

'No, just in to Reedham.' She had decided on putting some more questions to Harriet Bunting at her borrowed house in the neighbouring small town.

'Well, call a taxi.'

'That's expensive.

'One day won't matter. Then we'll sort your car out if you really need it.'

'Well, okay then.'

'But don't be long. I'm not going to be late this afternoon and I want to see you.'

Jasmine chuckled. 'Right. I'll make sure I'm ready and

waiting for you like an obedient little wife.' She ended the call. Viv had succeeded in making her feel on top of the world. Now she just had to phone for a taxi.

The taxi delivered her to the address that Harriet had provided. It was a pre-war detached house in a leafy part of the town. There were few cars parked in the narrow road, as the houses had driveways and garages. Jasmine paid the driver and watched him move off before walking up the gravelled entrance to the house. There was no car parked there so Tyler wasn't calling. She hoped that Harriet was home otherwise her visit was a waste of time and she was stranded.

She pressed the doorbell and waited. It was a minute or two before she heard steps approaching. The wooden door opened. Harriet Bunting peered out.

'Oh, it's you. What do you want?'

'I have some questions for you, Mrs Bunting.'

'More questions! Haven't I answered enough. Why don't the Police get on with finding who killed my husband?' Her eyes narrowed. 'But of course, you're not police are you.'

'I am assisting them,' Jasmine said.

Harriet snorted. 'But you have no authority. I don't have to answer your questions.'

'I think you should, Mrs Bunting. If you don't you may find that DI Shepherd will be here next to ask them.'

The woman glared at Jasmine, sighed and pulled the door open.

'Alright, if I must. You'd better come in. But I haven't got long.'

'I won't take up much of your valuable time, Mrs Bunting.' Jasmine stepped into a wood-floored hallway and followed Harriet into a lounge with large plush sofas in floral covers and lots of ornaments on tables and display cabinets. At Harriet's invitation, Jasmine sat on one of the sofas. She wasn't offered any refreshment.

Jasmine looked around. 'Your friend was very kind to loan

you this house.'

'Is that one of your questions? It sounded more like a statement.' Mrs Bunting sat herself in the other sofa some way from Jasmine and glowered.

'No, just making conversation.'

'I don't want conversation. Get on with it.'

Jasmine took a breath. 'We have been checking up on your alibi for Tuesday evening.'

'Really. How officious and unnecessary.'

'It has to be done, Mrs Bunting.'

The woman shrugged. 'So you proved that I spent the night with Tyler at the Royal Hotel, Faringdon. Well done, you.'

'But it wasn't just the pair of you was it, Mrs Bunting, at least for dinner.'

A startled expression appeared on Harriet's face. 'What do you mean?'

'You were joined by two other people for dinner, a man and a woman.'

There was pause. Jasmine guessed that Mrs Bunting was working out whether to deny the meeting, but she must have realised that Jasmine knew her facts and that the woman she had met was not quite what she appeared to be.

'Yes, well, so what? We were joined by friends for dinner. There's no law against it is there? We don't live in the kind of state where everyone's movements are controlled, and Big Brother decides who we can have dinner with.'

'No, of course not, Mrs Bunting. The point is that these two people can vouch for your presence at the hotel and therefore support your alibi.'

'But that is ridiculous. Why do I need someone to back up an alibi? You know I was there and that therefore I can't have been in Thirsbury when my husband was murdered and my home gutted.'

Jasmine tried an explanation. 'It is true that we have the evidence from the hotel that you and Mr Smith spent the night there, but you don't have to have been the person who swung the baseball bat or lit the fire to have been involved in the murder or the arson.'

Harriet stared at her as she considered her words. Realisation arrived. 'Are you suggesting that I *conspired* with someone to kill my husband.'

'It is a possibility that we have to consider,' Jasmine said as sweetly as she could manage.

'That suggestion is preposterous. What's more it's slander. I am not having you accusing me of such a thing.' She rose to her feet and took a step towards Jasmine.

Jasmine remained sitting, leaning back in the sofa and looking up at the formidable figure of Mrs Bunting.

'I am not suggesting you did anything Mrs Bunting, but we have to examine all possibilities. Any information that your dinner companions could provide to remove you from a list of potential suspects would be useful.'

Mrs Bunting stopped, glared at Jasmine then turned away and walked across the room. She looked out of the window at the front garden for a moment then turned around.

'No, I cannot tell you who they were. They trusted me to maintain their privacy. So however much you think it might help your investigation I can't tell you anything more.'

Jasmine decided that Mrs Bunting had to be pushed a bit further.

'I understand your loyalty to your friends when one of them was apparently taking the opportunity of meeting you to express their transvestite tendency, and especially as they paid for the meal.'

'*Transvestite tendency*! That's ripe coming from you. Do you think you are so much better than those men who dress as women just because you've had the operation that gives you the ability to fuck like a woman.'

'I don't consider myself better…'

'You're no more a woman than they are, and you're not a man either. You're a nothing, a eunuch, a cockless, ball-less, fraud.'

Harriet advanced towards Jasmine with her fists clenched in front of her. The thought occurred to Jasmine that she couldn't tell whether Harriet really meant her harm or if this was just a ploy to make it appear that way. Nevertheless, Jasmine reasoned that Harriet could cause her real harm, especially as she wasn't fully recovered from her surgery. She stood up and backed towards the door.

'I am a woman,' she insisted, 'My operation only confirmed what I believe is true.'

'Pah! Utter nonsense. You and your certificates and rights. You think they make you special. You're just another one with an itch you need to scratch.'

Jasmine was back in the hallway now, reaching for the catch on the front door.

'You mean like Evelyn,' she countered, 'We've seen the cage and the stool and the whips. Whose urges were they satisfying?'

Mrs Bunting hastened to her, fists raised. 'How dare you! Evelyn and I had a relationship that you wouldn't understand.'

The door opened, and Jasmine took a step back through it. She backed off the doorstep onto the drive. Harriet grasped the door and stood glaring at her.

'Yes, you run away, you freak, and don't expect me to answer any more of your questions.'

She slammed the door.

Jasmine turned and walked to the road, her breaths coming in rapid succession. *Well, that went well*, she thought. What was it that angered Harriet Bunting so much? Was it the suggestion that she was involved in her husband's murder or the threat to the privacy of her friends who stumped up the cost of the meal and the room at the Royal Hotel? What was the purpose of that meeting and what was behind this apparent bond between the two men and Harriet?

There was more to find out, but now she was stuck by the side of a road without transport. She rang the taxi company, but they couldn't provide a vehicle for half an hour. She tried to get in touch with Viv but his phone went to voicemail. Tom couldn't be asked to provide just a lift home. How far was it to walk? She hadn't got to know the area where she lived well since they had moved but she knew it was only a couple of miles away. She called up a map on her phone and started walking. Two miles? No distance!

She discovered that two miles was actually a considerable distance when you are still recovering from major surgery. The final gentle rise to the house felt more like an assault on a mountain. She made it, with an ache in her groin and collapsed onto the sofa in the lounge, with her coat still on.

The next thing she heard was the front door opening. She forced herself to sit up. Had she been asleep? Surely it wasn't time for Viv to get home yet. She glanced at her watch and was surprised to see that it was only four-thirty.

The door to the lounge opened and Viv entered, and froze.

'What's wrong, Jas? You've got your coat on.'

Jasmine looked down at herself and realised Viv was correct. She swung her legs off the sofa and felt a twinge in her groin. Viv obviously saw her grimace.

'Have you hurt yourself? You haven't opened up the incisions, have you?' He knelt by her side and rested a hand on her knee.

She managed a thin smile and placed her hand on his.

'No, I think I've just strained a few muscles that I haven't used enough for a while.'

'What have you been doing?'

'Just walking, but it was a bit further than I thought.'

'Where from?'

'Harriet Bunting's borrowed house in Reedham.'

Viv sighed. 'What were you doing walking? I said take a taxi.'

'I did. I got a taxi there but when I rang to get one to come home they couldn't come straight away. I didn't want to hang round outside so I started walking. I did try calling you.'

'I know, I picked up your call when I got out of a meeting. I came home straight away.'

'That's why you're early.'

'Well, I did say I wanted to be with you as soon as I could. What was wrong with waiting with Mrs Bunting till the taxi came?'

Jasmine snorted. 'I couldn't stay with her. I rather buggered up the interview. She got annoyed and all but threw me out.'

'Ah, I see. Your questions hit a nerve, did they?'

'I'll say and I didn't get everything I wanted from her.'

'Well, if you are going off to ask people questions that get them worked up we'd better make sure you have transport.'

'I'd like that.'

'We'll get your old Fiesta taken away and see about a hire car for you.'

Jasmine moved to get up.

'No, stay there. Relax,' Viv said, 'Let me take your coat. Cup of tea?'

Jasmine shucked off her coat and lay back on the sofa feeling looked after and mollycoddled. She shouldn't be like this. She should be out investigating, tracking down Evelyn Bunting's killer. But just for a few minutes… She closed her eyes.

15

SATURDAY 19ᵀᴴ OCTOBER
MORNING

The ring tone stirred Jasmine from a pleasant slumber. She found herself still entwined in Viv's legs and arm. Her hand reached out to pick up the phone as Viv moved beside her. She peered at the screen as she pressed the answer button. It was eight-thirty.

'Good morning, Jasmine.' It was Hamid's voice.

'Hi,' Jasmine replied still struggling to get fully awake. 'This is early for a Saturday. What are you up to?'

'Inspector Shepherd has got us in, looking into the insurance fraud he thinks Bunting and Griffiths were involved in.'

'Ah, yes, I can see that. Has he got a lead?'

Hamid made a non-committal sound. 'We're trying to get phone and email data on Griffiths and his employees to see if we can find any conspiracy.'

'That'll be fun for you. You don't need me...' It was the kind of task that Jasmine had found herself doing in the time between the start of her transition and leaving the force. She was good at it but that didn't mean that she enjoyed it.

'No. DI Shepherd hasn't asked for you. I was ringing to say I have the information on those two people that met Harriet Bunting in Faringdon.'

Jasmine felt a little burst of excitement. She heaved her leg out from under Viv's and slid around to sit on the edge of the mattress.

'That's great. Well done Hamid. Can you send them to me?'

'They're with you now.'

'Thanks. Er, does Tom know?'

'Yes. He says we have Harriet and Tyler's alibi's confirmed, so he doesn't see that these characters are important.'

'He's going with the insurance scam as the reason for the arson and murder?'

'He thinks something went wrong with the plan and Griffiths' accomplices killed Bunting as well as setting the building alight.'

'Possible,' Jasmine admitted although she wasn't convinced. 'Good luck in finding the evidence, and thanks.'

'No problem.'

They ended the call and Jasmine went into her inbox. She found the email there from Hamid giving the details on Harriet Bunting's generous guests. She read the information eagerly. The two men were Edward Wilson from Cheltenham and Montgomery Russell from Oxford. The first was apparently the one who had appeared dressed as a woman and paid for the dinner while Russell had covered the full cost of the room. Jasmine was keen to meet both. She jumped up and headed for the bathroom.

'Where're you going?' Viv asked sleepily.

'I'm getting up. Things to do.'

'Like what?'

'There are a couple of people I'd like to interview in connection with the Bunting case.' Jasmine called out from inside the en-suite.

'Oh. Where are they?'

'Oxford and Cheltenham.'

'Do you really need to speak to them? Can't Tom organise his people to do it?'

'I am one of his people. It's a lead I'm following. If my old car has had it I'll have to hire one.'

'Okay, Jas. If you say so.' Viv was sounding more awake. He hauled himself out of bed. 'I'll get on to it.'

Jasmine settled herself into the driving seat of the Nissan Micra, while Viv leaned on the open window.

'All okay for you?'

'Yes, thanks. I haven't driven a newish car since I left the force, but I think I'll manage.'

'Take care then. Don't overdo it. I'll see you later.'

'Yes, I won't be late, I promise.' Jasmine blew him a kiss and started the engine. Viv stepped back, and Jasmine set off across the forecourt of the hire car depot. Soon she was in the queue of traffic made up of Saturday morning shoppers heading into central Kintbridge but she parted company with them and headed north towards Oxford. She'd chosen to call on Russell first as he was the closer and he had paid the larger sum for the evening's entertainment, whatever that involved. She'd googled the address and found that it was in Jericho, an area of central Oxford popular with students and university staff alike. She knew where she was headed.

Speeding up the A34's dual carriageway, she found herself making comparisons between the hire car and the old red Fiesta. The Micra was comfortable, relatively quiet and covered the miles without complaint. The old car had performed a role when she needed it but had begun to complain bitterly about being pushed at its advanced age. The charms of the newer car gained her appreciation. She found herself in the Oxford congestion sooner than she expected but the last couple of miles to her destination were a slow crawl.

Finally, she entered the grid of streets of terraced and semi-detached houses that made up Jericho. Parking was on the straight, narrow roads and there were few spare spaces. Jasmine drove round for several minutes wishing for a police car pass that would allow her to park anywhere. Eventually she pulled into a space just vacated by a departing car. She got out, smoothed down her skirt and wrapped her coat around her. It was a sunny day, but still cold. She set off to find Montgomery Russell's home in Ramsay Street.

It was a two up, two down in a terrace. It looked small, but Jasmine knew that these homes were much sought after, in

153

walking distance to the colleges and the centre of the city. She pressed the doorbell.

Almost immediately the door was opened by a man of similar height to herself, but carrying rather more weight. He had short fair hair and was wearing a waistcoat over a check shirt with brown corduroy trousers. Jasmine guessed he was a college fellow or some other kind of academic.

He frowned as if surprised to see someone he did not recognise.

'Hello,' he said, 'Can I help you?'

He was polite at least, Jasmine thought. 'Mr Montgomery Russell?'

He nodded, still frowning. 'That is correct. Who are you?'

'Jasmine Frame. I'm a detective helping the Kintbridge police with some enquiries.' She took her identity card from her pocket and briefly showed it to him. He didn't show any interest in reading it.

'Kintbridge? What enquiries?'

'I believe you are acquainted with Mrs Harriet Bunting.'

His frown became one of puzzlement for a moment and then his expression changed to embarrassment. Jasmine noticed the rising flush.

'Um, yes, I, er, am.'

'You spent Tuesday evening in her company at the Royal Hotel, Faringdon.'

Now he looked scared.

'How do you know?'

'You paid for the room Mrs Bunting occupied even though you did not spend the night there yourself.'

Montgomery Russell was sweating despite the cold air. 'Er, yes, I did, but how…'

'Can you tell me why you did that and what the nature of your relationship with Mrs Bunting is.'

Russell was shaking visibly. He looked beyond Jasmine to see if anyone else was watching this scene play out. 'Um, you'd better come in,' he said, his voice shaking.

He backed away from the door allowing Jasmine to step into a small lounge. She pushed the door closed behind her.

Russell seemed to regain some of his composure in the privacy of his own house.

'Sit down, please, Miss Frame.' He gestured to one of the two large easy chairs facing a fire place. An old TV, not a modern flat screen type, occupied the corner of the room. Jasmine undid her coat and sat down. Russell sat beside her.

'Did *she* tell you where I live?' There was an emphasis on the female pronoun as if it stood for a name that must not be spoken.

'No. It's because you paid the bill with your credit card that we've been able to trace you.'

'She hasn't said anything?'

'About you, Mr Russell? No.'

A look of relief passed across Montgomery Russell's face and he relaxed into his seat.

'But we know that you spent the evening with Mrs Bunting and her friend Tyler Smith and another man who was dressed in female clothes who paid for the dinner you ate, or rather didn't. Apparently, it was Harriet and Tyler who did most of the eating.'

The scared look had returned to Montgomery's face.

'What is this all about? Why are you asking me these questions?'

Jasmine could tell that he was wriggling; trying to find any way he could to avoid describing his relationship with Harriet Bunting.

'We know about Mrs Bunting's relationship with her husband – that he always dressed in female clothes in a variety of let us say, eccentric styles; that she sometimes, we don't how often, locked him in a cage in their cellar and she beat him with a variety of whips;' She watched Russell's face grow redder as she recited Harriet's treatment of Evelyn, 'and that she kept his penis locked in a chastity cage.' The last drew a gasp from Montgomery and beads of sweat burst out of his brow.

He stuttered a defence. 'But, but, those things aren't against the law.'

'No,' Jasmine acknowledged, 'but the murder of Evelyn Bunting was.'

Montgomery gasped.

'Evelyn was killed while you were spending the evening with his wife.'

Montgomery shook his head. 'I didn't know. I don't understand, I, I...'

'The police need to know all that was going on that evening involving Mrs Bunting and her associates,' Jasmine explained. 'In particular, why did you pay for the bed and breakfast of Mrs Bunting and her companion?'

Russell sighed deeply. 'Alright. If I tell you, will it be confidential? I can't have it getting out to the students. I'll be … I'll be, I don't what.'

'If you are simply a witness then there is no reason why the nature of your involvement should become public knowledge, Mr Russell, but I can't promise anything until I have heard your story.'

He considered, took a deep breath. 'I paid for the room because I was told to.'

Jasmine was confused. 'Who told you to?'

'She did. Madame de la Clef.'

'Who? Oh, you mean Mrs Bunting.' Jasmine paused, translating the name. 'The Mistress of the Key?'

Russell nodded and looked away. His face and neck were a deep red.

'Can I guess?' Jasmine went on, 'The key to a lock that holds a chastity cage in place.'

Russell nodded again while staring at the floor.

'Which you wear?' He nodded. 'Now?' He nodded again.

Jasmine still wasn't fully sure what his admission meant. 'Why?'

Russell looked up, glared into her face, embarrassment gone. 'Because it gives me a thrill, no more than that, excitement. She holds the key.'

'You mean you can't get out of your, er, cage, unless she hands over the key?'

Russell nodded.

'And that is what you were doing on Tuesday. Mrs Bunting, Madame de la Clef, was handing over your key.'

Montgomery whispered, 'It was a bit more than that.'

'What do you mean?' Jasmine was even more confused.

Montgomery sighed. 'If I am going to have to tell you everything that happened that evening I think I need a coffee and something stronger. Can I get you one?'

'A coffee? Yes, please.'

Montgomery started to rise from his chair. 'How do you like it?'

'Black, no sugar. Thank you.'

Russell walked through the rear room into the kitchen beyond. Jasmine listened to the noises of the drinks being prepared. Meanwhile she wondered what in Montgomery Russell's story could provide more embarrassment than admitting that he wore a cage around his penis.

Montgomery returned carrying a tray on which were two fine china cups of coffee in saucers, a plate of chocolate biscuits and a large schooner of pale coloured sherry. He placed the tray on an occasional table beside his chair and handed Jasmine her cup and saucer. He sat and leaned across to her with the plate of biscuits. She took one while holding the saucer with her other hand. Jasmine nibbled her biscuit.

Russell settled back in his chair and took a sip of his sherry. 'I will try to explain. This may be a bit muddled. I have not told anyone before.' He paused, composing himself. 'I have made an arrangement with Madame, a contract if you like.' Jasmine listened eagerly. 'She is my mistress and I obey her. She holds the key to my cage and will only release me when she wishes and if I follow all her instructions to the letter.'

'You're her slave,' Jasmine gasped.

'In that respect yes. Of course, I live here and work and socialise but all the time I have the cage trapping my penis and

157

as soon as she makes a request of me I must respond.'

'What do you get out of this contract?'

'I told you, thrill, excitement. It makes me feel more alive than I ever have. To be owned by another person, a wonderful, beautiful, powerful goddess and to give her all that she wants and needs, gives me the utmost pleasure.'

'What does she want?'

'Worship.'

'Is that all? You can't do much with worship.' Jasmine thought she knew where this conversation was going.

'No, of course not. Madame has to be kept in the manner a goddess deserves.'

'You pay her.'

Montgomery nodded, '£50 a week to store my key and other expenses as necessary.'

Jasmine did the sums. It added up to a nice little sum each year, over two thousand pounds.

'The other guest on Tuesday, Edward Wilson, pays the same?'

Montgomery shrugged, 'Is that his name? I don't know how much he pays but I expect he is on a similar arrangement.'

'So you met Madame on Tuesday night to collect the keys so you could relieve yourselves.'

Russell went quiet again, 'It was a bit more complicated than that.'

'Oh, why were you and the transvestite meeting together then?'

'He's not really a transvestite.'

'What?'

'I think it was the first time he'd dressed up as a woman.'

'Why?'

'It was Madame's idea.'

'You mean Harriet told him to meet you dressed as a woman.'

Montgomery nodded, 'She probably told him what to wear.'

'And made him buy all the clothing?' Jasmine added.

'I expect so.'

'Right. Tell me what happened on Tuesday evening.' Jasmine sipped her coffee and awaited Montgomery Russell's tale.

'We met in the dining room, the four of us and ordered our meals. Madame had instructed Buttercup…'

'Buttercup?'

'That was the name that Madame made him, that is, Wilson you said his name is, use for the evening.'

'What name were you given?'

'Er…Willy.'

Jasmine suppressed a giggle. 'I see. Madame instructed you to do what?'

'We were not to eat too much and were only allowed water to drink.'

'While she and Tyler ate a full dinner and alcohol?'

'That's right.'

'When dinner was finished Madame told Buttercup and me to follow her upstairs to her room. It was very large with …'

'I know, I've been in it.'

'Oh, have you? Well when we got there, Madame asked me to remove the serapé she had been wearing over her dress. When I took it from her, her immense beauty was revealed.'

He seemed enraptured by the memory. Jasmine summoned her image of Harriet Bunting. Attractive perhaps, majestic maybe but immense beauty? She didn't think so.

'What was she wearing?'

'A dress of metallic silver satin. The top was like a corset, laced up to support but reveal the gibbous moons of her breasts. The bottom was a pleated skirt slit to her hips. She wore silver court shoes with four-inch heels on her feet. When she sat in one of the easy chairs, there was a glimpse of her white stockings with their lace tops attached to suspenders. She wore no knickers although her private parts were not visible.'

Jasmine acknowledged that it seemed to be a stunning outfit and smiled at his rapturous description

Montgomery went on. 'She told Buttercup to kneel on the

carpet in front her and then instructed me to stand by Buttercup's side and remove my clothes.'

'All of them?'

'All of them. I had to fold each item neatly and place it on the floor behind me and then when I was naked, except of course for my, uh, cage, I had to stand up straight facing Madame. She examined me and took photos with her phone and told me to turn around slowly. When she was satisfied she told me to go to the room bar and pour her a brandy.'

'Just for her?'

'Yes. I gave it to her and again stood in front of her. She took a few sips then told Buttercup to stand. She told me to undress him. I removed Buttercup's stilettoes, then the white silk blouse that he wore and the black leather miniskirt. He had on a white satin bustier. I think it is called that. It had the breast cups padded with something.'

'Silicone falsies from Molly's stock, I expect,' Jasmine said.

Montgomery shrugged. 'The suspenders were attached to white stockings. He had a little pair of silk knickers that just covered his genitals. Madame told me to kneel and remove them but to leave him in the other underwear.'

'A tranny dream,' Jasmine said.

'Then Madame picked up the big handbag she always carries and took out a small key which she put in my hand.'

'The key to your chastity cage?' Jasmine asked

'No. Buttercup's. Madame told me to release his penis. That was the first time I've touched a man's private parts, well, since I was at boarding school and we were just boys then.'

'But you did as you were told?'

'Oh yes. I always obey Madame. I placed the key in the lock, undid it and removed the cage, trying not to touch his penis and testicles as I did so. Of course, my fingers brushed him a little and as it came free it grew.'

'He was aroused.'

'I'll say. It happens when the restriction of the cage is removed.' Beads of sweat had appeared on Montgomery's upper lip and his cheeks glowed a bright pink.

'Hmm, I see. Go on.'

'I couldn't imagine what Madame would demand of me next and when she gave the order I admit that for a moment I doubted whether I could obey, but my own penis was aching, and I so desired my own freedom. I had to comply with Madame's wishes in order to get my own release.'

'What did she want you to do?'

His mouth opened but no sound emerged.

'Go on please,' Jasmine urged.

He swallowed. 'She told me to take his erect penis into my mouth.'

'She wanted you to suck his cock!' Jasmine was amazed, but then scolded herself. Of course that was what Harriet wanted. Two men in her power, neither of which she apparently wanted sex with, neither of them gay – at least they hadn't admitted to it. Forcing them into gay sex would be a delicious humiliation.

'No, not suck. Not immediately.' Montgomery took a deep breath. 'I just had to hold the head in my mouth at first. Buttercup was told to stand still, but he could barely manage it. His penis vibrated with pent-up energy on my tongue.'

'What happened next?'

'Madame stood up and took photographs of us in that position from all angles. Then she told Buttercup to fuck my mouth. He couldn't wait. He started thrusting into my mouth, pushing against the back of my throat. I gagged and tried to pull away, but he grabbed my head and held me as he thrust again and again. Madame urged him on. I think I was starting to faint when he came and filled my mouth with his semen. He made me swallow it.'

'Harriet enjoyed watching you?'

'I think so. I had closed my eyes but I think she filmed us on her phone. She made me lick up every drop of the cum from his penis. She sat down again and congratulated both of us on a "good show".'

'How did that make you feel?'

He turned away from her, avoiding seeing her eyes on him.

'Mr Russell,' she urged.

His voice had dropped to a whisper. 'In performing the act I felt abused, but learning of the pleasure it gave Madame made me proud that I had carried out her wishes and I hoped to receive a reward.'

'She released your penis, did she?'?'

'Oh no. It's never as straightforward as that. Madame told me to stand and Buttercup to kneel. She gave him the key to my cage and we did it the other way.'

'He sucked you off?'

Montgomery hesitated and Jasmine guessed that he was reluctant to admit his own arousal. 'Yes. I must admit to feeling relief at having my penis freed and an overwhelming desire to ejaculate. Madame does not always allow that.'

'She teases does she.'

Montgomery nodded.

'So, you've both come and Harriet has watched you both at it. What next?'

'I was instructed to fill her glass then to kneel with Buttercup in front of her. She drank and looked at us for a few minutes. I think she was just passing time and allowing us to recover.'

'Oh, what did she want next?'

He seemed to have recovered his willingness to talk. The words tumbled out now as if, having revealed so much, Montgomery had no embarrassment left. 'She told me to lie on my back on the bed. By this time my penis was becoming erect again. It seemed to have a mind of its own. I've never desired sex with a man but perhaps it was the presence of Madame or maybe it was because Buttercup was dressed in ladies' lingerie, I don't know, but I couldn't help being aroused.

She commanded Buttercup to kneel over me in the sixty-nine position. He was already engorged too. Madame told us to fellate each other again.'

Jasmine had an image of the two middle-aged, slightly overweight and wrinkly men going at it together. She wasn't sure that it was a pretty picture.

'Did you orgasm again?'

'Yes. After three months or more of chastity, the male organs are more than ready to deliver a second time. It did take longer than the first and my throat became sore from the banging it got from Buttercup but we both came within seconds of each other.'

'What did Harriet do?'

'I wasn't following all her movements, I couldn't with Buttercup's arse in my face but I think she circled around us with her phone, photographing and videoing everything.'

'She got plenty of evidence to blackmail you both.'

Montgomery looked blank. 'Of course. I hadn't thought of that.'

'Did she get any more action out of you?'

'No, that was it really. She made us lick each other's cock and balls and groin clean of all the semen and then we had to fix each other's cages back on. We handed the keys back to Madame. Then she told us to dress. Buttercup of course had to put her female clothes back on.'

'And then?'

'She told me to go and pay for the room and then leave.'

'Was that a surprise?'

'No, since Buttercup had paid for dinner I anticipated that I would be asked to pay for the room. While I was at the desk, Buttercup passed on her way to the car. We didn't speak to each other. Madame had said that we shouldn't.'

Montgomery, looking flushed and sweaty, drank the last of his sherry, picked up his cup of coffee and knocked it back in one gulp, then rested back in his chair.

Jasmine summed up. 'So, Harriet Bunting likes ordering two mature guys to do things to each other that they wouldn't ordinarily consider doing and she presumably gets a buzz from watching you, and what's more she gets paid for the playing out of her plans.'

Montgomery nodded, 'That's about it.'

'How many other slaves does Madame have I wonder,'

Jasmine said.

Russell shrugged, 'I don't know. I've met a couple of others on previous occasions. Madame always says she is busy and doesn't allow us to contact her.'

'She's earning a tidy sum if you are all forking out fifty pound a week.'

'I suppose so.'

That answered the question about Harriet's source of income. She could be making a couple of thousand pounds a month, plus expenses.

Jasmine had a sudden thought. 'What about Tyler? You didn't mention him at all. Did he enjoy the show?'

'He wasn't there.'

'What! He was with you for dinner. I have an eyewitness for that.'

Russell nodded, 'Yes, he had dinner, but he didn't come up to the room with us. I didn't see him again.'

'What time did you finish dinner? I know you didn't spend a lot of time in the dining room because the waiter commented on it.'

'Oh, that waiter. He was hanging around all the time particularly paying attention to Madame, but his eyes kept on focussing on Buttercup. I wasn't interested in looking at the time, but I suppose it was between seven-thirty and eight when we went upstairs. Why is that important?'

Jasmine was thinking rapidly. 'Because we had assumed that Tyler was with Harriet Bunting the whole time. But you see, it's actually not far from Faringdon to Thirsbury. If Tyler left as soon as you finished dinner he could be back in Thirsbury by eight-thirty or so. If he wasn't back at the hotel before you left then he had plenty of time to do it.'

'Do what?'

'Kill Evelyn Bunting.'

Montgomery gasped. 'No, he wouldn't.'

'Wouldn't he? He had the opportunity which we hadn't thought he had. Did he have a motive?'

Montgomery shook his head. 'I don't know. I didn't know him. He hardly spoke when we met. He looked after Madame.'

'How often did you meet him?'

'Twice, that's all. At my earlier appointment with Madame she had another, older man with her.'

'Gary Nicholls?'

'That was it.'

'He knew about Harriet's key-holding scheme?'

Montgomery shrugged, 'I imagine he must have done.'

'Can you tell me anything else about Tyler Smith or Gary Nicholls?'

Montgomery shook his head. 'I don't think so. My attention always is on Madame when I am in her presence. I'm jealous of Tyler, as I was of Mr Nicholls, because they are, or were, with Madame more often than me and administered to her desires in bed. But I knew I couldn't take their place so fulfilling Madame's wishes was and is my aim. Obviously, I noticed that Tyler is a much younger, fitter, more handsome man than Nicholls which perhaps explains why Madame changed the one for the other.'

Jasmine shifted forward on her chair, about to stand. 'Thank you, Mr Russell. You've been very helpful.'

'My thanks to you too,' he replied. He had a more normal colour now and appeared cheerful.

'What for?' Jasmine asked.

'I didn't think I could talk about what happened, but it has actually been a relief to describe it.'

Jasmine was eager to follow up the information about Tyler but she couldn't help but be intrigued by Russell's admission. She sat back in the chair.

'Why do you do it?'

'What?'

'All of it, wear the chastity cage, act as a slave to Harriet Bunting, allow yourself to be put through these humiliations, if that's what they are.'

Montgomery considered and then began to talk. 'It is quite a long time since I had a relationship with a woman, and it wasn't very successful, but I'm not attracted to men either. I've lead an almost asexual life I suppose. Except that I was finding myself aroused by my female students. I'm a history tutor. A couple of years ago there was one exceptionally pretty girl. I was afraid that I might make a fool of myself with her. I had read that wearing a cage can control desire. I bought one and fitted it to myself.'

'Did it work?'

'Sort of. They constrict the penis so that any slight erection is painful. Did you know that a normal, fit, mature, male has a dozen or more erections a day? It was quite a torment and sleeping was difficult at first as I am sure you can imagine. Or, perhaps a woman cannot.'

Jasmine could imagine. Until she began her hormone treatment and before she had her testicles removed, unwanted erections had mortified her. All that was behind her now that she had no penis.

Russell went on. 'The body is a quick learner. The effect is like Pavlov's dogs I suppose. It learns that arousal equals pain, so the erections stop happening.'

'Completely? But you said...'

'Only while you have the pressure of the cage around your cock and balls. As soon as it is released the feelings flood back as if the dam breaks. The cage controlled my feelings for my students, but I found that my willpower was weak. Often, I would use my key to release myself. Then I discovered Madame de la Clef's service. She takes the responsibility away and now I have to work for my release. I have to please her, worship her, obey her. Only if I do all that she asks can I get any relief. Do you understand?'

Jasmine shook her head. No, she couldn't understand what this man was prepared to go through in order to control his desires. On the other hand, she did understand compulsive urges. She had lived with them herself for a good part of her life and she thought of the steps she had taken to fulfil her own desires – transition, divorce from Angela, the pain and recovery of her most recent operation. She felt some sympathy for the man she had persuaded to reveal his most private behaviour. Perhaps revealing something about herself would be recompense. Her shake became a nod.

'Yes, Mr Russell, I think I do understand something of what you have said. Having that cage clasped around my penis would have been a torture. Giving control of my body to someone else is way outside my comfort zone, but I have been driven too.'

Russell stared at her. 'I thought there was something about you. Your voice, your figure. You're transsexual, aren't you?' Jasmine nodded. 'Have you had the change?'

'Yes, recently. I'm still recovering.'

'But you have achieved your goal?'

Jasmine smiled, 'Almost, there are still things in the future I suppose, and like you just mentioned, there are still giveaways that reveal my past. But I am close to being the woman I feel I am.'

'Well, good luck to you. And thank you again. You have helped me re-examine my own behaviour.'

'You're going to give up wearing your cage and paying Harriet Bunting to hold the key?'

'Oh, no. You've helped me to realise that it is the forfeits that Madame dreams up for us that make my life exciting. I'll be looking forward to the next act that she plans for me in a month or three.'

'Oh,' Jasmine was surprised. She was angry with herself now for revealing her past. This man didn't warrant her compassion after all. She stood up and pulled her coat back around her. 'Thanks for the coffee. There may be further questions.'

'I'll look forward to your visit Miss Frame.' He accompanied Jasmine to the door and let her out. Jasmine hurried up the street to the hire car.

16

Jasmine sat in the driving seat of the Micra wondering what to do. She should inform Tom Shepherd and the investigating team of her information concerning Tyler Smith, but she also had the address of Edward Wilson, Harriet Bunting's other "slave". She was keen to meet him to discover if he had any more titbits to tell her. She tried phoning Tom's mobile, but the call went to voicemail. She decided on a text instead and tapped out the message:

"Tyler Smith's whereabouts on Tuesday evening not known; alibi not true."

Then she started the car and negotiated the traffic to head west with Cheltenham her next destination.

She was travelling along the A40 when she realised that it was lunchtime. She wasn't particularly hungry, but the time meant one thing to her now. It was time for her exercise. It had been emphasised so much to her that she must dilate her vagina regularly that it had become a need.

She drove on through the Cotswolds and soon approached a roadside pub/restaurant, The Fox, a former coaching inn. She pulled into the car park and went inside. It was busy with most tables occupied but she found a table for two and ordered a sandwich and a glass of water. She ate quickly and having paid her bill headed into the ladies' room. She was relieved to find that all the cubicles were unoccupied so chose the end one. She tugged down her tights and knickers. Having peed she shuffled to the edge of the loo seat and spread her legs as much as her underwear and the partition of the cubicle would allow.

She had prepared for this eventuality by packing some lube and one of her dilators, the middle-sized one, in her shoulder bag. She couldn't go through the full sequence but the one she had would have to be sufficient. She smeared the lubricant on the glass cylinder and carefully inserted it. She tried to avoid the involuntary groan or gasp which sometimes escaped from her when she did this at home. She didn't want to give the wrong idea, or any idea in fact, to other ladies who entered the loo. The full length entered and she felt it stretching the channel, but it no longer hurt her. She rotated it, slipped it in and out a few times before removing it and then repeated the operation. One more time and she was done.

She listened carefully making sure that she was still alone. Clothing restored to respectability she stepped out and while washing her hands, cleaned the dilator. She dried it with a tissue and stuffed it in her bag just as the door opened and another woman entered. They smiled sweetly at each other and the woman went into a cubicle. Jasmine redid her lipstick and left the toilet relieved that she had done what she intended without embarrassing herself or anyone else. Before setting off again, she put Wilson's address into the maps app on her phone and saw her route marked out for her.

The instructions took her off the main road at the edge of the town and through the suburbs until she found herself in a narrow road with a row of semi-detached bungalows on one side. She drew up outside number eleven. There was a man kneeling beside a flowerbed in the front garden. He appeared to be digging up bulbs. Jasmine got out of the car and approached him. He was bald with a horseshoe ring of cropped hair and though older than Montgomery Russell was slimmer. He stood up as Jasmine approached.

'Can I help you?' he said in a voice that suggested he didn't really want to. He swung the trowel he was holding by his thigh.

'Mr Edward Wilson?' Jasmine said.

'Yes,' he said guardedly, 'Who's asking?'

Jasmine pulled her ID from her pocket. 'I'm Jasmine Frame, an investigator for Kintbridge Police.'

'You're not a police officer then. That's not a warrant card.'

'No, I am assisting the police in their enquiries.'

'Oh, yes. What proof do you have that you represent the police?'

'Um, none in fact. I just have some questions for you.'

'Questions? What about?'

'Your visit to the Royal Hotel, Faringdon on Tuesday evening with Mrs Harriet Bunting.'

He stepped towards her. The trowel was raised like a dagger pointing at her.

'What do you know about that?'

'I know you were there because you paid for dinner. Willy has told me what happened after dinner and I know you went dressed in drag.'

'How dare you!'

Jasmine stepped back hurriedly as he came forward waving the trowel.

'I'm sorry Mr Wilson. I'm not here because of what you were doing. It's about the murder of Mr Bunting.'

He stopped, the trowel still raised.

'What?'

'I am investigating the death of Mr Bunting while you and Willy and Mrs Bunting were at the hotel; also, the fire that occurred at the premises of Molly's, the business that Mr and Mrs Bunting own.'

Wilson shook his head. 'I don't know anything about that.'

'I don't suppose that you do, Mr Wilson. Look I'm not interested in what Mrs Bunting makes you do or why you let her boss you. Willy described that to me. But I'd like to ask you some questions about her companion, Tyler Smith.'

He took a step back from her, putting space between himself and Jasmine.

'You could be anyone, a journalist. I don't want my story all over the papers. My ex-wife would love it.'

'I'm sorry Mr Wilson. If you like I'll go away and come back with a police officer, but look at my ID. I'm a registered private investigator. I give you my word that I am working with the police to find out who killed Mr Bunting. Your information may be important.'

Wilson looked around as if realising that his neighbours may have been watching and wondering what the fracas between him and this young woman was about.

'Alright, you'd better come inside, but if I think you're stringing me along, you're out and it will be me reporting to the police. Got it?'

'Yes, Mr Wilson, that's fair.'

He marched off up the driveway to the door of the bungalow. Jasmine followed. When he entered the small porch, he stamped his wellington boots on the mat, tugged them off then stepped through the inner door into a hallway. It was painted white and unfurnished with nothing on the walls at all.

'That's far enough,' he said turning to face her. 'Close the door.'

Jasmine pushed the door closed.

'Now what are these questions?'

Jasmine considered how to start the conversation. 'You arrived at the Royal Hotel in the early evening…'

'Six-thirty was the time given.'

'Six-thirty, and you met Mrs Bunting, her companion, Tyler Smith and Willy.'

'Yes, I didn't know *Willy* until after we were introduced.'

'You had dinner together, and when it was finished you paid the bill.'

'That is correct, although why it should be of interest I don't know.'

'It was how we were able to identify you, Mr Wilson, that's all.'

'Hmmph. Invasion of privacy.'

'I'm afraid bank and credit card details are one of our means

172

of tracking people these days Mr Wilson. Anyway, you then went up to Mrs Bunting's room.'

He puffed out his cheeks and did not speak.

'Is that correct?' Jasmine insisted.

'Yes.'

'Can you recall what time that was?'

'Not exactly. I had other things on my mind.'

'I know Mr Wilson, but any idea?'

Wilson shrugged, 'Just after seven-thirty.'

'Thank you. Now who went up to the bedroom with you?'

'Mrs Bunting of course and *Willy*.'

'No-one else. Just the three of you?'

'That's right.'

'What about Tyler Smith? What did he do?'

Wilson looked blank. He shrugged. 'I don't know. He didn't come with us that's all.'

'Do you think he stayed in the hotel or did you see him leave?'

'I've no idea. We left him at the table. Look, I wasn't the slightest bit concerned by what Smith was going to do while we were with Madame.'

Jasmine smiled to show she was pleased with Mr Wilson's cooperation. 'Right, thank you. Now after you had been in Mrs Bunting's room for some time you came back downstairs and left. Is that right?'

'Yes.'

'Do you know what time that was?'

'No, I didn't look at a clock. I suppose it was around nine, perhaps a bit later. I lost track of time.'

I'm not surprised, Jasmine thought. 'Okay. Did you speak to anyone on your way out?'

'No, I went straight to the car park at the back of the hotel and drove home.'

'Good. Did you see anyone?'

'Willy was at the reception desk speaking to the manager or someone. I didn't stop.'

'Did you see Tyler Smith at all?'

'No.'

'Good. Thank you very much, Mr Wilson.'

He took a step towards her urging her back to the door. 'Is that all then?'

'Almost. That's all about Tuesday, but have you met Mr Smith before?'

'I don't know the man, but he's been with Madame on other, er, occasions.'

'How long ago do these occasions go back?'

'Oh, less than a year. She had another fellow before.'

'Do you know who that was?'

'Gary Nicholls was his name. I never spoke to him.'

'I see. When you met Mrs Bunting, Madame de la Clef, with one or other of these men did they always stay with you while you did whatever it was that Madame wanted you to do?'

Wilson stiffened when Jasmine used Harriet's full pseudonym and his hands formed fists as she completed her question.

'Sometimes, not always.'

'Did Nicholls or Smith join in the activities?'

'Look, *Willy* may have blabbed about Madame and what she asks of us but I'm not going to. The police can be as bad as the wankers on the papers in making private matters public.'

'Okay, I understand Mr Wilson. I don't want to embarrass you. What you get up to with Mrs Bunting is your business. I am just trying to establish if Tyler's absence on Tuesday evening was unusual or not.'

Wilson calmed a little. 'Nothing was usual or unusual. He hasn't been Madame's toyboy for long, so I don't know whether she normally has him with her when she tests us or not.'

'Thank you, Mr Wilson. I'll let you get back to your gardening. I'm sorry to have bothered you.' Jasmine backed to the door with Wilson hurrying her along.

'I tell you, if any of this reaches the papers or my ex-wife, you and the police will be hearing from my solicitors. No harm must come to Madame.'

Jasmine pulled the door open. 'I understand Mr Wilson but there may be other questions we need you to answer.'

'We'll see about that.' He pushed the door closed as she stepped into the porch.

Jasmine returned to the car and sat in it for a few minutes. She was disappointed that Wilson had not been as forthcoming about his relationship with Madame de la Clef as Russell, but looking at the neat homes of his neighbours with their tidy gardens she could perhaps understand his need for secrecy. The buzz of gossip would be deafening if they discovered what happened on his excursions to Faringdon and elsewhere. She had confirmed however that Tyler Smith had some questions to answer regarding his whereabouts on Tuesday evening and it was time she returned to Kintbridge to pass on her news.

Less than an hour and half later she pulled up outside her house and wondered why there was a blue and white Mini parked in the drive. She parked the Micra and walked into the house. Viv greeted her with arms around her and a kiss on her lips.

Jasmine eased herself away from him. 'Do we have a guest?'

Viv shook his head, 'No.'

'What's the Mini doing on the driveway, then.'

A broad smile spread across his face. 'That's your new car. If you like it, that is.'

'My car?'

'Yes. You can't go on with that old Fiesta. It's unreliable and probably unsafe. You need a newer car.'

'But I can't afford a Mini, even a second-hand one. That one's only three years old.'

'You don't have to afford it. I'll pay for it.'

Jasmine sighed, 'Oh, Viv. You don't have to buy me a new car. Even if my old one has given up, I can buy another.'

'What? Another clapped out wreck. I know what your finances are like, Jas. But look, we're a team now. What's mine's yours. You contribute what you can and I make up the rest. If you insist on going back to your detecting business I want you to have a decent car for your job. I'll put up the cost. You can call it a loan if you like and claim back the tax on it as an essential expense or whatever, I don't mind.'

'Well...' Jasmine was uncertain. She didn't want to be dependent on Viv's generosity, but she did enjoy being with him and she did need a reliable car. 'OK, a loan then.'

'Come and have a look at it. See whether you like it.' He took Jasmine's hand and lead her out of the house. The light was beginning to fade but they walked around the car. Jasmine admired the look of it but some doubts niggled.

'Don't you think it's a bit flash?'

'What do you mean, Jas?'

'If I'm on surveillance won't people notice a two-tone Mini parked nearby or following them? Perhaps a car that stands out less would be better.'

'Such as?' Viv was still grinning.

'Oh, I don't know,' she didn't have much interest in cars, 'another Fiesta, a more recent one, or that Nissan I had today.'

Viv shook his head, 'I wouldn't worry if I was you. There are plenty of these new Minis around now, they're as much part of the scenery as Fiestas or Micras. Give it a go.'

Viv opened the driver's door and beckoned for her to get in.

She made herself comfortable in the driving seat and surveyed the controls. She liked it.

'Have you paid for it? What about my old car?'

'I know the dealer. He let me borrow it to show you. Your old banger is still in the garage. They'll take it in part exchange.'

'Not much I bet.'

'No, but they'll tow it away. Look, let's get the hire car back, I'll follow you in this and then you can take it for a test drive. How does that sound?'

Jasmine was sitting in the old red Fiesta in the garage while Viv was cooking dinner. The deal was done and her old car would be collected on Monday morning. The smart, newish Mini, was on the drive registered in her name, but she wanted a few minutes with her old friend. It held lots of memories of the eight or more years that she had been the owner. It had been Angela's car at first. To be perfectly honest, it was pretty old even then. It was their transport in their first years of married life and then became her own car when they separated, and she transitioned. It had accompanied her on all her cases as a private investigator until now. It was part of her life as a woman.

'Hey, Jas. Come in.' Viv called out from the door between the garage and the house.

Jasmine pushed the door of the Fiesta open with a creak. 'Is dinner ready?'

'No. Tom Shepherd's here.'

Oh, god, she hadn't reported in, and there was so much to tell him. She got out and pushed on the car door. It closed but the lock didn't catch. She left it and hurried into the kitchen. Tom was leaning against a kitchen unit while Viv poured boiling water into a coffee mug.

'I'm sorry Tom. I should have got in touch. We've been sorting out my car since I got back.'

'So Viv said. What's this about Tyler? What have you been doing? Hamid said something about Oxford and Cheltenham.'

'That's where I've been. Come and have a sit down and I'll explain. You'll love it.'

Viv handed the mug to Tom and returned to his food preparation. Tom followed Jasmine into the lounge and settled his lanky frame into the sofa. Jasmine sat by his side.

'Go on then Jas. Tell me what you've got.'

'You know that Hamid and I found that there were two other people with Harriet and Tyler on Tuesday evening in Faringdon and they, the guests, that is, paid for dinner and the room Harriet stayed in.'

'Yeah, that sounded a bit odd.'

'The explanation is odder. Hamid got the names and addresses of the two guests – Montgomery Russell in Oxford and Edward Wilson in Cheltenham.'

'So you paid a visit to them.'

'That's right. Russell first. He was an affable middle-aged university type, a bit shocked at first when I showed up but gradually loosened up and told me all about it.'

'It?'

'Yes. Get this. He and Wilson, and some other blokes, are Harriet Bunting's slaves. Each of them wears a chastity cage like Evelyn, and she, Madame de la Clef, holds the keys.'

Tom's eyes had widened. 'Madame de la Clef? What does she get out of it? Some feeling of power?'

Jasmine chuckled, 'Probably, but that's not all. She charges for the service, about two thousand pounds a year in Russell's case.'

'What! Is he mad?'

'No, besotted with her perhaps, but quite sane in other respects.'

'He's in love with Harriet Bunting?'

'I don't think I'd call it love. She certainly has a hold on both of them and presumably the others.'

'Good god. What was this meeting on Tuesday for?'

'Well, from time to time, Harriet lets them out of their cages, but they have to perform forfeits before she will do so.'

'Forfeits? Like what?'

'On Tuesday, Wilson had to turn up at the hotel in drag, though he's not a transvestite. Or he wasn't before. Then he and Russell had to perform gay sex in front of Harriet.'

'Gay sex?'

'They fellated each other.'

'So they're gay?'

'No, they're not. They are both straight, at least they thought they were. This act was meant to be humiliating for them.'

'And was it?'

'Well, they both did it, so they must have been aroused.'

Tom frowned, 'And Harriet Bunting watched them.'

'And took photos and videos of them at it,' Jasmine added.

'For blackmail purposes?'

'That's what I thought of. It hadn't occurred to Russell that that might be a possibility. He was just glad to have pleased Madame and had his release from the cage, for a while.'

'They're locked in again now are they?'

'Oh, yes, until the next time.'

He shook his head, 'Well I don't get it, but I don't suppose there is anything illegal about it unless we can get Harriet Bunting for living off immoral earnings or for tax evasion if she doesn't declare her earnings.'

'That's what I thought,' Jasmine said.

'Okay, Jas. That's all very sordid and interesting but what has it got to do with the case?'

Jasmine grinned, 'Tyler Smith wasn't there.'

Tom frowned, 'What do you mean?'

Jasmine explained. 'Tyler Smith and Harriet Bunting both said they spent the night together at the Royal Hotel, but while Harriet was in the room with her two slaves, Tyler wasn't with them. Neither Russell nor Wilson saw him after they left the dining room soon after seven-thirty.'

Tom shrugged. 'Perhaps he stayed in the bar, or the residents' lounge if the hotel has one.'

'Of course,' Jasmine felt a little frustrated, 'we have to check that out, but the point is his alibi doesn't stack up and he had time to get to Thirsbury and back and be with Harriet soon after her two guys left. It's only three-quarters-of-an-hour each way.'

'You're right Jas, we have to check him out. I'll get Hamid on it tomorrow.'

'Tyler Smith could be Evelyn's killer or the one who torched the place,' Jasmine insisted. She felt that Tom was resisting her hunch.

'Perhaps, but I'm sure Neville Griffiths and his boys are involved.'

'Have you found anything yet? I thought there wasn't any evidence among Evelyn's phone or email records?'

Tom agreed, 'Yes, but we got permission to go into Griffiths' and Elvis Preston's records.'

'Elvis who?

'He's Griffiths' fixer. If he's not by his side fielding visitors he's out pursuing debtors.'

'Any luck?'

'Yes, we think we have a record of a couple of phone conversations he had with Bunting.'

'That could have been about paying the loan back,' Jasmine said.

'Yes, but Evelyn only paid the first instalment and missed at least two months payments. Preston would not have let that pass unless they had other plans; and Bunting did renew, and increase, his fire insurance in late September.'

'It's circumstantial, Tom.'

'I know but I'm sure Griffiths and Bunting were putting a plan together.'

'You need more evidence than you've got to make an arrest.'

'I know, that's the frustrating bit. I'm sure we're close to discovering something.'

'Well, I want to speak to Harriet and Tyler again, especially as I now know where Harriet is getting her money from and that she has a team of avid worshippers who will do anything, perhaps literally, to please her.'

'You go on with that line of enquiry, Jas.'

'It still leaves one person.'

'Who?'

'Gary Nicholls. We know he was a partner in the business and Harriet's lover. That seems to have ended in the last six months. He's the reason why Evelyn was in debt. We haven't spoken to him yet, have we?'

'No, we haven't been able to track him down. We've got his address near Kintbridge, but he hasn't been seen there for a couple of weeks. Neighbours don't know where he's gone. He has investments in a number of small businesses but none of them seem to have much contact with him. I can't see why he'd kill Bunting or be involved in the insurance scam.'

'I'll try his address again in the next few days.'

'Thanks, Jas, I haven't got the staff to keep an eye out for him.' Tom looked at his watch. 'I'd better be going. I don't want to miss Abi's bedtime again.'

'How's she doing, Tom?' Jasmine said wondering what it was like to live with a small child.

Tom looked dreamy. 'Gorgeous, except that I hardly get to see her. Soph says she'll never recognise me as her Dad if I can't be around when she's awake.'

'Well, you'd better get home. It's Saturday evening. Let the junior staff do the work.'

Tom laughed. 'Junior staff. Do you know, Terry Hopkins has taken to calling me "Boss"? I think he means it ironically.'

'Terry would never want to do your job. He likes being told what to do and grumbling about it.'

Tom hauled himself to his feet. 'I know you didn't get on, especially when you began, you know what, but he's a good copper.'

'Sort of,' Jasmine grudgingly agreed. She escorted Tom to the door and waved as he got into his car.

Viv shouted from the kitchen 'Dinner is served!'

17

SUNDAY 20ᵀᴴ OCTOBER
MORNING

Warily, Jasmine drove the Mini along the country road. One touch of the accelerator seemed to make it leap forward, something she wasn't used to with the old red Fiesta. She had an address and a vague idea how to reach it but thinking about driving the new car was competing with looking out for landmarks.

She came to a small village, not much more than a hamlet except there had been some recent house-building. Quite expensive housing, she noted. She slowed at a crossroads and turned left. This was the road. She pulled up at a large newly-built, arts and crafts style, house. There was a car in the driveway, a Volvo estate. It looked as though someone was home. She glanced at the clock on the dashboard. Just after eleven. A reasonable time on a Sunday morning to pay a visit.

Jasmine got out of the car and pressed the button on the key fob. Remote locking was a luxury she had not enjoyed on the old Ford, nevertheless she checked that the doors were locked. She walked up to the porch and pressed the doorbell.

A few moments passed before the door was opened. Jasmine observed the man. He was dressed in chinos and t-shirt, almost summer attire rather than late October even though the sun was shining. He was tall, over six foot, and there did not seem to be any spare flesh on him, but his pepper and salt hair betrayed his age – mid-fifties.

'Good morning,' he said in a somewhat surprised tone. 'Can I help you?'

'Gary Nicholls?' Jasmine asked.

He frowned. 'Yes. Who wants to know?'

Jasmine performed the familiar motion of pulling her id out of her pocket. 'I'm Jasmine Frame. I'm carrying out investigations on behalf of the Kintbridge Police.'

'Police?'

'We've been trying to contact you. You haven't been at home.'

'No. We just got back. Holidays.'

'You said "we"?'

'Me and Tracy, my, er, girlfriend. What's this all about? Why do the police want to contact me?'

'I can explain, Mr Nicholls, but can I come in and speak to your girlfriend too?'

'Uh, yeah. Come in. Trace is upstairs.' He stepped back from the door and called the name. A young woman in shorts and a sleeveless top, with sun-bleached hair and long sun-tanned legs appeared at the top of the stairs.

'What is it, Gary?'

'Come down. It's the police. Been trying to contact us, well me, I suppose.'

The girl, who appeared to be thirty years younger than Nicholls, skipped down the stairs and followed them into a spacious lounge with a picture window looking over the rear garden.

Nicholls beckoned Jasmine to sit on a large leather sofa. 'Now, what's this all about?'

'I believe you know Harriet and Evelyn Bunting,' Jasmine began.

'Yes.' The reply was guarded, not a simple affirmative.

'When was the last time you saw either of them?'

Nicholls laughed, 'Not for months. Why?'

Jasmine ignored the query. 'You said you've been on holiday. Can you tell me where?'

'Okay. The Maldives. We wanted some sunshine.'

'And when did you go there?'

'Two weeks ago. We had a fortnight. Well almost, the travelling, you know.'

'So you were out of the country all this past week?'

'Yes, that's what I said.' Nicholls looked annoyed and the girl standing by his side had a confused expression. 'Look, do you mind telling me what this is about?'

'Yes, Sir,' Jasmine said sweetly, 'On Tuesday evening, Evelyn Bunting was killed and there was a fire at Molly's.'

Tracy clapped a hand over her mouth and let out a little gasp. Nicholls frowned. 'Evelyn was killed in a fire at their place?'

Jasmine sucked her cheek. 'Not quite. I said, Evelyn was killed and there was a fire. They are not necessarily connected.'

Nicholls frowned. 'I don't get it. Do you mean Evelyn wasn't killed by the fire?'

'That's right.'

'How did she die then?'

'I can't say at the moment Mr Nicholls, but we are investigating the cause of death and how the fire started.'

'They weren't accidents then?'

'No.' Before he could ask another question Jasmine pressed on. 'We understand that you used to be a partner in the business.'

'Used to be. Not anymore.'

'You have no interest in the business undertaken at Molly's?'

Nicholls shook his head. 'None at all.'

'We understand that Mr Bunting paid you a sum to buy out your share in the business.'

Nicholls shrugged, 'Yes, that's business.'

'Do you mind telling me how much he paid you?'

'Well, it was between us, but I suppose it's general knowledge now if you've looked into Evelyn's affairs. It was one hundred thousand pounds.'

'That's quite a large sum.'

'It was less than it should have been given my level of investment over the years.'

'Oh, so your involvement in Molly's was purely financial, was it?'

'Er...' Nicholls paused and turned to his girlfriend. 'Hey, Trace, why don't you go and make some coffee. I could do with a cup after the journey. You too I expect, and you, Miss Frame?'

'Yes, please,' Jasmine replied. The girl stood and trotted out of the room.

'Does Tracey know about you and Mrs Bunting.'

Nicholls bit his lip. 'I was waiting for you to bring that up. My interest in the business was not purely financial as you put it, because I was in a relationship with Harriet.'

'Tracy doesn't know?'

'She knows I was previously in a relationship with an older woman, Harriet Bunting, but she doesn't know the, um, details.'

'Which are what exactly, Mr Nicholls.'

Gary Nicholls flushed. 'It was complicated. I met Harriet years ago and we started an affair. I knew she was married but I didn't understand at the time the er, nature of that marriage. Harriet got me to invest in the business and I got a bit hooked in.'

'You didn't approve of the business Evelyn was in?'

Nicholls shook his head. 'No, that was fine. Evelyn ran it well, knew his clientele, and his suppliers. It made money. At first anyway, until the internet turned things on their head.'

'So, what were your reservations?'

'They weren't reservations. It's just, um, a bit complicated to explain Harriet and me and Evelyn.'

'You mean Tracy may not understand Harriet's dominance of Evelyn and your role?'

Nicholl's glanced to the door then back at Jasmine. 'That's about it.'

'Well, can you explain it to me. You see I know Evelyn was trans. A sissy is the more descriptive term. Harriet kept him in female clothes and, I think the phrase is "in chastity".'

'Hmm, yes, that's it.'

'So, where did you fit in?'

'I was Harriet's stud.' There was a hint of pride in Nicholl's statement. 'Yeah, it was all about the sex between Harriet and me and, she was fucking hot. Still is in fact.'

'OK, so you had an adulterous affair with Harriet Bunting while she kept her husband as a sort of slave.'

The flush returned to Nicholls cheeks. 'Yes, well it was a bit more than that. You see, Harriet liked to have Evelyn with us when we, um, fucked.'

Jasmine struggled to speak in an even, unemotional voice. Inside she was screaming with hysterical laughter. 'You mean you had to perform in front of Harriet's cuckolded husband who was prevented from taking part in the proceedings.'

'Oh, he took part, alright.'

'Really, I thought Harriet kept his penis locked up.'

'He had a mouth and tongue.'

'Umm. I see.' Jasmine wasn't sure she could ask Nicholls to describe in more detail what happened in bed with Harriet and Evelyn.

'Look, is all this necessary?' Nicholls seemed to have just realised the intimate and personal information he had been freely giving.

'We are trying to establish who might have wanted to kill Evelyn Bunting and burn down the business. The relationship between Evelyn and his wife and her other relationships with men could be, probably are, important.'

Nicholls lay back in the chair, relaxing as if he was over the worst. 'Well, I've not got any interest in the business and my relationship with Harriet, and Evelyn, is over.'

'Why?' Jasmine thrust in the query, 'It looks like it was a cosy threesome.'

'Harriet ended it – the sex – and told Evelyn to buy me out so that I would have nothing more to do with them.'

'And you accepted that?'

Nicholls shrugged. 'What else could I do? She had gone after that youngster, Tyler. I was no longer the sex machine she wanted. I was happy to get out and have a normal relationship with a girl.'

Tracy reappeared carrying a tray with a jug of coffee and three mugs. Jasmine was pleased to see that there were also biscuits. The girl put the tray down on a large oak coffee table and began pouring. Nicholls mouthed a "thanks darling".

'Do you know how Harriet met Tyler Smith?' Jasmine asked.

Nicholls chuckled. 'Oh, yes. He was her personal trainer. Harriet got it into her head that to preserve her youth she needed to keep fit. Soon however she discovered that Tyler was good at other moves apart from squat thrusts and push-ups.'

'What does he see in her? She's quite a bit older.'

'Harriet can be very persuasive and, um, alluring. She soon got Tyler wrapped around her finger. Mind you he's getting everything he wants. She's insatiable.'

Tracy passed a mug of coffee to Jasmine and offered milk and sugar which Jasmine declined and a biscuit that she accepted.

'What about Tyler and Evelyn? Did they get on?'

Nicholls shook his head. 'I have no idea, but I don't suppose Harriet has changed.'

'What about the other men?' Jasmine asked. Nicholls frowned

'Other men?'

'Did you know about the men that Harriet provided a service for?'

Tracey held out a mug for Garry. He looked at it.

'Oh, love, is there any cream?'

The girl frowned. 'No, sorry. I thought you preferred milk.'

'I think I'd like cream today. Be a dear, Trace, and go and get some.'

'We haven't got any.'

'The village shop will be open. They'll have some.'

'You want me to go to the shop to get you some cream for your coffee?' The girl's face was all frown.

'There's a love. You don't mind do you? I'll make it up to you – promise.' Nicholls gave her the most lascivious smile that Jasmine had seen.

The girl smiled, 'Well, alright. For you Garypops.' She trotted out again. Jasmine sipped her coffee.

Nicholls leaned forward and whispered, 'You know about Harriet's gang of acolytes?'

'Acolytes?'

'Well, they worship her. You know what goes on?'

'I know that Harriet charges an immense fee to hold the keys to those men's chastity cages, and what's more, makes them take part in various acts when she releases them.'

'Yeah, they love it. The more pain and humiliation the more they like it.'

'How many are there?'

'Oh, I don't know. Not sure if I came across all of them. A dozen or so. Perhaps.'

'You met them? Did you take part in sexual activities with them like you did with Evelyn and Harriet?'

Nicholls roared with embarrassed laughter. 'God, no! I was just the chauffeur. Harriet doesn't drive you know.' Jasmine nodded. 'I just delivered her to her appointments with those weird guys and kept out of it.'

'Like Tyler.'

Nicholls shrugged, 'Yeah, I suppose he's her driver now.'

Jasmine put her empty mug down on the tray. 'The bond between Harriet and these men is strong.'

'I'll say. They'll do anything for her, buy anything for her.'

Kill for her, Jasmine wondered. 'Do you know who they are?'

'No. Harriet kept their real names to herself. She used to keep the keys and her notebook with their details, in her handbag, which she always has with her.'

'She told you what she made them do?'

There was chuckle in Nicholls' answer. 'She used to like telling me her plans for them and how they responded. She enjoyed having power over them.'

'And Evelyn and you?'

'What?'

'Having power over you?'

'She didn't...' Nicholls paused and considered. 'Well, I suppose she did. Not like Evelyn or those other guys, but yes, I suppose she got what she wanted from me.'

'And when she'd had enough of you, she discarded you.'

Nicholls frowned. 'I suppose it looks a bit like that.'

'Were you angry?'

'I was at first when she started seeing Tyler instead of me but then I sort of woke up.'

'What do you mean?'

Nicholls smiled as if he had regained control. 'I realised how much she had used me and how weird the set up with her and Evelyn was. When she said it was over between us I was quite relieved actually.'

'But you insisted on your payment.'

'Yeah. I wanted to get my own back. I said I'd leave them if they paid me my share of the business.'

'Harriet agreed straight away?'

'Yeah. She wanted me out of the way so that she could install Tyler in my place.'

'Did you know that paying you a hundred thousand pounds would all but bankrupt the business.'

'Can't say I cared by then.'

'Did you have a grudge against Evelyn Bunting?'

Nicholls looked confused. 'A grudge? No why should I. It was Harriet who was breaking the relationship. Harriet who I was angry with. Are you suggesting I might have killed Evelyn?'

'Just testing the possibilities.'

'I told you I wasn't here.'

'We'll check your alibi.'

Nicholls showed exasperation. 'Look, I'm sorry Evelyn is dead. He was an odd guy, but I knew him for years and liked him. Yes, I did, I liked the guy. There was no way I would kill him.'

'Or burn down the business?'

Nicholls shrugged. 'Why should I? I had nothing to gain from it and it wouldn't have been a way of getting back at

Harriet – she had little interest in it. I'm not the one you should be questioning about this. I think you're done now.' He stood up and glared at Jasmine. She got to her feet.

'Thank you, Mr Nicholls for being so open about your relationship. I'm sorry if I embarrassed you but we do need to get all the facts on this case. I agree that you don't seem to have a motive for either the murder or arson. Can you think of anyone who might?'

Nicholls shrugged, 'No, I can't. No one had anything against Evelyn. Why set fire to the shop? Unless… insurance?'

'That's a possibility,' Jasmine agreed.

'But Evelyn would be the one to benefit from any insurance payout. Why did he get killed? I don't get it.'

'Nor do we at the moment. But there are still questions to ask. Either I or a police officer may have more for you, especially as you knew the business.'

'Not a lot. Evelyn looked after everything. I was very much a sleeping partner.'

'Sleeping?'

Nicholls flushed again. Jasmine walked into the hallway. Nicholls opened the front door and Jasmine stepped outside. The door closed behind her.

Tracy jogged into the driveway, breathing heavily and grasping a carton of cream. She stopped and looked at Jasmine.

'Oh, are you leaving?'

'Yes,'

'But I've got the cream.'

'I'm sure Mr Nicholls would still like it in his coffee.'

'He doesn't usually have cream. That was just to get me out of the house wasn't it?'

Jasmine shrugged. She didn't want to come between the lovers.

'He didn't want me listening while you asked him about his last woman,' Tracy stated.

'Perhaps,' Jasmine agreed.

'Harriet wasn't it. He doesn't talk about her but sometimes

he says the name when he's asleep.'

'Does he really?' Jasmine wasn't particularly interested in Nicholls sleep-talking.

'He says another name sometimes,' the girl went on.

Now Jasmine was interested. 'Really? What name?'

'Evie. I thought it was another girl he had sex with, but you said the name of Harriet's husband was Evelyn. Do you think that was Evie?'

'Possibly. I can't be sure.' Jasmine didn't want to give the girl ideas.

'I didn't think Gary had sex with guys.'

Jasmine shook her head. 'I really don't know…'

'Which do you fancy? You're one of them trans people aren't you.'

How did I give myself away this time, Jasmine asked herself; *was it the voice or my appearance?*

'I'm a woman.' She stopped herself adding "now".

Tracy looked her up and down. 'OK. You look pretty good. Do men fancy you?'

'I've got a boyfriend.' Jasmine mentally kicked herself. She didn't need to get into this self-justification.

'Oh well. Takes all sorts I suppose. Gary's a real man, even though he's old.' The girl trotted on to the front door. Jasmine stared at her, wondering what the exchange was all about. Was it a tigerish, "keep away from my man" thing, or "I know more than you think"?

She returned to the Mini and started up. She turned in the road and headed slowly back towards Kintbridge. Where next? She reviewed her conversation with Gary Nicholls. There was no reason for him to be involved in the murder or arson but one thing he had said was at the forefront of her thoughts. Nicholls had said that Harriet's slaves would do anything for her, anything at all. Did that include setting fire to Molly's to get the insurance money, or disposing of Evelyn to please Harriet? She needed to speak to Harriet again.

18

'Gather round, people. Let's see what we've got,' Tom Shepherd called out to his team. They looked up from their papers or screens and shuffled across the office to cluster around the whiteboard. 'Right, who wants to start? Terry?'

Terry Hopkins took a breath, opened his mouth, and stopped. The door to the office had opened revealing the bulk of DCI Sloane. Tom looked at him in amazement. He had received no warning of the boss' imminent arrival.

Sloane approached the group, his face not giving away any emotion.

'Shepherd. Glad to find you here. Thought I'd call in for an update on your inquiry. It looks as though I came at the right time. Can't stop for long, taking the wife out for lunch.'

Tom continued to stare at his superior officer. Despite apparently being off-duty, he was still in his everyday grey suit. Tom shook himself.

'Good to see you Sir. We were just about to go over where we are.'

'Are you about to make any arrests, Shepherd? That's what I want to know. In a high-profile case like this, a murder and arson, it's important to make progress quickly.'

'Um, yes, Sir. Er, I don't think we are in a position to make an arrest just yet. The evidence is not strong enough. We're looking for communications between Bunting, that's Evelyn, Mr Bunting, the victim and Neville Griffiths' people regarding the fire at Molly's.'

'Ah, yes the arson. Insurance, do you think?'

'That's our theory, Sir.'

The DCI eased himself into a chair facing the group. 'Well? Evidence?'

Tom shrugged. 'There are some emails relating to the loan Bunting took out from Griffiths, but we haven't found anything in his phone records or emails to suggest a conspiracy to set the place alight. I think the contact would be with Griffiths' employee, Elvis Preston, but Bunting seems to have avoided speaking to him using his own phones.'

'Public phones only, eh?'

'Presumably.'

Terry coughed.

'Yes, Hopkins, do you have something.'

'Yes, Sir. CCTV from the centre of Thirsbury shows Preston's car was in the town on the evening of the fire.'

Sloane frowned. 'The centre of the town. What about nearer the premises.'

Tom replied. 'There aren't any cameras. Neither Bunting nor any of his neighbours have CCTV.'

The DCI growled with discontent. 'I know Preston of old. Nasty piece of work. Arson is well within his remit. Are you going to arrest him?'

Tom grimaced. 'The evidence is weak at the moment, Sir. We need to get a look at his phone details. He must have been in contact with Bunting, about repaying the loan if nothing else.'

'Get him in,' Sloane urged, 'then you can get hold of his phone. The evidence will be there, Shepherd, if you look hard enough.'

'Yes, Sir.'

'Did Preston kill Bunting as well as set fire to the place.'

Tom sucked in a breath. 'It's possible, Sir, but the murder could be a separate incident to the arson. Killing Bunting seems illogical when he was going to be the recipient of the insurance money.'

'Hmm,' Sloane pondered. 'What's Frame got to say about the

case? This Bunting chap was like her, wasn't he?'

Tom stopped himself from sighing. He was glad Jasmine wasn't present to hear Sloane liken her to Evelyn Bunting. 'I don't think they are that similar, Sir. Jasmine has been investigating the relationship between Evelyn and Harriet Bunting. It wasn't what you would call a typical marriage, Sir.'

Sloane snorted. 'Where is Frame? Isn't she in today?'

'It is Sunday, Sir. Actually, she was going to see if Gary Nicholls was at home. He's been away since before the incident.

'Nicholls?'

'The former partner in the business, who Bunting bought out precipitating his financial problems and dealings with Griffiths. Nicholls also appears to be have been a previous lover of Harriet Bunting.'

'Previous, you say. Who's the current one then?'

'Tyler Smith, a younger man,' Tom explained.

'Um, Sir.' Young detective Sassani raised a hand as if he was in class. Tom glanced at him.

'Yes, Hamid?'

'Miss Frame has shown that Smith's alibi for Tuesday night is not secure.'

'What's that?' Sloane said.

'Go on, Hamid,' Tom urged.

The officer took a breath. 'Miss Frame found that Smith was not with Harriet Bunting in the Faringdon hotel for all of Tuesday evening. In fact, I've now seen CCTV from the Royal Hotel. It shows Tyler Smith leaving in his Mercedes-Benz about seven-forty-five and returning soon after ten. He could have got back to Thirsbury in that time.'

'He did!' Sasha Patel said. Everyone looked at her.

'How do you know?' Tom said.

'I've been looking at the same CCTV as Terry. Tyler Smith's car was in the centre of Thirsbury at eight-thirty on Tuesday evening.'

Sloane stood up. 'Well, DI Shepherd, I think you have another suspect to interview. It sounds as though Mr Smith has some questions to answer. Good work. I'll leave you to get on.' He lumbered towards the door, paused and turned. 'Oh, and thank Frame for her assistance.' He departed.

Tom was left facing his team. 'Well, thanks, guys. Seems we have a couple of arrests to make. Let's see about tracking down Preston and his Polish mate and Smith. Terry, you and me for Preston. We'll need some uniform back-up for that I think. Sasha and Hamid, you find Tyler Smith. I expect he'll be with Harriet Bunting.'

The team started to disperse, but Hamid stood still. 'What about Jasmine?'

'What about her?' Tom asked.

'She hasn't been in touch this morning.'

Tom shrugged. 'She said she'd have a look at Nicholls' place. Perhaps he's not back yet and she's got nothing to report.'

19

It didn't take long to drive across Kintbridge, even though the Sunday lunch traffic was building up. She pulled up in the road a few yards from Harriet Bunting's borrowed house and was about to get out of the Mini when a car emerged from the driveway. It was a Merc, driven by Tyler Smith with Harriet in the passenger seat. She lay down across the passenger seat as it went past.

Jasmine started up the engine. At least this car was more reliable at re-starting than her old Fiesta. She did a quick three-point turn and was in time to see Smith turning left onto the main road. Jasmine followed, managing to insert herself into the flow of traffic while keeping her quarry in sight. At the centre of the small town they turned off the main road and drove over the canal and railway line through country and onwards, heading south. There were no cars between them now so Jasmine hung back. What was the reason for this journey, she wondered. Were Tyler and Harriet going out to a nice lunch together, or was there some other purpose?

They joined a busy A road, familiar to Jasmine, and she was able to ensure that there was always at least one car between her and Tyler. Soon they were on the outskirts of Basingstoke. Jasmine was a little surprised when they turned off into the car park of a budget hotel and restaurant – not Harriet's usual standard of accommodation. Jasmine followed and parked some distance from the Mercedes. She sat in her car and watched Tyler and Harriet walk into the building. Harriet was dressed in a smart woollen jacket and skirt with knee high boots in shiny black. They had very high stiletto heels which made Harriet rely on Tyler for support. Tyler carried a small holdall.

Jasmine got out of the Mini, straightened her skirt and hitched her bag over her shoulder. She crossed the car park to the entrance and took a swift look around. The restaurant was busy with young families and elderly couples. Harriet and Tyler were seating themselves at a table for four in a quieter, secluded alcove. Jasmine looked for somewhere where she could see but not be seen. She noticed a vacant table for two behind a tall pot plant, real or artificial, and she hurried to take possession of it. Harriet and her lover were examining the printed menus. What should she do? Viv was preparing a meal for later in the day when he expected her home. She didn't want to eat now. Perhaps a coffee and a light snack would be sufficient cover. Her glance was passing between her subjects and the menu when she was approached by a waitress. She gave her choice, a simple paté starter, quickly, so as not to draw too much attention to herself. Then she made a show of looking at her phone to feign disinterest in her surroundings.

Just a few minutes had passed when another person joined Harriet and Tyler. He was a slim man, middle-aged, with short, greying hair. He was dressed in a pair of nondescript brown trousers, a check shirt, plain red tie and a wind-cheater. He stood by the table until Harriet pointed to the seat opposite her. Then he sat and seemed to make himself shrink with his knees pressed together and arms folded in his lap. Another of Harriet's acolytes, as Nicholls called them, Jasmine was certain. She wondered what his forfeit would be to please his mistress.

Food was delivered to Harriet and Tyler but, Jasmine observed, none to the later arrival. Her own small dish was placed in front of her and she ate slowly, keeping an eye on the other table. She was surprised when, very soon, the three people all rose to their feet and started to leave the restaurant. There had been no sign of payment taking place.

Jasmine gulped her coffee, and scrabbled in her bag for her

wallet. She pulled out a ten pound note and dropped it on the table. That would surely cover her light lunch. She stood up and hurried in the direction the party had taken. In the foyer she saw Harriet and her supposed slave pass through a door into the hotel part of the building, but Tyler wasn't with them. Had he left them to carry out their "business"? She followed the pair at a discreet distance. They took the lift but there were only two floors. Jasmine galloped up the stairs, slowing as she reached the top. She peered around a corner to look along a corridor. Harriet was pushing a door into a room open and ushering her slave inside. Jasmine crept along the corridor as the door closed and locked with a loud clunk.

Jasmine stood with her back against the wall alongside the door. She listened carefully. There was no sound from this or any other room, just the usual drone of air conditioning. What should she do? Confronting Harriet while she had one of her slaves with her would be interesting, but the door was locked so she couldn't simply walk in on them. She didn't think Harriet would respond if she knocked, unless of course she thought it was Tyler. No, Harriet would have given him instructions not to disturb her while she was seeing to her slave. Perhaps she should just wait and surprise them when they emerged.

Minutes passed. No one else went along the corridor or came out of rooms. She was getting bored of standing. She crouched down, crawled to the doorway and pressed her ear to the wooden door. She listened carefully. Was that a rustle or a muffled voice?

The blow to the back of her head sent her sprawling along the carpeted corridor. Her vision blurred and pain filled her head. She pushed her hands against the floor to raise herself up. A hand grabbed the collar of her coat and dragged her onto her knees. He was leaning over her – Tyler Smith. The door of the room was open. He dragged her inside and let the door close behind them.

'Look what I found listening outside the door,' Smith said.

Jasmine was on her hands and knees. She bent her neck to

raise her head, sending arrows of pain piercing her mind. In front of her, on the patch of floor between the en-suite and the double bed, there was a chair in which Harriet sat. Her legs were stretched out in front of her. The mouth of the slave was pressed against the shiny black, patent leather boots. He knelt with his naked buttocks raised and his arms pinioned behind his back. There was a dog collar around his neck with a lead which ended in Harriet's hand

Harriet didn't move, but she looked down at Jasmine then up at her lover.

'What have you done now, Tyler?'

'I told you. She was snooping so I clobbered her.'

'Well, that's a pretty problem you've set me, isn't it?' She looked down at the slave and gave a tug to the lead. 'Get on with it.' His tongue emerged from between his lips and he proceeded to lick the leather boots.

'What was I supposed to do?' Tyler appealed.

'Well, you could have just watched her until we'd finished. Interfering little sneak that she is, there was nothing she could do while we minded our own business. I imagine she couldn't even hear anything outside the door; they're solid enough.'

Jasmine pushed herself into a sitting position while her head rocked and rolled. She felt sick. She felt the back of her head. There was no blood but she could feel a lump developing. She looked up at Tyler wondering what he'd hit her with. His gloved fist seemed to be the answer.

'Well, that's one count of actual bodily harm I can get you with,' she said. The words came out slightly garbled as if she was drunk, or concussed.

'You can shut up,' Harriet said. 'You'd better stop her interfering, Tyler. There's another set of cuffs in the bag, and a ball gag. Use Winkle's tie on her ankles. Better get her boots off first.'

Tyler squeezed past Jasmine to collect the items. This was her chance, Jasmine thought. She twisted round to face the door, heaved herself onto her feet and staggered two small steps towards the door. Her limbs were leaden and she felt as though she was on a storm-tossed boat. She thudded into the door.

'No, you don't. You're not leaving.' Tyler's hand grabbed her shoulder. She fell back onto him. His arms encircled her and he dragged her backwards into the bathroom. He rolled her over onto her stomach. The smooth floor felt reassuringly steady as her head continued to rock with the swell. He drew her hands behind her back and she felt cold metal against her wrists. There was a click as the handcuffs locked. She tried to move her arms to test them but they were immobile.

He moved to her feet undid the zips and tugged the boots off. He quickly tied her ankles tightly together. Then he crouched over her, grabbed her hair and pulled her head back forcing her mouth open. With his spare hand he stuffed a ball in her mouth. He released her head and fastened the strap of the gag behind her neck. She felt his weight leave her and then the door of the bathroom closed. The light in the windowless room went off. Jasmine lay still letting the throbbing pain in her head subside. At least she could breathe. The ball that filled her mouth was hollow and had holes to allow air to enter and leave. When her mind cleared a little, she rolled on to her back, pushed herself into a seated position and leaned her back against the shower cabinet.

Now what? The first thing that occurred to her was that it was just past lunchtime and time for her mid-day dilations. The regular exercise had become such a routine that it dominated her day. The fear of her vagina closing up was a powerful one but she dismissed it. One missed session wouldn't matter, would it? There were far more pressing questions, like how to get out of this mess. Why had Tyler responded so violently to her bit of covert surveillance? What would Harriet's reaction be? She listened to the muffled conversation going on in the bedroom. She couldn't make out a word of it.

It seemed like a long time but was probably only an hour or so when the door to the bathroom opened. The light came on. It was Tyler. He reached down and pulled her to her feet. With her ankles bound together she couldn't stand or walk. Instead he dragged her from the bathroom and dropped her, without any particular care, on the floor beside the bed. She rolled over so that she could see what was happening.

Harriet was still sitting in the one easy chair that the room provided. The slave, that she had called Winkle, was still naked but now was standing with his back to the window. His hands remained fastened behind his back. The chain of the lead hung down to his thighs between which Jasmine could see the steel cage trapping his penis.

Jasmine made a noise which emerged from the gag as a sort of gurgle. She hoped it would urge Harriet to remove it so she could speak. It didn't.

'You can stop making that noise. I don't want to hear your voice, you interfering piece of snot. If you don't shut up I'll get Tyler to make you.'

Jasmine guessed that Tyler was possibly quite eager to carry out that command. His sudden attack on her had allowed her to reassess her opinion of him. Not a besotted, spoilt toy-boy, but a violent, obedient servant who earned his moments of ecstasy with his lover. If he had returned to Thirsbury on the evening of the fire she could imagine him being the person that had murdered Evelyn. The evidence was piling up. All she had to do was get out of this alive.

'I'll get rid of her,' Tyler said in a voice that chilled Jasmine.

'Not here,' Harriet replied, 'You'll leave evidence however careful you are. We didn't come equipped to dispose of a body. There's probably some way we could be traced here even though the room's paid for in Winkle's name.'

'Hmm, right,' was Tyler's response.

'So we get her out of here, and get rid of her somewhere else,' Harriet said.

'Don't forget her car,' Tyler said, 'that blue Mini that we saw following us from Kintbridge.' He directed the last bit at Jasmine. *So much for my tailing skills*, she thought. Perhaps the Mini was a bit too visible after all.

'That's easy,' Harriet said, 'Winkle can drive it away and dump it somewhere a long way from here.'

'But I've got my own car,' the slave said.

Harriet glared at him. 'Quiet! You can come back later to collect your car. You're booked into this room till tomorrow morning. This is what we do. Tyler will drive his car round the back to the fire escape exit. Then you'll take her down the back stairs and put her in the car. Winkle will leave in the Mini and you'll come around the front to pick me up. We leave and no one's the wiser.'

'We're not going to take her back to the house, are we?' Tyler asked.

Harriet pondered. 'No, that's known to the police and they may give us a visit. I'll find somewhere else. One of the others can dispose of her. Someone is going to earn a lovely lot of pleasure.' She reached for her capacious handbag, rummaged inside and pulled out a small notebook. She turned the pages slowly until she found one that took her fancy.

'This one will do. I'll check he's in.' She picked out her phone from the bag and dialled a number. She held the phone to her ear. Jasmine could hear the ringing. It stopped and there was a voice.

'Good afternoon, Peewee. It's your Mistress.' There was some unintelligible reply, 'Yes, I know this is a surprise and an honour for you. You don't have to go babbling on. I have something for you to do. Do you have a spare room? You do. Very good. I will be bringing a person that I want you to look after for a few days. You don't have to ask any questions. I will ensure you are rewarded. We will be with you in an hour or two. Make sure you are ready for my arrival.' She took the phone from her ear and stabbed the screen with a finger-tip. 'There, done.'

Tyler grinned.

'Winkle, come here.' Harriet ordered. The slave scurried around the bed to be at her side. 'Kneel.' He knelt facing her. 'No, the other way, idiot.' He shuffled around on his knees.

Harriet reached forward undid the collar and released the hand cuffs. 'Get up and get dressed.'

He got to his feet, rubbing his wrists as he did so. He reached for the pile of neatly folded clothes that had been placed at the end of the bed. He pulled on the shirt and trousers, apparently, he went knickerless, tugged on socks and shoes and pulled the windcheater over his shoulders.

'Find her car keys,' Harriet ordered. Tyler picked up Jasmine's bag that had lain on the floor by the door since her enforced entry. He unzipped it and tipped it upside down. As he scattered the contents, Jasmine's phone began to ring and vibrate across the carpet. He stamped on it, shattering the screen into tiny fragments. The ringtone ceased.

Harriet clapped her hands slowly and lightly. 'Well done, Tyler. We've got bits of phone all over the floor now. Winkle, start putting them back in the bag. Make sure you get every piece.' The slave got down onto his knees and picked up the larger bits of the phone.

Tyler shuffled Jasmine's other possessions, picking up the keys to the Mini. He also picked up her dilator.

'What's this?' He asked raising it up for all of them to see. 'A dildo? A pretty boring one if it is.'

Harriet peered at it. 'Ah, I know. She's only just had her cock cut off. She has to stuff that up her new hole to keep it open. Is that right, you little fake?'

Jasmine nodded.

Tyler giggled. 'I'd like to see that.'

'You what?' Harriet laughed. 'You want to see what an artificial cunt looks like. Well, I suppose you're like all men. You'd stick your cock in any hole offered to you. Maybe I'll let you when we get her somewhere else, but I'm disappointed, Tyler. I thought it was only my delightful fanny you had a longing for.'

Tyler mumbled something like 'Of course, darling.'

'Come on, let's get a move on,' Harriet urged. 'Give the keys to Winkle, then go and bring the car round the back. We'll wait here for you to return.'

Tyler tossed the keys in the direction of the slave who was still bent over on the carpet. He fumbled them and they fell to the floor. Harriet tutted as he scrambled to pick them up. Tyler left.

Harriet addressed the slave. 'Go down to the fire exit and let Tyler in. Don't draw attention to yourself.' Winkle did as he was told. Harriet let out a sigh and stretched out her black booted legs. She looked down at Jasmine.

'What are we going to do with you? Tyler does over-react rather and then leaves me to pick up the pieces. Now I've got to deal with you and I'm not having you ruin my life.'

She closed her eyes as if taking a nap. Jasmine struggled against the handcuffs binding her arms behind her back, but they were secure. There was no chance of escape. She couldn't see how she was going to get away but she had to stay alert to any opportunity. The trouble was that the throbbing in her head was distracting her.

Some minutes later, Tyler and Winkle returned.

'There's no one around the back at the moment but we'd better get moving,' Tyler said.

'Well, don't stand around, get her down there. Help him, Winkle.'

The two men each grabbed one of Jasmine's arms and pulled her to her feet. They dragged her to the door, glanced up and down the corridor and then set off to the fire escape at the opposite end from the lift. The stairs were bare concrete and Jasmine's ankles got a bashing as they hauled her downwards. Tyler barged the fire door open and they carried her to the car just outside. The boot opened electronically and like the cliché sack of potatoes, Jasmine was dumped inside. The boot closed and locked. She was trapped.

The car began to move slowly and then stopped. Jasmine felt the suspension adjust as someone, presumably Harriet got in, the door clunked shut and then they were off. The speed increased and Jasmine was thrown around by the manoeuvres.

Then they settled down to a steady drive. Jasmine began to feel chilled as the cold air rushing under the car cooled the floor of the boot.

20

The car came to a halt. Jasmine rolled against the bulkhead. Then there was some more manoeuvring before the engine stopped. She felt cold and stiff. Her mouth was dry having spent an hour drooling through the gag. Swallowing was really difficult with the plastic ball filling her mouth. The boot lid swung open. She looked up to see sky and Tyler Smith leaning over. He dragged her into a sitting position. She saw that they were backed up a driveway between houses. There was a door open alongside the car. Harriet was standing in the doorway talking to a naked man. He was bent over, his head bobbing as if he couldn't bear to look at her. Jasmine corrected herself. He wasn't allowed to look at her.

Tyler put his arms beneath her and heaved. He lifted her out of the boot, staggered the few steps to the doorway and dropped her on the floor inside.

'Hurry up,' Harriet insisted, 'Get the door closed. We don't want neighbours watching, or seeing you naked, Peewee. Why on earth haven't you got some clothes on.'

'You said to be ready for your arrival,' the man whined, 'Mistress de la Clef always desires her slaves to be naked.'

From the floor, Jasmine looked up at the skinny, bald man. He looked to be in his late forties and of about average height. He had a silver cage around his penis and testicles, fastened by a sizeable brass padlock. Harriet slapped him around the face.

'Don't be cheeky, Peewee, and don't anticipate what I might want of you. Now don't waste time. Help Tyler get this object up to your spare room.'

Tyler reached down to grab Jasmine around her torso and drag her to her feet. Peewee took her ankles and together they carried her up the stairs and into a bedroom. She was dumped onto a double bed that had a bare mattress and chromed steel bars at the head and foot. Harriet pulled the curtains across the window. She turned and looked at Jasmine.

'That's convenient. We can fasten her to the bars. We don't want her wandering, do we. Where's the bag with the spare restraints, Tyler?'

'Still in the car, I suppose.'

'Well, go and get them.'

Tyler departed.

Jasmine made several attempts to swallow. The house owner examined her.

'She seems to be having trouble with the gag, Mistress.'

Harriet peered at Jasmine. 'You'd better take it off her. We don't want her choking on her own spit.'

The man reached around Jasmine's head to undo the straps of the gag. He tugged the ball from her mouth. Jasmine took a deep breath and closed her mouth. Her jaws ached.

'Don't make a sound,' Harriet said, 'Or you'll have it back in and feel the weight of my hand.'

Tyler returned with the holdall. Harriet took it from him and opened it up. She pulled out the dog collar and lead.

'Here put this on her and tie it to the headboard.'

Tyler took the collar and put it around Jasmine's neck. He fastened the buckle then pulled the lead tight to a bar at the head of the bed, wound it round a few times and tied a knot. Jasmine found she could only move her head from side to side a few inches.

'Now undo her ankles,' Harriet ordered. 'Hold her legs, Peewee, in case she foolishly decides to kick.'

Peewee held her feet while Tyler struggled with the knot that held the tie around her ankles. It had become tightened by her struggles. Eventually Tyler gave up and took a penknife from his pocket. He cut through the material and pulled the remains of the tie from her legs.

'Put the cuffs on her,' Harriet said.

Tyler looked at Jasmine's legs enclosed in tights. 'You said I could see what her fanny looks like.'

'Oh, god, Tyler. Do you ever think of anything other than sex?' Jasmine caught Harriet's eyes looking at her. 'Why not. Getting rid of her clothes might make her a bit more subservient. Don't undo the cuffs though. Use your knife.'

Tyler leaned over her. He undid the buttons of her jacket and then hacked at her jumper and vest-top. He peeled them back to reveal her bra and torso. He slid the blade of the knife under her bra between the cups. Jasmine struggled to stop herself shaking. Her fear of the knife was likely to cause him to injure her if she couldn't keep still. The material gave way and the cups popped off spilling out her enhancers.

'There,' Harriet sneered, 'I knew she was a fake. Hasn't got any boobs of her own to speak of.'

Tyler folded the knife and dropped it into his pocket. He reached down to Jasmine's side and pulled on the zip of her skirt. Then he tugged the garment down her legs revealing her tights. He stretched across her and inserted both hands into the waistband. With a grunt he pulled her tights and knickers over her hips and down her legs and off her feet.

Jasmine closed her eyes. She couldn't bear looking at the three people staring at her. Only Angela had ever seen her naked when she was a man and only Viv, other than doctors and nurses, had viewed her new physiology. She gasped when she felt her legs rudely dragged apart.

'She looks pretty normal,' Tyler said, 'She's got flaps and a cunt.'

'It's artificial, as I told you, Tyler,' Harriet said. 'Like a plastic flower it may look and feel real, but it doesn't produce nectar, can't make seed or turn into a fruit. She's an imitation. No more real than those blow-up dolls that wankers use. She can't satisfy you like a real woman.'

'Well…' Tyler sounded unsure.

'Come on. Let's get back. I can satisfy you far more than she could. Fasten her legs.' Harriet insisted. Her voice took on an authoritarian tone. 'Don't let her go, Peewee. I'll let you know what I want done with her.'

The slave muttered a quiet, 'Yes, Mistress.'

'And don't worry. You will receive your reward,' she added.

The cuffs were locked around her ankles and then the three left the bedroom. Jasmine listened carefully for any further conversation but could not make out any more words before she heard the door close and the car start up.

There were footsteps on the stairs, then on the landing, but they passed by the door. A few minutes later the door did open and the slave entered the room. He stood over Jasmine. He was dressed now. He looked down at her almost naked body without speaking.

'You have to let me go,' Jasmine said, 'Kidnapping is a serious crime.'

He didn't speak for several heartbeats but merely stared at her breasts and stomach and the re-growth of hair on her pubic mound.

'Was Mistress right? Have you had a sex-change?'

'Yes. That bit's true,' Jasmine said, 'but she's wrong. I'm not a fake. I am a woman.'

'You could have intercourse with a man.'

For a moment Jasmine worried that the man was contemplating raping her then she remembered that his penis was locked in a cage and that he couldn't have an erection. He was unable to have sex and indeed any arousal would cause him discomfort, even pain.

'I will, when I'm fully recovered,' she said, 'It's not long since I had the operation.'

He nodded and continued to gaze at her. She wondered whether he had ever looked at a naked woman before.

'I'm feeling a bit cold. Can you cover me up, please?'

He shook his head. 'Mistress said to keep you naked. I'll turn the heating up a little.' He left the room.

21

SUNDAY 20ᵀᴴ OCTOBER
LATE AFTERNOON

Tom Shepherd faced Elvis Preston across the interview table. Griffith's solicitor was alongside the fixer. Terry sat beside Tom and set the recording going.

'You know why we've arrested you, Elvis,' Tom said.

Preston glared. 'I've forgotten. Tell me again.'

Tom smiled at him. 'You have been arrested on suspicion of conspiracy to defraud the company insuring Molly's in Thirsbury and assisting in the arson of the premises.'

Elvis shrugged. 'Don't know what you are talking about.'

'You knew Evelyn Bunting,'

'Yeah. So what?'

'You knew he owed a large sum of money to your boss.'

Elvis shrugged again.

'State your answer to the question, please.'

'Yeah, I knew that.'

'You knew Bunting couldn't pay.'

'I knew he wouldn't pay.'

'Wouldn't?' Tom exclaimed, 'Can you imagine a person like Evelyn Bunting standing up to a thug like you and refusing to pay back the loan?'

'Who are you calling a thug? I work for a respected businessman.'

'I'm sorry Elvis, I wouldn't want to hurt your feelings,' Tom said. 'But come on. Evelyn was hardly in a position to tough it out. He saw a way out, though. Burn down the place and claim the insurance. He renewed, and increased, his cover a few weeks before the fire. But he couldn't be the one to do it. He needed someone else to start the fire and make it look like an attack on the business.'

'That's a nice story you're telling,' Elvis said. 'but I'm not one of the characters in it.'

'Are you sure. Elvis? You've had experience of setting a few fires.'

'That was a long time ago when I was a kid.'

'I imagine lighting a fire is bit like riding a bike. It's not a skill you forget. And we've got CCTV evidence of you near to the premises on the evening of the fire. You live in Kintbridge so what were you doing in Thirsbury in the evening if not to do a bit of fire-lighting.'

'It's a pleasant town for an evening out. Some good pubs.'

'Oh, so can you give us names of people who will vouch for your presence in one of them when the fire was being started?'

Elvis pursed his lips.

'Of course, as well as the fire there is the matter of who killed Evelyn Bunting, at the same time or perhaps a little before. As you were on the spot, perhaps you are in the frame for that as well.'

'I didn't kill the weirdo.'

'Weirdo?'

'This woman's clothes lark. Everyone knew he was a bloke.'

'Does it matter what people wear? It doesn't affect them getting into debt does it?'

'No, but it doesn't mean he didn't have a screw loose.'

'So, you didn't think much of Evelyn Bunting. Perhaps you weren't too bothered about murdering him.'

'I told you I didn't do that.'

'What did you do then, Elvis?'

Preston's mouth opened but no words came out.

'Answer me that, Elvis.'

'No comment.'

Tom grinned and stood up. 'We'll leave you to talk it over with your lawyer. Come on DC Hopkins.'

Tom walked out of the interview room with Terry close behind. In the corridor, Terry spoke quietly.

'He didn't like being accused of the murder.'

'Hmm, no. I think that denial's genuine, but I'm sure he was in on the arson.'

'I think you're probably right, boss, but we need a bit more to go on.'

'Yeah. Let's see if Sasha has got anywhere with his phone. It's been a few hours since we brought Preston in. The delay in getting hold of Griffiths' lawyer gave us a bit of time there.'

They hurried up to the office. Sasha was there alone, eyes focussed on the bright screen of her computer

'Still no sign of Hamid?' Tom asked.

'No. He's still at the house where Harriet Bunting is staying. There's no sign of her or Smith.'

'I wonder what they're up to. They've been out all afternoon. We can't keep a patrol car on standby for much longer. Give him a call, Terry. See if there's any news. Have you got anywhere with Preston's phone, Sasha?' He stood by DC Patel's side and looked at the screen.

'There's a lot of phone calls, Sir, a few are from call boxes. Three of them were made from a box near where the Bunting's lived.'

Tom clenched his fist and almost let out a yelp of joy. He restrained himself. 'That's brilliant, Sasha. Just what we were looking for. When were they?'

Patel peered at the screen, 'One was about two weeks ago, then a week later and the final one was on the evening of the fire.'

'Okay, so we've no proof that it was Evelyn making those calls but it looks likely. It must be them making arrangements for the fire.'

'Looks like that, Sir.'

Tom's mobile started ringing in his jacket pocket. He pulled it out, glanced at the screen, pulled a confused face and answered it.

'Hi, Viv. What can I do for you?' He listened while Jasmine's partner spoke.

'How long has she been out?' a pause, 'And she's not answering?' Viv went on a bit more. 'Her what? Her exercises? Oh yes, I remember her mentioning them. Okay, if you're worried, I'll put out a call for her car. What? It's not the old Fiesta. Okay, what's the number of the new car.' He grabbed a pen from Sasha's desk and scribbled a car registration on a piece of paper. 'Right, thanks, Viv. I'm sure she'll turn up. You know what she's like when she gets on a job. Bye.'

He ended the call and stood thinking.

'What was that, Sir?' Sasha asked.

'That was Jasmine's fella, Viv. He's expecting her for dinner and she hasn't turned up. She's hasn't been in touch since she went out this morning.

Sasha said, 'Jasmine is used to long shifts. It's not that long. Why is her boyfriend concerned?'

Tom was biting his lip. 'I think it's because Jasmine is still recovering from her operation. You know what. And Viv says she needs to do some exercises three times a day.'

'Exercises?'

'Yes, I can't go into what they are. Jasmine rushed off at lunchtime on Thursday because she needed to do them…'

'Oh.'

'Well, there's that and Viv said she promised to be home by now because he was preparing dinner.'

'Perhaps what she went out for has taken longer than she expected.'

'She was only going to see Gary Nicholls. I didn't expect her to wait there all day if he wasn't home. Perhaps she's been taken ill.

'What would you like me to do, Sir?'

'Give Nicholls a ring. See if he's home and ask him if he's seen Jas. I'll get a general call put out for her car. Viv says she's got rid of that old Fiesta and bought a Mini. About time.' He went into his office and sat at his computer.

A few minutes later Tom looked up as Sasha approached the office. 'Any news?' he asked.

Sasha had a worried frown. 'I spoke to Nicholls. He got back from his holiday this morning.'

'Did Jasmine call on him?'

DC Patel nodded. 'Yes. It was about eleven. He says she stayed for about forty minutes, had a coffee, then left. His girlfriend was there too. He says she will corroborate the time.'

Tom pondered. 'So Jasmine left there before mid-day. Where did she go? Nicholls didn't say?'

'I asked, but he didn't know.'

'I wonder. He must have said something that sent Jasmine off somewhere. Why didn't she call in? She will go off on her own.' He paused, then got up. 'I think we need to pay a visit on Mr Nicholls and see what he and Jasmine talked about. Come with me Sasha.' As they were leaving the main office, Tom called out to Terry. 'Keep an eye on things, Terry, and tell Hamid to stick it out with Bunting and Smith. I want Smith brought in as soon as they appear. And let me know if there's any news about Jasmine.'

'What's Frame up to now?'

'She's missing, Terry.'

Tom pulled up outside Nicholl's home. The brick-clad house glowed red in the sun, low in the west.

'It looks as though Nicholls has done pretty well for himself. Let's go and have a chat.' He got out of the Mondeo and Sasha Patel followed him up to the front door. He rang the bell. It was answered fairly soon by a young, blonde woman wearing a mini skirt over leggings and a tight top that revealed most of her breasts.

'Hello,' Tom began, 'we'd like to speak to Mr Nicholls. Is he home?'

The woman frowned. 'Who are you?'

Tom and Sasha both drew out their warrant cards and held them up. 'I'm Detective Inspector Shepherd and this is DC Patel.'

'Oh, you're real police, not like the one who called this morning.'

'You spoke to Jasmine?' Tom asked.

'The trans-whatsit?'

'Um, yes,' Tom knew how sensitive Jasmine was to being identified. She can't have liked being picked out by this young woman.

'She had lots of questions about Gary's old lover.'

'Harriet Bunting? Yes, we'd like to ask him about that.'

'You'd better come in then.' The girl stepped back, allowing them to enter the large hallway and then lead them into the lounge.'

Gary Nicholls rose from the sofa. 'Who is it, darling...' he began as Tom and Sasha followed her.

'It's the police, Gary. Real ones this time.'

Nicholls frowned. 'That woman I spoke to this morning said she was with the police. Wasn't she...'

Tom answered, 'Jasmine was asking questions on our behalf but she is not a police officer anymore.'

'Is that because she's not a real woman?' the young woman asked.

'Not at all,' Tom replied, 'and I think Jasmine would insist that she is a woman, especially now.'

'Oh, she's had the op has she?' Tracy said.

Tom frowned at her. Did Jasmine find her as insulting when she had been here? Did the woman realise what she was saying?

'Miss Frame is the reason we are here,' Tom said. He introduced himself and Sasha. 'you spoke to DC Patel a short while ago and said that Jasmine left you about mid-day.'

Nicholls answered. 'Oh, it was earlier than that. She wasn't here very long. About a-quarter-to twelve I suppose.'

'And she didn't say where she was going next?' Tom looked from Nicholls to his girlfriend.

They both shook their heads, then Nicholls let out a laugh. 'You've lost your investigator, haven't you? That's clever.'

Tom took a breath. 'Miss Frame has been out of touch for

over five hours. She is still supposed to be convalescing,' he glanced at Tracy who looked smug. 'so we're a little concerned about her whereabouts.'

'Well, I don't know where she went,' Nicholls said, 'that's what I told you on the phone,' he nodded his head at Sasha.

'We realise she didn't tell you where she was going,' Tom said, 'but we're wondering if you said something to her that might have sent her somewhere.'

Nicholls shrugged. 'We talked about the Buntings.'

'Your affair with Mrs Bunting and your part in the bankrupting of Evelyn Bunting's business.'

Nicholls drew himself up straight, his face red. 'I had nothing to do with that.'

'You accepted a hundred thousand pounds from Bunting.'

'I told your missing investigator that that was Harriet's doing. She wanted rid of me and I was happy to leave her to that toyboy of hers.'

'Tyler Smith.'

'That's him.'

Tom frowned. There was nothing unexpected there. 'Was that all you discussed?'

Tracy sidled up to Gary and flung her arms around his waist. 'What did you talk about when you sent me out for the cream, Garypops. I know you were embarrassed. You've never asked for cream before. Was it about you having sex with Evie Bunting?'

Nicholls stared down at her and blushed. 'How do you know?'

The girl smiled, 'You mention her name sometimes when you dream, and whatshername, Jasmine, told me that Evie is a man. Well, she didn't say that exactly, but I know what she meant. What's it like fucking a man, Gary?'

'It wasn't like that, not really,' Gary was sweating, 'and that wasn't what we talked about.' The girl pushed herself away from him.

Tom butted in to the exchange between the two lovers.

'What was it you *did* talk about then Mr Nicholls?'

Gary looked from his girlfriend to DI Shepherd and DC Patel. He sighed and subsided onto the sofa.

'OK. It's nothing I had any part in other than driving Harriet to her appointments.' He paused.

'What did you have nothing to do with?' Tom urged him on.

'Her men, her slaves. The ones she charges for holding their keys.'

'The keys to the chastity cages?' Tom wanted confirmation. Nicholls nodded. 'We know about that. Jasmine told me last night about two of the guys Mrs Bunting was with on Tuesday evening. Smith wasn't with her when she was, um, servicing them.'

'That's what I said,' Nicholls said, appealing to Tracy. 'I didn't stay in the room while Harriet made them perform for her.'

'But something you said might have set Jasmine thinking. What did you say to her?'

Nicholls shook his head. 'I don't know, I hardly knew those weirdoes. They just seemed to worship her like a goddess and would do anything she asked them to do.'

'Anything?'

'Well, I don't know, but they did everything Harriet told them to do, whether it was paying for the hotels or buggering each other. Harriet was always going on about the stuff she made them do. It tickled her.'

Tom was thoughtful, 'The men will do whatever Harriet Bunting ordered them to do?'

'That's what I said,' Nicholls glared at Tom.

'Including arson or murder?'

Nicholls looked worried, as if he realised that he could be an accessory to whatever criminal acts Harriet had made her slaves take part in. 'She never mentioned anything like that.'

'But perhaps, under pressure, she would use whatever resources she had,' Tom mused. He turned to Sasha. 'Do you think perhaps that was what Jasmine thought and decided to ask

Harriet Bunting some more questions?'

'Perhaps, Sir, but Hamid has been at the address Harriet Bunting is staying at since soon after mid-day and there hasn't been any sign of them, or Jasmine.'

'We need to find Harriet and Tyler and then perhaps we'll find Jasmine. Come on.' Tom faced Nicholls and Tracy. 'Thank you, Mr Nicholls for your assistance. We may have other questions later.'

Tracy smiled sweetly at them. 'I'll see you out.' She lead Tom and Sasha back to the front door. 'I hope you find your tranny helper.'

As Tom stepped across the door step he turned and glared. 'Jasmine has as much right to be called a woman as you, and she is a very competent detective. I suggest you choose the terms you refer to people by carefully, or else you might find yourself charged with using offensive language.'

The woman's face turned from smug to worried. She closed the door.

Sasha stood staring at the door. 'What's she got against Jasmine?'

'You tell me,' Tom said, 'I'm just a poor, bemused bloke.'

'Hmm,' Sasha mused, 'I think she's got confused by her boyfriend's history with the Buntings and is asserting her femininity and heterosexuality. You know some feminists have it in for transsexuals like Jasmine.'

'I wouldn't have considered Nicholls' girlfriend a radical feminist but perhaps you're right. Come on. Let's see if there's any news of Bunting and Smith – and Jasmine.' They hurried back to the police car. Tom called Terry Hopkins.

'Hi Terry. Any news?'

'Some. Bunting and Smith turned up. Hamid arrested Smith and is bringing him in.'

'What about Harriet?'

'You didn't want her arrested.'

Tom winced. Should he have asked for her to be brought in too? 'I know. Where is she?'

'Still where she's staying I expect.'

'Hmm, right. Did she or Smith tell Hamid where they'd been all afternoon?'

'I don't know. Hamid didn't say whether he'd had a conversation. I think he was chuffed that he didn't have to sit in the car any longer.'

'No word on Jasmine then?'

'Nope.'

'OK Terry. We're coming back.'

Tom Shepherd pushed open the door to the office and was pleased to see Hamid talking to Terry.

'Hamid. Did Bunting or Smith mention speaking to Jasmine.'

The young detective shook his head. 'No, I didn't ask if they had seen her. I didn't know...'

'Of course not,' Tom said 'but from what Nicholls said I'm sure Jasmine was keen to speak to Mrs Bunting again. Did they say where they'd been all day?'

'They said they had been out for Sunday lunch,' Hamid replied.

'Where?'

'I don't know. I didn't ask. I didn't think where they had been was important.'

'No, there wasn't any reason for you to ask. We'll have a chat with Tyler Smith in a minute.'

'He's being processed,' Hamid said.

An alert pinged on Terry's computer. He bent down to look at the screen.

'Hey, that's weird.'

'What is?' Tom said.

'There's a sighting of Frame's new car.'

'Where?'

'On the M6, near Stoke.'

'What on earth...' Tom leaned down alongside Hopkins and stared at the screen.

'Oh, god!' Terry shouted.

Sasha and Hamid gathered round.

'What's happened?' Sasha said.

Tom turned from the screen. 'The patrol car that picked up Jasmine's car, followed her but she refused to stop. She's crashed into the central barrier.'

All four of the detectives stared at the screen. Tom grabbed the phone and punched buttons. The other three stood looking on as he waited for a connection. He gave his name, asked a few questions, listened then put the phone down.

'Well?' Terry said, 'What's going on?'

Tom was deep in thought then looked at DC Hopkins as if just seeing him. He smiled.

'It wasn't Jasmine.'

The three officers appeared bemused. 'What do you mean?' Terry asked, 'It was her car, wasn't it?'

'Yes, it was. They've checked the number. It's still registered to the garage that Viv bought it from. But it's definitely the car Jasmine picked up yesterday.'

'So, what the fuck was it doing on the M6?' Terry asked.

'We don't know yet, but had presumably been stolen,' Tom explained. 'When the ANPR flagged it up, the patrol car tried to get it to stop but the driver speeded up. In trying to pass a car in the outside lane it hit the central reservation and rolled. When the officers got to the car they found the driver was some guy. They haven't been able to speak to him yet. He's not badly injured but he's been taken to hospital in Stoke. There's no sign of Jasmine.'

Terry asked, 'So where's Frame? Why hasn't she reported her car stolen?'

Tom shook his head. 'I don't know. Her phone isn't responding.'

'Perhaps Tyler Smith knows something,' Hamid said.

Tom straightened up. 'Yes, it's time we spoke to him. Sasha, come with me. Terry and Hamid, go and see Mrs Bunting again. Persuade her to come in for questioning.'

'Under arrest?' Terry said.

'There's no evidence that she was involved in the arson attack on her home or the death of her husband, so no, not under arrest. Be polite. Try to convince her that she's helping us.'

'What about searching for Jasmine?' Sasha asked.

'Where? We've got no idea of where she went after leaving Nicholls. There's a general call out for her. That will have to do for now.' The four detectives moved towards the door.

22

Jasmine tensed her muscles and pulled against the cuffs binding her wrists, to no avail. She rested, trying to ignore the ache in her head, listening for any sounds indicating what Peewee was doing. There was nothing, but she did slowly feel a little warmer. He must have turned the heating up as he had promised. That made her feel better; he was concerned for her welfare and comfort even if obeying Madame de la Clef was uppermost in his mind. Jasmine took the opportunity to review what she knew about the four of Bunting's slaves that she had so far met. They were all at or approaching middle age, apparently single and all seemed besotted with her. They might vary in physical characteristics, unless Willy could be considered the odd one out, being overweight while the others were slim, but they seemed to have the single desire to obey their mistress. They must have imposed their chastity on themselves, she presumed, prior to handing their keys to Harriet but having fallen under her spell they were like potter's clay in her hands.

After a time that Jasmine had failed to keep track of, she heard steps on the stairs again. The door to her room was pushed open and Peewee entered. He carried a tumbler containing a colourless, clear liquid.

'I thought you might need a glass of water,' he said.

A feeling of gratitude welled up in Jasmine. She had been trying to ignore her thirst and the dryness of her mouth.

'Thank you,' she said. She twisted on her back with her hands underneath her and lifted her head. He lowered the glass to her and she sipped the liquid. The cool water was the best restorative. She swallowed. 'What's your real name? I can't call you Peewee like Harriet Bunting does. That's her slave-name for you.'

He frowned as if weighing up what answer he should give. 'It's Clive,' he said finally.

'Thank you for the water, Clive.'

His gaze at her almost naked body made Jasmine nervous.

'How long is it since your operation?' he asked.

'Nearly six weeks,' she answered.

'You're still recovering?'

'Yes. It takes a long time.'

'You had your penis and testicles removed and a vagina constructed?'

'That's right.'

'That is serious surgery.'

Yes, Jasmine thought, *and if I can't get back to my routine of exercise soon it will all be wasted.* It was now time for her third dilation of the day and she had missed the second already.

'Why did you do it?' he asked. 'Why give up your penis?'

'I'm a woman,' Jasmine replied, 'I wanted to have a woman's body.'

He shook his head. 'I wouldn't want that.'

She decided to ask a question which might extend the conversation or end it. 'Why do you keep your penis locked up?'

His hand reached to his groin. 'My Mistress desires it.'

'But you must have chosen to give yourself to your Mistress. Why?'

'I was having thoughts.'

'What kind of thoughts?'

'Sinful thoughts, selfish thoughts.'

'Sexual fantasies?'

He nodded.

'You thought wearing a chastity device would control your desires?'

He nodded again.

'Does it?'

'Yes. If I even think of sex and I start to become aroused the cage presses against my flesh causing me pain.'

'OK, if that's the effect you want, but why did you give yourself to Harriet Bunting?'

He grimaced at the sound of Madame's real name. 'Possessing the key myself was too much of a temptation. I had to put it out of my reach and give the responsibility of freeing myself from my wicked thoughts to her. She has control. I only have to carry out what she desires of me. Nothing that I feel matters anymore.'

Jasmine couldn't understand. 'But she makes her slaves perform sex acts on themselves or on each other. A couple of them told me what they did. How does that help your sinful fantasies?'

'Because it is what Madame desires not what I wish, and those acts can only occur when She has given her permission.'

It was all nonsense, Jasmine considered. These men were deluded, and paying for it.

'You would do anything your Mistress told you to do in order to remain under her control.'

He nodded. 'You don't understand the joy that I and my fellow slaves get from pleasing Madame.'

'No, I don't.'

'You think we have given in to erroneous thoughts.'

'Yes.'

'But aren't you the same? You have denied your masculinity, removed the symbol of your manhood and accepted a role as a pseudo-female.'

Jasmine felt a burst of anger. 'I am a real woman. I have always been a woman even when I had a penis and testicles. Now I can have intercourse like a woman.'

'But as Madame said, you cannot bear fruit like a woman. You have no ovaries. You do not produce eggs.'

'Many women cannot have children,' Jasmine insisted.

'What then was your purpose in having the operation?' he

asked, 'Was it just so that you could have a man insert his penis into your new hole?'

His question made Jasmine gasp. Was that really all that she had gone through the pain and discomfort of her surgery for, at great expense to the health service. No. It wasn't called Gender Confirmation Surgery for no reason. Her possession of a vagina proved she was a woman. She did want to have sex with one man, Viv, as soon as she was healed fully. She was looking forward to the pleasure of that act and was hopeful that when her nerves had fully recovered she would be able to reach a climax as a woman. But that wasn't the point of her operation, was it?'

'That's important, but having a vagina confirms that I am a woman. That's what is important to me, and why I must exercise.'

'Exercise?'

'I have to keep my vagina open. If I don't it will close up and I won't be fully a woman anymore.'

He bent down to her. 'How do you do it?'

'I have to dilate three times a day.'

'Dilate?'

'Insert a tube, like a dildo.'

He stood up and chuckled. 'I have a dildo for a similar reason.'

Jasmine was confused. 'What?'

'Madame has told me I must prepare myself for my next appointment.'

Jasmine didn't understand at first and then realisation dawned.

'She wants to have one of her slaves bugger you!'

Clive's face turned pink.

'You're not gay. You haven't done that before have you?'

He shook his head.

'But your mistress is making you do it to earn you a few minutes relief from your cage.'

He nodded. 'She says I must prepare myself by inserting the

dildo every day.'

'How big is it?'

'I have two. I am using the smaller one. I haven't yet managed the larger.'

Jasmine thought of a way of achieving one or two of her desires.

In a coy voice she said, 'I'd like to see if yours are the same size as the ones I use.'

A hungry look appeared on his face. 'You'd like to use one of my dildos to do your exercise?'

'Perhaps. I hope you clean them properly.'

He looked offended. 'Of course. If I let you borrow them you will let me watch?'

She smiled. 'I can hardly stop you doing that.' It was the last thing she wanted but it suited her purpose.

Clive left the room but returned a few moments later grasping an object in each hand. He held them up to show Jasmine. She grimaced when she saw the dildos. One was a huge black implement, eight inches long and a couple of inches in diameter. She didn't want that anywhere near her groin. The other was a pink phallus of more acceptable dimensions no bigger than her middle dilator.

She nodded to the smaller dildo. 'I could use that one. Do you have any lube? I can't use it dry.'

He left again and returned with a tube replacing the larger tool. He unscrewed the top and squeezed an ample quantity of the gel over the phallus.

'You'll have to let me spread my legs,' Jasmine said.

Clive put the lubricated dildo down on the mattress and looked pensive.

'Madame said you must be kept bound.'

'But she also said you must look after me. I need this, Clive.'

'Hmm, okay.' He pulled apart the Velcro holding the cuff around her right leg and re-fixed it around a bar in the foot-board. 'There. How's that.'

Jasmine stretched her legs. Her right leg was free to bend or

227

stretch as she pleased. She didn't want to give Peewee Clive a glimpse of her vulva but the relief at being able to move overcame her reluctance. She parted her legs. Clive stared as if in a trance.

'Thank you, Clive. Now can you let me have a hand free to hold the dildo, please.' She rolled on to her left side so that the slave could get at her arms. He bent down and undid the handcuff around her right wrist and refastened it around one of the head-board's bars. Jasmine twisted round, her left hand now above her head and her right hand free.

'Give me the dildo please, Clive.' He placed it in her hand.

She parted her thighs and raised her right knee. She touched the tip of the dildo to her vulva, and gasped. The first touch on her clitoris was always a surprise, perhaps because the contours of her flesh were still new and unfamiliar and the nerves not yet fully recovered. She rubbed the greased tip of the tool against her labia, to give them some lubrication.

'Do you want to come closer, Clive,' she said softly, 'You want to see, don't you?'

He leaned over the bed, his head between her legs. She pushed the dildo against her hole, ever so gently. The tip passed between her lips, entering her. She gasped again. It wasn't painful, rather the opposite.

'Come on Clive, closer. See how it's entering me like a real cock could. Like your cock could if it was free.'

Her taunt encouraged him to bend closer, his head approaching her groin. She lifted her foot so that it was over his shoulder. He peered at the implement protruding from her vagina. She pushed it lightly and it slid further in. Clive's head followed it.

She brought her right thigh down across his neck. Trapping his head against her left thigh. She squeezed, applying all the force she could muster in her thigh muscles and hips. His arms flailed and his legs kicked out. His fingers grabbed at her legs but failed to find a grip. She caught his left arm in her hand and twisted. His screech was muffled by the thigh compressing his throat. His body heaved but she hung on, squeezing with all the power she could muster.

She could feel her energy draining away. Her level of fitness had not been maintained during her convalescence. She gasped for breath. A strange rasping sound came from his mouth as air failed to enter his lungs. He was weakening too. She mustn't give up. This was her one chance of freedom. She pressed her thighs together as hard as she could.

His arms and legs went limp. His struggles ceased. She held on for a few seconds longer. Then released him. His body slipped from between her legs and he slumped to the floor beside the bed. Was he dead? She didn't know but she had to get free – quickly.

Her left wrist was still above her head, but she could see the catch that locked the handcuff. Her right hand undid it. Her hands were free. Now she just had to release the lead attached to the neck collar. The chain had pulled tight but by pushing at it, she was able to loosen and untie it. Her upper body was free at last. She pushed herself up and winced. The pressure from her thighs had forced the dildo deep into her vagina. She lay back and felt between her labia for the base of it. Her heart was beating fast. Had she damaged herself? Was she haemorrhaging? She grasped it and slid the dildo out. She looked down. There no sign of blood but she felt sore, as if she had been violated. She breathed again and reached forward to tear the Velcro apart from the cuff around her left ankle. She slid across the bed, every muscle in her body aching from being bound and immobile for a few hours and then forced into violent action.

A moan came from the floor. Jasmine rolled off the bed, the dog lead trailing beside her. She knelt beside Clive. He was alive at least. She was glad she hadn't killed him. He wasn't a bad man, just misguided. She crawled back onto the bed and removed the two pairs of cuffs. She reused them on Clive's limbs. When she was sure he was secure and breathing she sat on the bed shaking.

A few minutes passed before she felt ready to move and that

was only when Clive spoke in cracked semi-whisper. 'You tricked me.'

'Perhaps you obey women too easily.'

'Not all women.'

'Some then. Are you feeling okay?'

'My throat hurts.'

'But you can breathe?'

'Yes.'

'Right, you can stay there then.'

He moaned and strained at the bindings but failed to free himself. Jasmine forced herself to stand. Her legs ached, her body ached, her groin was sore and her head felt full of needles. She stepped over the slave and placed a hand on the wall to steady herself. She staggered through the door and down the stairs relying on the banister to keep herself upright. In the hallway she started to look for a phone. She could have asked Clive where it was but she hadn't thought of it and wasn't going back upstairs to speak to him. She went into the first room, a living room, surveyed the contents and saw a handset sitting in a cradle on a sideboard. She picked it up and dialled a familiar number.

23

The line phone rang. Tom paused in the doorway. Terry Hopkins was at the back of the quartet leaving the office.

'Get that, Terry,' Tom said. DC Hopkins turned around and hurried to the desk. He picked up the phone.

'Violent and Serious Crime Unit, DC Hopkins speaking. Hello?' He took the phone from his ear and called out. 'It's Frame.'

The other three officers scrambled around each other to get back into the office.

'Let me speak to her,' Tom reached out his hand. Terry passed him the handset.

'Jasmine? Where are you?' a pause, 'What do you mean you don't know?' A longer pause. 'Are you alright?' a short pause. 'Right, I'll hold, you have a word with this guy.' He took the phone away from his ear.

'What's happened to her?' Sasha asked.

'She was kidnapped, taken in the boot of a car somewhere. She's in a house, she doesn't know where but has managed to overpower her captor.'

'What's she doing now?' Terry grumbled.

'Gone to ask him where they are.'

'Is she harmed?' Hamid asked.

'She sounded okay. A bit shaken perhaps but otherwise normal.' A voice came from the handset. Tom lifted it to his ear.

'I'm here, Jas. Where are you? Ringwood. That's right down in Dorset isn't it. Okay Hampshire. Right. Have you got the address?' He beckoned for a notepad and pen. Sasha placed them on the desk in front of him. 'Okay, give it me. I'll get the local guys out to you ASAP. Are you sure you're safe for a few minutes? Right, good, stay on the line.' He handed the handset to DC Hopkins. 'Keep talking to her Terry. She says she's safe but I'm not sure.'

He grabbed a phone from another desk and started tapping keys.

Terry spoke into the phone. 'It's me again; Terry. Who abducted you, Jasmine?' he listened. 'DI Shepherd thought you might have gone to speak to Bunting. We've got Smith in custody. No, not Bunting. We'll arrest her now. Oh, another thing, your new Mini was involved in a RTC on the M6. Yes, the M6. Probably a write-off. Do you know the guy who was driving it? What was he called? Winkle? What sort of name's that? Oh, I see, a nickname.'

Tom returned. 'Let me speak to her, please Terry.' Hopkins handed over the phone. 'Jas? The local police are on their way, blue lights and sirens. Should be there in minutes. What do you mean you have to get decent? What did they do to you?' He took the phone from his ear and looked around at his colleagues.

'She's gone to find some clothes to wear before the response team turns up. Seems Bunting and Smith stripped her.'

'They raped her?' Sasha cried.

'No, Jas didn't say that, but they did something to her.'

'They're monsters,' Sasha said.

'Hmm, yes. We need to interrogate Harriet Bunting. Terry, Sasha, go and arrest her.' Without another word DCs Hopkins and Patel left the office at a run.

Tom was still holding the phone loosely in his hand when there was the distant sound of sirens. He lifted it to his head, 'Jasmine, are you there? Jasmine! Okay, you go to the door. We'll see you soon.' He ended the call and put the phone down.

'The Hampshire guys have her. She's safe.' Tom said, for his own benefit as much as Hamid's. 'I think we need to have a chat with Tyler Smith, don't you Hamid?'

DC Sassani nodded and together they walked out of the office.

....

Jasmine ran up the stairs. Well, she tried to run, but her complaining muscles refused to carry her fast. She got back to the bedroom. Clive was still trussed up on the floor, she was relieved by that, but he was wheezing, which troubled her. There was no time to look after him now. She needed some clothes on her lower half. She scanned the room. There, flung in a corner, were her tights, knickers and skirt. The police would be here any moment, so just the skirt then. She grabbed it and stepped into it. Hurrying back down the stairs she struggled with the zip.

Sirens were approaching. She heard a voice. It was Tom on the phone. She went into the living room, picked up the handset.

'Yes, I'm here. Got to go, they're here.' She thumbed the end button and dropped the phone onto the sofa. There was banging on the front door and shouts of "Police!". She hurried into the hall. No sense in them bashing the door down. She pulled it open. Two uniformed officers stood in the porch. She saw their eyebrows rise and remembered to tug her anorak and the remains of her top around her body.

'We were told that an incident was in progress here,' the closest police officer said.

'Yes, that's right. Come in. My captor's upstairs in the bedroom.'

The officer pushed past her and climbed the stairs slowly, calling out that he was a police officer. The second officer stepped inside and stood examining Jasmine. There was a strange expression on his face. She realised that the dog collar was still around her neck with the lead trailing over her shoulder. More sirens signalled the imminent arrival of more police.

A call came from the top of the stairs. 'Hey, Kev. Come up here,'

Kev followed his partner up the stairs. Jasmine looked out of the door as the second police car screeched to a halt. She was unsure what to do so just stood watching. Two more officers jumped out of the car and ran towards her.

Kev came back down the stairs speaking into his radio. 'We need an ambulance here,' he said. He looked at Jasmine and frowned.

'Can you come in here please, er, Miss,' he said urging Jasmine into the lounge. 'What's been going on here then? The guy upstairs has bruising on his neck and is having trouble breathing. There's a dildo on the bed. A BDSM scene got a bit out of hand?'

'No, officer, I was being held against my wishes.'

'You were? It's the other guy who is bound like a turkey at Christmas.'

'I know,' Jasmine said, exasperation creeping into her voice. 'I managed to get away and put the cuffs on him, so he couldn't catch me again.'

The second pair of police officers entered. Kev looked at them.

'This is a crime scene, upstairs anyway. Looks like some kind of sex scenario. There's an injured male in the bedroom. You'd better look after this, er, woman.'

'Is she under arrest?' One of the newcomers asked.

'I'm the injured party,' Jasmine complained. The two men and one woman glared at her.

Kev glared at her. 'Get her out of the way while we assess the situation.'

'I haven't got anything on my feet,' Jasmine pointed out. The officers looked down at her bare legs and feet.

'Where are your shoes?' Kev asked.

'I don't know. Basingstoke, I expect.' She looked at the officers' uniforms noting the Hampshire Constabulary badges and insignia.

'How did you get here then?' Kev went on.

'In the boot of a Mercedes.'

The officers raised their eyebrows.

'Get something to cover her feet and put her in your car,' Kev said. The female officer went out.

'There's no Merc outside. Is it in the garage?' Kev asked.

'No, they've gone,' Jasmine said

'They?'

'Harriet Bunting and Tyler Smith.'

Kev looked confused. 'Who are they?'

'Suspects in a case I was working on.'

'You're a police officer?' Kev didn't seem convinced and looked her up and down.

'No, but I was helping out.'

'Who's the guy upstairs?'

'I only know him as Clive.'

Kev frowned as if trying to decide whether to believe what he'd been told.

The female officer returned with a pair of elasticated plastic overshoes. Jasmine took them from her outstretched hand and snapped them over her feet.

'Right. Off you go,' Kev said, 'We'll secure the house for SOCO.'

The woman took Jasmine's arm and tugged her towards the door. Jasmine thought about struggling and complaining but decided this maybe wasn't the time. She could get Tom to sort things out soon. Let the officers do their duty. She allowed herself to be taken to the police car and be put into the back seat. Once she was in, the officer closed the door. With the child-locks operating she wasn't going anywhere. The woman got into the passenger seat. More vehicles were arriving, police cars with lights flashing and sirens sounding.

'What's your name?' the PC asked, 'I need to make a note.'

'Jasmine Frame.'

The officer scribbled it down and spoke into her radio describing to the control centre what was happening. After a few more minutes, an ambulance arrived. Clive would be having a trip to the hospital rather than a custody cell, Jasmine thought, but she hoped he wasn't badly hurt. She didn't want that on her conscience replacing the satisfaction of having escaped from him.

The officer's partner returned and got into the driving seat.

'We've been instructed to get this one to the station,' he said, starting the car.

'Which police station?' Jasmine asked.

The driver twisted around to look at her.

'Southampton. Put the seat belt on please and unless you're not feeling well I suggest you say nothing until you're in the interview room.'

Jasmine tugged the seatbelt across her chest and locked it in place. *I'm still the guilty one as far as they're concerned*, she thought. I hope Tom has told them what's happening. The driver manoeuvred around the other parked vehicles and then they sped off into the night.

....

Tyler Smith was slumped in the chair. He didn't move when Tom and Hamid entered the interview room and presented a bored expression.

'What did you do to Jasmine Frame?' Tom began. Smith jerked as if shocked. Suddenly he looked alert, not bored.

'What do you mean?'

'You abducted Jasmine and took her to Ringwood. Why?'

Smith looked pale and worried, but he didn't speak.

'Tell me, Mr Smith, what did you do to her?'

Tyler shook his head. 'I'm not saying anything. I want a solicitor.'

Tom sighed, a resigned, annoyed sigh. 'You'll get your solicitor, but you will answer questions, because Jasmine will be back soon and she'll have a story to tell. You will be charged with kidnapping, holding someone against their wishes and whatever other offences I can make stick. You and Harriet Bunting. And that's before we start on the murder of Evelyn

Bunting and the arson at Molly's. So, if you want to reduce your time in prison you had better start telling the truth.'

Tom stood and strode out of the interview room. Hamid jumped up with surprise and hurried after him. Tom kept up his determined pace all the way back to the office. As they entered, his phone rang. He dug it out of his jacket pocket.

'Hi, Terry. What's up?'

'She's not here,' DC Hopkins said.

'Bunting's gone? What about the car?'

'The Merc's still here. She doesn't drive does she?'

'I don't think so. She had Smith drive her everywhere.'

'Well, she's not in the house. She's done a runner.'

'Anybody see her leave?'

'Patel's knocking on doors. I spoke to one set of neighbours. They saw nothing. But it's a quiet neighbourhood. She could easily have slipped out without anyone noticing.'

Tom pursed his lips. 'OK, Terry. You and Sasha get back here. We'll put out a call for her and think about where she might have gone.'

Tom ended the call.

Hamid stared at him. 'Harriet Bunting's missing?'

'She's slipped out of our hands, Hamid. Now that tells us a lot about her guilt doesn't it? She doesn't know that we know about Jasmine. She just thinks we've called in Tyler for questioning about the fire and murder. I think her nerve has broken and now she's desperate. Who has she got who can help her?'

Hamid shook his head.

'These guys that Jasmine's been learning about. Her sex slaves.'

'The ones she keeps the keys for?'

'That's right. We need to get Jasmine back quickly. She's got all we know on those strange fellows. Let's find out what's happening down in Hampshire.'

24

The chair was hard. She didn't feel very comfortable. In fact, she felt sore all over and her head and groin were still throbbing. At least she had a mug of coffee, the familiar, cheap, instant variety found in all police stations. She warmed her hands on the mug resting on the table. Jasmine wasn't used to sitting on this side, waiting for someone to come and ask her questions.

It wasn't long before the door opened and an unfamiliar detective entered. He was male, white, with a short beard, the unshaved type of beard. Jasmine didn't get up to greet him, waited for him to say something. He looked at her, glanced at the sheet of paper he was holding then sat down opposite her and looked at her again.

'Jasmine Frame?'

She nodded.

'I'm DS Dobson.'

'How do you do.' Jasmine treated him to a smile. He didn't return it.

'You were picked up in Ringwood this evening at a house belonging to…' he glanced at the sheet, 'Clive Lawton.' He looked at her as if expecting some comment.

'I didn't know his surname,' she said.

'Mr Lawton was found conscious but with an injury to his neck. He's been taken to hospital.'

'I hope he gets well soon.'

Dobson frowned. 'Can you explain how he was injured and what you were doing at the house.'

Jasmine smiled. At last she could explain. 'Mr Lawton was holding me prisoner, but I managed to escape and in doing so he came to some harm.'

'How exactly did you injure him?'

'I crushed his trachea between my thighs until he passed out.'

Dobson grimaced. 'Was that degree of violence necessary?'

'I think so. My arms and legs had been bound and my neck fastened to the head board. I had persuaded Clive to release one arm and leg, but he wouldn't have let me go completely unless I over-powered him.'

'And why were you in this position? Was it some kind of sex game?'

'No. I told you. He was holding me prisoner.'

'Why?'

'On the instructions of Harriet Bunting.'

The DS looked confused, peered at his sheet of paper again then back at Jasmine. 'Who is she?'

'She's a Mistress, a dominatrix if you like. She controls men like Clive Lawton who are her slaves.'

DS Dobson shook his head as if finding Jasmine's story incredible. 'How does she control these "slaves"?'

'She holds the keys to their cock cages.'

The man's eyes widened. 'I don't understand. Where do you fit into this? You're a woman. Aren't you?'

Her anorak was still wrapped around her, so the state of her clothes was not visible. She smiled. Recognition. To be identified as a woman was a sort of justification.

'That's correct. I was helping the police in Kintbridge investigate Mrs Bunting.'

'Kintbridge Police?' He searched the sheet of paper. 'Oh yes, the call came from DI Shepherd. He gave us the address in Ringwood, but the rest of the message was pretty garbled.'

Jasmine sighed. Her poor opinion of communications between different police forces seemed to be accurate.

'Tom didn't know what was happening,' she said.

'Tom?'

'DI Shepherd.'

'Oh, I see. Are you assisting in the investigation of Mrs Bunting for this sex slave ring then?'

'No. I don't think that side of it is illegal. The slaves are consenting adults. I'm helping to investigate the murder of Mrs Bunting's husband.'

Understanding was joined by annoyance on DS Dobson's face. 'I see. You should have notified us if your investigation was taking place in our area.'

Jasmine said, 'I hadn't intended being in your area. I had followed Mrs Bunting to the edge of Basingstoke which was where I was kidnapped. I was carried to Ringwood in the boot of her car.'

'Ah, so Mr Lawton was not involved in your abduction.'

'Not originally. Now can you please let me go so that I can get back to Kintbridge. I need to report to DI Shepherd.' Jasmine started to rise, her limbs complaining

'Um yes. Stay here please for a moment. I'll need to get my senior officer's permission to release you. We'll have to corroborate your story.' He got up and hurried from the room with less authority than when he had arrived. Jasmine sank back into her seat, clenching her fists with irritation.

The detective was back in a few minutes, in an excited state this time.

'The guvnor says you can go but we'll need a statement to explain what happened to Mr Lawton; and there's a phone call for you. DI Shepherd.'

Jasmine jumped up, her aches forgotten. She strode to the door with Dobson at her side.

The detective led her down the corridor to the custody area. He pointed to a phone handset lying on the counter. Jasmine grabbed it.

'Hello? Tom?'

'Jas? You're there?'

'Yes, almost under arrest for what I did to Clive.'

'Clive?'

'Peewee, Harriet's slave. He was my gaoler.'

'Oh. You'll have to fill me in.'

'That doesn't matter. Have you got them?'

'Who?'

'Harriet and Tyler of course.'

'Ah. Smith is under arrest, but Harriet Bunting has gone.'

Jasmine felt her stomach tighten. Damn; she wanted to ask Bunting a few questions.

'Any clues to where she's gone to?'

'No, we hoped you might have some ideas. Look I want to get you back here as soon as poss., but I haven't got a car to send down for you.'

'Well, I haven't.' She recalled being told that her new car, the pretty Mini was a write-off in Cheshire.

'I'll give Viv a call. He'll come and get you. He was worried about you.'

The thought of Viv being worried gave her a funny tickle down her back. 'That's a good idea. Tell him to bring some of my clothes and shoes.'

'I'll do that. I'm really going to have to know all that they did to you.'

'I know.' She wasn't looking forward to describing the more intimate parts of her ordeal.

'Look, go and have a rest somewhere. I'm sure Viv will be with you as soon as he can.'

'Thanks, Tom. Just have a word to the guys here to make sure they believe I'm working for you.' She handed the phone to DS Dobson who had been standing a few feet behind her. He spoke to Tom for a few seconds then put the phone down and turned to Jasmine.

Jasmine spoke. 'I'm going to be picked up, but it's going to take a while. Can I wait somewhere comfortable, and, if at all possible, get something to eat?' There was a growing hole in her stomach that was making itself felt more than the various aches and pains.

'Oh, yeah. You'd better come to our rest room. I can get you something from our canteen.'

'That's the best thing I've heard for most of today,' Jasmine said with relief. Dobson led her away.

Jasmine was almost asleep when she heard the door opening. She half-raised her eyelids and then she was awake.

'Viv!' She jumped up then regretted it as her muscles and groin complained.

'Jas! What have they done to you?' He dropped the holdall he was carrying and stepped towards her with his arms outstretched. Jasmine realised that she had allowed the anorak to flop open and her torn clothes were revealing an expanse of skin including her paltry little breasts. They embraced and Jasmine felt joy at feeling the man in her arms. But she pushed him away.

'You brought my clothes?' she asked. Viv nodded at the bag. 'Good. Go back outside and don't let anybody in until I'm ready.' She urged him to the door, and as he disappeared she fell on the bag. She opened it, pulled out the clothes and tut-tutted about what a man might think were essential. She found a bra and a pair of knickers, her new, slinky, almost-not-there, pair. She discarded the remains of her clothes, felt a quick thrill at being naked in the officers' restroom, then quickly dressed. Soon she felt almost herself in a skirt, tights, t-shirt and jumper but Viv hadn't packed cosmetics. Her face must be a mess after the day's events, but she didn't have a mirror to see the damage. She stuffed the torn clothes in a rubbish bin, put the rest in the bag, donned her anorak again and with the bag in her hand stepped through the door, straight into Viv's back.

He stumbled forward and turned. 'You said, guard the door.'

'Yes, thanks. I just need the loo and a mirror and then we can go.' They walked up and down the corridor until she found the Ladies' toilets. She went inside, into a cubicle and sat. After her pee, which she was relieved to discover did not hurt, she gave her anatomy a brief examination. Finding herself uninjured was a relief. She pressed the flush and emerged to wash her hands and face. She peered into the mirror. Would she have to venture into the world without make-up? On this occasion, the answer was, yes. It was unfortunate as her features still displayed something of her male past without the mask of foundation and lipstick. Still, she was relieved to be free and back on the job.

She stepped out to find Viv joined by DS Dobson.

'Thank you for your assistance, Miss Frame,' the DS said, 'I hope you have a pleasant journey home.'

'Thanks. It will be,' she replied.

'I'll let you out,' the detective added, leading them to the exit.

Jasmine stirred from a fitful sleep. Her head was resting against the passenger door of the Audi. How long had she been asleep? She wasn't sure but as she looked through the window at a damp, dark evening she realised that they were approaching a roundabout in a town. It was the slowing down that had woken her. They were nearly home; they were in Kintbridge. Viv drove straight on at the roundabout.

'No, Viv. I need to go to the police station,' she said. He glanced at her, only just aware that she was awake.

'What are you talking about, Jas? We're going home.'

'I have to report to Tom. Harriet has gone. I need to help them find her.'

Viv drove on. 'You've had an ordeal today, Jas. You're still recuperating. You need to rest.'

'I've just had a rest, thank you very much. I've got to work. Turn around and take me to the police station. Please.'

Viv glared at the road ahead and sighed. At the next roundabout he drove all the way around it so that they headed back.

He growled in an unfamiliar tone. 'I'm not happy about this, Jas. You should be home.'

'I'm sorry, Viv, but this is my job. I need to do it.'

He didn't reply but turned off into the police station approach. The car stopped at the entrance. Jasmine opened the door.

'Thanks, Viv. I do appreciate you picking me up.'

'Don't be long,' he said, 'Come home to rest.'

'I will, as soon as I can.' Jasmine closed the door and hurried up the steps to the entrance. The Audi moved off with a petulant burst of acceleration.

As Jasmine pushed the office door open she saw all the team there. They looked at her, rose to their feet and approached her. Even Terry Hopkins stood up and joined in the welcome.

'There you are,' Tom said, embracing her in a rare hug.

'Are you okay?' Sasha Patel asked.

Jasmine extricated herself from Tom's arms. 'I'm fine,' she said, not prepared to admit the truth. 'Now what have you got on Harriet Bunting?'

Tom grinned and backed away from her. 'You're okay to work?'

'That's why I'm here Tom. Viv wanted to take me home to rest, but if you've lost Harriet I want to help you catch her.'

Tom's eyebrows raised. 'A bit of vengeance called for?'

'Perhaps.' Jasmine examined her feelings about the woman who had abducted her. Yes, she wanted to see her in a locked cell and answering questions, truthfully for once. 'But, mainly, I want to help you close this case.'

Tom smiled and beckoned them all to gather round. 'We've had a bit of luck while you were on your way back.'

'Good,' Jasmine said, 'What is it?'

Tom went on, 'None of the neighbours saw Mrs Bunting leave the house. She had either walked or she had taken a taxi. We called the local cab companies and one told us they had picked her up and taken her to Reading railway station.'

'But you didn't catch her there,' Jasmine said.

'No, we were too late for that,' Tom admitted. 'We've been looking at the station CCTV and just before you came in Terry spotted her.' He looked at DC Hopkins.

'She got on a train,' Terry said.

'Where to?' Jasmine felt exasperated by the pace of the story.

Terry looked triumphant. 'Swansea.'

'When does the train arrive?' Jasmine asked.

Tom glanced at the wall clock. 'About now. We've put a call into the transport police at Swansea station to arrest her.'

'If she travelled all the way,' Jasmine said.

Tom lost his smile. 'There is that. If she got off at an earlier station we've missed her.'

'We're waiting for the call from Swansea,' Terry said.

Jasmine felt impatient and she wasn't confident that Harriet would be spotted getting off the train in Swansea. 'Where else did the train stop?'

Sasha looked at the nearest computer screen. 'Swindon, Bristol Parkway, Newport, Cardiff, Bridgend, Port Talbot and Neath.'

'That's quite a few stops,' Jasmine said, 'Shouldn't you be asking for CCTV from each of them.'

Tom sighed. 'Of course. Terry, Hamid, get on it.' DC Hopkins sent Jasmine a scowl but moved to his desk with DC Sassani. 'I'm glad you're back with us, Jas,' Tom said in a gentle voice, 'You can tell us what Harriet Bunting is up to.'

Jasmine was pleased to feel needed but despite her insistence to Viv that she wanted to work, she was feeling the effects of the day's hardships.

'Thanks, Tom. I hope I can, but I think I need to sit down first.'

'Oh, God, yes!' Tom reacted as if he'd been given an electric shock, 'What am I thinking? I forgot what you've been through, and you're supposed to be recovering.' He took her arm and guided her to a chair. She sat, pleased to relax into the seat.

'It's OK, Tom. I'll be fine, but it has been an eventful day. Now you want to know where Harriet is going.'

Tom leaned against a desk next to Jasmine while Sasha stood nearby, listening to the conversation. 'That's right. Where's she running to?'

'I've no idea,' Jasmine chuckled. 'I guess she's off to meet another of her slaves, but who or where, I couldn't tell you.'

'Well, I didn't expect you to have all their addresses,' Tom admitted. 'But how many are there?'

Jasmine counted up. 'There's the guy who loaned her the house in Reedham and the four I've met, Willy in Oxford and Buttercup in Cheltenham. They're the two she met in Faringdon. Then there is Winkle, who she met in Basingstoke.'

Tom interrupted, 'Is he the guy who went off in your new car and had the collision?'

'That's him. Written off is it?'

''Fraid so.'

Jasmine sighed. How would Viv respond to the news that the new car he'd bought for her had survived just one day in her hands?

'And then there's Peewee, who she dumped me on in Ringwood.'

Tom pondered. 'Could she be visiting any of them?'

Jasmine shrugged, 'I suppose she may have changed trains and gone to Oxford or Cheltenham, but there are another six or more who I don't know anything about.'

'That many?'

'Yes,' Jasmine said, 'She was collecting a tidy sum from her clients, and I imagine that they would do anything for her.'

'Anything?' Sasha asked

Jasmine nodded. 'Anything.'

Tom scratched his chin which was showing bristles. 'How do we find out who they are and where they live. Did she keep records?'

'Oh yes,' Jasmine said, 'A little book that she keeps with her at all times. You won't find anything in the house she was using.'

'But she did meet them,' Tom said.

'Yes, not often. Every few months, to give them tasks and hand over their keys for a few minutes relief.'

'She had to travel to the meetings,' Tom said, 'She doesn't drive herself, so she had a chauffeur. Tyler.'

'Don't forget that the meetings were often in hotels. I don't know how often she went to their homes.'

Tom stood up, a renewed eagerness in his stance. 'Tyler Smith's downstairs. He can tell us what he knows.'

'Will he?' Jasmine said, 'He may just "no comment" you.'

Tom deflated. 'Hmm. You're probably right, but we can give him a try. Sasha, go and get him taken to an interview room, with his solicitor if he's turned up.' Sasha Patel hurried off.

'There is another thing,' Jasmine said.

'What?'

'Tyler's only been on the scene a fairly short time. He may not have taken Harriet to meet all the men, let alone driven her to their homes.'

'What are you getting at, Jas.'

'Gary Nicholls was her lover and driver for a lot longer.'

'So he was,' Tom said with a sense of wonder.

'Let's ask him,' Jasmine said.

'Good idea, Come with me, Jas.'

Terry called out 'Hey, Boss. She didn't get off the train in Swansea. Or if she did the officers there missed her.'

Tom headed to where Terry and Hamid were bent over computer screens with phones to their ears. 'What about the other stops?' he asked.

'We're speaking to each of the station officers,' Terry said, 'The train was pretty full so quite a few people got off at each station. They're looking through their CCTV to see if there's anyone matching Bunting's description.'

'Good. You stick at that Terry and let me know if anything comes up. Hamid go and join Sasha and see if you can get anything out of Tyler Smith.'

'Where are you off to, Boss?' Terry said.

'To have another chat to Gary Nicholls.'

'He'll be delighted to see you again,' DC Hopkins said.

'I'm sure he will be,' Tom agreed, 'or his girlfriend will be.'

Tom Shepherd headed towards the door. Jasmine pushed herself out of the chair and hastened to follow him.

25

Sunday 20TH October

Late Evening

A light came on over the entrance porch as Tom and Jasmine approached Gary Nicholl's house although no interior lighting could be seen.

'Are they in?' Tom asked as he pressed the doorbell. Jasmine didn't answer but had her fingers crossed that their journey wasn't wasted. Her hopes were answered when a light appeared through the small window in the door and then the door was opened by Gary Nicholls.

'You again,' he said, not cheerfully, as he looked at both of them. 'You've caught up with each other then.'

Tom didn't offer an account of their day. 'I said we may have more questions, Mr Nicholls. May we come in.'

For a moment Nicholls looked uncertain whether to give in to the request, but then he pulled the door wide and stepped aside.

'Make it quick,' he said.

Jasmine followed Tom into the hallway. Nicholls closed the door behind them.

'We need your assistance to find Harriet Bunting,' Tom said.

Nicholls looked disbelieving. 'I don't know where she is. I haven't seen her for months.'

'But you may be able to help us determine where she's gone,' Jasmine said.

'Gone?'

'She's left the house she was staying at in Reedham,' Tom said.

'With Smith?' Nicholls spat out the name.

'No, we have Mr Smith in custody. Harriet Bunting left soon after,' Tom said.

'She didn't go by car then.'

'No,' Tom continued, 'She took a taxi to Reading station and we know she caught a train which went to Swansea, but she got off at a station between Reading and there.'

Nicholls shrugged. 'So? Why call on me?'

Jasmine stepped forward. 'Because you might know where she's headed. We think she's meeting one of the men for whom she keeps a key. You know what I'm talking about.'

'Yeah, her weirdoes.'

'Who she does pretty well out of,' Jasmine added.

Nicholls nodded grudgingly, 'OK, so she did.'

Jasmine went on. 'We think you drove her to meetings with the men, perhaps to their homes. We're wondering if you can recall one who might have met Harriet off her train.'

Nicholls eyes widened in incredulity. 'You're expecting me to remember the address of someone who might be living somewhere between Reading and Swansea?'

'We hope so,' Jasmine said, smiling sweetly.

'Bloody heck.' Nicholls turned and headed into the lounge. Tom and Jasmine followed. Nicholls went straight to the drinks cabinet ignoring Tracy who was sitting on the sofa.

'Oh. It's you,' she said in a not very welcoming tone. 'What do they want Gary?'

Nicholls turned to face her with a tumbler containing a large quantity of whisky.

'Go and have a bath or something, darling. I'll be up shortly.'

The girl sulked. 'Is this more about your affair with the Bunting woman?'

'Sort of,' he admitted, 'Now go on and leave us. I won't be long.' He blew her a kiss with his spare hand. She stood up, swung her head and stalked out of the room.

'You don't want your girlfriend to know about your relationship with Harriet Bunting?' Tom said.

'She knows about the relationship,' Nicholls growled, 'It's the other stuff that Harriet did with her blokes that she won't understand.' He slumped into one of the large armchairs and sipped his drink. Tom and Jasmine sat on the vacated sofa.

'Do you think you can help?' Tom asked.

'Shush,' Nicholls said, 'I'm thinking.'

Tom and Jasmine sat quietly allowing him to ponder. He took frequent sips. Within a few minutes the glass was empty.

'There was a guy who lived in a bungalow in Cheltenham,' he said.

'Edward Wilson, known as Buttercup,' Jasmine said.

'I don't know his real name. I don't remember a Buttercup.'

'That might be a recent name,' Jasmine said, 'Since Harriet made him dress as a woman.'

Nicholls snorted. 'That was one of her favourite forfeits. She had enough experience with Evelyn, although he liked being a sissy.'

Tom intervened. 'Can you describe the man you met, Mr Nicholls?'

Nicholls considered for a moment. 'Fifties-ish, medium height, brown hair, receding, slim.'

'Sounds like Wilson,' Jasmine said, 'I don't think she'll have contacted him. She knows we know of him.'

Nicholls frowned. 'I remember a couple of others. One of them lived close to the M4/M5 junction.'

'Near Bristol,' Tom said.

'That's right. A village called… Almondsbury. That's it.' Nicholls looked delighted.

'No distance from Bristol Parkway,' Jasmine said. 'Any others?'

Nicholls held his head. 'Yes, we went to a place just south of Swindon once. Wootton Bassett.'

'That's two possibilities, then,' Jasmine said, 'Any more?'

Nicholls shook his head. 'I can't remember any more of them in that direction.' He stood up and took a few staggering steps to the drinks cabinet. He refilled his glass.

'Do you have any names, or addresses?' Tom asked, his notebook at the ready.

'I told you, Harriet never said their real names. I only ever knew the nicknames she gave them.'

'OK. What are the two you've mentioned called?' Jasmine asked.

Nicholls thought for a few moments. 'The guy near Bristol was Todger and the other one was Dong.'

'Nice,' Jasmine said.

'We can hardly go around their neighbourhoods asking if anyone knows Todger or Dong,' Tom said, 'What about their addresses?'

Nicholls shook his head.

'You drove Harriet there,' Jasmine said, 'Can you pick out your route on a map?'

Nicholls breathed deeply. 'Perhaps.'

Jasmine raised her hands. 'I haven't got a phone. Tom, let's have yours.'

Tom reached in his pocket and drew out his smart phone. He tapped the screen a few times and handed it to Jasmine. The screen showed a map of their current location. Jasmine searched for Wootton Bassett and handed the phone to Nicholls.

'Can you pick out where Dong lived?'

Nicholls peered at the map, moving his fingers over it. Finally he stopped.

'There, I think.'

Tom stood up and leaned over the phone. He scribbled in his notebook. 'What about the other one. Todger.'

Nichols returned to fingering the screen. 'I remember the road. A number of houses all looking pretty much the same. Not sure which one it was,' he said passing the phone to Tom. Again, Tom wrote down the address.

'Are you sure there are no others you can remember?' Jasmine said.

Nicholls shook his head and shrugged. Tom's phone rang. He stood up and went out of the room with the phone at his ear.

Jasmine waited with her heart beating fast in anticipation. Nicholls sipped his whisky and appeared to be getting sleepy

Only seconds passed before Tom returned, smiling broadly.

'It's Bristol. CCTV shows her getting off the train and getting into a Ford Focus. Can't get a number though.'

'It's Todger then.' Jasmine said.

'Let's hope she hasn't got another slave down there which Mr Nicholls doesn't know about.'

'Uh?' Nicholls said.

Tom said, 'It's alright, Mr Nicholls, we'll leave you and your girlfriend now. Thank you for your help.'

'We'll see ourselves out,' Jasmine said.

They almost ran into the hall and out of the house to the car. Tom was driving away as Jasmine fastened her seatbelt.

'Are we going to Bristol?' Jasmine asked.

'You bet,' Tom said as they accelerated along the country road towards the M4 junction. 'I'm not giving Harriet Bunting any more time than I can help. Let's see if we can get the local police to nail her.' He tapped the dashboard to open a phone line.

It was an over an hour later when Tom drove slowly along the streets of the dormitory village. There were two police cars parked in the road. Tom stopped the car and he and Jasmine got out. They were approached by a uniformed officer. Tom flashed his warrant card.

'DI Shepherd from Kintbridge. We asked you to check out an address here.'

The officer stood upright, confident. 'The message we got was to find out which house is occupied by the owner of a Ford Focus.'

Tom nodded. 'That's right. That's the only information we have other than the house being on this street.'

The officer grunted. 'Well, the car wasn't in sight when we arrived, so we knocked on a couple of doors. One of the neighbours told us the owner of the Focus lives at number ten.'

He pointed down the dark road lit by a couple of dim streetlights. 'It's owned by a Mr. Cherry. Lives on his own so we were told.'

Tom began to walk down the road with Jasmine and the officer following.

Jasmine asked, 'Have you called at number ten?'

The PC replied, 'No. We were told to wait for you. But we've kept it under observation. It doesn't look as though there's anyone in.'

Jasmine's heart sank. She was hoping that this would be the end of the trail and that Harriet Bunting would soon be in custody.

They stopped and looked at the front of number ten, a 1970s detached house with large curtained windows and white-painted walls. There was no car in the drive and no lights on inside.

Jasmine spoke again. 'Have you asked the neighbours if they saw Mr Cherry this evening?'

The officer nodded. 'Yes. The people at number twelve said they saw him drive away soon after eight.'

Tom looked at Jasmine. 'That would give Cherry time to get to Bristol Parkway to pick her up. But they didn't come back?' The PC shook his head.

Jasmine was trying to think like Harriet Bunting. 'Harriet may be on the run but I'm not sure she is prepared to give up her way of life yet. She's found a new chauffeur in Todger but would she want to slum it by shacking up with him.'

'What do you mean, Jas?' Tom said, looking mystified.

'I mean that she likes to stay in nice hotels.'

'You think she's got Todger, Mr Cherry, to take her somewhere for the night.'

'And probably persuaded him to pay while she allows him a little relief.'

Tom pondered. 'But where? There must be dozens of suitable places round here. How do we work out where she is?'

'Perhaps we won't have to,' Jasmine said.

'Go on.'

'She never spent more than a couple of hours with her slaves. They were kicked out pretty soon. She only stays the night with her lovers, Gary Nicholls and Tyler Smith.'

'You mean Cherry won't be staying with Harriet Bunting and will come home when she's finished playing with him.'

'Perhaps.'

Tom nodded. 'So, we wait here until he arrives to tell us where Harriet Bunting is staying.' Tom turned to the PC. 'We'll only need one of your cars as back up. You can let the other go. But get your car out of sight. We don't want Cherry spooked if he arrives back and finds a police car outside his house.'

The PC nodded and hurried off.

The autumn cold was beginning to penetrate Jasmine's anorak. 'We can get back in your car, Tom, and wait for him to return.' She glanced at her watch. 'It's almost eleven-thirty. They've already had three hours in each other's company. I don't think Todger will be long if my guess is correct.'

As they got back to the Mondeo, one police car drove off and the other reversed down the road and around a bend. Jasmine got into the passenger seat and pulled the anorak around her. Tom pulled out his phone and made a call.

'Sasha? Did you interview Smith?' a pause, 'Did you get anything from him?' another pause. 'That's the response we expected. We're just outside Bristol. Yes, Bristol. A possible lead on Bunting. I'll speak to you again soon.' He finished the call.

'No joy with Tyler?' Jasmine asked.

'No comment, as you expected. He's staying loyal to his lover. For now.'

The lights of a car appeared behind them. Jasmine and Tom simultaneously lowered their heads. The car, a Ford Focus, drove slowly past.

'It's him,' Tom hissed.

The car turned into the driveway of number ten.

'Come on,' Tom said and opened his door. Jasmine opened hers and in a moment was almost running in pursuit of Tom's long-legged strides. They reached the drive as the man was approaching the front door. He turned as they got near to him. His surprised face was illuminated by the streetlight.

'We're police, Mr Cherry. We'd like to ask you some questions.'

Cherry froze. 'Police? Questions?'

'Where have you just come from?' Tom asked. Cherry was between him and the door. Jasmine moved to his side and she saw the two uniformed police officers coming up the drive.

Cherry looked at each of them. 'I... I've been out.'

'Where Mr Cherry?' Tom said in his most authoritative voice.

'For dinner.'

'Where, is what I asked.'

Jasmine watched the thoughts passing across the face of the middle-aged man. He was thinking whether lying could possibly preserve the secret whereabouts of Harriet Bunting.

'I'm expecting the truth,' Tom said, 'Any lies will see you in court.'

Cherry's mouth opened and closed a few times before he spoke. 'The...The Grove Hotel.'

'Where's that?' Tom asked.

'A few miles away,' Cherry said, his voice shaking, 'the other side of the motorway.'

'Who were you having dinner with?'

Cherry shook his head. 'No one. I was on my own.'

Tom snorted. 'Really? Don't give me that. Who was she?'

The man shook his head violently again.

Jasmine intercepted Tom's next question. 'Was it Madame de la Clef?'

Cherry looked at her with wide eyes. His mouth opened and his tongue lolled.

'Did she let you have your key?' Jasmine said in a stage whisper.

The whole body of the man shook. He nodded.

'I think that's all we need,' Tom said. 'You're coming with us, Mr Cherry. You can show us the way to this hotel.' He took the man's arm and dragged him away from the doorway. He called to the police officers. 'Follow us. We're going to The Grove Hotel. That's where the person we're after is staying.'

Tom tugged the man along the road to the Mondeo. Jasmine tagged along by his side prepared at any moment to grab him if he decided to escape. Tom shoved him up against the car, pulled the rear door open and pushed the man inside. Jasmine got in beside him while Tom got in the front. Tom leaned around to face their prisoner.

'Now give me directions.'

Cherry directed them out of the village and onto an A road. Jasmine examined him. Like Harriet's other slaves, Cherry or "Todger" was middle-aged but slim and fit. He had short, greying hair and a small moustache which was darker. He sat upright, avoiding Jasmine's gaze by looking out of the window into the night.

'What time did Harriet contact you?' Jasmine asked.

Cherry looked at her and said nothing for a moment. He was deciding whether to answer the questions and reveal his story.

'Answer her,' Tom ordered. Jasmine saw his eyes in the rear-view mirror looking at them.

'Um, it was half-past five.'

'Were you expecting a call from your mistress?' Jasmine said.

Cherry held himself upright. 'One expects nothing from Madame. One puts oneself at her service.'

'Oh, so you were prepared to drop what you were doing to respond to her wishes?' Jasmine realised that she was sneering.

Cherry shrugged. 'I was not doing anything important. It is a pleasure to serve Madame.'

'Were you surprised to find she was on her way to meet you?' Jasmine went on.

'You need to take the next right,' Cherry said. Tom nodded and turned the car. Cherry looked at Jasmine. 'It was a little unexpected but not unknown for Madame to want to test me at short notice.'

'Keeps you on your toes, does she?' Jasmine said.

'Madame is thorough in her pursuance of her desires.'

'Did you book the hotel before you picked her up at the station?'

Chery nodded. 'Madame asked me to make arrangements.'

'You met her and went straight to the hotel?'

'Yes.'

'And what did you do when you got there?'

'Madame needed to eat.'

'You bought her dinner?'

'Naturally.'

'And then.'

'We went to her room.'

'Which you paid for?'

'Of course.'

He had answered all her questions in an even tone, as if proud of his actions. They were travelling along a country road, passing fields and hedgerows.

'Did she tell you why she needed your help tonight?' Jasmine went on.

Cherry snorted. 'Madame does not explain her actions.'

'But you were unhelpful when we met you. You didn't want to tell us that you'd been with Harriet Bunting.'

He was quiet.

'Why?' Jasmine insisted.

'She told me not to say where I had been or that I had been with her.'

'You disobeyed your mistress.' Jasmine smiled sweetly at him and was pleased by his reaction. He shivered. 'What did you do in her bedroom?'

He shook his head and kept his mouth shut.

'What did she make you do?' Jasmine insisted.

'It's private,' he whispered.

'Perhaps, but you are going to tell us,' Jasmine said.

'Hold on,' Tom said. The car slowed. 'There's a junction coming up. Which way do we go?'

'Keep to the right,' Cherry said. 'It's not far now. The Grove

Hotel is on the right.'

They speeded up again.

'You can answer Mizz Frame now,' Tom said.

Jasmine watched the man swallow and take a breath.

'She made me undress. Then she used the key to release me.'

'She touched your cock and balls?' Jasmine said.

'She was wearing gloves,' Cherry said. 'Then she told me to kneel with my arms behind my back.'

'While she watched your reaction, I presume,' Jasmine said. Cherry nodded. 'Is that all?'

'She told me to remove her shoes and stockings and then kiss her feet.'

'Did you enjoy that?'

'It is a great honour to touch any part of Madame.'

'You have a foot fetish.'

He shook his head.

'She just wanted to test you?'

'She didn't need to. I will obey her always.'

'You didn't just now when you told us where she was staying.' Jasmine saw his face turn pale in the darkness of the car. 'What else did she ask you to do?'

'That was it.'

'Nothing else?'

'She told me to put the device on again.'

Jasmine chuckled. 'That must have been difficult for you. Surely you were hard. Didn't she let you come?'

He shook his head.

Tom spoke as he turned the wheel. 'I think we're here.' Jasmine saw the sign with "The Grove Hotel" in large painted letters, as they turned into the car park. Tom halted the car in front of the entrance. The police car drew up beside them.

Jasmine undid her seat belt, disappointed that she had not completed her questioning and embarrassment of Cherry.

Tom got out and opened the rear door.

'Come with us, please, Mr Cherry. You can guide us to Mrs Bunting's room.' Tom took his arm and led them into the hotel

259

with Jasmine and the two police officers close behind. The young man seated at the reception desk looked up with surprise when he saw them approaching.

Tom released Cherry's arm. 'This gentlemen booked a room this evening which is occupied by a Mrs Harriet Bunting.

'Ah, yes. Mr Cherry, isn't it,' the receptionist said. Cherry nodded but looked unhappy.

'We are police,' Tom said, showing his warrant card, 'I'd like the spare key for the room please, just in case Mrs Bunting does not want to let us in.'

'Oh, yes, I see,' the young man muttered. He felt around in his desk drawer then reached out with a card in his hand. 'This is the master keycard.'

'Good. You can accompany us,' Tom said. He gave Cherry a gentle shove. 'Lead on Mr Cherry. Show us to the room.'

The party followed Cherry up the stairs and along a corridor. They stopped outside a bedroom. Tom rapped on the door. There was a faint reply of 'Who is it?'

Tom nudged, Cherry.

The man looked from Tom to Jasmine and took a breath. 'It's Todger, Madame.'

The reply was louder. 'What are you doing back? I told you to go home.'

'Um. I have some people with me, Madame. Police.'

There was a cry from inside the room.

'Open the door please Mrs. Bunting,' Tom called. There was no reply. Tom turned to the receptionist and nodded. The man stepped forward and slipped the keycard in the slot. When the door beeped he pressed down on the handle. The door swung open. Tom and Jasmine stepped forward into a large bedroom.

Jasmine saw Harriet Bunting standing by the bed facing them. She was in an ankle-length white satin nightdress with her hair in curlers. She faced them.

'You!' she screamed and ran at Jasmine, her fists raised. Jasmine stepped back lifted her hands to defend herself, but Tom grabbed Mrs Bunting as she passed. He gripped her shoulders. She struggled for a moment and then subsided, hanging over Tom's arms.

'I'm arresting you for the abduction and false imprisonment of Jasmine Frame,' Tom said, then turned his head to the leading police officer who was behind him. 'We're in your jurisdiction. You can say the rest of it.'

The PC came forward reaching to his belt for his handcuffs. He clipped her wrists behind her back as he went through the statement of rights.

'Take her back to your station,' Tom said, 'We'll follow and sort out the transfer to Kintbridge.'

The PCs led their prisoner out, followed by Tom, Cherry and Jasmine.

26

Jasmine glanced at her watch as Tom brought the Mondeo to a halt outside her home. It was gone three a.m. and she felt drained. It seemed like an age since she had left the house yesterday morning and she felt she could hardly summon the energy to get out of the car.

'I'll let you know when we're interrogating Harriet Bunting,' Tom said. 'I'd like you there.'

'You can't let me interview her.'

'No, of course not. It has to be an officer. But I'd like you to listen to her responses and give me guidance.'

'I'll be delighted.'

'But go and get a good night's sleep. I'd like to get at her as soon as we can, but it will be a while before we get her back from Bristol.'

It had taken a couple of hours booking Harriet Bunting into custody at the Bristol police station. Then there had been the paperwork to transfer her to Kintbridge and arrange the transport. Her belongings, left in the hotel room, had been bagged up as evidence and were sitting in the boot of Tom's car. Harriet herself was allowed some rest in a cell before her journey home to face interrogation.

'We can charge her and Smith for what they did to you, Jas, but it's the murder and arson I'd like to get one or both of them for.'

Jasmine paused with her hand on the door lever. 'We still don't have much evidence, do we?'

'No. Nothing concrete.'

'So, it's your interrogation that's going to have to persuade one of them to tell the true story.'

'That's why I need you, Jas. Sleep on it.'

Jasmine stepped out of the car and watched as Tom drove off. She hauled herself up the driveway. It was only when she reached the front door that she remembered that her key along with the other contents of her bag was lost. She would have to ring the doorbell. Was Viv in bed asleep, she wondered.

The door opened. Viv, in a dressing gown, frowned at her.

'Good god, Jas. Where have you been?'

'Bristol,' she said attempting a smile.

'What on earth for?'

'To make an arrest.'

'That's a police officer's job. Not yours.'

'Tom needed me.'

'Doesn't Detective Inspector Thomas Shepherd realise that you're still weak and need to convalesce?' There was a tone to Viv's words that Jasmine was not familiar with. Could he actually be jealous?

'Yes, he does, but I wanted to do my job.'

'Oh, what job is that?'

'You know what I do, Viv. I'm a detective.'

'You were a detective. Now you are a woman who needs to look after herself.'

Jasmine was incredulous. Was this the Viv who looked after her, who provided her with a smart home, who bought her a fancy car? The Viv who had said he loved her? She shivered. It wasn't just from standing on a doorstep on a cold October night.

'Can I come in please, Viv? I'm freezing.'

'Oh, you want to be at home now do you. You've finished detecting for tonight?' He stepped back from the door and she slipped inside.

'What's up, Viv?' she said, closing the door. 'Why are you being like this?'

'I'm surprised at you, Jas. I thought that all you wanted was to be a woman.'

She looked at him feeling confused. 'I did. I do. I am.'

'Well, why aren't you looking after yourself instead of taking the risk of undoing the surgeon's work.'

'Yes, I know I missed some of my dilations today. But one day won't matter. I'll do it now before I settle down.'

'It's not just that Jas. You could get injured running around after murderers. Heck, you got knocked around enough today. Doesn't that make you think again?'

Perhaps it was just concern for her that was making Viv act weirdly.

'Look, Viv. I appreciate you looking after me, and today has been a bit extraordinary, but doing my job is part of me. It's part of me as a woman. I'm not going to spend the rest of my life ducking out of investigations because I've now got a cunt instead of a dick.'

He looked away from her. 'There's no need to be crude, Jas. Look, go to bed. You're tired. We'll talk about this later.'

'Talk about what?'

'Your job, as you call it.' He climbed the stairs leaving her speechless and shaking with fury.

She went to the kitchen, drank a glass of water, then went to her bedroom, the bedroom they had shared for the last few nights. Viv wasn't there. She undressed, showered, slipped on a nightie and went to lie on the bed, alone for the first time in days. She performed her exercises, delighted and relieved that inserting the dilators was no more painful or difficult than previously although she ached all over from the day's pressures. At last she slipped under the duvet and settled down. She expected to drop off to sleep immediately but she didn't. Thoughts kept circulating around her mind, not about the case, but about Viv. She had thought they were a couple and that they were setting up a home and a life together. A life where they both had careers and interests as well as love for each other. Had she misinterpreted Viv's intentions? Was it that he *really* wanted a stay-at-home wife, one who he could now have normal intercourse with? A wife who would do as he instructed?

Jasmine stirred. A noise had woken her. There it was again. A knocking and a bell ringing. She sat up in the bed. Someone was at the front door. Why hadn't Viv answered it? Her eye caught her watch on the bedside table. 10:15. She had been asleep after all. Viv must have gone to work without waking her.

The ringing came again. She swung out of bed, grabbed her robe from behind the door and hurried downstairs while flinging it over her shoulders. She reached the door as she wrapped the dressing gown around herself.

She pulled the door open. DC Sassani was standing there.

'Ah, you are in. The DI said you would be.'

'Hi, Hamid. What are you doing here?'

'DI Shepherd sent me to fetch you. He realised you didn't have a car or your mobile and we don't know the number of your new house phone.'

'Oh yes, I forgot. He did say he'd let me know when he wanted me. You'd better come in while I get dressed.' She opened the door wide and lead the young DC into the lounge. 'Would you like some coffee?'

'Yes, please.'

'So would I. Do you mind making it? You'll find everything in there.' She pointed into the kitchen.

'OK. Black, no sugar. I think that is how you like it?' Hamid said as he moved into the kitchen.

'That's it. I won't be long.' Jasmine hurried back upstairs. Actually, "not long" was a pretty imprecise period of time. She didn't need a shower so her trip to the bathroom was relatively short but, not knowing how long she would be at the police station, she decided she couldn't afford to forego her morning exercises. Then she had to dress and, finally, do her make up.

She returned to the lounge to find Hamid sitting on the sofa with an empty mug. Hers waited on the coffee table with no hint of steam rising from it. She picked it up.

'I think it's probably cold,' Hamid said.

Jasmine gulped down half the mug. 'Warm,' she said, telling the truth in that warm filled a large range between cold and hot.

She took another mouthful and put the mug down. 'Right, let's go.' She collected a coat from the hallway and stood by the front door.

She let Hamid out and followed him. As she pulled the door closed she remembered she had no key, no bag, no possessions. She hoped Viv would be in, and in a better mood, when she returned. She pulled the door closed.

As they drove off in Hamid's Ford Focus she faced him.

'Is Harriet back yet?'

'On her way,' Hamid said, 'DI Shepherd says he will interview her as soon as she arrives but wants to speak to you first.'

The sense of being wanted made Jasmine happy. 'And Tyler Smith?'

'Still in custody. The DI says he wants them both in interview rooms at the same time.'

'Good. We need to get their stories disagreeing.'

'He's let Elvis Preston go though,'

Jasmine frowned. 'Oh, why?'

'Seems he was seen in a Thirsbury pub on the night of the incident.'

'Doesn't mean that he didn't have time to start the fire, or beat Evelyn Bunting to death for that matter.'

'No, but DI Shepherd says we should concentrate on Bunting and Smith. We can speak to Preston again later if necessary.'

'Any reason why Tom's less interested in Preston and his boss?'

'I don't know the details, but I think Harriet Bunting's phone and other stuff in her handbag are proving to be interesting. Forensics have managed to get more out of Evelyn Bunting's laptop as well.'

Jasmine was excited. Perhaps there was more evidence after all. They just had to trap Tyler Smith or Harriet Bunting, or both of them, into an admission of guilt for Evelyn's murder and the fire at Molly's. But what were the motives?

They were soon at Kintbridge Police Station and climbing the stairs to the V&SCU office. Hamid held the door open for her and she looked in to see Sasha Patel's and Terry Hopkins' heads down over their computers. Tom came out of what had been DCI Sloane's office as they entered.

'Hi, Jas,' he greeted her, 'How are you this morning?'

'Fine. Better than you by the look of it.' She noted the DI's pale complexion and dark eyes.

'I did manage a couple of hours last night, but we've got work to do.'

'Anything I can do to help?'

'I hope so. Come and sit down.' Tom pulled out a couple of chairs by the whiteboard. They sat down, close to where DCs Patel and Hopkins were working. Hamid pulled up his own chair.

Tom said, 'Tell us what we've got from Harriet's bag, Sasha?'

The young woman lifted a clear evidence bag. 'There's a zip-up bag that contains twelve key rings, each with one or two small keys. They are labelled with a number.'

'I can guess what they are,' Jasmine said.

Sasha grinned. 'Yes, we can. The numbers would seem to match the pages in this book.' She held up another bag. It contained a slim book resembling a diary with hard covers.

'Her little black book?' Jasmine said.

'Well, its dark red actually,' Sasha said, 'but it contains details of twelve people, all men. It gives their names and, er, nicknames, their addresses and contact details, and some information about each of them.'

'Information?' Jasmine asked.

Sasha's face seemed to have turned pale pink. 'Hmm, they seem to be descriptions of the men's likes and dislikes and the, er, tasks she has set them.'

'I think I get it,' Jasmine grinned, 'It's her record of her slaves' performances and what she has planned for them.'

Tom intervened. 'I don't think there is anything illegal in any of that, unless we can get her for failing to declare an income.

She's not procuring prostitutes, of either sex, or living off immoral earnings – well not technically. It's the diary and phone records which are more useful to us, aren't they, Sasha.'

DC Patel nodded. 'Her diary has a note of all her appointments with her, um, men, and with Tyler Smith. She also had a couple of meetings with Neville Griffiths.'

'Did she?' Jasmine expressed surprise, 'I thought it was Evelyn that handled all the business dealings.'

'So did we,' Tom said, 'But it's the phones that are most interesting. Come on Sasha. You're stringing out the story.'

Sasha Patel smiled. 'Well I haven't been through them all yet but Harriet has kept all her text and voice messages from Tyler Smith.'

'That's useful,' Jasmine said thinking that this really could be a breakthrough.

'It is,' Sasha said, 'There's lot of mundane and, er, intimate stuff, but there are also instructions to do this or that. She received a short message from Tyler last Tuesday evening at nine-ten. It's just one word, "Done".'

'Duh, I wonder what that means,' Tom said.

'There's one thing it could mean,' Jasmine said, 'He's murdered Evelyn.'

'And started the fire?' Terry added.

'Could be,' Tom agreed in his normal voice.

'He sent it just before heading back to Faringdon,' Jasmine said, 'You said he got back at around ten.'

Tom nodded. 'Right, well we've got that to present to Smith and Bunting and see how they explain it.'

'Is there anything else?' Jasmine asked.

'Yeah,' Terry Hopkins said, 'We've got some more of Evelyn Bunting's emails out of his crocked laptop.'

Jasmine's raised her eyebrows. 'And they're interesting?'

'Sort of,' Terry replied, 'He sent a blackmail threat to Nicholls.'

Now Jasmine really was interested.' 'Blackmail?'

'Yeah. Bunting threatened to tell Nicholls' new girl friend

about his dealings with Harriet Bunting's gang of slaves.'

'But Nicholls didn't deal with the slaves. He just chauffeured Harriet to her meetings with them, like Tyler Smith did,' Jasmine said.

Terry shrugged.

'He must have been getting desperate,' Jasmine mused, 'Realising that paying Gary Nicholls off had ruined the business finances. Perhaps he was hoping he could get some of it back. We know that Tracy is a bit scratchy about Nicholl's relationship with Harriet and he didn't want her to know about Harriet's side line. How did Nicholls' respond?'

'He didn't,' Terry said, 'He ignored it. Treated it with the contempt it deserved I suppose.'

'So, Evelyn had to look for other ways of getting some cash,' Jasmine said, 'Like fire insurance money?'

'We're wondering about that,' Tom said. 'The insurance cover was increased a short while ago, but in none of his communications with Griffiths or Preston is fire mentioned.'

'Well, he wouldn't want to leave a trail would he,' Jasmine said.

'No,' Tom continued, 'but his last messages to Griffiths were urging him to buy him out of the business.'

'Buy him out?' Jasmine was surprised. 'He was prepared to hand over Molly's to Neville Griffiths?'

Tom nodded. 'Including the building. That was his offer.'

'What was Griffiths' reply?'

'No deal,' Terry answered, 'Doesn't look as though he wanted to get involved with weirdoes buying artificial female body parts.'

Jasmine scowled at Terry. 'Evelyn was providing a service to a particular group of transgender people.'

'Not a very lucrative one though,' Terry glared back at Jasmine, 'Not now the business has gone online. Shops like Molly's have had it.'

Jasmine took her eyes off Terry. Her thoughts on Evelyn Bunting were changing. 'So you think perhaps we were wrong and it wasn't Evelyn that planned the arson. She was thinking of retiring.'

Tom nodded. 'That's the way our thoughts are going.'

The phone on the desk rang. Tom answered it, listened for a moment and put it down.

'Harriet Bunting has arrived. She's in interview room one and Tyler Smith is being put in the other. They've both got lawyers with them so we're ready to go. Sasha with me. Jasmine you come and watch. Terry and Hamid. You carry on digging through Tyler and Harriet's communications.'

Tom headed for the door with Sasha and Jasmine behind. As they went down the stairs, Tom called over his shoulder.

'Oh, some news for you, Jas.'

'What's that?'

'We found your handbag in Tyler Smith's car. We'll let you have it back once it's been dusted for fingerprints.'

'Oh, thanks,' Jasmine was delighted to know that she would get some of her possessions back.

'And the remains of your phone were found at the Basingstoke hotel. No use to you though. Even the SIM was busted.'

'I'm not surprised.' Jasmine recalled Tyler grinding it into the floor of the hotel room.

'And forensics are checking out the boot of Tyler's car for your DNA. Just to provide evidence to confirm your story.'

'Great.' Jasmine was quite certain she had shed skin cells and dribbled some saliva while tied up.

They reached the ground floor. All three of them entered the viewing room where screens showed the CCTV pictures of the two interviewees. Tyler was slumped in a chair looking bored while Harriet sat nervously upright. Jasmine noted that she'd been given a mundane outfit consisting of track suit bottoms and sweat shirt. She was certainly not her usual immaculate self. Jasmine hoped she was feeling vulnerable and susceptible to Tom's questioning. Sitting beside the two arrestees were the duty solicitors. A uniformed officer stood by the exit from each room.

Tom bent down to examine the two screens then stood up. 'Let's have a go at Tyler first. Looks like he needs waking up. Harriet can stew for a little longer. Keep an eye on them, Jasmine, and let us know if you have any ideas.'

'How?'

'Send a note in with one of the uniforms. Come on Sasha.' The two detectives left. Jasmine sat herself down in front of the screens. She saw Tom and Sasha enter the room containing Tyler Smith. They sat down opposite the young man who didn't move.

Tom's voice came over clear and loud. 'DI Shepherd and DC Patel have entered the room. Interview with Mr Tyler Smith commencing at,' he looked at his watch, 'Eleven-oh-four a.m. Monday twenty-first October. Good morning Tyler. I hope you had a good night.'

Tyler mumbled and shifted in his chair but made no effort to sit up.

Tom began, 'You are under arrest for the abduction of, and assault on, Jasmine Frame. We will have her statement about that and plenty of evidence, such as the discovery of her handbag in your car. There's also the statement of William Morley who I think you know as "Winkle". He took Miss Frame's car without her permission from a certain Basingstoke Hotel where we have your presence on CCTV. Morley wrote off the Mini on the M6. He's in hospital but is answering questions.'

Jasmine was interested to hear news of her car but was more intrigued by Tyler's reaction. He stirred and straightened up. His expression seemed to show realisation that he was in trouble.

Tom went on, 'But what I'm really interested is what you were doing in Thirsbury on Tuesday evening between about eight-thirty and nine fifteen.'

'I was in Faringdon.'

'Not between those times you weren't,' Tom said, 'We have CCTV of you leaving the hotel in Faringdon and returning around ten, and more from Thirsbury High Street between those times. Why did you leave Harriet Bunting and her companions, drive back to Thirsbury, spend less than an hour there and then drive back to Faringdon?'

'No comment.'

'Why did you send a message to Harriet Bunting at nine-ten saying "Done"? What had you done Tyler?'

'No comment.'

'I'd think about it if I were you, Tyler. I think you were at Molly's between those times. We'll have DNA and fingerprint evidence of you being there.'

Tyler sat up and glared at Tom. 'I was there a lot. That won't help you.'

'Ah, but we have the murder weapon. The implement used to beat Evelyn Bunting to death.' Tom leaned forward and fixed a stare on the suspect. Smith glared back. Nothing was said for a moment.

'No comment.'

Tom stood up and walked out. DC Patel followed.

Jasmine swung her seat around as Tom entered her room.

'What do you think, Jas?'

'I think you rattled him, Tom. He was paying attention by the end even if you didn't get more than a "no comment". He knows he's in trouble. Keep reminding him that he's not going anywhere because of the abduction charge.'

'Will do. Now it's time for Harriet I think. Keep an eye on Tyler for us, Jas.'

Tom backed out of the small room and he and Sasha appeared on Jasmine's second screen commencing the interview with Harriet Bunting. She was attempting to put on a haughty look but it was spoiled by the scruffy pink sweatshirt.

'Now, Harriet,' Tim said, 'Let's consider Tuesday evening. The time when your husband was being murdered and your business and home in Thirsbury was set alight.'

'You know I wasn't there. I was in Faringdon.'

'Ah yes, a romantic night away with your lover, Tyler Smith, joined by your two compliant gentlemen friends, who I believe go by the names, Buttercup and Willy.'

Harriet sniffed but said nothing.

'But you weren't all there all the time, were you? Tyler left after dinner and did not return until about ten. He drove all the way back to Thirsbury. Why did he do that?'

Harriet shrugged, 'I don't know. He is a free man.'

'Unlike Buttercup or Willy, I understand.' Jasmine thought she detected a chuckle in Tom's voice. 'But let's get back to Tyler Smith. If it was nothing to do with you, why did he send a text to you saying "Done", at nine-ten, before starting the journey back to join you?'

Harriet shook her head but remained silent.

'Come on Harriet, we need an answer. "Done" implies a task completed. What task did Tyler carry out on your behalf? A task that required notification that it was complete?'

She shrugged and glared impassively at Tom.

Tom tried a different tack. 'You like being in charge don't you. You took charge of the abduction of Jasmine Frame when she turned up unannounced at your lunch in Basingstoke. You give instructions to your slaves. You dominated Evelyn.'

Harriet Bunting didn't deny any of Tom's statements. Jasmine actually noted a slight relaxation of her body indicating acceptance. Harriet wielded power as her right. She didn't mind that being presented to her as fact.

Tom paused, then took up his speech again. 'I don't think Tyler Smith would go anywhere unless he was under strict orders from you.' Harriet didn't blink. 'So what order did you give him on Tuesday evening?'

Jasmine saw Harriet catch her breath. She had realised that her lack of denial of her control over the men in her life had drawn her into a trap.

'It was of no importance,' she said, looking away.

'Oh, but it was,' Tom replied, 'Because when Tyler left Molly's to return to you, Evelyn was dead and your property was on fire.'

Harriet snapped back, 'That was nothing to do with the

instructions I gave Tyler.'

'What were those instructions?'

She gaped. Jasmine watched with a smile. Harriet must answer now. A "no comment" would look like an admission of guilt.

After a considerable delay while Tom watched her, she spoke. 'He was to put Evelyn to bed.'

'Surely Evelyn was capable of doing that himself.'

Harriet shook her head. 'No, he had to be stripped, shackled and locked in his cage.'

Tom nodded, 'Ah, I see, the cage in your basement dungeon.'

'That's correct.'

'This was a regular ritual.'

'Most nights.'

'Evelyn was left on a thin mat in a cage in the basement while you slept on a king size bed with your lover.'

'It was what Evelyn liked.'

There was silence. Jasmine sympathised with Tom's failure to find an immediate response. How did one empathise with a person who accepted such treatment as Evelyn suffered or indeed with the woman who administered it?

Tom recovered however. 'Tyler didn't carry out your instructions, did he? Evelyn was found, dressed, on the ground floor, having been bludgeoned with his own antique baseball bat. So why did Tyler send a message to you saying "Done"?'

Harriet didn't respond. Jasmine saw her face freeze with her mouth slightly open.

'Can you give me an answer Mrs Bunting?'

She shook her head.

'What were the actual instructions you gave Tyler?'

A more violent shake of her head.

'Did you tell Mr Smith to dispose of your husband?'

Still no reply.

'I need an answer from you, Mrs Bunting. For the record.'

She whispered, 'No comment.'

Tom went immediately on. 'Well perhaps you will comment

on the conversations you had with Mr Neville Griffiths.'

Harriet's face showed shock. The change of topic had surprised her.

'Business,' she said. 'Mr Griffiths had made a loan to us.'

'But you told us before, that Evelyn handled all the business matters. You took no interest in Molly's. Of course, we know now that you had other business interests involving twelve men. So, what was the purpose of your calls to Mr Griffiths.'

'He was demanding money.'

'Wasn't Evelyn handling that?'

For the briefest of moments, Harriet's nose wrinkled. Jasmine saw it. What was the cause of her distaste? Having to deal with Griffiths or the fact that Evelyn wasn't?

'I was helping.'

'How?'

There was a pause which went on and on. This time Jasmine could almost see the cogs in Harriet's brain turning. What lie would she tell now?

'We were negotiating the sale of the business.'

'And the property?'

'Um, yes.'

'I can't imagine that Neville Griffiths' offer was generous especially as you already owed him a hundred grand plus interest.'

'We hadn't agreed a price.'

Tom leaned forward as if to make a killing thrust. 'But Griffiths must have been fairly confident that the business and your home could be his for a pretty low price.'

Harriet shrugged in grudging agreement.

Tom went on. 'So, it wouldn't have been in Griffiths' interests to burn the place down would it. We know the fire was deliberately started and encouraged by a liberal sprinkling of petrol. If it wasn't Griffiths who set the fire, who was it?'

Harriet looked blank.

'The only people to benefit from the fire, assuming the insurance company was convinced that you weren't responsible yourselves, were you and Evelyn. With Evelyn dead, you are the sole beneficiary.' Tom was sounding triumphant now. 'Admit it, Mrs Bunting. It was you that planned the fire at Molly's and the murder of your husband.'

'No!' Harriet screeched.

Tom stood up. 'Think about it Mrs Bunting. You are not leaving here because of the charge of the abduction of Jasmine Frame. Pleading guilty to the arson and murder might mean that you get out of prison in your lifetime. If you don't, you'll die in a cell. Evelyn may have liked being imprisoned in a cage but I don't think you will.'

Harriet looked away as Tom walked out of the room with DC Patel close behind.

He joined Jasmine. 'What do you think, Jas?'

'You've got her,' she said feeling elated.

'Not quite,' Tom said in more measured tone. 'She hasn't admitted it yet.'

'But you've got a logical story now,' Jasmine said. 'Harriet is bored with Evelyn and a business that is failing. Now she's got her slaves and a young lover, she wants a change. Griffiths doesn't want the business because it has no future, so the insurance scam was the only option.'

Tom nodded, 'But it was executed badly. The use of petrol was a forensic giveaway, and implicating Evelyn by making it look as though he had spread it ruined the story.'

'I think she expected Evelyn's body to be burned to a crisp. For someone who excels at giving orders I don't think she gave Tyler instructions that were precise enough.'

Tom nodded. 'He's the one who's carrying the can. Literally as far as the petrol goes. He killed Evelyn and started the fire, didn't he?'

'I think so.'

'Perhaps I can make him admit what he did and implicate Harriet to share the responsibility.'

'That's it! Put him on the spot. Suggest that it was all his idea, his plan, so he gets all the blame and we'll see how loyal he is to his lover.'

Tom chuckled, 'How fickle can love be, eh?'

'Too right, Tom. We're nearly there.'

Tom hurried from the small room, and Jasmine saw that he was feeling confident of success. Could he break down Tyler Smith?

She saw his image and Sasha's reappear in the room with Smith and his solicitor. Tom and Sasha sat down without a word. Jasmine saw the two men eyeing each other. At last Tom announced the recommencement of the interview.

'Do you have anything to say to me, Tyler?' Tom said. The young man shook his head.

'Well, we have it from Harriet that she did give you instructions to return to Molly's. Certain things that you had to do before your headed back to her bed in Faringdon. You presumably felt you had completed those tasks because of that message you sent to her. "Done", you said.'

Tyler looked glum but didn't answer.

Tom tried again. 'Mrs Bunting says that her instructions were to put her husband to bed. That is, to strip him of his women's clothes, bind him in chains and lock him in that cage downstairs in the cellar.'

Tyler looked confused.

'Was that it, Mr Smith? Were those the instructions she gave you?'

'Er...'

'Because that's not what you did was it. You thought that if you killed Evelyn and made it look as though he had spilt the petrol, you assumed that Harriet would get the insurance money.'

'No.'

'You saw a chance to get rid of the sissy husband and the failing business and get Harriet all to yourself. You knew she was bored with her husband and fed up with the shop. You hoped to please her by taking the initiative, so you planned and carried out the murder and the arson. You're going to prison for a long time for planning and carrying out those crimes, Smith.'

'No, no!' Tyler was rising from his seat.

'No?' Tom's voice was quizzical, 'Sit down Tyler. What's wrong with that interpretation of the facts?'

Tyler slumped back onto his chair. 'She told me to do it.'

This was it. Jasmine clenched her fists to stop herself clapping. Surely Tyler was going to confess.

In a slow voice, Tom asked, 'What did Mrs Bunting tell you to do?'

'She told me to drive back to Thirsbury and set fire to Molly's.'

'Is that all she said?'

Tyler took a breath. 'She said to make it look as though someone else had started the fire.'

'Did she say why?'

'She said there was an insurance policy that she could collect on.'

'She didn't tell you that it was Molly's insurance policy and that if either of the owners were shown to have been involved in the fire then the insurance was void?'

'Um...'

'Um, what, Mr Smith?'

'Harriet said the money would come to her.'

'It would have if you hadn't created the impression that Evelyn Bunting was implicated in the arson. The insurance company would not pay out if that was the case. You were just supposed to ensure that Evelyn died in the fire weren't you.'

'No, Evelyn wasn't meant to die.' There was a look of anguish on Tyler's face. Jasmine was surprised. She had convinced herself that Harriet wanted Evelyn out of her way.

'What was supposed to happen, Tyler?' Tom said

Tyler Smith took a deep breath and looked at Tom with appeal in his eyes. 'Harriet decided that the only way out of the financial mess the shop was in was to burn it down. She said it had to look like someone had attacked the place with a petrol bomb. So I travelled back with the petrol can. Once the fire was lit I was supposed to get Evelyn out.'

'You were supposed to be his rescuer?' Tom sounded sceptical.

'That's it. But he wouldn't do it.'

'Do what?'

'He wouldn't let me start the fire. He didn't want to lose the business. I suppose he was attached to it.'

'It was his. His life's work,' Tom agreed, 'Harriet may have been a joint owner but didn't show any interest in the day to day running of it.'

'That's right,' Tyler said.

'So, what happened when you got back to Molly's?'

'I started spreading the petrol, but Evelyn tried to stop me. He was really wild. He was bashing at me with his fists. I pushed him off, he came at me with that old bat. I grabbed it off him and swung it. He... he fell.'

'You killed him with one blow from the baseball bat?'

'I didn't mean to, but he was dead.'

'So, you decided to finish the job Harriet had given you and let Evelyn's body be consumed by the fire.' Tyler nodded slowly. 'Tell us what you did.'

'I left Evelyn where he was. I couldn't touch his body. I just ran out of the building.'

'What did you do with the baseball bat?'

'Er, I don't know. Dropped it somewhere I think. In the shop?'

Tom nodded. 'And when you were outside?'

'I had a cloth. I lit it with a lighter, smashed a small window in the door and pushed it through. The petrol caught alight. It was faster than I expected. I barely got away before the front of the shop blew up.'

'You overdid the petrol, Tyler. The fireball at the front of Molly's attracted attention so the fire service arrived before the whole building was alight. You left Evelyn at the back of the building where the fire didn't quite reach and because a little petrol had spilled on him when you fought, we thought he had spread it.'

Tyler looked down at his hands resting on the table.

'You ran away, sent the message and drove back to your lover,' Tom concluded. Tyler nodded.

'You, Tyler Smith, killed Evelyn Bunting and set fire to Molly's.'

Tyler nodded.

'Answer please, Mr Smith. For the record.'

'I didn't mean to kill him.'

'But you did.'

'Yes.'

'And started the fire.'

'Yes.'

'Thank you, Tyler. That's all.' Tom rose from his chair.

Tyler looked up, his face pained. 'But Harriet made me do it.'

Tom paused, not quite straightened up. 'Made you? You followed her instructions, if not quite to the letter, but "made you" do so? I don't think so.' He pulled himself to his full, imposing height.

'No, she did. She made me.'

Tom sat down again. 'How?'

'I can see it now,' Tyler said.

'What?' Tom said, a note of impatience in his voice.

'I fell in love with her. She did things to me that made me want to be with her all the time, made me want to please her.'

'Ah, she seduced you. Is that what you're saying.'

'Yes. I admit it was the sex. I wanted it. She gave it.'

'I don't think you can use lust as an excuse for murder. Motive perhaps.'

'No, you don't understand. She's a sorceress, a witch. She makes men do things they would never think of doing. If you saw what she makes those old blokes do, you'd believe me.'

Tom didn't reply immediately. Jasmine recalled the things she'd been told by Harriet's slaves. She certainly seemed to have a hold over them.

Tom finally spoke. It didn't sound as if he believed Tyler's story. 'So Harriet Bunting has a magic power which she wields over men young and old.'

'Yes,' Tyler nodded his head eagerly. 'I admit I fell for it. I would do anything she wanted of me, even do things to Evelyn that disgust me.'

'What things?'

Tyler froze with his mouth half open. 'I can't say.'

'Can't or won't?'

Tyler shook his head. 'Can't. I… I'm not gay.'

'Oh, that. She told you to have gay sex with her crossdressing husband.'

'Yes.'

'And that disgusted you.'

'Yes.'

'Well, Mr Smith, that has just provided another motive for why you wielded the baseball bat with such ferocity. The disgust you felt for Evelyn added weight to the blow you gave him.'

'But…'

'Forget it, Tyler. Yes, I can see that Harriet Bunting spellbound you, but you are not getting out of charges for murder and arson as well as kidnapping and imprisoning Jasmine Frame. You and Mrs Bunting will be in court together.' Tom stood and walked out of the room at speed.

He went straight into the other interview room with DC Patel hurrying along behind him. Harriet Bunting looked up as he entered. The expression on her face revealed her realisation that her denials were pointless. But would she give in without a fight, Jasmine wondered.

Tom eased himself down into the chair without saying anything. Harriet watched him uneasily.

Tom began. 'The plan was for Tyler to make the fire at Molly's look as if some third party was responsible, perhaps someone unhappy about the business that was being engaged in, a transphobe. But Tyler wasn't an expert arsonist; he was a little too liberal with the petrol in the front shop. And he had a problem. Evelyn.'

Harriet looked as though she wanted to ask a question but

thought better of it.

Tom continued. 'He didn't want to go along with your plan. Wasn't prepared to see his life's work go up in flames. He still had hopes, maybe, that he could get through the financial problems, repay Griffiths and get his goons off his back. He tried to stop Tyler but Tyler, perhaps more enthusiastically than you might have expected, bludgeoned him to death. Evelyn's murder rather spoiled the arson story, didn't it?'

'What do you mean?' Harriet asked, drawn into the story.

'Arsonists may have planned to pour some petrol through the letter box or a broken window and set the shop alight. They wouldn't really commit themselves to entering the property, engaging with the owner and then leave his body in the back room. Tyler's poor execution of your plan resulted in the death of your husband and the exposure of the arson as a scam. He may be good in bed but he was a useless tool for your purpose.'

'He said he'd done it,' Harriet mumbled, her cheeks reddening with fury. 'he didn't tell me he'd killed Evelyn.'

'Nevertheless, it was your plan,' Tom said. Harriet shook her head. 'Your plan to burn down Molly's and claim on the insurance.'

Harriet looked venomous. 'I didn't want Evelyn dead,'

'Perhaps not,' Tom said calmly, 'You thought that Evelyn would comply with your scheme, that Tyler would, in public eyes, appear to rescue him from the flames. This story of Tyler being sent to lock Evelyn in the basement was just an excuse for his return to Molly's while you were otherwise engaged.'

'Evelyn shouldn't have tried to stop Tyler.'

'He was defending his business.'

'Business. Pah! Evelyn didn't know how to run a business. Not when things got into difficulties.'

'Difficulties? Such as ditching your previous lover, Gary Nicholls, and buying out his share. That's what tipped Molly's into the red and sent Evelyn to Neville Griffiths for a loan, wasn't it?'

Harriet didn't reply.

'In fact, it was your meddling in the business and your lust that ended with your property destroyed, your husband dead and you, and your lover, facing a long prison sentence. Isn't that the truth?'

She appeared to slump. Jasmine watched the scene thinking it resembled one of those horror films where the evil siren ages in moments, face cracking and turning to dust, or the formerly imperious, formidable sex-goddess becoming a shrunken, withered, old crone. Harriet's head tipped forward and she sobbed.

'Did you plan to burn down Molly's and claim the insurance?' Tom asked.

'Yes,' came the mumbled reply.

'Clearer, please Mrs Bunting.'

'Yes.'

'Did you instruct Tyler Smith to carry out your plan?'

'Yes.'

'Did you withhold knowledge of the circumstances surrounding your husband, Evelyn Bunting's death and continue to shield his killer from arrest?'

'Yes.'

'Thank you, Harriet. You will be charged along with Tyler Smith for those offences and others relating to the assault on and abduction of Jasmine Frame. You will probably be held on remand while the case is prepared. You may return to your cell.'

Tom rose and walked out of the room. He joined Jasmine in the observation room with Sasha Patel grinning behind him.

'You did it, Sir,' Sasha said.

'Good work, Tom. You finally got the full story out of them.' Jasmine congratulated him while feeling a little jealous that she hadn't done the interrogation herself.

Tom waved away the plaudits. 'They weren't hard-cases. For all her domineering of men, Harriet Bunting was a novice at criminal intrigue, and Tyler is just a hunk.'

'Nevertheless, you got their confessions,' Jasmine repeated.

The door opened and another person entered the already

crowded room. There was barely space for the bulk of DCI Sloane. Jasmine, Sasha and Tom were forced to stand shoulder to shoulder, or shoulder to elbow in the case of DC Patel and DI Shepherd.

'Ah, Shepherd, Patel,' Sloane said looking up and down each of them in turn, 'and um, Miss Frame. I was told you were here carrying out interviews. Any progress in this arson/murder case?'

Jasmine couldn't wait for Tom to answer. 'DI Shepherd's cracked it. He's just secured confessions from Harriet Bunting and Tyler Smith.'

'Has he, by God,' Sloane said, 'Well done, Inspector. Murder and arson?'

Tom bit his lip. 'I'm not certain about premeditated murder, Sir. Tyler Smith has admitted killing Evelyn Bunting but says it was not intentional. Evelyn tried to stop him setting the place alight.'

'But Smith used extreme force in order to carry out the plan,' Sloane added.

'Yes, Sir.'

'So Mrs Bunting can't be charged with conspiracy to murder?'

'No, Sir.'

Sloane nodded. 'Nevertheless, a good result. What brought them to this sorry state?'

Tom shrugged. 'Money and sex, Sir, like lots of cases.'

'Hmm,' was the DCI's comment.

Jasmine decided it was her turn to speak. 'Harriet Bunting has, or rather had, a particular allure, Chief Inspector.'

Sloane's eyebrows rose. 'Allure?'

'Smith called her a witch,' Tom said.

The DCI looked at Jasmine. 'Explain, Frame.'

Jasmine took a deep breath. 'Harriet was an attractive woman, fit and shapely. She also apparently had a strong liking for sex, kinky as well as vanilla, straight if you prefer. She accommodated, indeed fed, Evelyn's attraction to sissy, submissive and masochistic activities and satisfied her more traditional appetite with Gary Nicholls. I think, though that something happened in recent years. She got bored with Nicholls, and also perhaps with Evelyn's unchanging pattern of desires. Perhaps it was a recognition that she was middle-aged, and that Molly's was failing, even without the financial burden of buying out Nicholls. Nevertheless, she was fully aware of her powers. She found that there was a market among certain types of men for a dominant woman who would manage their desires, put them in scenarios that they wouldn't naturally seek out but which heightened their arousal. And she found she could still seduce a younger man, her personal trainer, Tyler Smith. I think her success as Madame de la Clef made her feel that she could achieve anything. The problems that Molly's had got into had to be solved. She thought she had the answers, but Tyler wasn't up to it and she misread Evelyn's devotion to the business.'

'Hmm,' Sloane said again, 'That's quite a theory, Frame. Not sure I follow all your reasoning, but it certainly seems that the practices this woman engaged in lead her to serious crime. What do we do about these men she dominated?'

Sasha Patel spoke, 'We've got their keys that Harriet Bunting kept in her bag.'

'Keys?' the DCI asked.

'To their, um, devices,' Sasha answered, 'They can't release themselves unless we give them back.'

'Aren't they needed as evidence?' Sloane said.

Tom shook his head, 'I don't think they are a factor in the case against Smith and Bunting, Sir.'

'In that case, release them,' Sloane said, 'in time.'

Jasmine said, 'I could use Harriet's red book to make sure that they are returned to the correct men.'

Sloane nodded. 'Thank you Frame. That seems appropriate. Well, good work, Shepherd. I'll let you get on with the processing.' He backed out of the cramped room allowing Tom, Jasmine and Sasha to breathe easily again.

27

MONDAY 21ST OCTOBER
AFTERNOON

Tom drew his Mondeo to a halt outside the house where Jasmine lived. She looked at the building feeling somewhat different about it than she had done. She had thought it a comfortable refuge, a place of companionship and even love with Viv, her home with her partner. Now she wasn't so sure. She felt reluctant to get out of the car as it signalled the end of the case, the termination of her relationship with Tom, Sasha, Hamid, even Terry.

'Thanks for your help, Jas,' Tom said.

'I didn't do much,' Jasmine replied, 'You got the confessions out of Harriet and Tyler.'

'Yes, but if you hadn't pursued Harriet's outings as Madame de la Clef, and got yourself kidnapped, we might not have ruffled her enough to get the breakthrough. Thanks for offering to see to Madame's retirement.'

Jasmine looked at the clear evidence bag that rested on her lap. It contained a bunch of small keys and a hard-cover notebook. 'It will be interesting to see how Harriet's slaves react to getting their keys handed back to them.'

'They may want you to carry on holding them. Could be a little earner for you.'

Jasmine saw that Tom was grinning at her. She snorted. 'I don't want to have to think about men's bits for longer than I have to.'

'Well, what will you do now? Back to the private investigator work?'

'Soon. I want to get fully fit before I have to spend my time chasing after benefit cheats, and errant husbands and wives.'

'Of course. How are you feeling?' There was concern in Tom's voice. 'With all the excitement I keep forgetting you're still recovering from major surgery.'

'That's in the past now,' Jasmine said, smiling, 'I'm a bit tired and sore, but that is more down to the last couple of days than the op. I feel I'm there now, Tom. The woman I've felt myself to be for most of my life.'

'Well, good luck, Jas. I hope it won't be long before we're working together again. Sloane seems keen to involve you, not that he'll be around much longer.'

'And then it will be up to you whether you bring me in.'

'The more often the better.' Tom glanced at his watch, 'Look I'm sorry Jas. I'd better get back. There's a pile of paperwork waiting for me.'

Jasmine opened the car door. 'Sorry, I'm holding you up. Mustn't keep you from the bureaucracy.'

She stepped onto the kerb and pushed the door closed. Tom waved and drove away. Jasmine stood and watched the car disappear around the bend in the road then turned and trudged up to the front door. It was then that she remembered. Her keys and other possessions had not been returned to her. They were still sitting in a box of evidence recovered from Tyler's car. Neither did she have a mobile phone. She pressed the door bell not expecting a reply as Viv's car wasn't parked in the drive, although the garage was now available to him. There was no reply. She looked to the left and right. The neighbours on both sides seemed to be out. She looked at her watch. Viv might be back in an hour, if he was in a hurry to get home and see her. Or, maybe he'd be longer. She had nothing to do but take a walk. Actually, that seemed a pleasant thing to do. It was dry, not cold, and still light.

She set off along the road then turned off onto the paths up the hill behind the house. The views across Kintbridge were pleasant, the smells of the autumn trees were refreshing and the gentle exercise was invigorating. There was a lot to contemplate – the past, the present and the future.

The sun had sunk below the horizon when she returned to the house. Viv's Audi was standing on the drive. She went up to the front door and pressed the bell.

The door was flung open. Viv stood in the gap holding the door. 'Jasmine. There you are. I thought you'd be here when I got home.'

'Why?'

'After yesterday. Your ordeal. Surely Tom Shepherd didn't have you working today?'

'Of course he did. There was a case to crack.'

'But you're not fit.'

'Fit enough, Viv. Look can I come in. It's getting cool outside.'

Viv, stepped back. Jasmine stepped into the hall appreciating the warmth. She closed the door and took off her coat.

'We need to talk,' Viv said as he moved towards the kitchen.

'About what?' she followed him.

'Well, there's your car for a start. I've been speaking to the insurers. They accept that the Mini is a write-off and that it was stolen from you, but they are arguing that you were using it for your business when it was only covered for private use.' He filled the kettle with water then put it down on the work top. He flicked the switch.

Jasmine raised her hands in frustration. 'How else am I supposed to get around, Viv? I'm a private detective. Of course I needed that car for my work.'

'Well, that's another thing, Jas. Are you really intending to go back to that lark?'

Jasmine frowned. 'Yes, I am. It's how I earn my money. Investigating is what I do.'

'Hmm. I'm not sure that's the best thing for you, Jas. It's dangerous.'

'Not much, but what's changed?'

'You have, Jas. You're a woman now.'

'I've been a woman for a long time.'

Viv looked away from her. He got a couple of mugs from the wall cupboard. 'Yes, but a you're really a woman now.'

Jasmine sighed. 'I have a vagina. So what?'

'No one can tell what you are anymore.'

'So that makes my job more dangerous?'

'It makes you vulnerable.'

Jasmine felt a knot of anger forming in her chest. 'Is that what you mean, or do you mean, available, as in available to fuck. Now I no longer have a penis dangling between my legs to put them off, I'm a target for any sex pest and rapist who has sight of me.'

'Jas.'

'What do you want to do, Viv? Lock me away to keep me safe? Keep me to yourself? Let me go mad with boredom? Is that what you want.'

'Now you're being silly, Jas. I just said that we need to talk about it.'

'Maybe we do need to talk, Viv, but I'm not going to be kept in a gilded cage as your little housewife. I will be the woman I want to be and that includes being an investigator.' She turned away from him and headed out of the kitchen. 'I'm going for a shower and then I will do the exercises that ensure that in the future I can be a sexually active woman. Then, maybe, we can talk again.'

She mounted the stairs, breathing heavily, tears trickling down her cheeks. Apparently, she still had to fight to be herself.

THE END

Jasmine Frame will return in her fifth novel

An Impersonator's life

While contemplating her future and the decision to have breast enhancement, Jasmine is employed by a famous but elderly female impersonator. He has been receiving threatening letters and emails and wants to know who is responsible. Jasmine immerses herself in the world of the stage where no-one is real. She questions her own motivation to model herself on her image of the ideal woman. When a death occurs, Jasmine is a person of interest for the investigating team lead by DI Tom Shepherd. She has to find the murderer to protect her self-image and to keep her promise to her client.

ACKNOWLEDGEMENTS

Molly's Boudoir is the fourth novel following the transition and career of Jasmine Frame detective. It is the third to be prepared for publication by Alnpete PrePress. Once again I would like to thank Sofia for her copyediting. Her comments are always relevant and her suggestions always improving. Thanks also to Pete and Alison Buck for turning my manuscript into a format fit for publication. Thanks also to Barbara and Lou for reading a rough copy of the novel and allowing me to convince myself that it was worth pressing on. Scott Wood has again designed a striking cover that I think looks good whether viewed at postage stamp size or on a poster.

In this story Jasmine at last goes through her Gender Confirmation Surgery. They say you should write about what you know but while I consider myself to be genderfluid, I am not transsexual and have not and do not intend to go through that operation. I have therefore relied on accounts by transwomen of their experiences, in particular those of Jules Jacques as described in her book, Trans A Memoir (pub. Verso ISBN 978-1-78478-164-4). I admire the determination of all transwomen, and transmen, to achieve the physical attributes of their gender identity. There are many other people, the world over, who question the gender stereotypes in the societies in which they grew up and live. Whether they feel confident to proclaim their identities or feel they have to put on a mask to protect themselves, this book and the other Jasmine Frame stories are a symbol of solidarity.

There are a variety of characters in this story, some who engage in practices that some readers may consider weird. While I try to make the characters as plausible as possible they are all figments of my imagination and none are based on real people. Similarly, although the locations are based on places in the Newbury area you won't find an establishment like Molly's in the town that Thirsbury is modelled on (at least I don't think so).

Finally, thank you, dear reader for getting this far. If you enjoyed this book please write a review or tell your friends. If you haven't read any other Jasmine Frame stories, details about the novels and novellas follow.

P R Ellis

JASMINE FRAME NOVELS
Available in paperback and e-book

Painted Ladies
A Jasmine Frame Story

Jasmine Frame was scared of knives when she was a policeman. Now she finds herself on the trail of a knife killer, but it's not just her skin that is in danger. Her identity as a woman is under threat.

Published 2013.

Bodies By Design
The 2nd Jasmine Frame Novel

Three months after the events of *Painted Ladies*, Jasmine responds to a call for help and finds herself involved in a murder case by the special request of DCI Sloane. But who or what was the victim? What was the motive? Jasmine's investigation leads into the murkier regions of the transgender scene. Meanwhile, she is about to take an irreversible step to lose her masculinity. What are the parallels between her situation and that of the murder victim?

Published 2015.

The Brides' Club Murder
The 3rd Jasmine Frame novel

A country house hotel. A death. Ten suspects. Jasmine Frame has a weekend to identify the killer before the attendees of the Butterfly Ball disperse. She must pretend to enjoy the strange activities of the Wedding Belles, but, with her gender reassignment still some way off she is uncomfortable confined with a party of transvestites. Nevertheless, she relishes a mystery. What drove a member of the group to kill and are they prepared to kill again?

Published 2017.

Praise for the Jasmine Frame novels

Painted Ladies

"…Jasmine is a very engaging character, well written and believable. Her emotions and feelings are central to the book and, I hope, will shed light on a situation that cannot be easy to accept and live with in face of everyday prejudice. However, this is a crime novel and stands on its own as such. I found it a page-turner and really enjoyed reading it…"

Susan White, Eurocrime

"…Painted Ladies is the first literary examination, that we have seen, of the trans community in the role of both detective and victim, a rare and exquisite treat…"

Jake Basford, So So Gay Magazine

Bodies By Design

"I had enjoyed Painted Ladies and was pleased to find that Bodies by Design was if anything even better. Like PL, BBD shows the great range of types of sexual/gender identity – not exhaustively."

Sue King

The Brides' Club Murder

"This is the third outing for Jasmine Frame, and the character development is progressing well, as we follow Jasmine on her personal transition journey. This is interrupted by a suspicious death at a local hotel, hosting the gathering of the Wedding Belles and, this year, a real wedding. Jasmine is forced to go undercover for the conference in an attempt to identify the killer.

It's an enjoyable read, in the style of Agatha Christie, as Jasmine explores the means, motives and opportunities of each of the Wedding Belles. I felt this novel was a little more 'cosier' than the previous two.

While this book works as a standalone novel, to fully understand Jasmine's personal journey I would recommend reading the first two novels in the series first."

Simon Whaley

JASMINE FRAME NOVELLAS
AND ANTHOLOGIES
(e-book only)
Discovering Jasmine

James Frame is 17 and struggling with his desire to be Jasmine. When sister, Holly, discovers Jasmine she suggests a venture into the outside world. Jasmine meets a transwoman facing severe hate and finds herself drawn to protect her.

Published 2015.

Murder in Doubt

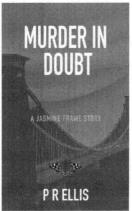

James Frame is starting at university and experimenting with revealing Jasmine to his new friends including a young woman called Angela. When a new acquaintances, a transwoman, is found dead Jasmine is certain it is murder and sets out to prove it.

Published 2016.

Trained By Murder

Four stories, four locations, four deaths and four dilemmas give Jasmine Frame a training in the art of detection. As James she is embarking on a career in the police force and a marriage to Angela, while wondering what part Jasmine will play in her life. She strives to keep Jasmine secret from her colleagues but the urge to be female is ever-present. The examples and experiences of the transmen, transwomen and crossdressers that she meets influence her decisions. She has choices and decisions to make and crimes to solve.

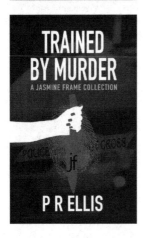

Published 2018.

ORDER FORM

To order copies of the paperback editions of the Jasmine Frame novels, fill-in the order form below

Title	Cost (inc p&p)	Number required	Total cost
Painted Ladies	£8.99		£
Bodies By Design	£9.99		£
The Brides' Club Murder	£9.99		£
Molly's Boudoir	£9.99		£
		Total	£

Send your order to paintedladiesnovel@btinternet.com

Or post to:
Ellifont, Flat 20 Llangattock Court, Dixton Road, Monmouth NP25 3PX

Payment can be made by cheque payable to P R Ellis

Or by PayPal to the account attached to paintedladiesnovel@btinternet.com

Volume 1 of Evil Above the Stars

Seventh Child

Peter R. Ellis

September Weekes is accustomed to facing teasing and bullying because of her white hair, tubby figure and silly name, but the discovery of a clear, smooth stone at her home casts her into a struggle between good and evil that will present her with sterner challenges.

The stone takes her to *Gwlad*, the Land, where the people hail her as the *Cludydd o Maengolauseren*, the bearer of the starstone, with the power to defend them against the evil known as the Malevolence. September meets the people's leader, the *Mordeyrn Aurddolen*, and the bearers of the seven metals linked to the seven 'planets'. Each metal gives the bearer specialised powers to resist the manifestations of the Malevolence, formed from the four elements of earth, air, fire and water, such as the comets known as *Draig tân*, fire dragons.

She returns to her home, but is drawn back to the Land a fortnight later to find that two years have passed and the villagers have experienced more destructive attacks by manifestations. September must now help defend *Gwlad* against the Malevolence.

Seventh Child is the first volume in the thrilling fantasy series, *Evil Above the Stars*, by Peter R. Ellis, that appeals to readers, of all ages, of fantasy or science fiction, especially fans of JRR Tolkien and Stephen Donaldson. If old theories are correct until a new idea comes along, does the universe change with our perception of it? Were the ideas embodied in alchemy ever right? What realities were the basis of Celtic mythology?

ISBN: 9781908168702 (epub, kindle)
ISBN: 9781908168603 (256pp paperback)

Visit bit.ly/EvilAbove

Volume 2 of Evil Above the Stars

The Power of Seven
Peter R. Ellis

September Weekes found a smooth stone which took her to *Gwlad*, the Land, where the people hailed her as the *Cludydd o Maengolauseren*, the bearer of the starstone, with the power to defend them against the evil known as the Malevolence. Now, having reached Arsyllfa she is re-united with the *Mordeyrn Aurddolen* with whom, together with the other senior metal bearers that make up the Council of *Gwlad*, she must plan the defence of the Land.

The time of the next Conjunction will soon be at hand. The planets, the Sun and the Moon will all be together in the sky. At that point the protection of the heavenly bodies will be at its weakest and *Gwlad* will be more dependent than ever on September. But now it seems that she must defeat Malice, the guiding force behind the Malevolence, if she is to save the Land and all its people. Will she be strong enough; and, if not, to whom can she turn for help?

The Power of Seven is the second volume in the thrilling fantasy series, *Evil Above the Stars*, by Peter R. Ellis, that appeals to readers, of all ages, of fantasy or science fiction, especially fans of JRR Tolkien and Stephen Donaldson. If old theories are correct until a new idea comes along, does the universe change with our perception of it? Were the ideas embodied in alchemy ever right? What realities were the basis of Celtic mythology?

ISBN: 9781908168719 (epub, kindle)
ISBN: 9781908168610 (288pp paperback)

Visit bit.ly/EvilAbove

Volume 3 of Evil Above the Stars

Unity of Seven
Peter R. Ellis

September is back home and it is still the night of her birthday, despite her having spent over three months in *Gwlad* battling the Malevolence at the seventh conjunction of the planets. She no longer has the *Maengolauseren* nor the powers it gave her. It is back to facing the bullies at school and her struggles with her weight and studies, but she worries about how well the people of *Gwlad* have recovered from the terror of the Malevolence. She is also unsure what happened to Malice/Mairwen as the *Cemegwr* said that *Toddfa penbaladr*, the universal solvent, would join the twins together. Is Malice inside her? Could she turn to evil?

She must discover a way to return to the universe of *Gwlad* and the answer seems to lie in her family history. The five *Cludydds* before September and her mother were her ancestors. The clues take her on a journey in time and space which reveals that while in great danger she is also the key to the survival of all the universes. September must overcome her own fears, accept an extraordinary future and, once again, face the evil above the stars.

Unity of Seven is the third volume in the thrilling fantasy series, *Evil Above the Stars*, by Peter R. Ellis, that appeals to readers, of all ages, of fantasy or science fiction, especially fans of JRR Tolkien and Stephen Donaldson. If old theories are correct until a new idea comes along, does the universe change with our perception of it? Were the ideas embodied in alchemy ever right? What realities were the basis of Celtic mythology?

ISBN: 9781908168917 (epub, kindle)
ISBN: 9781908168818 (256pp paperback)

Visit bit.ly/EvilAbove

September Weekes returns...

Cold Fire
Peter R. Ellis

London, 1680. The famous philosopher, Sir Robert Boyle, is about to demonstrate the results of his investigations of the phosphorus and its cold fire to fellows of the Royal Society and other guests. Far away at the edge of Wales an alchemist learns of the discovery and, helped by his young assistant, attempts in his own way to form the mysterious material, little suspecting that his work threatens to open the universe to the evil power of the Malevolence.

Summoned by the Brains, September, the *Cludydd o Maengolauseren*, arrives charged with halting the Malevolence's storm of destruction. But how? She finds herself out of her time and in a world not quite her own. Nevertheless her experience of the Malevolence tells her that she must do something. The fantastic beasts she encounters may come to her aid, if she can work out how to save them from the Cold Fire.

For September, hardly any time has passed since she was trying to save *Gwlad* in Peter R. Ellis' thrilling fantasy series *Evil Above the Stars*. Now, in the first of *the September Weekes novels*, she appears to be closer to home, at least in space if not time. But not everything is as she'd expect it, and she still seems to be wearing her school uniform! Combining science, fantasy and adventure, this is a novel truly worthy of the designation Speculative Fiction.

ISBN: 9781911409168 (epub, kindle)
ISBN: 9781911409069 (264pp paperback)

Visit bit.ly/Cold-Fire

MEET THE AUTHOR

P R Ellis goes by the names Peter or Penny. He/she (whatever) is transgender or gender fluid or non-binary.

What that means is that I was born male, lived most of my life male but I have a feminine side (?) that I have been able to reveal for the last sixteen plus years. My ideas about myself and where I fit in the gender spectrum or map have changed during the course of my sixty-plus years. I now think of myself as "me", i.e. not two people, not one person sometimes acting as another, but someone who while physically male likes to express feminine preferences in dress, appearance and perhaps other attributes, if not all the time, then whenever convenient.

I was a science teacher, have always been a writer, and now, having retired from the career that paid the bills, am indulging myself by writing what I want to write and trying to get it published. As well as the Jasmine Frame stories, I write fantasy and SF, articles on science and still, occasionally, science education resources.

Lou and I live in Monmouthshire where we do all sorts of things.

You can follow me and Jasmine on my blog www.ellifont.wordpress.com